A PAINTED
‑GODDESS‑

OTHER NOVELS BY VICTOR GISCHLER

Suicide Squeeze

Gun Monkeys

The Pistol Poets

Shotgun Opera

Go-Go Girls of the Apocalypse

Vampire a Go-Go

The Deputy

Three on a Light

Stay

Gestapo Mars

A FIRE BENEATH THE SKIN TRILOGY

Ink Mage

The Tattooed Duchess

A PAINTED GODDESS

A FIRE BENEATH THE SKIN: BOOK 3

VICTOR GISCHLER

Text copyright © 2016 Victor Gischler
All rights reserved.

Published by 47North, Seattle

www.apub.com

Amazon, the Amazon logo, and 47North are trademarks of Amazon.com, Inc., or its affiliates.

ISBN-13: 9781503954762
ISBN-10: 1503954765

Cover design by Megan Haggerty
Illustrated by Chase Stone
Interior maps by Tazio Bettin

Printed in the United States of America

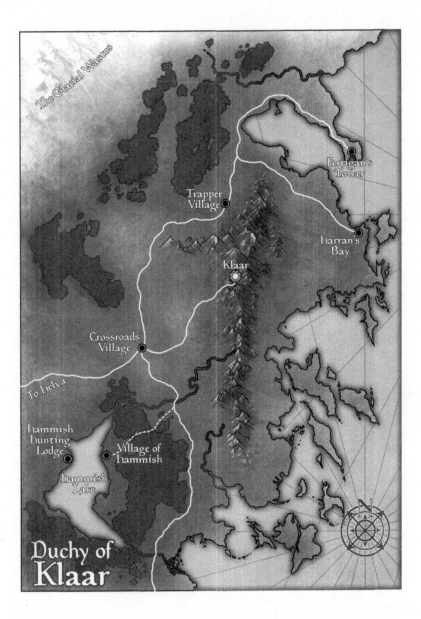

The Glacial Wastes

Ferrigan's Tower

Trapper Village

harran's Bay

Klaar

Crossroads Village

To helva

hammish hunting Lodge

Village of hammish

hammish Lake

Duchy of
Klaar

N

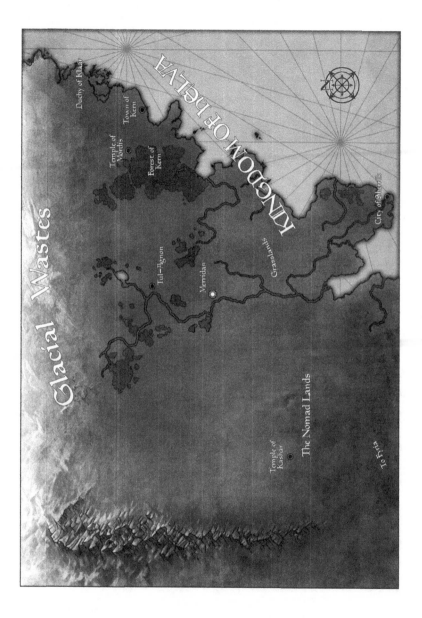

PROLOGUE

Spread along the southern end of the western mountains, yet still north of the Nomad Lands, an ancient evergreen forest surrounded a large, calm, crystal-blue lake. On an island near the middle of the lake, a temple perched on a raised bank, overlooking the water. Centuries ago, the faithful had labored for years to construct it, using large gray stones. The structure was circular with arched doorways and fat columns all around. A gurgling spring fed a tranquil fountain in an open courtyard at the center of the temple. It was a place of quiet contemplation and prayer.

Usually.

It was not a temple in the typical fashion, not a branch temple serving a city's parishioners, offering weekly services, nor was it like the conveniently placed roadside shrines where worshippers could pray or leave offerings. There was nothing convenient about this temple's location, and that was by design. It was the mother temple of Zereen, goddess of clouds, mists, and fog. As such, it was distantly located and difficult to find. Pilgrimages would be fairly pointless if they were too easy.

The pilgrim circled the entire lake, searching for a bridge or ferry landing. He found none.

Of course. Six weeks walking here and now I have to swim the final few hundred yards? Thanks, Dad.

The pilgrim's family was a devout lot. Each child made the pilgrimage upon reaching adulthood at age twenty. The pilgrim was the last of six children. The send-off parties were the talk of the town. He suspected his parents had discussed having more children just to send them on pilgrimages and have an excuse for another party. Although there were always plenty of excuses. His older brothers and sisters were already providing grandchildren.

He stood on the bank and looked across the water at the temple. The idea of coming all this way only to arrive soaking wet at the temple after a long swim didn't appeal to him. He looked back into the depths of the forest behind him. He'd passed a number of fallen evergreens. Vines were plentiful also, and he had his hand axe. Fashioning a quick raft before nightfall was doable, and then he and his gear could arrive dry and presentable.

It took longer than he thought to build the raft. He camped at the edge of the river, huddled over a small campfire, and the next morning dragged the little raft down to the water.

He was glad he'd waited until morning. A thick fog lay over the water, the temple a vague shadow on the island. It was a fitting way to approach the Temple of Zereen. What was it his hometown priest was fond of saying? Zereen is about transition. You travel through the fog, faith leading you to the mystery on the other side.

Or something.

He stood on the raft and poled it out into the lake. It wasn't exactly the most well-constructed craft, and water splashed over his ankles. No problem. His boots were good, watertight. The raft would get him there.

Halfway across, he spotted the glow of a lantern, yellow light fuzzy in the fog. As he approached, a figure materialized on the far side, holding the lantern aloft as if expecting him. A short figure, though it was difficult to tell if it was a man or woman in the billowing robes and the hood pulled forward.

"Welcome, pilgrim." A light and airy voice.

A woman's voice.

"Hello!" he called back.

The shabby raft nudged against the bank, and the pilgrim hopped across with his gear slung over one shoulder. He bowed to the woman in the robe and introduced himself.

"Welcome, pilgrim. You're the first of the season to arrive." She pulled her hood back. Pale and beautiful. Her hair was so blond it was almost white, eyes the color of the sky. She wasn't any older than he was.

"Hello." He smiled so wide it almost hurt his face. He'd made it at last. "Hello."

"Please follow me," she said. "You've come so far. Come and take refreshment."

She turned, walking slowly back toward the temple. He followed.

"Who are you?"

"Leena," she said. "An acolyte."

"How did you know I was coming?"

"Not me," she said. "The high priestess. She knows when one of the faithful approaches. It is a gift of foreknowing. A gift from Zereen."

They passed beneath a wide archway and into an open stone room. Arched doorways and windows and a high ceiling. A constant light breeze passed through, cool, the sound of it soothing. The place had a holy feel to it.

Which, the pilgrim supposed, was the point.

"Follow me," Leena said.

They walked through the temple.

"Do you know why this is the *mother* temple?" Leena asked.

"Because it's the first one?" said the pilgrim.

"It is," Leena said. "But it's more than that. A mother temple is a special place for any religion. It is a window, a small place where our world intersects with the world of the gods. This is a place where we can actually feel the presence of Zereen herself."

Oh yeah. That sounded familiar to the pilgrim, something he'd heard the adults talk about as a child. It sounded made up.

She led him through another arched doorway, and they found themselves in a wide green courtyard, roof open to the sky. Leafy vines twisted and crept up the stone walls. Lush grass and well-trimmed rosebushes. A magnificent fountain sat in the center of the courtyard. A thick column rose up from the center of a wide pool. The top of the column was ringed with stone dragons, and water sprayed from the mouth of each, creating a rain-shower effect down into the pool. The way the raindrops hit the stones below created a constant mist in the courtyard.

The cool mist and the sound of the simulated rainfall gave the place a natural, holy feel. Maybe this was really all religion was, thought the pilgrim. Clever staging. Giving worshippers that vague feeling they were connecting to something larger.

Leena gestured at a carved stone bench near the pool's edge. "Please. Sit. We are preparing refreshment for you, and you will join us tonight at a welcoming banquet. But after such a long journey, many pilgrims elect to sit and contemplate, pondering the many life choices that have brought them so far."

So far, the pilgrim's parents had made most of his life choices for him, but he was game to play along and seated himself on the bench.

He stared at the trickling water and waited. It wasn't unpleasant. Relaxing. A goblet of wine would have added something to the experience, in his opinion, but it wasn't his place to point that out. Something to consider if he ever started his own religion.

He stared into the shimmering pool and let his mind wander. When he returned, he would discuss with his father whether he'd come into the family business. Father was a merchant and knew trade like the priests in this temple knew their tenets. Father bought things, kept them in a warehouse for a while, then sold them again. Somehow a profit was the result. The pilgrim would have preferred to study at the university in Tul-Agnon, but that could be expensive, even for his father. Anyway, there was a girl from a good family back home of marrying age with a nice wide backside. His family had been talking to her family. If she were ready to start making babies, then maybe . . .

He sat up straight, blinked at the pool.

He leaned forward, squinting.

A vibrant blue light played through the pool, jerking like lightning just below the surface of the water.

The pilgrim turned back to the acolyte. "Uh . . . I think I saw something."

Leena picked her head up. She'd been standing with eyes closed in calm meditation. "Excuse me?"

"I thought I saw something."

"What?"

"I don't know," the pilgrim said. "A light."

Leena smiled. "Often the pious are overcome with the joy of being at the mother temple and think they see things as the mind gropes to make a personal connection with Zereen."

The pilgrim frowned, looked back at the pool. The blue light pulsed and flared brighter.

He turned back to Leena. "No," he insisted. "*Something's* going on in there."

Leena's serene smile faltered. "I *assure* you that it's not uncommon for—"

The pool bubbled and churned, and blinding blue light erupted from the pool, filling the courtyard.

Leena stepped back. "Oh."

There was a sudden sharp sound like fabric ripping, but ten thousand times louder. A jagged line grew up from the pool and opened wide.

A roar and a blast of frigid air knocked the pilgrim back off the stone bench. He staggered to one knee, dazed, and looked to see Leena also struggling back to her feet.

The temple shook, the ground beneath the pilgrim's feet rumbling. There was an earsplitting racket like the world breaking in half, and a huge figure tumbled out of the blazing hole that opened in midair over the pool. She was ten feet tall, hair a golden, shimmering blond that seemed to taper way into the air like mist. Robes flowed around her more like fog than fabric. She held a gleaming silver sword in one hand. Her beauty was mesmerizing and terrible.

Leena fell to her knees, prostrating herself. "Zereen!"

The goddess? The pilgrim blinked at her. Looking at the goddess *hurt*, such was the power of her glorious appearance, but he couldn't turn away.

Zereen stumbled and fell across the stone bench, shattering it. She lifted her sword, turned back to the shimmering rent in the air.

And another figure emerged.

Taller and more fearsome than the goddess Zereen, a figure in spiked armor, holding a lethal-looking morningstar in one spiked gauntlet. A dark glow hung around him as if he were sapping the light from the world. Flames for eyes sizzled from the shadow beneath the spiked helm.

The armored god swung the morningstar down at Zereen. She lifted the sword to block. When steel crossed steel, the ringing crack sent a pain through the pilgrim. He touched one of his ears. Blood on his fingers.

The armored god brought the morningstar down again, but Zereen rolled to one side. The morningstar struck the ground, and the shock wave knocked the pilgrim off his feet. The god advanced on Zereen, stepped on the stonework surrounding the pool and crushed it. Water flooded the courtyard.

The pilgrim splashed away, lurching to his feet. He turned and ran.

Back in the cavernous halls of the temple, he paused, trying to remember which way he'd come in. He'd been following Leena and not really paying attention.

What had happened to her? Never mind. Just run.

The wall ahead of him exploded, the grappling deities crashing through, locked in combat. A flying stone block spun past scant inches from the pilgrim's head. The armored god had an iron grip on Zereen's throat. She no longer held her sword, pried uselessly at the mighty gauntleted hand choking her.

The pilgrim ran for the first doorway available. He followed a narrow hallway, passing small wooden doorways, some of which were opening, frightened faces appearing and wondering what was happening. Priests and acolytes joined him as he fled down the hall. The temple shook. People screamed.

A thunderous sound somewhere behind him, and the temple shook so violently, a thick roof beam fell, crushing a priest right in front of him. The pilgrim leapt over fallen beam and priest both and kept running.

He found a door, threw it open, and mercifully found himself outside. He sprinted for the water's edge. He was at a different part of the shoreline, and the little raft he'd built was nowhere in sight.

He dove into the water.

It was a cold shock, and he swam hard, looking ahead for the far bank but not able to see it through the fog. He stroked and kicked until his limbs ached. Finally he saw land, felt the bottom under his feet. He staggered up the back, dripping and shivering.

The pilgrim looked back.

An orange glow blazed through the fog. Something burned. The temple's silhouette looked crumpled. A roar of pure rage rose from the island. The ground shook.

The pilgrim ran deep into the forest and didn't stop until the cataclysm of the temple was many miles behind him.

CHAPTER ONE

The scholars in the lower levels of the Great Library didn't even glance at them. They'd seen expeditions come and go as a matter of routine. They were busy. They had many ancient books and scrolls to pore over. They didn't have time for idiot dead men leading goat carts to certain doom.

Brasley sighed and followed Olgen down the main walkway through the stacks. It was nearly as wide as a boulevard in Merridan. Tables and chairs, rows and rows and rows of bookshelves on either side. Books were expensive things, and so many in one place was a marvel.

And we're only just on the first level, Brasley thought.

Talbun followed closely behind him, leading the goat cart. She seemed pensive, possibly because she'd been on another expedition into the Great Library years ago and had barely come out again with her life. But she was a wizard, and who knew what worried wizards? She was so painfully gorgeous, it was hard to believe she was old enough to be Brasley's great-something-grandmother.

Well. The world is full of surprises.

He thought suddenly of his wife, Fregga, which surprised him. If he were killed somewhere in the heights of the Great Library and never got back to her, it would upset him to no end.

And that surprised him too.

She loved him. Brasley was so obviously the most abhorrent cad, and yet Fregga loved him. And that made him love her back. Dumo help him, it was true. He vowed on the spot to return to her. He would survive the Great Library and return to her, whatever it took.

Which, frankly, was a sort of easy vow for him since he'd really planned to do everything in his power to live anyway. The notion he might die was really the most unpleasant prospect he could think of. None of this shit was his idea after all. Rina had come to him—on his *honeymoon*—to say she'd needed him.

Nobody had ever needed him before. How could he refuse? He couldn't.

Because you have mule dung for brains, you damn fool.

The walkway led them under a twenty-foot-high archway and a raised portcullis. Guards on either side lazily waved them through.

Olgen turned back to them, offering a gap-toothed grin. "This is it. Out of the library proper and into the danger zone. Don't worry. The first five levels have been explored thoroughly, sort of a buffer zone."

Brasley forced a smile. "Excellent."

The walkway angled upward gently and curved gradually from right to left.

"It's not completely evident at first because the slope is so gradual," Olgen said. "But this walkway actually circles the interior of a large tower. It takes us up ten levels with plenty of opportunities to hop off wherever you like. Most parties go straight up to the top and figure it out from there."

"How far up have you been?" Talbun asked.

"Here."

"Here?" Brasley said incredulously. "This spot?"

"No, milord, sorry," Olgen said. "I wasn't trying to be that specific. I meant here in the buffer zone. I bring in first-year engineering students to look at the walkway and the other architecture."

"Why?"

Olgen gestured at the walkway beneath his feet. "Look how smooth. All the roadways, most of the architectural features, all superior to what builders can do now. The first-year students come to have a look for themselves. I show them around."

"You're not worried about it?" Brasley asked. "Going up to the dangerous levels?"

Olgen's grin wilted. "Should I be?"

For the love of Dumo, we're all dead.

"Never mind," Brasley said. "Just take us up."

They trudged in relative silence for an hour, Olgen pausing just once to mark the fact they were now leaving the buffer zone. It didn't mean much. Most of the expeditions had come this way. They passed the sixth, seventh, and eighth levels, doorways at every landing that led a different direction into the inner reaches of the Great Library. At each landing, Brasley glanced at Talbun, and the wizard shook her head. At the ninth landing, she nodded.

"Here." Brasley gestured at a doorway no bigger or any more interesting than any normal doorway found in a hundred other castles.

Olgen frowned. "Are you sure, milord? It's my understanding most of the expeditions go to the top of this tower and then proceed from there."

"Right here," Brasley said. "Let's explore."

They moved through the doorway into a narrow hall. The goat cart cleared with six inches on each side. On the broad walkway as they'd spiraled upward, it was as if they'd been in a large indoor city. Now in the close quarters of the hallway, they might as well have been in Castle Klaar or the manor house of some nobleman.

Olgen led the way, although he'd clearly never been here before. He seemed not to know the difference. He was the guide, so he went first.

"I'm supposed to turn back once we hit unexplored territory," Olgen said. "But I can't resist going a little farther. I just want to find a good place for a map reference."

Brasley let him edge ahead, hung back until he was walking shoulder to shoulder with Talbun.

"This the way you came before?"

"Yes," she said.

"On the way in, or on the way out?"

"Out."

Olgen rounded a corner and screamed.

Brasley and Talbun left the goat cart and sprinted after the guide.

They rounded the corner and found Olgen backed up against the wall, holding his chest, panting and bug eyed. He pointed at something across from him. "H-he surprised me."

Brasley's eyes fell on the corpse across from Olgen. It had been there a while. Skin gray and shriveled, almost a skeleton. A crossbow bolt stuck out through rusty chain mail just over the heart. A notched sword in one hand and a dagger in the other.

"He startled me," Olgen said.

"He can't hurt you," Brasley said. "A member of some long-forgotten expedition who didn't make it. That's my guess. Name lost to memory, I expect."

"Edgar," Talbun said. "His name was Edgar."

CHAPTER
TWO

Fregga stood on the porch of the Hammish hunting lodge and watched the riders come. Three of them galloping toward, the late-afternoon sun glinting off armor and weapons.

She cradled a cup of hot tea, tried not to feel nervous but failed. Who would they send if something happened to Brasley, she wondered. Or her father. Or both. Something could have happened to them on the road. These were dangerous, upsetting times.

Furthermore, she didn't really trust Brasley too long on his own. She'd barely begun the process of wrapping him around her finger. Brasley was the sort of man that was a long-term project. Such a handsome rogue, but he knew it was the problem. Yes, she had her work cut out for her, but she'd whip him into shape.

Of course he'd actually have to be around and not off getting killed with Duchess Veraiin for her to be able to do that. *Oh, please don't be off getting yourself killed, you ridiculous man.*

She sipped tea.

The riders were close enough now that Fregga could see they were women. A trio of—what were people calling them now? Oh, yes. The Birds of Prey. The all-female guard unit that protected the duchess and Castle Klaar.

Not that Rina Veraiin needed protecting.

The riders reined in their horses ten feet from the porch, and the one in the middle offered a curt nod, which Fregga had come to understand as a legitimate gesture of respect here in the northern wilderness. In Merridan, a messenger would be expected to dismount and offer a proper bow. Fregga was getting used to the informal, rustic atmosphere of Klaar.

"Hello, Baroness Hammish. I'm Darshia." A tall redhead with broad shoulders. She seemed a little too pretty to don armor and swing a sword, but she certainly wasn't small. "I've been sent by her ladyship Stasha Benadicta, steward of Klaar."

Oh, Dumo help me. Brasley's dead. He's dead and they've come to tell me. A hand went reflexively to her round belly. She was beginning to show just a little more. The baby would be all she'd have left of Brasley.

"Lady Benadicta knows that the baron is away on business with Duchess Veraiin," Darshia said. "She asked me to say that if you're enjoying your peaceful solitude here at the lodge, then please just consider this a courtesy call. On the other hand, if you feel you would enjoy some company, she invites you to be her guest at Castle Klaar."

Fregga stared at the redhead for a long moment. "What?"

"You're invited to Castle Klaar," Darshia repeated. "If you've a mind, milady."

They hadn't come to tell her about Brasley. A gesture of courtesy from Klaar's steward. That was all. She wasn't a widow. Not yet.

She blew out a ragged breath she didn't know she'd been holding and started to laugh.

The Birds of Prey exchanged curious glances.

"Forgive me, ladies," Fregga said. "It's just that it's such a delightful invitation and unexpected. I accept, of course."

"If we leave now, we can make it by dinner," Darshia said. "Although if you'd prefer a fresh start in the morning and time to pack . . ."

"No," Fregga said. "I can pack quickly. It will be pleasant to dine in the castle this evening."

"Forgive me, Baroness," Darshia said. "But can you ride? I mean . . . uh . . . in your condition."

"I'm not so far along quite yet," Fregga told them. "If I could trouble one of you to saddle the brown mare in the stable, I'll just duck back inside and pack a few things."

"Of course." Darshia gestured to one of the other women, who dismounted and jogged toward the stable.

"Uh, Darshia, is it?"

"Yes, milady."

"Darshia, have you by any chance heard anything of my husband, Brasley?"

Darshia smiled. "If you mean recent news, I'm sorry, no, milady. However, I have heard a thing or two about him."

"Oh?"

"He is extremely fond of his own hide," Darshia said. "And in all of Helva there is no one more adept at preserving it."

A moment of hesitation and then Fregga smiled deeply. It was just what she'd wanted to hear.

◆ ◆ ◆

"The trip down to Lake Hammish and back was good?" Stasha Benadicta asked.

"If you mean uneventful, Lady Steward," Darshia said. "Then yes. I think Baroness Hammish is relieved to be here. I think she's looking forward to dinner and some company. It was good of you to invite her."

"I should have before this," Stasha said. "A pregnant woman alone. If I hadn't been so preoccupied, I would have."

"She's worried about her husband."

"As are a great many women these days," the steward said. "How goes recruiting at the Wounded Bird?"

The castle guard—the so-called Birds of Prey—had all once been prostitutes at a brothel called the Wounded Bird. Circumstances were such that many of them learned the sword and gave up life on their backs. Stasha Benadicta had once been madam of that brothel.

"Two last week," Darshia said. "None this week."

Stasha raised an eyebrow. "So few? I'd predicted more would seek an alternative to letting sweaty men ride them every night for coppers."

"There were more," Darshia said. "I refused them."

"Oh?"

"They were whores."

Stasha Benadicta narrowed her eyes. "*You* were a whore."

"Yes," Darshia said. "I've been there. I've lived among them, been one of them. There were some I'd call 'sister' all the way to my grave. There are others who'd call *me* sister, and then steal my last copper when my back was turned. I won't stand shoulder to shoulder with any woman I don't trust."

"Two last week and none this week," Stasha said.

"That's right."

"What does that bring us up to?"

"Fifty-eight."

"Not much of an army, is it?" Stasha said.

"The Birds of Prey are the castle guard," Darshia said. "Klaar has an army."

"Klaar does," Stasha said. "I don't."

Darshia let that comment settle a moment. "The new general?"

"My previous credentials running a brothel are not enough to inspire confidence in him, it seems," Stasha said. "For the time being, I'm not forcing the issue."

"I see," Darshia said. "I'm sorry."

"Don't be sorry," Stasha said. "If I can't accomplish what needs to be done with fifty-eight, then it wasn't meant to be."

Darshia hesitated, not wanting to ask. She couldn't help it. "Accomplish what, Lady Steward?"

Stasha opened a desk drawer, pulled out a folded piece of parchment and placed it on the desk between her and Darshia. "You recognize this?"

"Yes."

Darshia and the Birds of Prey had been tasked with rooting out all of the traitor Giffen's minions left in Klaar. She'd chased them down alleys and into dank basements. When she'd cornered and killed the last one—a brute named Bolger—he'd been carrying that parchment. She'd brought it back to the steward, intentionally not reading it, hoping she wouldn't be asked to. She didn't want to know.

"You didn't read it." Not a question.

"Not my place."

"Isn't it?"

Darshia wasn't sure what to say. "Milady?"

"What is your place exactly?" Stasha asked. "As you see it."

"The Birds of Prey guard Castle Klaar. We guard the duchess," Darshia said. "When she's here."

"And what's guarding the castle been like?"

Darshia shifted her feet. She wasn't sure where this was going. "Keep the wrong people from stumbling in." She smiled weakly. "Keep drunk nobles from stumbling out."

Stasha laughed softly. "Is that all, really? You're a leader."

Darshia shook her head. "A leader?"

"You're captain of the Birds of Prey, no?"

"I'm no captain."

"I realize the Birds have no formal command structure," Stasha said. "There's been no time to establish one. I guess everything has sort of evolved. But Tosh is gone and the girls look to you. You might not wear a badge of rank, but you're their captain. And that's how I think of you too."

Darshia didn't know what to say to that, so she said nothing.

"So you're a leader, and you're important," Stasha said. "And I need you."

"I'm no captain," Darshia said again. "I'm just . . ."

"What? A whore? None of us are anything until we decide to be. A captain. A steward. We're living in a dangerous and confusing time, but also a time that's letting us step up and be exactly who we say we are. We just have to be brave enough to state it in a calm, clear voice, and damn anyone who says otherwise."

A long moment of silence stretched between them.

"Tell me what you need," Darshia said. "And I'll do my best."

Stasha pushed the folded parchment across her desk at Darshia. "Read it."

Darshia plucked the parchment from the desk, saw that the wax seal had been broken. She unfolded it. A single page, but it felt like lead in her hands. She read:

> I have the final component. I'll be at the usual place
> on Dumo's Day. If one of your people can't make it
> then, I'll show up at the same time the next three days
> in a row, but I can't linger longer than that. Make sure
> your man knows the password and has my gold.

The note was unsigned.

"A mystery," Darshia said. "And not a lot to go on. Dumo's Day is next week."

"Except we know who has the answers," Stasha said. "I'm paying a visit to Giffen later. We'll see how he's enjoying his cell."

"I suppose you have some dirty work for me," Darshia said.

"Not so dirty as mine," Stasha said. "Please find Lubin and Bune and ask them to join me in the dungeon. I have no intention of leaving Giffen's cell without the information I want."

◆ ◆ ◆

Giffen heard the keys jingle and the footsteps. Torchlight growing gradually brighter as they approached his cell door.

What now? Giffen wondered. *Can't they leave me in peace?*

He didn't mean that. Day upon day in utter darkness. Even the most hostile visitor was a welcome change of pace. And each visit was an opportunity. Giffen gathered information. He was biding his time. Somehow he'd get free, and then he would make every man, woman, and child in Klaar pay for their abuse of him.

The lock rattled, and the cell door creaked open, sudden torchlight making him wince.

It was that whore peddler Benadicta again. Two enormous bruisers in tow. His bruises still ached from the pasting they'd given him. He'd see those oafs dead as well, although he'd likely have to hire a gang of ruffians to make it happen. Benadicta he'd gladly kill with his own hands.

"To what do I owe the pleasure?" he asked.

"We caught your man Bolger," Stasha said.

"Congratulations," Giffen said dryly. "Am I meant to be impressed?"

"You're meant to listen," Stasha said. "Because this involves you."

"Please do go on," Giffen said. "I'm aquiver with anticipation."

"Bolger had a note on him when he was taken. Sealed. He was delivering it to you."

Stasha took out the note and read it to Giffen.

As he listened, he kept his face carefully blank, not wanting to react. He immediately realized his mistake. She was used to seeing him sneer. A blank expression was a dead giveaway. Giffen rolled his eyes as if he were bored, but it was too late. A hint of a smile at the edges of Stasha's mouth. She knew. Giffen had the answers she wanted, and she knew it.

"We already know how this goes," she said. "You can tell us or be beaten and then tell us anyway."

"A beating. You've done that already," Giffen said. "What of it?"

"It can always get worse," Stasha Benadicta said coldly. "We can take your thumbs. We can leave here with arms and legs. We can make you go away a little piece at a time. It might take all year."

Giffen tried to swallow, but his mouth and throat had suddenly gone dry.

CHAPTER THREE

Hot and steamy and uncomfortable.

That's how Alem felt lying facedown on the mossy rock, his clothes clinging wet and heavy, the morning sun already baking the world. He'd been told this was still a mild part of the year in the tropics, the real heat coming deeper into the summer. But these were minor concerns.

Alem was alive.

Maurizan had fallen overboard the previous night when Miko's scow had been caught in the grip of a tremendous storm. He'd seen her topple over the gunwale and then dove in after her without thinking.

Because you're a stupid thick idiot thicko, he thought.

He'd lost track of her, bobbing in the water, waves crashing down on him. He'd lost track of the boat too. Lost track of the land. The currents took him at their whim. He'd finally bumped up against something that nobody would call a proper island, just a stretch of rock humped up out of the sea with moss and lichen growing over it. He'd sprawled there, rain lashing him, until he'd finally fallen asleep.

He sat up now, limbs aching, and shaded his eyes against the rising sun. Alem stood, turned a slow circle. Open, empty sea stretched in almost every direction, but there was a small island east only a couple hundred yards away. He could probably swim it but would have preferred not to. And who knew what sort of creatures lurked the depths? Sharks were a common enough terror, but he'd heard of a lot worse. Things with tentacles that wrapped around a man and dragged him to the bottom, for example.

And there could be strong currents. He might try swimming straight for the island only to find he was being carried sideways out to sea. His boots were soft leather. He could take them off and tuck them into his belt. They'd hamper his swimming, but he'd need them again when he made land. Yeah, it was doable.

Still, he wasn't up for it.

On the other hand, Alem couldn't live on thirty square feet of rock in the middle of the ocean for the rest of his life either. He'd need water eventually. Food.

And if Maurizan washed up on some island, maybe that was the one. He had to find out.

So. Boots tucked into belt. He eased back into the water.

At least it was cooler. He swam toward the island, forcing himself to go slowly. Getting a cramp or tiring out halfway there wouldn't help him.

Arms stroked. Legs kicked. Head above the water for a gulp of air. He fell into a rhythm. After a while he paused to get his bearings. The island didn't look one inch closer.

Damn it.

♦ ♦ ♦

Tosh knelt at the prow of the scow-schooner, eyes peeled for any foreign objects floating in the water. Kalli scanned the ocean to port, and

Lureen and Viriam were doing the same thing starboard and aft. Miko manned the tiller, uncharacteristically quiet and somber.

They were all worried about Alem and Maurizan. They'd all grown close, traveling together these past weeks, surviving a ship-to-ship attack from the Perranese, barely escaping from the mobs in Sherrik before the city sealed itself for siege.

Miko had been sailing for hours, crisscrossing the area where Alem and Maurizan had gone overboard. Not a sign of them. Not a hint.

"Tosh."

Tosh tore his attention from the sea and looked back at Kalli. "You see something?"

"No," Kalli said. "Nobody has."

"So?"

"So it's a big ocean," Kalli said. "Miko says we barely got through that storm ourselves. He says the chances of Alem and Maurizan surviving are—"

"Don't." Tosh turned away from her. "Don't say it."

Silence for a moment except for the wind and the scow slicing a path across the water.

"Okay, so what do I do?" Tosh asked. "Just leave them?"

"You're the boss," Kalli said. "I just thought you might want to talk about it."

Tosh turned his head and saw Viriam and Lureen were watching his conversation with Kalli. Likely they'd discussed this before electing Kalli to come talk to him.

"Maurizan still has the map," Tosh said. "But Miko has seen it. He still knows where we're going."

"She and Alem could be together if they made it to land," Kalli said. "They might follow the map. We could find them there."

Tosh nodded, thinking it through. "It might be our best bet. To keep going. It's where Alem and Maurizan would go."

"Yes." Kalli was nodding too. Encouragement.

It was what he needed to hear. It was a plan to find their lost friends instead of a decision to abandon them.

Just the sort of lie a man could cling to.

Shivering and wet.

Maurizan hugged herself and shifted, gravel crunching beneath her. She was afraid to move in the pitch darkness. She sensed an open cavernous area. The place smelled dank and salty. The water's edge was only a few feet away.

When she'd fallen overboard during the storm, panic had seized her. She could swim but not well. The sea was something angry and immense that wanted to crash down on her and drag her to its cold depths. Never had she felt such helpless fear. She'd known she was going to die. No other scenario had been conceivable.

Until the Fish Man.

Even when he'd been saving her, it had seemed ridiculous. Miko's tall tale of the Fish Man, glimpsed here and there by sailors—often drunk—skimming just below the surface of the water. It was supposed to be a legend. Nonsense. Lies.

But the Fish Man was truth.

He'd grabbed her in the water, swimming so incredibly fast, diving, breaking the surface again just in time for her to gulp air before plunging back below the surface. This had happened over and over again until the routine of it had numbed her. When he'd taken her down for the last time, it had been longer. Her lungs were about to burst, and she'd struggled, but the Fish Man held her with an iron grip. Just when she was desperate, about to give up on ever tasting air again, they broke the surface into total darkness. Maurizan sucked in ragged breaths as the Fish Man dragged her out of the water and dropped her on a dry patch of gravel.

She'd heard a splash and then silence. Gone.

Now she waited, wondering if the Fish Man would ever return. She dozed, started awake, dozed again.

Finally there was another splash, and she held her breath, listening, waiting.

Footsteps on the gravel. Movement.

Her hands fell to the daggers at her belt. The Fish Man could have left her. Could have let her drown. Could have done anything. Maurizan held tight to the hilts of the daggers but didn't draw them.

A scraping, more movement.

Maurizan slowly and quietly kept backing up until her back was pressed against the cavern wall.

A sharp sound and something flared in the darkness. A spark. The sharp sound again, flint striking steel and then a bright-orange flare of light.

And there stood the Fish Man in the glow of the lantern he was lighting.

He wasn't so tall. A couple of inches taller than Maurizan. The broad shoulders and thin waist of a swimmer, someone who spent a lot more time in the water than he did walking on land. Legs muscular, skin white and smooth. Hairless except for the unkempt thatch of blond on his head and another between his legs.

She realized where she was looking and turned her head quickly, but her eyes darted back for a peek without her meaning it. "Who are you?"

"Kristos."

Kristos. It seemed a strangely ordinary name for the legendary Fish Man.

"Could you put something on, Kristos?"

"Sorry." He gestured at himself. "This is the best for swimming." His accent was heavy and unfamiliar, and the words came out *Dees iz bezt for sweeming.*

"Where are you from?"

"Helva, like you," Kristos said.

"You don't sound like it."

"I have been many years with the Moogari," he said. "My accent is like how they talk."

Moogari. Terrific, thought Maurizan. *Probably what they call the local cannibals.*

But so far the Fish Man hadn't been eaten. Maybe he'd gone native.

He turned to reach for a long stretch of dry, rough cloth hanging from a hook on the cave wall. It had a pattern on it of leaves and vines, a wrap like she'd seen natives wear in the South Sea islands. Well, in paintings anyway. She'd never been there.

Kristos turned away from her as he tied the wrap around himself, and that's when she saw it and gasped.

Kristos's head jerked back to her. "What is it?"

"The Prime," said the gypsy. The tattoo down his back, the ornate circle between the shoulder blades, and the runes trailing down either side of the spine.

"You know this word?" Kristos said. "You've seen this tattoo before?"

"Yes."

"Where?"

"My mother," Maurizan said. "And grandmother." She'd seen Rina's too but didn't see any need to mention it.

Kristos's eyes narrowed with curiosity. "Who are you?"

Maurizan tightened the grip on her dagger hilts. "Who are *you*?"

"I saw you fall from the boat, rescued you, and brought you here," Kristos said. "I went back to find the others, but the boat had sailed away. I have lived here a long time. You are safe here. I saved you."

"Thanks." She didn't ease the grip on her weapons.

"When I was a child, my family and I traveled by sea from the Red City to Fyria. My father was a merchant. We were caught in a storm like you, and the ship went down. I washed ashore and the Moogari found me. I've been a man of the Scattered Isles ever since. What about you?" Kristos asked. "You are far from home. And you know the Prime. I think you have a story to tell, yes?"

She nailed him with her eyes, looking him over, deciding. She let go of her daggers.

The gypsy reached into her vest, came out with a piece of parchment. It was still damp, and she unfolded it carefully. She held it out to Kristos. "Bring the lantern closer. Look."

He approached slowly before leaning in to look at the map, the lantern held aloft. It took him a moment, but then his face changed as comprehension dawned.

"I see," he said. "I wondered when somebody would come."

CHAPTER
FOUR

Rina stared at the dagger tip an inch from her eye. She tried again and failed to tap into the spirit. Cold fear welled up in her. She was paralyzed but completely awake and aware of her situation. A prisoner of the Perranese, they'd apparently dumped her unconscious into the back of a cart, where she now sat unable to move, a foreign wizard threatening her with a dagger and worse.

What had he called himself again? Jariko. That was it.

"Be calm, Duchess," Jariko said. "We are simply going to have a chat, you and I."

Rina strained, reached with her willpower, desperately trying to touch the spirit. It was as if the spirit were covered with some greasy film, a slick barrier that prevented her from latching on. She flailed at it, dug at it, scratched it, but her grip on the spirit kept sliding away.

"Ink magic is ancient and powerful," Jariko said. "The secrets of it were thought by many to have faded into legend, but I crossed the Eastern Sea with an ink mage named Ankar, a brute of a man covered head to foot in tattoos. Rumor is you defeated him, although I find that hard to believe."

Rina barely heard the man. Outwardly, she appeared limp and life-less, a rag doll slumped in the back of a shabby cart. Inwardly, she raged, flinging herself against the walls of her own consciousness, trying to do anything to move or blink or reach the spirit. If she could tap into the well of her own spirit, it would turn the tables. *Come on, move a finger, wiggle a toe, blink. Anything!*

"For obvious reasons, a wizard cannot ink the Prime upon his own back," Jariko said. "Not even the acrobats of the Imperial Circus are *that* flexible." He chuckled, mildly pleased with his own humor. "Which means *you* know a wizard, and *he* knows the secrets of the Prime."

He shifted his dagger to menace the other eyeball. "There are a number of dire spells I can bring to bear, which will convince you to see things my way, but sometimes the old-fashioned ways are best. The simple idea of something pointy being inserted into one's eye is quite appalling to most people. You probably think your eyeball will pop like an overripe piece of fruit, squirting juice everywhere. Not so. It's actually a quite different experience altogether. Would you like to find out firsthand?"

Jariko brought the tip of the dagger to within a hair's width of her eyes. In her mind, Rina shrieked terror.

"Now, I'm going to ask you questions," Jariko said. "You will answer. It's just that simple. If you *don't* answer, well, that's when things become complicated. I think we'd all prefer to keep things simple, don't you? Yes, of course you do. Now, I want to know the name of the wizard who inked your Prime. I want to know where he's located. If differ-ent wizards inked your other tattoos, I want to know the names and whereabouts of these spell casters too. I want to know the circumstances that brought you into contact with them and why it is they found you worthy of such power. I intend to be very thorough in my interrogation, so there's no point in holding anything back."

Her vacant eyes stared back at him.

Jariko turned away abruptly, anger twisting his features as he spit a string of obscenities in his own tongue.

When he faced her again, his smile seemed strained. "The joke's on me, I'm afraid. The potion coursing through your veins renders you temporarily paralyzed. Naturally, that would also render your tongue and mouth paralyzed. Of course you can't answer me. Even clever fellows like me trip themselves up by overlooking something simple."

What was he saying? Pay attention. Calm down. Panicking isn't getting you anywhere, girl. Rina saw two fully armored Perranese warriors standing at a respectful distance behind Jariko—likely there to rush in and help him should the mad duchess prove too much for the wizard. Obviously there could be more men behind her, but no sense worrying about maybes.

Okay, a wizard and two soldiers. What are you going to do about them?

"We've been keeping you unconscious," Jariko continued. "The theory being that it wouldn't occur to you to slaughter us all if you were asleep. All well and good, but then of course you can't answer my questions that way either. The paralysis potion accomplishes more or less the same thing, but you're conscious, so I can question you."

They'd chosen well how to keep her captive. Asleep she would be helpless. But Jariko was mistaken if he thought paralysis would bind her in the same way. Tapping into the spirit was an act of will. She didn't need to move, but she did need to be conscious. Jariko might have unwittingly given her the opening she needed.

Rina redoubled her efforts reaching, attempting to get a grip on the spirit, but it kept sliding away, so tantalizing close. She felt frustration and anger building in her and immediately tamped it down. No time. She had to focus. Eventually the wizard would get tired of his own voice.

"It's a matter of degree, obviously," the wizard said. "I mean, you're not *completely* paralyzed, are you? The heart must pump blood. Lungs must draw breath. You're functioning. It's a matter of dosage, you see."

Grabbing for the spirit, trying to latch on to it wasn't working. It had always been so effortless before. She didn't usually pay attention to how it was done; it had become second nature in the past weeks.

"The dose I gave you will wear off very gradually," Jariko explained. "It will be quite some time before you can move your arms and legs, but something smaller might be accomplished. If we wait a bit, you might be able to blink your eyes, and then we can have a conversation of sorts. One eyeblink for yes. Two for no. That sort of thing, if you follow me."

Just keep talking, you arrogant asshole.

It was difficult to concentrate, staring directly at the dagger point. Jariko had been right. The idea of that point plunging straight into her eyeball was enough to—

Wait. Dagger point.

She had attempted to latch on to the spirit like she was grabbing a handful of dry grass. Of course, that was all wrong. The old wizard Weylan had called it "tapping" into the spirit. Like drying to draw ale from a large keg. So too was the spirit a deep well within her. Except now there was some sort of slimy layer over the surface, something that kept her from getting through. The effects of the potion, most likely.

The dagger point at her eye had made her realize her mistake.

Rina envisioned her willpower as a physical thing, long and straight like a blade. She molded it with her mind, honed it to a fine point. She put all of the willpower behind it and *thrust*.

The greasy film over the well of spirit stretched, resisting. Rina summoned all of her inner strength, insistent, demanding. The sharpened point of her willpower *would* break through. She would not accept anything less.

I. Am. Master. Of. Myself.

She was vaguely aware that something distracted the wizard. Jariko turned his head at the sound of a galloping horse. The two Perranese guards drew their swords, both suddenly looking alert.

Jariko shouted orders at them, brought the dagger up to fend off whatever was coming, and shifted just enough to block Rina's view of what happened next.

◆ ◆ ◆

Bishop Hark had seen the best opportunity he was likely to get.

He'd crept in as close to the Perranese camp as he'd dared. He'd watched, waited, and hoped. Frankly, it had seemed hopeless. Hark intended to do everything within his power to free Duchess Veraiin, but taking on hundreds of Perranese warriors seemed a poor way to go about it.

And then, the one with the long moustache and the robes—some sort of sorcerer, probably—had, inexplicably, taken her farther from the rest of the camp. He had only two guards with him. Suddenly, the situation had become manageable.

Although applying the word *manageable* to a situation that involved a wizard was dubious at best.

Dumo always asks us to look on the bright side. This often involves inventing *a bright side.*

The trick was speed. Hark was educated enough to know something about how a wizard's spell worked. They had to say a litany of nonsense words, and if the spell were interrupted, then it would fail. So . . . kill the bloody wizard first. Simple.

He'd raised his mace, spurred his horse, and ridden like all the underworld blood demons of Hadronetes were after him.

Hark's steed thundered into the small clearing, the bishop twirling his mace over his head, ready to serve up crushing death to whoever stood in his way. The old man in the robe barked orders at the soldiers, and they drew weapons, moved to take up positions between the bishop and the wizard.

So much for killing the wizard first.

The Perranese wore wide helms that flared outward. Probably good for defending against a rain of arrows. Terrible against anything coming from below.

Hark rode hard at the first warrior, swinging the mace under-handed. He smashed it up into the first warrior's chink, which shattered, teeth and blood flying, jaw cracking. The soldier dropped his weapon, staggered, and collapsed.

The other warrior swung at him, but the sword glanced off the bishop's thick breastplate. Hark brought the mace down onto the warrior's helm. A metallic crunch. The warrior stepped back, shaken, and brought his sword up to fend off the next blow.

Instead, Hark urged his horse forward, slamming into the soldier and knocking him to the ground.

Bishop Hark leapt from his horse before the soldier could recover and brought the mace down hard on the man's face. He smashed it nearly flat, blood spraying to either side. The warrior's legs twitched, and then he went still.

Hark turned back to the wizard.

The old man in the robes had one hand lifted, a pinch of some powder between thumb and forefinger drifting away on a mild breeze. His mouth worked frantically to utter the words of some spell as precisely as possible.

Hark sprinted for him, mace raised to stave in the man's skull.

Dumo, grant me the speed to engage my foe before he's able to—

The wizard completed the spell and pointed a bony finger at Hark.

The wizard's hand bucked, and a blue bolt of lightning shot out and struck the bishop in the breastplate.

Hark went rigid, every part of him buzzing with fire, blue light crackling all around him. He trembled violently, halting steps taking him nowhere.

He pissed himself.

He blinked, discovered he was on his hands and knees. He tried to right himself but found his limbs in rebellion. He tingled unpleasantly all over, his hair seeming like it was straining to leave his scalp. He coughed, spit bile.

The bishop found himself frozen like that. He couldn't stand or move; he just shook and felt sick and knew he was going to die. With enormous effort, he slowly picked his head up, squinted at the wizard. Hark tried to focus on the man, but his vision was a blur. It looked like the wizard was raising his hands, perhaps readying another spell.

I guess I'm just not dying fast enough for the bastard, Hark thought.

◆ ◆ ◆

Rina pushed.

It was all in her mind, of course, but it helped her to think of it as pushing. She mentally put her shoulder against her willpower and thrust the point deep into the grimy layer that kept her from touching the spirit.

The barrier stretched, growing thin and weak at the driving point of her sheer insistence. Her willpower was like a lance thrusting home.

And then the barrier . . . ripped.

Rina was through to the other side and tapped the deep well of her spirit. The power flooded into every part of her, filled every corner. And with it, as always, came the complete and perfect awareness of herself. If she wanted, she could count every hair on her head, knew the width of each fingernail, the landscape of every tooth, the position of each freckle.

But to free herself of the paralyzing potion, she would need to look inward even more deeply.

Her consciousness dove below the flesh of her arm, traveled up the bone to one of her fingers. She went inside one of her veins and got caught in the flow of her own blood. She examined every drop until she found what she was looking for.

They looked like glowing blue crystals, spiked and clinging to the drops of blood like sandspur. The potion.

Tapping into the spirit gave Rina total control of her own body. She simply needed to know what had to be done and focus. She ordered the corrupt blood to flow out of her finger, clean blood to replace it. A second later she was able to wiggle that finger. It felt stiff and ached, but she could do it.

She repeated the process with the other four fingers and then the rest of the hand. She opened and closed her fist, working the muscles.

Rina ignored the screams of pain and the crunch of weapons smashing armor. Whatever was happening was none of her business for another few seconds. She needed one good arm. That was all.

She forced the potion up past her elbow, then past her shoulder. Her arm was free of it now.

Jariko cast a spell, and the small clearing flashed with blue lightning.

Rina rolled her shoulder. It felt like a rusty hinge, but it could move.

It could strike.

She reached out with her one good arm and latched on to the wizard's wrist just as he was preparing to cast another spell. Jariko looked back, eyes wide with horror and realization.

The strength of the bull tattoo flowed into Rina's hand. She squeezed. Jariko's wrist crunched and snapped like a fistful of dry twigs. The wizard screamed. She jerked hard, pulling him down into the cart with her. He fell across her legs, looking up at her, terrified.

Rina let go of his wrist and latched on to his throat. She guessed how she must look. The rest of her was still paralyzed, her head lolling to one side, eyes glassy and unblinking. It must have seemed as if her arm moved independently of the rest of her. As if it were possessed by some demon specter.

She squeezed once, and Jariko's neck snapped, eyes rolling back in his head.

Rina sat in the cart for long seconds, listening. Whatever had happened, it was over now. She saw bodies on the ground in front of her but couldn't turn her head to see anything else.

She focused, repeating the same trick as before, chasing the potion from her other arm, legs, head. She pulled it from every part of her body until it was a knot of bright pain in the middle of her stomach. Rina pushed the dead wizard off her, crawled to the edge of the cart, and gagged.

At first nothing came up. She gagged again, chest and throat burning. Rina's mouth suddenly tasted sour, and she spit. She still had the potion gathered in her gut.

Her back hunched, mouth opening so wide her jaw hurt. She vomited a long stream of hot fluid that spattered on the ground, steaming and sizzling. It was a mix of blood and digestive fluid and Jariko's potion. The smell hit her, and she spewed a second gout of vomit on top of the first.

She collapsed trembling in the back of the cart. A slick sheen of cold sweat covered her body. Rina was still tapped into the spirit. She pushed away all pain and discomfort, commanded her limbs to obey. She lurched to her knees. Then to her feet. She stepped over the first two bodies, her eyes going wide at the third.

Bishop Hark!

She knelt next to the man who was down in the mud, gently turned him over. "Bishop."

Hark's eyes flickered open. His mouth worked but no words came out.

"Easy," Rina said. "I've got you."

Rina hadn't seen everything that had happened, but it was an easy guess that Hark had been on the receiving end of whatever spell Jariko had cast.

"I'm sorry," Rina said. "I know you're hurt, but we've got to go. I don't know where we are, and I don't know how many other soldiers might arrive at any second. I don't know anything. Can you tell me which way to go?"

Hark lifted a hand. It shook. He pointed west and a little north. "Your h-horse. And y-your arm-muh-mor."

"Okay. Don't talk anymore. I'm going to put you on your horse. It might hurt. Sorry."

Hark nodded, head shaky. It wasn't completely clear if he understood what was happening.

Rina gathered him up, his stout form draped over one of her shoulders, and stood. Even with the bull strength, the fully armored bishop was no easy burden. She took him to a hidden horse and tossed him over the saddle. He grunted but seemed otherwise unhurt.

We've got to go. We need to move fast before more soldiers come.

She took the horse's reins and headed out in the direction Hark had indicated.

Rina remembered she was still tapped into the spirit. Having undergone incredible torments to touch the spirit again, she was reluctant to let it go, but she knew the dangers of hanging on too long. She could drain herself, burn herself out. Her spirit well was deep but not inexhaustible.

She released her hold on the spirit.

Immediately she fell to her knees, going dizzy and sick, every muscle in her body aching. Obviously the only thing that had let her function was being tapped into the spirit. She was wiped out. Hours—days?—of slumping paralyzed in the back of a Perranese cart had taken their toll. Her muscles and joints were stiff. Impossibly, she was alive, but she wouldn't stay that way if she couldn't summon the will to move.

She willed herself to her feet, legs quivering, sweat breaking out on her forehead and under her arms. She breathed in through her nose, exhaled raggedly out of her mouth. She closed her eyes tight, waited for the dizziness to pass, then opened them again.

A cry rose from deep in the forest behind her. The distant clank of armor and rustle of men gathering and coming through the wood.

Move, you stupid girl. Get out of here.

Rina tugged at the reins and headed west, each halting step a stab of pain in her limbs. She forced herself to move quickly in spite of the pain, weaving between the trees, putting one foot in front of the other with dogged determination. A minute later, she was no less panicked. Five minutes later, and she started to feel she'd put some safe distance between her and the Perranese.

Ten minutes later she'd found her horse with her weapons and armor. She felt almost whole again once she donned the armor and strapped on her weapons. A general sort of fatigue weighed her down, but the awareness she'd escaped a very close call buoyed her up again. She was damn lucky to be alive. It was a lesson, really. No matter how powerful she felt, no matter what kind of strength the tattoos gave her, there were no guarantees. Anything could happen. At any time.

She went to Hark still draped over the horse.

"Bishop Hark," she said. "I think we're in the clear, but we'd better keep moving. They could catch up to us easily."

No response.

"Bishop Hark." She felt his neck.

He lay pale and motionless.

CHAPTER
FIVE

"Edgar who?" Brasley asked.

"One of the hired toughs we brought along to guard our backs," Talbun said. "He made it this far. We were ambushed at the last."

Olgen, Talbun, and Brasley stared down at the corpse.

"Ambushed?" Brasley frowned. "This place is abandoned, isn't it?" His eyes darted from Olgen to Talbun and back again. "Are you saying the Great Library is *not* an abandoned ruin?"

Olgen cleared his throat. "Well, no. I mean, that is to say, there is dispute among the scholars about whether or not there remain living inhabitants in the depths of the Great Library, but those theories are not necessarily pertinent here. The far more likely explanation is that this fellow fell victim to one of the other expeditions."

Brasley's eyes widened. "One of the other expeditions?"

"Yes."

"An expedition like us?" Brasley asked.

"Yes."

Brasley cleared his throat. "Am I to understand that expeditions prey upon other expeditions?"

"Hardly ever," Olgen said. "But yes."

"Well." Brasley blew out a tired sigh. "Fantastic."

"Sadly, not all expeditions are motivated by the wonder of discovery," Olgen said. "Some are simply out for some quick coin, and it is easier to rob their fellow explorers of treasure than it is to find it for themselves."

"I feel like this might be something that could have been mentioned sooner," Brasley said. "Like *before* entering the library."

Olgen turned to Talbun, face puzzled. "You knew him?"

"Yes."

Olgen looked at the body, then back to her. "But the corpse has obviously been here for many years."

Talbun frowned and narrowed her eyes. "So?"

"So . . . uh . . . nothing." Olgen rapidly elected to focus his attention elsewhere. "There's a small room up here. I think I'll have a look." He stepped lively down the hall away from them, lantern held aloft as he went.

Brasley moved to stand next to Talbun. They both looked down at the corpse the wizard had called Edgar.

"Part of your expedition?" Brasley asked.

"Yes."

"Did you see who killed him?"

"I killed him," Talbun said.

"Well," Brasley said. "That's perfect. I do love a good story."

"There's no time to go into the details."

"I'll settle for the basics."

"We had a disagreement over an artifact we'd found," Talbun said.

"So you shot him with a crossbow?"

"*He* tried to kill *me* first. Look, Brasley, I'm the all-powerful wizard here, remember? I don't answer to you or—"

"Milord! Milady! Come have a look," Olgen called from down the hall.

"We can continue this later," Brasley said.

They were quickly walking toward the sound of Olgen's voice when Talbun stopped abruptly to gawk at a narrow arched doorway that had caved in, a ton of cracked and broken building blocks completely blocking it.

"What is it?" Brasley asked.

"It's a cave-in."

"The place is ancient," Brasley said. "There are probably cave-ins all over the place."

"You don't understand," Talbun said. "This is the way I came out last time I was here. I'd hoped to go *back* this way."

Brasley pushed one of the larger blocks. It didn't budge. "Yeah, I don't think that's going to happen."

"Come on," Talbun said. "Let's see what the guide's found."

Olgen stood at the edge of a doorway, peering into a small room. Brasley and Talbun looked past him into it. Nothing.

"I'm missing something," Brasley said.

Olgen pointed along the walls. "Look at those very thick ropes. See how they disappear into the ceiling one way and then down into the floor also?"

Brasley squinted at the ropes. "Ah. Yes. This is obviously . . . the rope room."

"No, begging your pardon, milord," Olgen said. "Do either you or milady have a background in engineering?"

"Sorry, no," Brasley said. "My line is more drinking and womanizing. Although I am recently married."

"Ah. No, I meant scholarly pursuits." Olgen turned to Talbun. "Milady?"

"Magical studies," Talbun said vaguely.

"I believe this is a lift," Olgen said.

"A what?" Brasley asked.

"I think I know what he means," Talbun said. "A means for moving up and down within the Great Library. I've heard rumors of such."

Olgen beamed. "Just so, milady. It is a miracle of engineering only whispered about in the high places of the university."

"There's nothing special about ropes and pulleys," Brasley said.

"Please don't misunderstand, milord," Olgen said. "This isn't anything as simple as that. It is a perfectly balanced system that allows you to go up or down to any level in the library. If the stories are true, that is. Engineering is not my field, but I can't pass up this opportunity to examine the mechanisms. Without a doubt the university will want to send master engineers to examine the lift . . . if that is indeed what this is."

Brasley gestured into the room. "By all means. Have a look."

Olgen set foot into the room. Then another foot. He entered slowly, hands drawn up to his chest as if he didn't want to accidently touch anything, eyes wide.

Talbun followed. "If it's still operational, the lift might be useful. Could save us a lot of time."

Brasley rolled his eyes. "*If* it still works and *if* we can figure out how to use it. Everything in this damn place is falling apart, remember?"

He led the goat cart into the room.

Iron doors slammed closed behind him, sealing them in the room.

"Are you fucking kidding me?" Brasley said.

"What did you do?" Talbun demanded. "Did you touch something?"

"I didn't touch a damn thing," Brasley insisted.

Looking back, Brasley saw two rows of short levers, at least a dozen for each row. Next to that was a larger lever shoved all the way into the up position.

"One of these levers opens it up again, I expect."

"*Don't* touch anything," Talbun said.

"Our combined weight must have triggered the doors to close," Olgen said. "That's a guess, obviously."

"Well, I don't fancy being trapped in such a small space," Brasley said.

"Just stay calm," Talbun said.

"I'll be calm enough when I'm not trapped anymore," Brasley insisted.

"I imagine those small levers choose what level the lift takes us to," Olgen mused. "Or maybe a combination of levers. Fascinating."

"No, not fucking fascinating," Brasley said. "Very annoying. I want out of here. I don't like being confined. Not with a goat especially."

"Let's just figure this out," Talbun said.

"If all these smaller levers decide which level we go to, then this big lever must open the door." Brasley grabbed the lever.

Olgen's eyes shot wide. "Milord!"

Talbun lunged for him. "Brasley, no!"

Brasley yanked the big lever all the way down.

There was a distant clunk, and in a split second they were all thrown to the floor as the lift sped upward at a staggering speed.

Brasley heard somebody screaming and realized it was him, his face pressed flat against the cold stone floor. The little room sped up and up.

And up.

CHAPTER
SIX

Brasley struggled to push himself back to his hands and knees, but the lift flew upward at such a velocity, he could barely move. Ropes and pulleys rattled as they passed each level. The goat bleated panic. Olgen nearly matched the goat's terror, screaming sheer guttural fear.

If he could get to his feet, maybe Brasley could grab the big lever and flip it up again. Maybe it would stop their reckless ascent, and then they could—

There was the crack and smash of the world breaking. The little room shook so violently, Brasley knew he was going to die.

The lift stopped.

Because it had smashed into something.

"We must have collided with the top level." Olgen looked pale, a sheen of sweat on his face.

Brasley gestured to a set of iron doors similar to those that had closed behind them on one of the lower levels. "Do you think one of the levers would open those?"

"Don't fucking touch any more levers," Talbun barked.

Something creaked and groaned and snapped, and the floor tilted abruptly.

Brasley threw his arms out to his side for balance. "I would like to be on the other side of those doors, please."

Olgen set his lantern down and went to the doors, stuck his fingers into the seam where they closed together, and tried to pry them apart. "Stuck fast."

The floor lurched again. Grinding noises came from somewhere above them.

Brasley looked pointedly at Talbun. "Can't you do anything? You know." He tapped the side of his head with a finger. "Something from up here?" *Come on, woman. What's the point of being a wizard if you can't magic us out of this?*

She nibbled a bottom lip, considering. "Maybe. But I'm pretty sure it would incinerate us too."

"And we're still thinking the levers are a bad idea?"

Something groaned, the sound of metal bending. The little room shook.

Talbun raised her hands, doubt on her face. "I guess we've got to try something."

"Wait!" Brasley rushed to the cart just as the floor tilted again, almost knocking him off his feet. He rummaged the supplies in back and came out with a long metal pry bar. "I thought the supply vendor was just milking me when I bought these tools, but thank Dumo I did."

He waved Olgen out of the way and jammed the end of the pry bar into the crack where the doors met. He worked it back and forth until he edged it in a few inches, and then he put all of his strength into prying one way and then another, muscles straining, face going red.

"Olgen, help me!"

The young man crowded in and gripped the pry bar, adding his strength to Brasley's. They gnashed teeth and grunted, and the doors . . . budged!

"Keep going!" Brasley shouted. "We're getting it."

The doors slid back haltingly, making an ugly scraping sound of metal on metal.

"We may have knocked the doors off their tracks when the lift hit so hard," Olgen said. "Probably there's rust too."

"I don't care," Brasley said. "Just put your back into it."

There was another cracking sound above them, and the room shimmied, floor tilting slightly one way and then the other.

"Hurry!" Talbun urged.

"Oh, hurry? Really?" Brasley pushed the pry bar with everything he had. "Why didn't I think of that?"

Something gave and both doors slid to the side enough for Brasley and Olgen to get their hands and shoulders in. They pushed, the doors sliding rough until they were open enough for the humans, goat, and cart to get through.

"Come on!" Brasley grabbed the goat by the reins. Olgen and Talbun went through ahead of him.

Brasley backed through the doors and out of the lift, dragging the goat behind him. "Titan, you stupid beast, let's go already."

Because the floor of the lift had tilted, it was six inches lower than the floor beyond the doors. The front two wheels stuck, jamming the cart in place. The goat kept on with its panicked racket.

"Help me!" Brasley shouted. "It's stuck."

Talbun and Olgen reached past him, each grabbing hold of the cart. They heaved and managed to pull the front wheels over the hump. Titan took that moment to discover a reserve of strength and bounded past them, pulling the cart into the chamber.

There was a series of snapping sounds.

Brasley leaned forward to look into the lift.

The floor of the lift gave way, tumbling back down the shaft and taking the lantern with it. The floor bounced off the sides, shattering into pieces, plummeting, thick ropes and pulleys chasing after it. The falling lantern cast strange shadows. The lantern and debris seemed to fall forever until there was a final crash, the last echo rising until it reached Brasley in the darkness, and then all was silent.

A long dreadful moment settled over the three.

"Is everyone okay?" Talbun's voice somewhere behind him.

"I am, milady," Olgen said. "Milord?"

"Alive," Brasley said. "Everyone stay put. The last thing we need right now is to trip over each other and break our necks. I'll find one of the other lanterns."

Feeling his way in the dark took longer than he'd anticipated, but he found the cart, felt his way through the gear until he found the lantern and the flint and steel. He struck a spark, and soon they had light again.

Brasley checked the gear while the others looked around to figure out what sort of place it was they'd suddenly found themselves. They'd been lucky in one respect: if Titan and the cart had fallen back down the shaft with the lantern, they'd have *nothing*. They'd be crawling through the dark with no food or water.

Brasley saw Olgen standing at the edge of the shaft, looking back down. "Careful. It's a long drop."

"One of the legendary engineering feats of the Great Library. A perfectly balanced and self-contained system of weights and pulleys," Olgen said. "And we wrecked it."

"Never mind," Brasley said. "It brought us here, and anything this high up must be important. Maybe we've had a lucky accident. Come. Let's see what Talbun's found."

They came up behind her where she stood looking up at a set of tall double doors, carved from some black stone. There was a golden circle at the center of the doors. It was covered in ancient runes Brasley couldn't hope to read. Golden chains went from the circle to the four corners of the door.

"It's a seal," Talbun said. There was a faraway quality to her voice.

"Sealed? Damn," Brasley said. "So we can't get in."

"It's not a seal to keep us out," Talbun said. "It's to keep something in."

CHAPTER
SEVEN

Miko hung on the tiller, guiding the scow along a narrow passage between two islands. He seemed to know where he was going, or at least Tosh hoped so because he certainly had *no* idea where they were.

He's crazy but you've got to trust him, Tosh thought. *He knows the Scattered Isles like the back of his hand.*

Tosh hoped.

How had he been drawn into this? A common soldier, then a deserter, then a cook in a whorehouse, and now on a mission he didn't completely understand for a duchess hundreds of miles away, in a foreign land so hot it made him sweat between his thighs until he had a rash.

Tosh sighed. He didn't much like boats either.

"Tosh," Lureen called from the prow. She pointed ahead of them to a small island.

Tosh squinted into the waning light. A twisting pillar of smoke rose into the air. A campfire maybe.

He turned back to Miko. "A settlement?"

Miko shrugged. "Maybe."

"Cannibals?"

"Maybe."

"Should we avoid it?" Tosh said.

"No," Miko said. "We go there."

"What for?"

"This place is the place," Miko said. "From the gypsy-girl map."

Shit.

♦ ♦ ♦

Nobody paid much attention to the man in the cloak as he hobbled through the marketplace. He made a slow circle of the Great Library, looking for a likely place.

Traffic in and out of the Great Library was limited to the front gates. There were no side doors, no rear entrance. There was nothing special about the other three sides of the huge structure. The city of Tul-Agnon went on as usual. He'd passed through a fetid slum and kept circling and now found himself in a market. It was closing up now, getting late into the evening. A few taverns would stay open, but none of the shops. Good. He could attend to his business without prying eyes upon him.

He ducked into an alley between two closed shops that had been built right up against the wall of the Great Library, paused a moment to listen. When he heard nothing, Ankar threw off his cloak. If anyone had been there, they would have seen a hulk of a man, covered head to foot in exotic tattoos. All except for one metallic leg that gleamed in the moonlight. He'd had the leg made by one of the university's best engineers. It would never be as good as his old leg, but he was surprised how well it worked. He'd been practicing with it, and his limp was only very slight now. In battle, he doubted whether it would hamper him very much at all.

Ankar climbed the side of one of the shops. This was the easy part.

Once upon the roof, he ran a hand across the smooth stonework of the ancient builders. Ankar would not need the permission of the university scholars to enter the Great Library. He had his own methods. No ordinary man could hope to scale the smooth outer surface of the library.

Ankar was no ordinary man.

He tapped into the spirit.

He had a tattoo that gave him the strength of a mountain troll, another that made his skin hard as iron. He didn't need handholds. He could make his own. He jammed a fist into the stonework two feet above his head, pulled himself up. He kicked a foothold and kept going. It might take him all night, but he'd get there.

Slowly but surely, Ankar climbed.

◆ ◆ ◆

Darshia didn't want to know how Stasha Benadicta had gotten the information out of Giffen, but she could imagine. Giffen had never struck Darshia as a particularly courageous man. She doubted he'd held out long if Bune and Lubin had been their usual persuasive selves.

The first piece of information they'd extracted had been the password. *Fire toad.* She supposed it had been chosen for the fact it was unlikely anyone would utter such words accidently. The second bit of information was the name of the man she was supposed to meet. A man of southern-island blood called Harpos Knarr. In Klaar, a man with the dark skin of the southern islanders should be fairly easy to spot.

The final bit of information had been the location of the rendezvous.

The statue of the First Duke stood in what had once been Klaar's main square before the second castle was built. Although in fairness the first castle wasn't much of a castle. More like one of the great wooden halls favored by the northern chieftains from whom the First Duke was a descendent. The king of Helva had made him a duke as part of a treaty—the settling of some long-forgotten dispute—and had granted him the lands of Klaar. The great hall and the first buildings had been erected ten years before construction of the Long Bridge.

A century later, another duke built a proper castle in an attempt to dispel the widely held notion the citizens of Klaar were rustic, backwoods bumpkins barely a step removed from the barbarians of the north.

It hadn't worked.

Darshia considered the bronze statue of the First Duke. He did look every inch a barbarian. Broad shouldered, hair and beard wild and shaggy. He wore heavy furs and had been posed heroically, a huge battle-axe held aloft in one hand. An eye patch over his left eye. The stories of how the First Duke had lost the eye ranged from the dull to the outlandish. The cumulative effect of his appearance made him seem striking, imposing, and virile.

I seriously doubt he ever had to pay for sex.

The old town square was in a reasonably good neighborhood, where the patrols still lit the street lamps. Most of the shops were closed at this hour—tailor, glassmaker, apothecary—but it was reasonably cheerful with the warm glow of lantern light in the windows, and a small chapel to Sharine, the moon goddess, across the square. Most people worshipped Dumo, of course, but the moon chapel did a fair bit of business this time of the evening. All in all, the square was far from deserted, but it certainly wasn't crowded either.

Which means Knarr wants to do his business in public . . . but not too public.

Darshia circled the statue again, scanning the square as she strolled. Knarr hadn't shown the first night, and she was about to give up on him now. He was nearly an hour past the agreed time. A few more minutes and she'd call it quits.

A man in heavy blue robes emerged from the moon temple, walking rapidly toward the statue of the First Duke. His hood was pulled forward, hiding his face, but even in the dim illumination of the street lamps, Darshia could see the hands clasped in front of him were a dark brown. Darshia didn't need to move to intercept him. He was walking right toward her.

And then passed her without so much as a glance, continuing on to the statue in the middle of the square.

"Fire toad," Darshia said in a low voice.

Harpos Knarr froze in his tracks. Slowly he turned to look at her, eyes gleaming from the darkness within his hood.

"Did I say it wrong?" Darshia asked.

"Forgive my reticence. Giffen's underlings aren't usually so . . . appealing." He pushed back his hood. He was a little older than she thought he'd be, gray hair over each ear, hairline receding. He was clean shaven with an open face and an easy smile full of white teeth. He seemed amiable and fatherly.

Darshia wasn't falling for it.

"Do you have it?" Darshia asked.

"Do you have the gold?"

Darshia had a bag slung over one shoulder. She wore only a plain dress, no armor, no sword hanging from her belt. She didn't want to send the wrong signal. But there was a short dagger in the bag next to the gold. So far, there seemed no need for it, but situations like this were known to change rapidly.

She took out the gold, jingled the purse.

Knarr reached into his robe and came out with something wrapped in soft leather. He handed it to her. It fit into the palm of her hand but was heavy. She dropped the object into her bag.

Knarr reached for the gold, but Darshia pulled back.

"Not so fast," Darshia said. "Sorry to put you on the spot, but I have some questions. I'd like you to come with me, and we can discuss—"

He was surprisingly fast, reached out, latched on to Darshia's wrist, and drew her close. The unmistakable feel of cold steel against her ribs told her Knarr held a dagger.

"Forgive me, madam," Knarr said. "But I'm afraid I have neither the time nor the inclination to answer awkward questions. I have no desire to mar what I'm sure is lovely skin underneath your dress, but I must insist on my payment. Simply hand it over, and I'll be on my way and we can avoid an unpleasant altercation."

"Nobody wants anything unpleasant." Darshia turned her head to speak to the others who were approaching at a fast walk. "Do we, ladies?"

Knarr looked to see the approaching Birds of Prey, a dozen of them in full armor, hands on the hilts of their swords, expressions stern. They formed a circle around Knarr and Darshia.

Knarr considered a moment and then stepped back from Darshia. He flipped the dagger over in his hand and gave it to Darshia hilt first. "It would be rude of me to refuse the hospitality of such lovely—and well-armed—ladies."

CHAPTER
EIGHT

Alem lay shivering in the sand. He couldn't quite decide if that were better or worse than baking on a hot rock, which was how he'd started the morning. Every muscle screamed pain. It had been a much farther swim than it had looked.

He curled there a long time, listening to the surf. The upside to his situation was that he was far too exhausted to think about the things he didn't want to think about anyway. He didn't want to think of Rina hundreds and hundreds of miles away, planning her marriage to another man. He didn't want to think about Maurizan possibly drowned or worse. Had she really been taken by Miko's Fish Man? The world was crazy.

But Alem was relieved for the moment from such concerns. All he could think about was that he was incredibly thirsty and hungry.

And stranded on an island in the middle of nowhere that might have cannibals on it.

He forced himself to his feet and took stock. His worldly possessions amounted to the ragged wet clothes he wore and his boots. He'd also managed to hang on to his coin purse but didn't imagine there was anywhere nearby he might spend his coin. The moon hung huge and bright, and he took a good look at the island in front of him. Palm trees. Undergrowth not too thick. The smart thing would be to sit tight and wait for daylight.

He couldn't think why he should all of a sudden start doing the smart thing now.

Alem pulled on his boots and cautiously moved inland.

Water drove him to explore. The inside of his mouth was salty and dry. There *had* to be water somewhere.

Under the canopy of palm trees, it was much darker, moonlight filtering through here and there. Alem tripped over a vine and almost went down. Some small animal rustling in the brush to his left startled him. He was already regretting his decision to venture into the darkness.

Water. You need water and soon.

He realized he'd been walking on a narrow trail the last few minutes, following the path of least resistance between the trees. Probably a game trail. And if animals made the trail, then it might lead to water, right?

And a few minutes later, he heard it, the telltale trickle of flowing water. He picked up speed, hope blooming in his chest.

Alem felt and heard himself splashing in it before he saw it. He went to one knee, shoving aside the ground foliage, and felt along the ground, his hand wet and cold as he found the shallow stream. He scooped water frantically. It was so cold and wet in his mouth there was a moment of pain, but then pleasure as he scooped more. He spit out pebbles and dirt. The slow trickle of water could barely be called a stream.

He trudged uphill, and soon the stream was ankle deep and then knee deep. He scooped in big mouthfuls of water until his belly stretched full. He dunked his head. Alem hadn't fully realized how desperate he'd been until relief flooded him. He felt refreshed and alive.

Immediately a deep fatigue soaked his bones. The long swim and critical thirst had sapped him. He trudged out of the water until he found a dry spot, collapsed, and fell into a deep, dreamless sleep.

It seemed only a few minutes later that his eyes popped open again, but it must have been hours because it was full daylight. He sat up, groaned, every part of him stiff, but he felt a world better than he had the night before. He crawled a few feet back to the stream and drank deeply.

He stood, looked back the way he'd come the night before, and could glimpse the sea between the trees. He hadn't really come as far inland as he'd thought. Everything seemed different at night.

Alem's clothes clung to him, salty and damp. He looked around to make sure nobody could see him—which was idiotic since *of course* nobody was around—and stripped naked. He soaked his clothes in the pool, wrung them out, and hung them on a nearby tree limb to dry.

He put his boots back on and decided to follow the stream uphill. He wasn't thrilled to set off exploring completely nude, but sitting around watching his clothes dry didn't appeal to him either.

As the hill steepened, the stream became wider and foamy, cascading down rough boulders. He looked ahead and saw that the face of the hill became sheer gray rock for a ways, and the stream flowed from the wide mouth of a cave entrance. Alem climbed to the edge of the cave and peered inside. If he were stranded for long on this island—Dumo forbid—he would need some kind of shelter.

He entered slowly, rough gravel crunching beneath his boots. Once inside, he saw that the stream was fed from deep underground, but to the side, the cavern widened to a dry area, the ceiling rising enough to make standing straight no problem. It wouldn't be a bad spot. A place out of the sun or rain. He scanned about for a likely spot to—

Alem screamed when he saw the man. He stumbled back, tripping over his own feet.

He fell back into the water and was swept out of the cave, tumbling and splashing back down the slope until he was thrown up against a boulder. He grunted, holding his ribs, and staggered out of the water.

Thicko. Watch what you're doing. You've come too far to break your own neck like some clumsy oaf.

He trudged back up the hill and into the cave.

Alem approached the corpse carefully. He stood off to the side so as not to block the sunlight. Quite a few years ago, this man had obviously had the same idea about using the cave for shelter. How many years ago, Alem could only guess. The corpse's skin was dried out and shriveled tightly against his skull. Patches of skin coming off on the hands, and bone showing through. He was sitting on an upended bucket, back against the cave wall. His tunic was about to fall into dust but looked to have been fine material with intricate swirling patterns of gold and silver and copper. The man's turban suggested he might be from Fyria. There was a sea chest next to him, along with the frayed coils of rope, rusted spears. A rusty woodman's axe leaned against the cave wall. The survivor of some long-ago shipwreck, maybe? Perhaps he was a lone survivor who found his way to shore, took refuge in the cave, and never left again.

Which is bad news for me. I'm guessing not a lot of ships pass this way.

Alem opened the sea chest. Tools inside, crusted with rust.

Something caught Alem's eye, a glint of sunlight on bright metal.

The corpse's tunic was tucked into a cracked leather belt, the fabric billowing over and almost covering something but not quite. He pushed the tunic back, revealing the hilt of a sword. It was untouched by any blemish, unlike the man's rusted belt buckle and buttons. Not ruined like the spears or the tools in the sea chest.

Alem gripped the sword's hilt, hesitated, then drew the blade from its scabbard.

The cavern blazed with light, the straight blade glowing bright white like liquid flame. The sword was perfect, straight and without a nick or notch. It was longer than the short swords of the city guard but a bit shorter than a great knight's long sword. It seemed simultaneously lighter than air and also indestructible.

"Well, then." Alem grinned at the corpse. "Seems even dead men have interesting tales to tell."

CHAPTER
NINE

Rina pulled the horses into a thick stand of bushes and spread the bishop on a bed of pine straw. Hark's breathing was shallow, his skin clammy and cold, but she didn't dare light a fire.

She peeked through the bush's thick foliage at the road, well lit by the moon. It had been a while since patrol, a dozen hard-riding Perranese warriors. There had been a moment of apprehension when they'd reined in their horses only forty yards from her hiding place. They'd conferred for a few seconds, and then half had ridden on up the road, the rest going back the other way.

Rina was reluctant to tap into the spirit. She was already so fatigued, but she needed information. She tapped in and closed her eyes and instantly saw the world from the point of view of her familiar Zin, a green forest falcon. She flew above the trees, wheeling, the landscape spreading out before her. She ventured far from her hiding spot, turning a slow circle over several miles and back again.

She released her hold of spirit and familiar both. She'd found out what she needed to know. There were a number of other Perranese patrols scouring the countryside, but none coming for her position. Zin had shown her there was a town about ten miles up the road. When the coast was clear, she'd make for it. Hopefully Hark would be fit to ride by then.

She checked her gear. It was a fortunate thing the bishop had thought to bring her horse, all of her armor and weapons. But she didn't put them on.

She lay down. Someone should really have kept watch, but she was too exhausted to care. What would happen now? Where would they go from here? Rina knew these were important questions, but her thoughts were a senseless jumble. Her eyes slammed shut, and she was asleep in seconds.

Yano approached Commander Tchi, who was frowning at a map he was attempting to read by moonlight.

The ten men with Yano had been handpicked. This had been a long time coming, and Yano wanted it handled just right. Tchi conferred with one of his lieutenants, which was a shame, but they couldn't wait forever to find the commander completely alone. It had to be now. They couldn't count on a better opportunity.

The men slowly moved into a loose circle around Tchi and the lieutenant, trying not to be obvious about it. They were understandably reluctant, and their swords hissed slowly from their scabbards. The lieutenant was slow to react, but Tchi sensed immediately what was happening, his hand going for his sword hilt.

The men moved in quickly once they saw the commander go for his weapon. The lieutenant died quickly and surprised, three blades penetrating him various places through the torso.

Tchi drew his sword and sliced across his opponent's throat in one smooth motion. Blood sprayed, and the soldier dropped his weapon, staggering back, clutching at the wound.

Two more crowded in at him from different sides, but Tchi spun, sword flashing out, parrying blades and striking again with savage speed. One of his attackers stepped back, a long bloody line down his forearm. The other tried a thrust to his belly, but Tchi came over his blade and jabbed him in the face, sending him away screaming.

"All together, you cunts!" Yano shouted. "Gang pile the bastard."

The remaining warriors rushed Tchi all at once.

Two grabbed his sword arm, but only after a third took a stab in the belly. They pulled Tchi down to the ground, blades entering him from every angle. The commander didn't scream, just kept struggling to the end, until he finally went still. The soldiers got up, backed away from him, breathing hard. They shot anxious glances at one another.

"Had to be done," Yano said. "We agreed. Be strong and remember the story. Our patrol found the girl, but she killed the commander and the lieutenant. We barely got away. Right?"

Nobody said anything. "The men saw what she could do back at the enemy camp. They'll believe it. Now you men get your minds right. You hear me? Everyone square?"

The men nodded, mumbled agreement.

"Y-Yano." A weak voice.

Yano looked down and saw that Tchi was still alive. He drew a dagger and knelt next to him.

"Y-you're a traitor." Tchi coughed flecks of blood over his bottom lip and chin. He was fading fast. "Your n-name will live on . . . in . . . disgrace."

"I am only a traitor in a technical sense," Yano said. "You're the one putting your men in danger. I told you she was dangerous. I told you to kill her while you had her in your power. I will return to camp and gather the men, and when the patrols return, we will go south.

We already know the fleet is landing at Sherrik. We've done our part, Commander. They'll rotate us home, or, if not, at least we'll be with our own army. Either way, we'll be better off without you leading us to death."

Yano stabbed him through the eye with the dagger.

◆　◆　◆

Rina heard the bishop stir just after first light.

"How are you feeling?"

Hark sat up and groaned. "It's you. Thank Dumo. I had such dreams. What happened?"

"What's the last thing you remember?" Rina buckled her black breastplate as she spoke.

"They had you in the back of some cart," Hark said. "I killed the guards. And then . . . the wizard. I thought he had me."

"He did," Rina said. "But you took his attention away just enough. It was close. Thank you for coming for me."

Hark stood slowly, taking in his surroundings. "Only too happy."

"Why you?"

He blinked at her. "Your grace?"

"I thought maybe Brasley."

"He wanted to," Hark told her. "But Talbun said she needed him to go with her north to the Great Library. I was at hand and volunteered to effect your rescue." Hark rubbed his neck and frowned. "Such as it was."

Rina strapped on her bracers, buckled her sword belt. She felt right in the armor. Maybe *right* wasn't the correct word. Ready. She felt ready.

"I asked how you felt. Can you ride?"

"I feel weak, but yes. I won't fall out of my saddle."

"I've sent Zin ahead and the road is clear," Rina said. "There's a town south. We can buy supplies."

"And then?"

"And then we keep going south. We head for Sherrik."

"I thought you might want to catch up with your friends," Hark said.

She sighed, shook her head. "Their head start is too big. No, Talbun and Brasley are on their own. I trust them to get the job done. Our way is south. If you still want to help me, that is."

"Of course, your grace."

The old death priest's words echoed in her mind. *The southern path pays a debt.*

Rina still wasn't sure what that meant. She didn't know what waited for her in the south, but she could guess it involved danger on top of danger. For herself and anyone around her.

"I won't think ill of you if you want to return to Klaar," Rina said. "You've done your part."

"With respect, your grace, serving you is only a small part of my consideration," Hark said. "I sense that we're living through a critical turning point of history, and the best view of it will be near you. If I'm to have some hand in it, if I can help in some way, then I think coming with you is most likely how that will happen." He shrugged. "A wizard threw lightning at me, and by Dumo's will I survived. I think I'm meant to go on."

Rina smiled. "Good. Truth is I didn't really like the idea of going by myself."

They mounted and galloped the road south until they came to the small town Rina had seen through the falcon's eyes. They refilled their water skins from the town well and stocked up on food in an open-air market. Rina noticed the prices were significantly higher than she'd expected, and few of the vendors responded to her haggling. She remarked on this to a man selling turnips.

"The refugees, milady," said the man selling turnips. "They come through in waves, buying up everything in sight. It drives the prices up."

"Refugees?"

"From Sherrik," he said.

That didn't sound encouraging.

Hark munched an apple as they rode out of town. It looked like the color had come back into his face. When Rina had thrown the man unconscious over his own horse, she hadn't been confident he would make it.

An hour later, they met the first group of refugees.

About two score of them, looking bedraggled and hollow eyed, men with young children on their backs, all carrying their worldly possessions in bundles and baskets.

"Brother," Bishop Hark hailed one of the men. "What word?"

The man looked up, blinked at the bishop as if coming out of a daze. His clothes marked him as possibly some upper-class merchant, but he trudged through the mud with everyone else. "Me? Are you talking to me?"

"Indeed, my good man," the bishop said. "What news from the south?"

"Sherrik is sealed," he said. "Anyone inside is going to stay there. Anyone outside isn't getting in. The Perranese fleet is on the way, might be there already." He slogged on, shaking his head and muttering defeat.

Hark turned to Rina. "Now what?"

"We keep going," she said. "And when we get to Sherrik, we knock on the front gate and ask to be let in. I'm told I can be very persuasive."

CHAPTER
TEN

The rough cavern walls gave way to carved stone. The floor smooth and even. They walked a wide hallway, the ceiling stretching high above them into the darkness.

"What is this place?" Maurizan asked.

"The hall of the ancient wizards," said the Fish Man.

That caught Maurizan's attention. Had she come as far as the place marked on her map? If her mother were right, then there were secrets of ink magic somewhere in the depths of this place . . . if they'd survived the centuries.

They were coming to a T intersection, and from around the corner Maurizan saw the flickering of firelight casting jagged shadows and heard echoing voices.

Maurizan slowed her walk. "Who's down here?"

"The Moogari," Kristos said.

"Why do they want to see me?"

"Maybe they don't," he said. "But you want to see them."

"Do I?"

"Your map," Kristos said. "The Moogari are the ones you want to see even if you don't know it."

"Who are the Moogari?" She was still worried they might be cannibals. According to Miko, there was apparently a cannibal behind every palm tree on the Scattered Isles.

"They belong to this place," Kristos said. "They are those who served the ancient sorcerer."

"You mean their descendants still live here?"

"No." Kristos smiled enigmatically. "Not *descendants*, no."

Now she stopped walking altogether. "Okay, you need to explain what you're talking about before I take another step."

"Do you want the Prime or not?" Kristos asked.

Maurizan's eyes widened. The directness of the question startled her. "Who says I do?"

"Do not be foolish. The Moogari hold the secret." Kristos turned so she could see his back. "Like me. They inked the Prime on my back many years ago. They served the old wizard and know his secrets. Your mother had the Prime and your grandmother. You wish it also."

She didn't deny it. Why should she? Rina had robbed Maurizan of her chance for the Prime. Okay, that wasn't quite true or fair, but it was how Maurizan felt about it. Weylan's dying act had been to ink the Prime on Rina before Maurizan could make the trip up the mountain to the reclusive wizard's cave. Rina herself might not have robbed her, but fate had.

"I want the Prime," Maurizan said. "Tell me what to do."

The Fish Man grinned. "Come with me and meet the Moogari."

He motioned for her to follow, and she did. When they rounded the corner, Maurizan stifled a gasp. She had been expecting to see some reclusive tribe of people.

They weren't quite people.

The Moogari had arms and legs and eyes and moved around as people, but they were clearly not human. Their skin was a strange rubbery

67

pink, hair a pale blue, straight and fine. They didn't have proper noses, just nostril slits, and they were strangely thin, like they'd been stretched. Maurizan couldn't tell male from female. They all wore the same loose gray robes. Or maybe there wasn't a male or a female at all. Did they mate?

But Kristos said they weren't descendants. Dumo, could he mean these were the originals, that they were as old as the place itself?

It didn't seem possible.

"They were a slave race," Kristos said as if reading her thoughts. "Created by the master wizard of this place to carry out his whims. I have learned their language, and they have told me their stories."

She watched them a moment. They went about apparently normal business, mending clothes, tending a cookpot over a small fire in an enormous fireplace big enough for Maurizan to stand in. About a dozen of them.

"Do they have children?"

"No," Kristos said. "There are only these you see here and a few more off tending errands. I don't think it has ever occurred to them to have lives of their own or to leave this place. They were created to serve. They know nothing else."

One of them looked up and saw Maurizan and Kristos. He immediately began to jabber to his fellows in a language she'd never heard before, although it was now apparent where Kristos had picked up the odd accent.

One of them broke off from the others and scurried to stand in front of the Fish Man, offering him a crisp bow and rattling off more syllables in his strange tongue.

Kristos answered in the same language, then turned to Maurizan and said, "They ask if you have come for the tattoos. What shall I tell them?"

"How did they know?"

"It is what they do," he said. "They would ask the same of anyone."

Maurizan hesitated, swallowed hard, then said, "Tell them yes. I've come for the tattoos."

Kristos translated, and there was a sudden, excited exchange of talk among the Moogari. In seconds they surrounded the gypsy girl, attempting to gently take off her clothing.

"Hey!" She pulled back from them, alarmed.

"It is the way," Kristos said. "You must be bathed. Your skin must be clean and perfect. Trust them. They have no designs on your virtue. They are not capable."

Maurizan frowned at the Fish Man. "And what about you?"

A wan smile. "I have no interest in such things, but if it makes you feel better, I shall withdraw."

"Wait. Withdraw?" Her eyes darted to the Moogari eager to undress her. She didn't want the Fish Man around watching her bathe, but the idea of being alone with these strange nonpeople was suddenly unsettling.

Find some courage, okay? This is what you've wanted for as long as you can remember.

"Leave me with them," she said. "It's okay."

He grinned, turned to leave without another word.

The Moogari seemed to take this as some sort of signal and went about undressing her again. At least they weren't rushed or rough about it. She imagined it was what it must be like to be a proper lady with handmaids in attendance.

Sort of.

Indeed they were quite polite, folding her clothes and setting them aside, hanging up her belt and weapons near the fireplace. From somewhere, they'd produced a large brass tub and were building a fire under it. Maurizan flashed on a memory, her mother and grandmother describing what it was like to get the Prime. The pride. The excitement.

But each time it had started with a bath.

When Maurizan was naked, they helped lower her into the tub. The water was the perfect temperature, and soon she felt her muscles ease. She wondered if maybe this wasn't half the point. Her skin needed to be perfectly clean for what was to come, yes, but it couldn't hurt if she were also relaxed. The Moogari began to scrub her with sponges. They were so polite and sexless that she felt no apprehension about this.

Eventually one of the Moogari offered a hand and helped her from the bath. Others surrounded her with soft towels and dried her. One of them put her red hair up in a bun so it wouldn't hang down her back. She was escorted to a padded mat and through hand gestures was made to understand she was supposed to kneel.

She went to her knees.

Maurizan heard one of the Moogari chanting in his strange tongue, and she glanced to the side, saw him arranging needles and bottles on a small table, a thick leather-bound book open next to him.

Everything that had been relaxing about the bath vanished now. She remembered more of her mother and grandmother's stories. The discomfort. The *pain*. The hot pinpricks down their spines. It was the price one paid for the Prime.

The Moogari formed a circle around her, hands clasped in front of them, heads bowed reverently, all save the one who came up behind her, still muttering his incantations. When the first needle plunged into her soft skin at the nape of her neck, it was all she could do to keep from screaming.

◆ ◆ ◆

At last it was finished.

Maurizan's knees were sore, every muscle aching. For a time, she thought it would go on forever, the fire beneath her skin as the Moogari sewed a trail of pain down her spine with the tattooing needle. They all stood back from her now, the one who'd worked the needle motioning for her to stand.

She tried it and almost failed, legs shaking, her whole body trembling with the strain. Her mother had tried to warn her, but nothing could have prepared the gypsy for the sheer physical toll. And yet . . .

When she stood, she sensed something.

Something on the horizon of her consciousness. Something so close. If she could just . . . reach out . . . and . . .

Maurizan tapped into the spirit.

Power flooded through her, filling her, lifting her. Perfect awareness threatened to overwhelm her, and yet she could control it. Through sheer willpower, she was the perfect master of herself. Every smell, every sound, every sight. Her mind arranged it and made a perfect picture of the world around her.

She heard light footfalls behind her, bare feet on the grit of the floor, and could tell from the weight distribution and the rhythm of the movement that it wasn't one of the Moogari. She turned, knowing it was Kristos.

Maurizan was aware of her own nudity, and somewhere distant feelings of embarrassment reared. These feelings weren't useful, though, and she made them go away.

"You're tapped in now, aren't you?" Kristos said. "You feel it."

"Yes."

"They've given you the other ones too, I see," he said. "The three stripes and the fish."

"Yes."

The Moogari had tattooed three stripes like gills on the left side of her throat and a small fanciful fish on each of her ankles. They were identical to the Fish Man's tattoos.

Kristos dropped the wrap from around his waist. "Come. Let's try them out."

He turned and sprinted down the corridor. Maurizan followed, running effortlessly.

She had previously considered herself an athletic person. She trained with the other gypsies with the daggers just like all of them did from the time they were old enough to hold the blades, ducking, dodging, spinning, striking. She'd thought herself quick and graceful.

Now Maurizan could barely recognize that slow, clumsy woman she used to be. She sprinted after the Fish Man, running faster—running *better*—than she ever had. It wasn't that she had tattoos that specifically made her stronger or faster like Rina had. It was a perfect understanding of herself, knowing exactly where to place her foot with each stride, how each muscle worked to propel her, the perfect posture, controlled breathing. Her body was a tool she'd not even half known how to use before.

She smelled the salt water even before turning the corner. The hallway slanted down into a dark pool.

Kristos, without breaking stride, ran until he reached the edge of the pool and then launched himself like a spear, diving into the water and disappearing below the surface with hardly any splash at all.

Maurizan didn't hesitate, diving in after him.

She sped through the water with ease, naturally, as if she were born to. The fish tattoos tingled on her ankles. The gill tattoo pulsed with each breath. She effortlessly glided after Kristos toward a patch of light ahead of them. A second later, they emerged from the ruined sorcerer's stronghold into open sea.

They swam side by side, two feet below the surface of the water, the sun glittering on the waves above. Kristos smiled at her, and she felt herself smiling back. He pointed down and took off for the depths, indicating she should follow.

Maurizan sliced through the water like a harpoon, grinning madly. Excitement built in her, and she welcomed it.

A second later, she and Kristos hovered within a school of fish, thousands of them each about the size of her hand, bright blue scales with golden stripes catching the sunlight from above. They swirled around her. She floated weightless, caught in the dream.

Maurizan remembered her mother warning her about staying tapped into the spirit for too long. How she could use herself up if she were careless or greedy. But now that she had the Prime and held the spirit, she couldn't see how she'd ever lived without it, how normal people stumbled through their drab gray lives. She drank in the spirit until she overflowed with it. Just a few minutes longer.

Just a little bit more.

CHAPTER
ELEVEN

Brasley rolled over and opened his eyes. It was very much the same as having his eyes closed. He tried to blink the darkness away and failed.

Then he remembered where he was.

Ah, yes. The delightful pitch-dark place with the sealed door at the top of the shaft with the wrecked lift. He felt around in the darkness. He'd set the lantern close the night before, but he was still disoriented and his groping couldn't find it at first. There'd been talk of leaving it on, but of course they couldn't risk burning through the fuel so quickly. Even on the darkest winter night in the middle of a forest, there'd been a glimmer of starlight. The darkness in the enclosed heights of the Great Library was so complete Brasley would actually have been impressed if he hadn't been so certain he was going to die here.

In the occasional morbid moments he imagined his own death, it was usually something like a dagger tossed into his back by an angry husband as he climbed out of his wife's bedroom window.

Or falling into a nice long sleep after far too much wine and never waking up again.

Not trapped in the Great Library of Tul-Agnon to rot slowly in the dark.

He found the lantern and lit it. The others were already sitting up, clearly waiting for him to conclude his fumbling.

"I presume everyone had a comfortable night on the cold stone floor?" The bedrolls Brasley had purchased when outfitting the expedition might as well have been drawn on the floor with chalk for all the comfort they provided.

Brasley set the lantern in the center of the landing and fed Titan a handful of oats and then rationed the animal a bit of water. Then he went to the lift shaft and looked inside. It was still ruined, not that he'd expected anything different.

"We might have enough rope to climb down to the next level," he said.

Talbun tsked behind him, and Brasley could sense her rolling her eyes. They'd already had this conversation the previous evening, and nobody had liked the climbing-down-the-shaft option. After yesterday's spectacular smashing of the lift and the subsequent pounding the shaft took as the debris plummeted, ricocheting off the sides as it went, there was legitimate doubt about the shaft's stability. Tying a rope to the wrong support beam might result in a long, lethal drop.

Then there was the goat and the cart. Lowering them by rope would be problematic at best. At worst . . . well, Brasley pictured their mangled bodies in a bloody heap at the bottom of the shaft with the goat and cart on top of them.

So climbing down the shaft was out, and that left the door.

The sealed door.

With who knew what sort of perilous instant death on the other side.

He sighed. He didn't want to be here. He missed Fregga.

The shadows shifted, and Brasley turned to see Talbun holding the lantern up to the seal again, squinting at it with a mix of curiosity and apprehension.

"Nothing's going to change no matter how much we stall and think it over," she said. "We go inside. Today. Now."

Brasley raised a finger. "Point of order. What about instead of now, later? And instead of open the door, have breakfast?"

"Brasley!"

"Okay, okay." He turned to the guide. "Any last-minute advice before we open the dangerous door of mystery, Olgen?"

Olgen started, surprised to be included in the conversation. "Me? I'm not even supposed to be here."

Brasley smiled. It was difficult, but he did it. "Nevertheless. If something on the other side of the door turns out to be the sort of thing that might kill us, I imagine that would include you regardless of the fact that, as you say, you're not supposed to be here. Thus it would behoove you, as a matter of self-preservation, to relate to us any tidbits of information you might think relevant to the current situation."

"Well." Olgen cleared his throat. "I mean, it could be *anything* in there. No one from the university has ever been this far up into the Great Library, at least no one that's lived to return and tell about it. The Great Library is the most ancient puzzle in the world."

"So to sum up," Brasley said. "We should prepare ourselves for anything that's ever been known or imagined, mundane or magical, animal, vegetable, or mineral in the last thousand years or so."

"Just so, milord."

Brasley drew his sword and looked at Talbun. "Proceed."

She passed her hand over the seal, mumbling arcane words. Pinpoints of cold blue light danced and jerked over the seal like insects looking for a way to burrow inside.

Olgen stepped forward, wonder on his face. "You're a spell caster? I didn't know you—"

Brasley put a gentle hand on his shoulder and eased him back. "Give her room, boy."

Olgen stepped back.

There was a sharp pop, more felt than heard, and Talbun had to scramble away quickly as the chains clattered to the floor. The seal tumbled from the door in pieces, acrid smoke rising from it.

"What happened?" Brasley said.

"An opening spell," Talbun said. "A powerful one. Sort of all purpose. Like I said before, the seal was meant to keep something in, not us out. Otherwise, I don't think I could have broken it. The magic felt . . . old. And very strong."

There was a muffled *whumf* and a sucking sound as the doors swung outward, eddies of air swirling around them. The temperature seemed to drop suddenly, and Brasley shuddered at a sudden chill. When the doors stood wide, Talbun lifted the lantern and entered. Brasley swallowed hard, sword in hand, and followed, Olgen in tow.

They halted a dozen paces inside the doorway, the black floor smooth as glass spreading out ahead of them. The chamber in which they found themselves was so large, the lantern light touched neither the walls nor the ceiling. The three of them stood on a small island of dim illumination in the vast darkness.

Brasley's palm was sweaty on his sword hilt. *I wish whatever was going to jump out and eat my face would just get on with it. The suspense is killing me.*

A flicker of light overhead. Their heads snapped up. Another flicker. Faint. More flickers off to the sides. Slowly the lights brightened. Enormous glass globes hung from the vaulted ceilings. What seemed to be flakes swirled in a frenzied circle within each sphere like a tiny blizzard, the glow increasing with the agitation. The globes extended a hundred yards to the right and left and ahead of them, illuminating wide hallways of highly polished back stone.

Carved into the walls down both sides of each hallway were rectangular indentions like large picture frames without the pictures, six feet high and three feet wide. The halls were dust free and perfect, no sign of the deterioration they'd seen elsewhere in the Great Library.

Talbun stared up at the globes, mouth agape.

"A spell?" Brasley asked.

"Several spells, I would imagine," Talbun said. "Something to energize the particles in the globes. A spell that detects when people walk in and then turns on the lights. Another to preserve everything for centuries. That's just off the top of my head. But that's not the most amazing part. I'm wondering why, in a place where rust and dust rule, these halls are completely unblemished."

Brasley looked around. In the full light of the globes, he could see that the halls of gleaming black stone indeed looked brand new. Nothing was dirty or had fallen into disrepair. It didn't have the look of a place that had been abandoned for centuries, as if they arrived mere seconds after the cleaning staff had departed. Even the old, musty smell was absent here.

"I don't think the seal was just a seal on the door, on this place," Talbun said. "I think it was a seal on time."

"I don't understand."

"I have—had—a spell that created a time bubble," she said. "This might be similar, although much more powerful obviously. I think time has been frozen here, preserving this place until somebody came along."

Brasley frowned. "But why would somebody preserve an empty—"

The sliding sound of stone on stone stopped him short. All the rectangles lining the walls were doorways, and they were sliding to one side, revealing darkened passages behind them.

A second later, scores of people scurried out of all the new doorways.

People might not have been the right word.

They were all clearly female but just as clearly not quite human. They were all the same height, about half a head shorter than Brasley. Skin as white and as clear as milk, hair a coppery red, glinting metallic beneath the glow of the globes. Their features were odd, eyes completely black, noses pressed just a little too flat, mouth a tad too wide. They weren't all *exactly* identical, but the variations were so slight, they might as well have been.

They wore black shirts of some shimmering material and matching pants hemmed at the ankles. No shoes.

At the sight of the milk-skinned women swarming the halls, Brasley, Talbun, and Olgen drew together in a tight circle. Talbun drew the short dagger from her belt. Olgen hadn't brought a proper weapon, but he held the pry bar in front of him ready to whack anything that got too close. Even the goat took up a defensive position.

"What in blazes are *they*?" Brasley said.

"You think I know?" Talbun snapped.

"Olgen?"

"Sorry, milord. Nothing about them in any of my university texts."

"They don't seem hostile." Talbun lowered her dagger. "They don't actually seem to notice us at all."

They fell into lines, groups breaking off and going one way or another up and down the halls, bare feet slapping on the smooth floor.

One of the women broke off from one of the groups and approached Brasley and the others. She had three white stripes circling her left sleeve, and he wondered if it were some indication of rank. She stopped four feet from Brasley, bowed deeply, and spit out a string of words in a language he'd never heard before.

"Okay, what do I do now?" he asked.

"Wait," Talbun said. "It sounds familiar. Almost like Fyrian."

"We're a long way from Fyria," Brasley said.

"It's said that all sorcery began in Fyria," Talbun said. "As a result, all spell casters study the language. But I speak *fluent* Fyrian, and I'm not really catching what she said. It just sounds so tantalizingly familiar."

"Begging your pardon, milady," Olgen said. "But the language might be ancient Fyrian."

"I've just told you, I *speak* Fyrian," the wizard said.

"I mean *ancient* Fyrian, milady."

"I *know* it's an ancient language," Talbun said sharply. "I *speak* it. Have you gone deaf?"

Olgen blanched. "My apologies, but I mean a language that predates Fyrian, spoken by the first dwellers in Fyria who in later centuries would become the Fyrians we know today."

Talbun's eyes narrowed. "What?"

"I would never have known either, milady," Olgen said, placating. "My studies of the ink magic led me to it. Old Tohler, the master of languages and dialects, showed me the precious few tomes the university has on the subject." The guide's voice took on an academic tone, as if he were delivering a lecture. "Evidently the first wizards to create magical tattoos needed words more elemental, closer to the properties the tattoo was attempting to duplicate, and it's believed that ancient Fyrian is likely the first spoken language on the entire—"

"Hey," Brasley interrupted. "This is all very fascinating, but I think the young lady expects some sort of reply."

Talbun sighed. "Can you speak it?" she asked Olgen.

Olgen's eyebrows went up. "Speak it?"

"Aloud," Brasley said. "With your mouth."

"I've only ever read it," Olgen admitted. "Maybe?"

"Try," Talbun said.

Olgen cleared his throat. A pause. Then: "I don't know what to say."

"Tell her we'd like some wine while we browse the menu," Brasley suggested.

"Can you be serious?" Talbun said.

But it was too late. Olgen was already translating, stumbling through the syntax, groping for vocabulary.

"What are you doing?" Talbun said. "Don't take that idiot seriously."

Olgen shrank from her, abashed. Brasley frowned.

The copper-haired woman with the stripes on her sleeve jabbered frantically, and three nearly identical women fell out of the line jogging past to scamper in three different directions. Additional jabbering from the one in the stripes, and a dozen more scurried in seemingly random lines away from her, bare feet like a summer rain shower on the smooth floor.

"What did you tell her?" Talbun asked.

"Only what Baron Hammish asked me to," Olgen said. "I think. I told you, I've never spoken ancient Fyrian out loud."

"From now on you only translate what *I* tell you to," Talbun said. "Understand?"

Olgen's eyes shifted to Brasley.

"We'll talk about it later," Brasley said.

Talbun made a low growl in her throat. "No, we bloody will not talk—"

The three women who'd darted away earlier—at least Brasley thought it was the same three—returned abruptly. One held a silver tray with a dazzling crystal wine decanter filled with red wine. Another held a similar silver tray with three crystal wineglasses. The woman in the middle unstoppered the decanter and filled one of the glasses, then handed it to Brasley with a respectful nod.

Brasley brought the glass halfway to his mouth, paused, glanced sideways at Talbun.

The wizard shrugged, as if to say, *Might as well.*

Brasley drank.

He lowered the glass.

He didn't move.

Talbun started to reach for him, then stopped herself. "Uh . . . Brasley."

"This," Brasley said, "might be the best wine I've ever had." He remained frozen, staring into the wineglass.

"Uh . . . what are you doing now?" Talbun asked.

"I'm trying to think what I should ask for next," Brasley said.

CHAPTER
TWELVE

Her Perranese captors had carried Rina steadily south as she'd lain spelled and unconscious in the back of the cart. As a result, she and Bishop Hark were only a few days' fast ride from Sherrik's landward gates.

The size and frequency of the refugee groups increased the first day until finally there was just a line of them, disheveled, downtrodden, and defeated, their bleak faces hollow and haunted. The next day the number of refugees gradually decreased, and the road was empty of them by the third day. Scavengers rummaged the discarded baggage the refugees left in their wake and scuttled away like startled crabs as Rina and Hark galloped past.

They topped a low hill and caught their first sight of the city. Or rather sight of the wall that separated them from the city, carved of great gray stones and forty feet high. The gates were double doors fifteen feet high and forged of iron. From this vantage, Sherrik looked more like a grim fortress than the glittering cosmopolitan jewel Rina had always heard about.

Hark must have seen the look on her face and guessed her thoughts. "Most travelers and merchantmen approach from the sea, where Sherrik presents its better face."

They reined in their horses before the gate, craning their necks to look up at the top of the wall.

"Hello, the wall," called Hark. "Hello, the gate."

A second later, two silhouettes appeared atop the wall, leaning out to look down at them, helmed men with spears. "Be off!" one shouted down at them. "The city is closed."

"Then open it!" shouted the bishop. "We didn't travel all this way to be told to go home."

"Don't give a shit if you walked barefoot all the way from the Glacial Wastes with King Pemrod on your back. I said get lost!" yelled one of the guards. "Or you can start sprouting crossbow bolts if you prefer."

Hark looked at Rina. Rina shrugged.

Hark went red and blew out an annoyed burst of air. "I am *Bishop* Feridixx Hark, and I ride with *Duchess* Rina Veraiin."

"Right, and I'm the great sorcerer of Fyria."

"Fools!" Hark bellowed. "Are Sherrik's walls manned exclusively by the mentally infirm, or is there someone with half a brain up there who can make a proper decision? Think fast, for I'm not made of patience. Perhaps I'll have a word with your Captain Sarkham and have you stationed on the seaward wall so you can be first to greet the Perranese when the fighting starts. And be warned that I will snatch out of midair any bolts you loose at me, break them in half, and return them to you up your arses. Go now and find an officer!"

The silhouettes put their heads together, conversing, and then one left in a hurry.

The hint of a smile on Rina's face. "Haven't seen you so furious before. Or was that the wrath of Dumo you were channeling?"

"Well." Hark looked slightly embarrassed. "Somebody had to set those louts straight, and a duchess shouldn't have to deal with such lowly matters."

"Thank you for sparing me from such grubby matters," she said. "I am a fine and delicate flower after all."

Hark cleared his throat and looked away. "I just hope Sarkham is still master of the city guard. It's been some years since I've visited Sherrik."

A moment later, the other silhouette appeared again and pointed to his left. "Go to the west door, sir. They'll take care of you there."

Rina and Hark turned their horses from the main gate and followed a narrow track west around the city wall. As they went, a shallow ditch along the wall widened into a moat fifty feet across, two feet of muddy water at the bottom. Fifteen minutes later, the track intersected with a narrow road that led away north, probably to outlying villages. A narrow bridge spanned half the moat, then stopped. A wooden drawbridge was up on the other side. A small stone building guarded the intersection.

Rina dismounted and knocked on the guardhouse door. "Anyone there?"

No answer.

"I imagine they've all pulled back to the other side of the wall," Hark said.

A minute later, the clank of heavy chains drew their attention. The drawbridge lowered, revealing a portcullis no larger than an ordinary doorway. The drawbridge thudded into place, completing the way across. Hark and Rina led their horses across the span, the portcullis raising as they arrived and lowering again after they entered the narrow walkthrough, barely big enough to accommodate the horses. Rina glanced up, imagining murder holes and all sorts of other nasty defenses. If an army wanted to take Sherrik, she didn't think squeezing through here would be the best way to do it.

They emerged through another portcullis into a courtyard on the other side. Walls rose up high and close all around them, and soldiers atop the walls pointed crossbows down at them. Three soldiers walked toward them, two men with spears and a third who looked like an officer, if the gold badge pinned to his tunic was any indication. He wore a breastplate with chain mail underneath and a simple, open-faced helm. A long sword hung from his belt on one side and a dagger on the other. He had a well-trimmed black beard and moustache with just a little gray creeping in at the sides, a sharp nose and deep brown eyes.

Rina felt an air of gentle authority radiating from the man, but maybe that was just something she hoped.

The officer grinned suddenly and stepped forward, clasping hands with Hark.

"Good to see you again, Bishop," he said. "Although you've picked an odd time to visit Sherrik. Can you really snatch crossbow bolts out of midair?"

Hark laughed. "Please don't ask me to prove it. And my thanks for letting us in, Captain Sarkham. You're looking well. Jeela and the children?"

"Gone to Kern out of harm's way," Sarkham said. "Jeela has cousins there."

"Good, good. Glad to hear it." Hark turned and gestured to Rina. "Captain, please allow me to introduce—"

"Duchess Veraiin." Sarkham bowed politely. "Welcome to Sherrik and to General Braxom's side door."

Rina raised an eyebrow. "General Braxom's side door?"

"The door and bridge were ordered built nearly two hundred years ago by the general of Sherrik. A man called Braxom."

"Why?"

Sarkham grinned. "Because he's a general, and generals get what they want."

Ah.

Sarkham glanced back at Hark, looking mildly embarrassed. "Forgive me, old friend, but it's the duchess you should thank for your safe passage into the city. When the duke heard who was at the gate, he ordered you both be admitted immediately. He waits for you even now."

Rina nodded to him. "Well, then. I don't suppose it's polite to keep a duke waiting, is it?"

◆　◆　◆

In the tall grass, behind a fallen log, two Perranese scouts watched the duchess and the bishop cross the bridge and enter the castle, the drawbridge pulling up again behind them.

"Well, they're in now, and that's all there is to that," said the first. "There's no getting her back now."

"Suits me fine," said the second one.

"Maybe we should have tried to take them."

"The two of us? Pull the other leg. You know what she can do."

"I suppose you're right," said the first.

"What about the door and the drawbridge?"

"Even if we got the bridge down and the portcullis up, that tunnel looked pretty narrow from here. We'd get slaughtered going in single file. Go back and tell Yano what we've seen and that I'm going to keep circling the city west to see if there's a better way inside."

The other Perranese warrior slithered away on his belly in the long grass, keeping out of sight of the watchful eyes atop Sherrik's wall.

CHAPTER THIRTEEN

When Stasha Benadicta showed up again in his cell with those two bruisers Bune and Lubin in tow, Giffen sensed it would be different this time.

He'd always had a ratlike cunning for self-preservation, and some instinct told him that he might have another beating coming. Previously, he'd made the beatings stop by simply telling the evil woman what she wanted to know.

But this time was . . . different.

How it would be different or why Giffen thought such a thing remained to be seen. Perhaps he was wrong. Maybe there'd be no beating at all. Wouldn't that make for a nice change of pace?

Stasha Benadicta gestured at him as if indicating a pile of goat shit that needed to be cleaned up. "Bune."

Bune seized him by the back of the neck and slammed him face-first into the stone floor of the cell. Giffen spit blood, blinked, and saw stars. The great oaf held him pinned against the floor.

Not that Giffen had any immediate plans to get up.

So it's to be another beating after all, Giffen thought. *If I had a sharp gentleman's blade and two minutes alone in the dark with that bitch* . . .

"I need to know something," Stasha said.

Bune gave Giffen's neck a squeeze for emphasis.

"I presumed as much. It's not as if you come down here to socialize." Giffen put as much contempt into the words as he could muster, considering his face was being pushed into the cold stone floor.

"Good," Stasha said. "Then you understand our relationship."

"No," Giffen said. "It's going to be different this time."

"Is it?"

"Yes." *It has to be. I can't go on like this. Eventually I'll run out of useful information, and then there will be no need to keep me around.*

No need to keep me alive.

She knelt next to him, had something in her hands. It was wrapped in soft leather. She began to unwrap the object. Giffen watched her, held his breath.

Stasha revealed the object. It was a flawless ruby the size of a walnut, valuable beyond reckoning in and of itself, but it was no mere gemstone. The ruby was set in a silver disc with obscure runes set at different stations around it. On the reverse side of the disc were four metal prongs of various lengths, ranging from an inch to three.

Giffen had never laid eyes on the object but recognized it immediately.

The last piece. She knows.

"We met the man at the place and time you told us, Giffen," Stasha said. "He had this with him. Care to tell us about it?"

She doesn't know? "Didn't he tell you?"

"He told us what he told us," Stasha said. "Now *you're* going to tell us. And if what you tell us doesn't match what he told us . . . well, someone's going to have to be held responsible for that, aren't they?"

"It's the last piece. The one that opens the doorway." He pressed his lips together tight, refusing to say more. That would either match up with what Harpos Knarr told her or it wouldn't.

Stasha nodded slowly. "Good. Thank you, Giffen. Then you can imagine what questions are coming next. Why don't you be a helpful chap now, eh?"

"No."

"No? You want to bring Bune and Lubin into the conversation again. We know how that goes."

"That's the point, isn't it?" Giffen said. "You don't think I know what happens once I'm no longer useful. No, Lady Chamberlain, we need to work out something else. I realize I can put off a beating by telling you what you want to know, but then what? We're going to start thinking long term, you and I."

Stasha bit her lower lip while she thought about that. "What do you want?"

"Out of this dungeon."

"No."

"I don't expect you to set me free. I'm not a fool. But lock me in some room with a bed and light. I can't tolerate this dank hole any longer."

"You tell me what I want to know first."

"No," he said. "We need to figure some way to trade what we want. I don't trust you, and I can't imagine you trust me. I have three pieces of information I know you will need. As we go along, other issues might arise, and perhaps I will have answers, but at the very least, I possess *three* items of information, which are essential, and I am the *only* one who has this information. On that you must take my word. Here is what I propose. The first item of information is an object you must possess."

"I thought *this* was the final component." Stasha indicated the ruby in her palm.

"To the doorway, yes," Giffen said. "But where is it? How to find it? Without my help, you could look for a hundred years and never get close."

"Go on, then," Stasha said.

"I tell you what the object is, and in return, you move my incarceration to a more hospitable location," Giffen said. "It will take you some time to locate this thing, and I don't fancy rotting down here in the meantime."

"Tell me what it is," she said.

"No, first your promise," Giffen insisted. "I tell you, and you let me out of this sodding hole. Then when you've found it, I'll tell you how to use it."

Stasha considered, then said, "You have my word."

"The duke's signet ring," Giffen said.

Stasha frowned. "What of it?"

"Klaar is one of the oldest holdings in Helva," Giffen said. "The Veraiin house is centuries old. The ring is more than just a symbol of Klaar, more than just an heirloom. It's been handed down from one generation to the next to guard a very specific secret. I am privy to that secret. When you find the ring, I'll tell you the rest."

Giffen allowed himself a smug smile. Searching for the ring would keep the bitch busy a good long while, and in the meantime, he could enjoy a proper bed in a room not crawling with rats and that didn't stink of his own excrement. During the Perranese occupation of Klaar, Giffen had searched high and low for the ring and had finally assumed the brat Rina had taken it with her when she fled the city.

Stasha considered Giffen for a moment, her face blank. Maybe she was trying to decide whether Giffen were telling the truth.

Stasha Benadicta dipped two fingers into her blouse between her breasts and came out with a thin silver chain. At the end of the chain hung a ring.

"Do you mean this ring right here?" Stasha asked.

Giffen gaped. *Damn the woman.*

CHAPTER
FOURTEEN

Darshia stuck her head into the Birds of Prey barracks and counted the girls. Nine. The rest were either on guard duty or attending to personal matters. She thought about picking the three she wanted, but the fact was they were all good. They trained hard. They wanted to be Birds of Prey. They were proud of it. It wasn't just some job. It was a way out of an old life.

And into a new one.

"Hey!"

All nine of them stopped what they were doing and looked up. They knew the sound of their captain's voice.

"I need three volunteers right now," she said. "Armor up and follow me."

She turned and left without waiting to see who volunteered. Let them work it out among themselves. A second later, she heard them clanking down the hall behind her, buckling on sword belts and strapping on armor. She glanced back over her shoulder. All nine of them followed her, slipping on bracers and straightening helms.

Okay, full points for enthusiasm, but we'll need to work on listening skills later. They were all coming along well with the sword training, but they were newbies and hadn't quite gotten the hang of being a military unit. *Listen to yourself,* Darshia thought. *As if you were some old war veteran.*

There was a pang of grief as she thought about Prinn. She wished her friend were at her side now. She wished Tenni were still alive. She'd have been proud to see what the Birds of Prey had become. She wondered where Tosh was, if he was okay.

She shook her head, dispelling the thoughts. *Focus on what you're doing.*

Darshia led them up the stairs and down the hall to the residential wing of the castle. At one time, the duke, his wife, and his daughter had occupied the wing. Now it was empty, two of them dead and Rina off on some mission.

Stasha Benadicta stood waiting for them at the end of the hall in front of a closed door. She stood back straight, chin up, hands clasped primly in front of her. She had an air of authority. She made a good steward, Darshia thought. Not everyone respected her because of where she'd come from, but Duchess Veraiin had been smart to leave her in charge.

Darshia stopped in front of the steward, nodding respect.

Stasha looked past her, raising an eyebrow at the women in tow. "So many?"

"I can send some away if you want," Darshia said.

"Never mind," Stasha told her. "Follow me."

She went through the doorway behind her, and Darshia followed. The room within was spacious and well lit, a bay window taking up almost one entire wall. A writing desk. Cushioned chairs arranged facing a cold fireplace. Shelves with many books. A thick rug. A small sideboard with a stoppered decanter half full of wine, and a pair of pewter wine goblets.

A man stood with his back to her, scanning the titles of the books. He turned, and Darshia recognized him immediately.

Giffen.

Last Darshia had heard, the man was rotting in the dungeon. He'd bathed and had been given a clean robe, but she still felt slimy just looking at him.

She held her tongue, but hatred must have flashed in her eyes because Giffen sneered contempt at her.

"Ah, the red-haired harlot," Giffen said. "With a gaggle of whores in your wake. Last time we saw each other, my hands were around your throat, if I remember correctly. I'd have finished the job if one of those oafish brutes hadn't come to your rescue."

Darshia's hand fell to the hilt of her sword, the muscles in her jaw working. *One more word, you maggot. Go ahead, just one more word out of that stinking mouth.*

"Be civil, Giffen, or I'll forget any agreement we have," Stasha said. "I can only protect you up to a point. There are enough people in this castle who'd be delighted to see you dead as soon as I turn my back. And I'll make a *point* of turning my back if you don't behave."

Giffen sniffed and turned away from Darshia. "Very well. It's not worth my time anyway."

"Let's get on with it," Stasha said. "Tell us why we're here, Giffen."

Giffen gestured at the room around him. "The duke's private library. He wasn't much of a reading man, not like his father, but it was a good, quiet place for a drink." He gestured at the chairs by the fire. "Often we would sit side by side on a cold winter's night and discuss Klaar's troubles."

"You're trying my patience, Giffen," Stasha said. "And if you keep talking about the man you murdered as if you were old friends, then I will let Darshia and the rest of these women hack you to bits until what's left is unrecognizable."

Giffen went to the fireplace. Just under the mantel was the stone carving of a face. In an instant of clarity, Darshia realized it was the face of the First Duke, the same one she'd seen on the statue in the old town square. The eye patch was unmistakable, crossed axes under the face.

Giffen reached a hand out, palm up. "The ring, if you please."

Stasha hesitated. She pulled out the chain from her modest neckline and took it off over her head. She unfastened it and removed the ring, stepped forward, and placed it in Giffen's hand, frowning the whole time.

Giffen slipped the ring onto his finger, looking smug, as if he'd won some petty victory. Again, Darshia suppressed the urge to put her sword through his face.

Giffen inserted the ring into the First Duke's good eye and pressed until there was an audible clunk of some mechanism clicking into place. He rotated his fist 180 degrees to the right, stone scraping on stone until the First Duke's head was upside down. Giffen pressed hard, shoving the face back into the fireplace, and Darshia felt the next clunk vibrate under her feet, as if something were sifting into place below them.

A loud crack, and then the fireplace began to turn, the wall shifting out, dust falling from the ceiling. Giffen stepped back as the fireplace rotated. It finally stopped, revealing an arched opening behind it and stairs spiraling down into the darkness.

"Get something so we can see," Stasha told Darshia. "Lanterns or torches."

Darshia waved her hand, and one of the Birds of Prey left at a run to obey.

"Castle Klaar is one of the oldest structures in Helva, along with the royal palace in Merridan, the Great Library in Tul-Agnon, and the duke's pyramid in Sherrik," Giffen explained. "Back then the most powerful families had much better relationships, and their reign over Helva was considered a golden age. One of the keys to their close relationship lies below." He gestured to the stairway.

The girl who had gone for the lanterns returned breathless, one in each hand. Darshia took one of them and nodded to Stasha. Ready.

Stasha looked at Giffen, her face a grim, unreadable mask. "Lead on."

CHAPTER
FIFTEEN

The flat-topped pyramid that served as the ducal palace stood in the center of the city and dwarfed all structures around it. Centuries ago it had been a keep unto itself, and over the decades the city had grown up around it and the wall around the city until Sherrik had become known as the fortified jewel of southern Helva, a place of culture and trade, but also a place of high walls guarded by men with long spears.

Sherrik's streets—and especially its waterfront—usually bustled with activity as merchant ships from southern waters and western lands trafficked its piers and wharves, trade caravans setting out on northern routes to bring exotic goods to the rest of Helva. For centuries, the dukes of Sherrik had kept the peace, kept tariffs low, and kept out of the way as the city prospered, letting trade find its own natural ebb and flow.

Now the hooves of Rina Veraiin's horse echoed on the empty cobblestone streets. Windows stood empty except for the occasional haunted face of some brave—or foolish—person who'd elected to stay behind and ride out the siege. She and Hark galloped behind Captain

Sarkham, who rode ahead of them on an enormous black mare. Two more guards brought up the rear. They passed through an open-air market, the stalls empty, vendors either hiding at home or fleeing the city. The other side of the market opened into a wide boulevard, columned buildings of gray stone on either side. To Rina they seemed like the halls of government, housing the bureaucracies that ran the city, but it was only a guess. She'd never visited Sherrik before. The streets and sidewalks were as deserted here as everywhere else, and she found the eerie quiet more disturbing than the clamorous racket of a battle. Almost.

Ahead of them, the great pyramid of Sherrik rose above all other structures. From a distance it looked simply like fifteen progressively smaller blocks of square stone piled one atop the other, the top flat, unlike the smoother pyramids of Fyria, which rose to sharp points. As she moved closer, Rina saw that each level above the first was ringed by a railed balcony as wide as a city street, tall narrow windows lining the walls. They passed through a large gate into a wide courtyard. The great doors of the pyramid loomed at the head of a broad stone stairway before them.

Rina and Bishop Hark dismounted, and grooms led their horses away.

"Do you know the duke?" Rina asked from the side of her mouth.

"I met his father," Hark said. "My understanding is that the young duke is brash but smart enough to let his advisors run the daily affairs of the city."

"Can he handle a siege?"

Hark shrugged.

Fantastic, Rina thought. *The perfect time for my first visit to Sherrik.*

Sarkham led them up the steps and through the great doors, which stood open on enormous iron hinges. They passed through a few anterooms until they emerged through a side door into the pyramid's great reception hall.

Every lord, baron, and duke has a room like this, Rina mused. *A big hall and a big chair raised up so we can greet visitors and show who's boss. A visible and obvious projection of power. Klaar's reception hall could fit ten times into this place.*

Their footfalls echoed as they walked the polished floor to the raised platform in front of them. A line of seven chairs dominated the platform, but at the moment only the center chair was occupied. A gray-haired man in a black robe bent to whisper into the ear of the man sitting in the center chair. A brief flurry of whispers and nodding heads.

The man with the black robe straightened and faced Rina. "May I present Emilio Barakas Hansfel Sherrik, the duke."

A history lesson from one of her old tutors tickled Rina's memory. *Oh yeah. The original duke had named the city after himself.*

Bishop Hark bowed. Rina's bow was more of a respectful nod. As duchess she was Duke Sherrik's equal.

Technically.

The duke rose from his seat and raised a hand in greeting. "Duchess Veraiin, Bishop Hark, you're most welcome to my city." He went to the edge of the platform and took a short set of side stairs down to the floor and jogged toward them. "As we're on the brink of war, let's dispense with the stuffy formalities, shall we?"

"That's hospitable of you," she said. "I hope you'll call me Rina."

"And I'm Emilio." He stopped in front of her, staring openly at her face. "Forgive me. I'd heard about the tattoos. They *are* striking."

Rina's instinct was to reach for the tattoos around her eyes, but she resisted.

"I'm envious," the duke said. "You look positively *fierce.*"

Rina forced a smile, not quite sure if she were pleased with the comment or not. By now she was used to the stares, but most people refrained from saying anything.

"And you also look . . . formidable," she told him.

The duke's armor had been painted a bright gold and was trimmed in red enamel. The emblem of the sailing ship silhouetted against the setting sun—the symbol of the Sherrik house—blazed across the breastplate. It was armor made for parades and fancy dress balls. There wasn't a scratch on it. Rina doubted the armor had been within a hundred miles of a battle.

Emilio looked down at himself. "You don't think it makes me look too much the dandy? It was custom made and fits well at least." He turned to Hark. "Welcome, Bishop. We haven't met before, have we?"

"No, your grace," Hark said. "But I was an admirer of your father."

"Yes, a terrible thing his passing so suddenly last year," Emilio said. "Rest assured I have everything under control and am taking steps to make sure the city is well defended."

"I have no doubt of it, your grace," Hark said.

No trace of insincerity. *He'd make a good politician*, Rina thought.

"You've faced these Perranese devils before," Emilio said to Rina. "And won. I'd very much like your opinion on the city's defenses."

"I'm no general," Rina said. "We got lucky in Klaar and surprised the Perranese."

"Nonsense. Come, follow me. I want to show you something." He turned and stalked away, not bothering to look and see whether anyone followed.

Rina and the bishop hurried to catch up. Guards fell in behind them.

He's like some kid, eager to show off something or other. It seemed only some vague trace of ducal dignity kept Emilio from breaking into a jog. *Kid. He's a year or two older than I am. If that.*

Rina suddenly felt old beyond her years. She'd seen so much, been through so much in such a short time. She had responsibilities. They weighed her down. She spent every day second-guessing herself.

Emilio appeared unburdened by such doubts.

They headed up broad stairs, gently spiraling around the inside of the palace. A moment later they emerged through a large archway onto a wide veranda. The sun beat down, but bright linen canopies had been erected, tables and chairs beneath, making a pleasant little pavilion. Servants sprang into action, filling wine goblets. Others brought platters of food.

"Please, help yourself. Be comfortable. Be at home." Emilio grabbed a goblet of wine as he passed a servant with a tray full of them. He motioned for Rina and the bishop to follow him.

They went to a table near the edge of the veranda. The spot offered a good view of the city spread out before them to the southern wall. They weren't high enough to see down into Sherrik's famed harbor, but the glittering blue sea was visible beyond. *It's beautiful*, Rina thought. Hard to believe the view would soon be filled with an enemy fleet.

She reached into a small bag hanging from her belt and came out with a chuma stick. "Do you mind?"

"Chuma! I don't partake myself, but please go ahead," Emilio said.

A servant appeared as if by magic with a brand from the fire, and Rina puffed the chuma stick to life, blowing a long gray cloud out over the city. She immediately felt a slight ease in her tension. She'd ridden a long way and had been filled with various anxieties. She looked out over the city again, puffing. It would have been a nice place for a holiday if they hadn't been on the edge of war.

They stood around a table about ten feet by five feet with a red silk sheet thrown over it. There was something lumpy beneath the sheet. Rina didn't have to wonder long what was underneath. Emilio whipped the sheet aside with a dramatic flurry.

"Behold," he said proudly. "The city of Sherrik and its defenses."

Rina stuck the chuma stick into the corner of her mouth and leaned forward to squint at the duke's revelation.

It was a painstakingly accurate model of the city—every building, wall, and street accounted for. Metal figures in armor—probably cast in lead—had been painted with the livery of Sherrik. Wooden carved sailing ships had been placed entering the harbor. They flew Perranese flags.

Emilio pointed at the figurines atop the outer wall facing the harbor, careful not to knock them over. "Obviously we can't have a figurine for every single soldier. The ones with white helmets represent a hundred troops. The red helmets represent five hundred troops. As you can see, we have five thousand men stationed along the harbor wall, where we expect the brunt of the attack." He made a lazy circular motion with his finger, indicating the rest of the city's perimeter. "Another thousand stationed around the other walls." He indicated a wide boulevard that spanned the width of the city in a straight line from the harbor defenses to the northern wall. Halfway between the two points was a building marked with a little red flag. "We can move troops to strengthen either the harbor defenses or the gate to the north should they land troops up or down the coast to march inland and attack us that way. The flagged building houses additional troops sent by cousin Pemrod. I had initially planned to station them at points around the wall but thought instead to hold them in reserve until we see how the enemy deploys."

Rina listened to the duke with a growing sense of dread. She hadn't really known how close she'd come to hitting the mark earlier when she'd thought of him as a kid. *He's a child, playing at war with his toy soldiers. He's giddy with the idea of this battle. Has he ever heard the screams or smelled the blood or bowels loosened in the throes of death?*

Emilio pointed to a space between the harbor wall and a larger wall back a few hundred paces within the city. "If they take the harbor wall, we can fall back behind this inner wall, conceding this dockside market area. Naturally, I don't expect it to get that far, but a commander must always be prepared."

He'll get everyone killed. He has no idea what's coming.

But neither did Rina. All she knew for sure was that if she was never in another battle for the rest of her life that would be just fine. Her instincts told her fate had something else in mind.

She blinked, looking back at the duke, realizing he was asking her a question. "Your grace?"

"I asked if you thought my preparations sufficient," Emilio repeated. "I welcome any suggestions you might have."

She looked back at the toy soldiers. "I . . . I don't know."

"The defenses seem sensible," Hark said. "I suppose it's difficult to plan when you don't yet know the size of the enemy force."

"Hmmm, yes." The duke's eyes were still on Rina.

He's still playing but doesn't want Hark as his playmate. He's waiting for me to say something.

A memory stirred. Rina's father preparing for the oncoming invaders.

"How are your stores?" she asked.

Emilio raised an eyebrow. "Pardon?"

"If they have a siege in mind, they might not bother to storm the walls at all," Rina said. "They can blockade your harbor and choke the roads inland if they land enough men."

Emilio brightened. "An excellent point. Our supplies are good and will stretch even further with so much of the population gone from the city, and we have deep wells for fresh water. My people estimate the stores should easily last—" The duke turned suddenly to speak to someone behind him. "Maxus, how long did the chamberlain's clerks estimate the food stores would last?"

Rina turned also to see a man come forward from a shaded spot beneath the canopy. He'd been standing quietly; she hadn't noticed him before.

"Eighteen months at present consumption," Maxus said. "Longer if we go on half rations or even quarter rations."

"There, you see?" Emilio said. "And by then we could easily have ships down from Kern to break the blockade. I'm sure even now, King Pemrod is rallying more troops to our cause. We'll throw these Perranese bastards back into the sea, I promise you."

Rina's eyes were still on Maxus. "I'm sorry, I don't believe we've met."

"But of course, I should have introduced you," Emilio said. "Bishop Hark, Duchess Veraiin, this is the wizard Maxus Fench, my chief advisor."

Maxus bowed. He was so tall and thin, Rina imagined she heard his bones creak. He was completely smooth and bald up top. His braided beard, a mix of black and white, hung almost to his belt. Nose like a beak, eyes a dull brown. A robe of deep scarlet, cinched at the waist with a tasseled green cord.

"It's a special treat to see you out and about in the sunlight, Maxus." Emilio turned to Rina. "Usually our master magician locks himself away in his tower, pouring over dusty books and fiddling with potions and whatnot."

Maxus's grin was filled with yellow teeth. "When I heard the duchess arrived, I had to see for myself. Forgive me. Professional curiosity. May I?"

He moved closer to examine the tattoos around Rina's eyes.

Her instinct was to back away from him, but she didn't want to be rude. She endured his scrutiny. He squinted at her face like she might be some exotic species of insect.

"Fascinating," Maxus said. "This doesn't look like Weylan's work."

Rina blinked surprise. "You knew him?"

"A long time ago," Maxus said. "We haven't crossed paths in nearly three decades."

"Then you might not have heard," Rina said. "He died."

A look passed across Maxus's face, more curiosity than grief. "I'm sorry to hear it. How did it happen?"

"A long story. The tattoos around the eyes were done by another." She was tempted to tell him the lightning bolts on her ankles came from a wizard named Talbun just to see if he knew her. Sometimes it seemed as if these wizards all ran in the same cliques.

But she held her tongue.

"As you can imagine, ink mages are something of a rarity in this day and age," Maxus said. "I'd love a demonstration."

Emilio stepped forward, clearing his throat pointedly. "Now really, Maxus. Duchess Veraiin is our guest. Not some dancing bear for your amusement. I must apologize, Rina."

Maxus bowed. "I apologize also. I meant no offense." His eyes came back up to Rina's. "A familiar, yes? The feathers at the corners of the eyes suggest some bird. Perhaps strong of wing, maybe enough to get a look at our foes. Surely, if I am too forward, it's worth it to get some advanced word of our enemy before they arrive."

"You heard what I said, Maxus." But the duke's eyes bounced between Rina and the wizard now. The idea of getting a look at the enemy clearly had his attention. "You're making an assumption about the duchess's abilities that might not even be true." His gaze rested on her, the unasked question hanging in the air. *Is it true?*

"Master Fench appears to know something of ink-mage tattoos," Rina said.

A slight shrug from Maxus, mock humility. "Those who practice the arcane arts have exotic hobbies."

Rina looked at the duke. "It's true."

There was a moment of awkward silence as everyone looked at each other, wondering what would happen next.

"It will take some time," Rina said at last. "My familiar is a forest falcon. I'll have to call him. I can't be disturbed. Probably better if I sit since I don't know how long this will take."

The duke snapped his fingers and barked orders. Servants scurried. Rina puffed the chuma stick, a sense of resignation settling in her chest.

"There's something else," Rina said to Emilio. "There's a Perranese force north of the city. I escaped from them. I don't know how close they are. A few hundred men. Hardly enough to storm the city, but enough to harass your scouts or act as spotters for the incoming fleet."

Emilio scratched his chin. "Perhaps a patrol."

"You have horses?"

"I can mount thirty men within twenty minutes."

"A suggestion. Tell them not to engage. Just find out where the enemy is."

The duke thought for a moment, then nodded quickly. He snapped his fingers again for a runner and sent the orders.

A servant brought a wicker chair with thick cushions. Rina sat. A half dozen guards ringed her, facing outward.

"No one will disturb you," the duke assured her. "Do you need anything else?"

She puffed the chuma stick one last time. "No."

Rina settled back into the chair. Closed her eyes.

And tapped into the spirit.

◆　◆　◆

Zin waited at the forest's edge just north of Sherrik, spread his wings, and soared into the air at Rina's call, flying over the city and out to sea.

Rina would never get used to the sensation of flight.

And she'd never tire of it. It was still as thrilling as the very first time.

She looked down at the blue sea through the falcon's eyes and dove low, skimming along the waves.

No. It wasn't a time to play. She had far to go, maybe to the limit of Zin's range. That meant altitude. She flapped hard and climbed.

Impossibly high now. She caught a current and rode it out to sea. Fast. Faster than she'd ever flown before, faster than she could run with the lightning tattoos. It was cold.

How long? An hour? Two? Time seemed to warp into meaninglessness as she looked down to the unbroken blue sameness below.

Through the bond they shared, she sensed Zin's concern. He was nearing the limit of his range. He'd need to turn around soon or he wouldn't make it back.

Glide on the current. Conserve your strength.

The falcon's fatigue was a palpable thing, even as the spirit kept her from feeling it. A peculiar paradox.

Turn back. Turn back now!

Zin didn't communicate to her in any language but with pure, raw feelings.

And he was frightened.

This isn't working. And yet she willed the bird on.

The sun looked like shimmering gold on the water. Like liquid metal. Little black bumps dotted the gold, thousands of them.

Zin folded in his wings, making a sleek projectile out of himself and dove toward the water. The scene congealed into focus the lower he went, the waves giving the flat blue of the sea texture again, the black bumps taking shapes.

Ships.

Rina flew between them, from ship to ship, darting and wheeling between sails and masts, Perranese banners flapping in the wind. The occasional sailor looked up at her, the foreign face a jarring reminder. The men on these ships were traveling a long way to take her homeland for themselves.

Why? What did they want?

It didn't matter.

She told Zin to climb. High. Higher than before. He had to find a current going back the other way. Through their bond, the bird's knowledge became hers, the ways of the sky and the wind.

By the time she found a current going back to Sherrik, she was so high that the bitter ache from the cold was almost more than Zin could bear, but he spread his wings, let the current take him.

How many miles? How long?

Zin wasn't going to make it. Rina could feel the falcon's emotions, could feel the panic welling up inside of him, the bird's heartbeat increasing, his wings so sore, the idea of flapping them became a torment.

Rina could feel the falcon giving up.

She passed some of her spirit to the bird.

Rina hadn't even known it was possible. A reflex. Just as she could push pain and fear away while tapped into the spirit, now too did Zin ignore the blinding ache in his wings, the biting cold, the fear of death.

Zin flew on. The thought of letting the falcon go never once crossed Rina's mind. He was too much a part of her.

Finally, a shape humped up from the horizon.

Hope sprang as the walls of Sherrik took shape. Every muscle in the falcon burned, but they were too close to quit now. A jetty thrust out a hundred yards from the mouth of the harbor, a red marker pennant fluttering in the breeze. The falcon landed on the jetty collapsing, trembling, and spent. Rina knew Zin would not have been able to fly another hundred yards, but he'd made it. Safe.

Rina released her hold on the falcon.

She'd never hung on to the bond with Zin this long before, and releasing it was like riding a bowstring as it snapped back into place.

She felt as if she were being yanked backward—

The sky blurred past her, alarmed faces, her head spinning, and then she was facedown on the veranda's hard stone floor. She blinked her eyes clear, looking up into the faces of Hark, Emilio, and the wizard Maxus, the guards pushing in behind them.

"Don't crowd her," the duke commanded. "Let her breathe."

Rina trembled, covered with sweat.

The bishop knelt next to her. "Your grace. Can you hear me? Are you okay?"

"Ships." Her voice was barely a croak. She cleared her throat and tried again. "Ships. At least ten thousand."

The guards murmured at that. The duke frowned.

"Impossible," he said. "I've consulted closely with my military advisors, and there aren't that many ships in the entire Perranese Empire."

"With good wind and fair weather, they'll be here in three days," Rina said. "And then you can count them yourself."

*   *   *

CHAPTER
SIXTEEN

Maurizan awoke, the Moogari a swarm of activity around her, stoking the fire, preparing food, washing her clothes.

She looked down at herself. She wore a thin linen gown and sprawled on a pallet of straw. Memories flooded back. She'd swum with Kristos for hours, feeling as at home in the depths as a dolphin, swimming and diving and surfacing again. The gypsy girl was at play. She'd never felt so free and alive.

Until Kristos had led her back to the ruined fortress of the ancient wizards. She'd released her hold on the spirit and collapsed. Too much too soon. Exhaustion had overwhelmed her. She'd felt hands lift her up and carry her along. The Moogari. They'd gently dried her and dressed her and eased her onto the straw pallet. She slept forever and ever.

Until now.

She sat up, and one of the Moogari rushed to her with a small ceramic bowl and offered it to her. A steaming broth. She tasted it. Fish. Salty. Some kind of soggy, leafy vegetable like spinach. She was still wondering at the different flavors and textures when she looked down and saw she'd emptied the bowl. They brought her water, clear and cool. She drank.

Maurizan stood, her legs still a bit wobbly. Her mother and grandmother had warned her not to drink too deeply of the spirit. It could affect her the next day just as if she'd had too much wine.

Or she could drain herself completely. There were worse consequences than fatigue and a headache.

She looked around for Kristos, but there was no sign of the Fish Man.

The Moogari didn't stop her from exploring, but every hall ended in an abandoned room or a pile of rubble from a cave-in or a dark pool of water leading down to another level of the fortress. Whatever the cataclysm was that had destroyed the place, it had done a pretty good job. Kristos had explained that the Moogari were a race created by the old masters to tend the fortress. They were bound to the place, but by a spell or some sense of duty, Maurizan couldn't guess. It was still difficult to understand why they hadn't moved on. She wondered if Kristos had ever suggested it to them.

She returned to the Moogari and tried to ask where Kristos had gone. Communication was impossible, but they seemed to understand the word *Kristos* and motioned her to follow them.

Maurizan paused to buckle the two fighting daggers on to her belt, one on each hip. Her clothes were clean but still wet and drying by the fire. Her boots were nowhere to be found, and no matter how much she mimed putting them on, she couldn't make them understand.

"Never mind, damn it," she said. "Let's get on with it."

They led her down a narrow hallway, bare feet slapping on the stone floor. She hadn't gone this direction earlier when she'd been exploring. Moogari ahead of her and behind carried torches to light the way. The hall opened into a wide chamber with a vaulted ceiling. It was barren of furnishings. Across the room was a ten-foot-high iron door, an iron bar locking it shut.

The Moogari slid the bar to the side, pulled a metal ring, and the door creaked open. She followed inside.

They were at the top of what must have been a grand stairway many years ago. Now the stone steps went down into dark water. The Moogari pointed at the water and jabbered. The only word she caught was *Kristos*.

"What do you mean?" Maurizan asked. "You mean Kristos is down there, or he wants me to go down there?"

More pointing and jabbering.

"Great. Fantastic." She sighed and unbuckled her belt, letting it drop. She pulled the gown up over her head and tossed it aside. Strange how quickly she was getting used to being naked in front of other people, or maybe it was more that the Moogari weren't really people.

It didn't matter. She buckled the belt around her waist, daggers dangling, and that seemed the oddest of all. Her standing there nude, daggers on her hips. What a sight she must be.

She wondered what Alem would think and allowed herself a little smile.

One of the Moogari approached her, held out his hand. Some sort of offering. A glass sphere the size of an apple filled with water. Something swam within. Maurizan took it and squinted at it. A hundred tiny translucent fish swam inside of it, each no longer than a fingernail. What she was meant to do with the glass orb full of tiny fish, Maurizan couldn't guess.

Seeing her consternation, the Moogari took the sphere back and shook it violently. The fish swam madly in a clockwise circle around and around. A second later they began to glow a brilliant blue-white, casting light as bright as any lantern.

Of course. It's not like I can take a torch with me under the water.

The Moogari slipped the sphere into a small bag of mesh-like fishing net. The bag was attached to a leather cord tied in a hoop. She bent her head as the Moogari hung it on her, the net with the glowing orb hanging between her breasts.

"Okay," she said. "I'm naked and glowing. I guess it's time to take a swim now?" She gestured at the water.

The Moogari nodded, also pointing at the water.

"Well, then. No sense in putting this off."

Maurizan turned and dove into the water.

She tapped into the spirit and sped like a fish into the depths, gliding effortlessly. This wasn't like before with Kristos, not a warm swim with bright, tropical fish flitting all around and the sun shimmering overhead. It was cold down here. The orb with the little fish cast an eerie glow on the stone.

She paused at the bottom of the stairs to take in the place. It was a great hall, the glow from her little orb too weak to reach the ceiling. The floor was mosaic, some complicated design, the brightly colored stones worn smooth by use and dulled with time. Rows of arches lined the sides of the hall, ten-foot stone statues filling the space between each arch.

Maurizan swam to the nearest statue, held out the glowing orb in front of her to better examine the figure. The stone was intricately carved. She was not an expert on such things but supposed it had been sculpted by a master. The lifelike face was drawn and thin, its cheeks sunken. Eyes cold and cunning. A sparse beard and moustache. Flowing robes. A necklace with numerous unfamiliar and arcane objects hanging from it. His hands were frozen in midgesture, as if he weaved something invisible in midair.

Yeah, this guy has wizard *written all over him.*

She made a slow circuit of the great hall, pausing to look at each of the statues. Some were women, but most were men. Each loomed tall and ominous, some slight variation in pose. Some held staffs aloft.

Others held a large tome open in front of them—spell books, Maurizan supposed.

A hall of wizards, forgotten by the centuries. They were all probably really important people once upon a time.

Now they were the silent guardians of an ancient and watery tomb.

She ducked under one of the arches and swam down a short hall that ended in a pile of rubble. Some cave-in that had happened decades ago. *Where's Kristos? Am I supposed to find him down here somewhere?*

She swam back through the grand hall of wizards and through another random arch, into a maze of empty halls and rooms. Perhaps at one time these rooms had been richly furnished and used for various purposes, but after centuries of salt water, nothing was left but barren stone. Dust rose up in swirling eddies like lazy ghosts whenever she swam close to the floor, the remains of . . . who could say?

Maurizan swam back to the hall of wizards and contemplated going back up the stairs. Maybe she could try harder to make the Moogari understand her questions. She couldn't stay tapped into the spirit forever, and swimming in circles wasn't accomplishing anything.

She was still trying to decide, when she felt it.

Something cold. Like a chill current descending on her from above, but also like an emotion, like a sense of dread floating down so softly and seeping into her bones so gradually, she didn't even realize it was happening until she suddenly felt herself in the iron grip of fear. Panic bloomed in her so quickly it almost paralyzed her.

Only the fact she'd been tapped into the spirit saved her. She took hold of the fear, pushed it away to some distant part of herself, and locked it away.

She craned her neck to look up, held the orb aloft, its light stretching toward the high ceiling but falling short. She swam upward, slowly, cautious, the orb held out in front of her.

The ceiling had once been another gorgeous mosaic depicting the night sky. Planets and stars and constellations. At one time it must have been quite striking, but again, time had taken its toll.

A great fissure twenty feet wide and twice as long marred the center of the mosaic, from which an oily darkness oozed. It leaked out, dissipating into the rest of the water. Did it flow out somewhere, or was the whole place permeated with the stuff?

Maurizan started to swim closer but froze. Something stirred in the murky darkness. The fear she'd bottled up earlier thrashed to get out. Anyone else, anyone not tapped into the spirit, would have fled in wild panic, but Maurizan was master of herself. She wanted to know what she faced. Was this what Kristos had meant her to see?

She squinted into the inky depths of the fissure. Perhaps she only imagined she saw movement in there. Maybe it was only a stray current stirring the oily—

The tentacle lashed out, snaking through the water so fast that even tapped into the spirit, Maurizan almost wasn't quick enough to dodge it. The tentacle curled back to lash at her again, but she'd already twisted in an aquatic somersault and was kicking hard back toward the steps.

Her rapid departure had nothing to do with the fear she still held at bay. No, this was a matter of pure common sense. Whatever the monster was, she'd seen enough of it. A cold and logical desire for self-preservation sped her back up the wide staircase. She shot through the water like a sleek shark on the hunt.

Except you're the one being hunted, stupid girl.

She swam until the water became too shallow, then trudged up the last few steps, releasing her hold on the spirit. A mild fatigue settled over her, but nothing like last time. She was pacing herself better, getting used to it.

The Moogari were gone. Maurizan would have stood in utter darkness if not for the sphere of little glowing fish. She ran to the big iron door, pulled on the metal ring with both hands.

It didn't budge.

No. She yanked on it again with the same result. *No no no no—*

She pounded on the door with both fists. "Hey! Let me out of here."

No reply. They'd barred the door and left her.

She pounded on the door again. Harder. "Open this door, you freaks! Swear to Dumo, if I get my hands on you bastard sons of—"

The water roiled behind her. She turned, backed against the iron door, eyes shooting wide with panic. The water bubbled and foamed like a boiling pot, something rising from the depths.

And then she saw it.

The tentacles came out first, thrashing about wildly, spraying seawater and slapping against the walls and ceiling of the chamber. The bloated, hideous body followed, breaking the surface. A hard green shell covered its back. Claws like a crab's raised high in the air, lifeless black eyes on short stalks. Its oily flesh oozed from the breaks in its carapace where the tentacles grew out. Its enormous maw opened and closed, flashing rows of teeth like spearheads.

The creature was an ancient sea dweller from depths none had ever seen. When the cataclysm that broke the continent into the Scattered Isles happened, it came up through caverns dark and old into a part of the ruined fortress sealed away from the rest. Maurizan knew none of this. All she knew at the moment was abject terror, and she screamed.

She tapped into the spirit, the situation snapping into focus, fear subdued as she readied herself.

The creature swiped at her with a huge claw, and she ducked underneath. It missed her by inches, denting the iron door behind her with an echoing clang. Even as she rolled away, another part of her brain cataloged a score of similar dents in the door.

No wonder they keep it barred.

The tip of a tentacle looped around her left ankle and dragged her toward the water. She swiped at it with a dagger, and the blade bit deep. A dark green ichor sprayed from the wound. The beast squealed—a high-pitched, hissing, gurgling sound—and yanked the tentacle back.

She dodged another tentacle that lashed at her like a whip even as another part of her mind calculated escape. There was no going back. The door was shut and barred and was going to stay that way.

That meant she had to go forward.

She launched herself at the water, the monster's claws snapping above her. She entered the water straight and fast, as if she'd been shot from a crossbow, and swam hard before the creature realized what she was doing. She swam between its crustaceous legs and under its bloated belly and was through to the other side. She glanced over her shoulder and saw a half dozen tentacles making a grab for her but falling short.

Don't look back. Just keep swimming.

But where?

If she hadn't been tapped into the spirit, she'd have never had a chance, but her brain scrolled logically through the options. Her earlier explorations had found only dead ends and cave-ins. The beast would corner her and rip her apart.

That left only one choice.

And Maurizan didn't like it.

She swam with all her speed for the ceiling, a pale flash through the water. The oily ooze from the fish had dwindled to a trickle, but it was still enough to give her pause. She felt the beast coming fast behind her and plunged into the darkness.

The foul stuff nearly swallowed the light of the orb. She could see only a few feet in any direction. Again, without the perfect calm that came with being tapped into the spirit, the fear of being lost in the dark would have paralyzed her. The disgust would have revolted her.

Be calm. Think.

She closed her eyes.

A current, coming in from the side, cooler and not so foul.

She swam toward it.

All of this transpired in a split second. The beast was already crawling back into the crevice after her.

Maurizan found the source of the current. A crack in the wall about three feet wide. No way the creature would be able to follow, but Maurizan had no idea what might be on the other side.

Who cares? Something worse than a giant tentacled sea monster trying to eat you? Don't be ridiculous!

She darted through to the other side, and immediately the water was cleaner. Her eyes tried to see everywhere at once. Looking for a way out.

A tentacle followed her through the crack and snaked tight around her waist. She tried to pull away, but the tentacle squeezed. She felt her ribs bend and bruise. She winced with the pain.

The beast put its gaping maw right up against the crack, rows of razor-sharp teeth exposed. It reeled Maurizan in with the tentacle.

She struggled, slashed a deep cut into the tentacle that held her. This time the beast held on.

It vomited a cloud of black sludge at her. It was so vile that Maurizan almost lost her hold on the spirit. The beast squeezed harder. She felt a rib crack but set aside the pain.

She went back to work on the tentacle with the dagger, but instead of slashing, she began to saw through it. The creature thrashed on the other side of the crack in fury and pain. Stonework fell away, the crack widening, the monster's maw working as it pulled Maurizan closer.

Now. It's got to be now!

She sliced completely through and kicked hard, swimming away, the limp remains of the tentacle falling away.

The beast thrashed with rage and frustration, but she was beyond its reach.

She kept swimming, found herself in a long hall. It might have been any hall in any ordinary castle except it was filled with water. Sooner or later she'd need to release the spirit. And that meant she'd need air to breathe. If she just kept swimming in one direction, maybe she'd eventually—

The orb's glow flickered and dimmed.

She held up the sphere, squinted at it through the netting. The tiny fish within swam sluggishly now. Half of them had gone dark altogether. She shook the orb like she'd seen the Moogari do, but that made it worse. The exhausted fish stopped swimming entirely.

The light went out.

Leaving only the cold and the dark.

CHAPTER SEVENTEEN

The sword was magnificent, expertly forged, flawless, and obviously magical. It was a priceless prize fit for royalty.

At the moment, Alem was using it to knock fruit out of a tree.

He'd built a small fire in the mouth of the cave, slept fitfully. The next morning, his clothes had dried. He'd put them on and buckled his new sword and scabbard around his waist and headed up the hill. He'd thought to get as high as possible and have a look around.

He'd paused near the top when he saw the fruit hanging from a high limb, red colored and fuzzy. It had looked sweet and edible, and he'd been starving.

Now he'd shimmied out on a limb and was swinging the sword, trying to knock the fruit loose. He'd seen similar fruit being sold in the bazaar when he'd been in the Red City, and his mouth watered at what he imagined they'd taste like.

Even if the fruit tasted like cheese left out all day in the sun, he still planned to eat it. He was just that hungry.

Alem swung at the fruit again, the tip of the sword just missing where it hung from the branch. He scooted farther out on the branch. It creaked beneath him. He held his breath.

Please. Don't. Break.

He connected this time, and a clustered bunch of the fruit fell to the ground. Alem blew out a sigh of relief. Now just to back down the way he'd come and—

Alem turned his head, looked out over blue water. He hadn't realized he'd come this far up the hill, and from his vantage in the tree he could see down the other side and also to the next island not far away. It would be an easy swim if he wanted to get there.

Frankly, it wasn't much of an island and maybe not worth the trouble. He had edible—he presumed—fruit here and fresh water and a cave for shelter. The island across the narrow channel looked like the point of an old man's hat sticking up through the water, circled by a thin band of white beach. The island humped up gradually until the very top, at which point it shot up unnaturally straight, as if the hill had suddenly grown a large chimney. The more he looked at it, the stranger it seemed that a rock formation would be so symmetrical. He supposed that in the wide world nature would occasionally . . .

Alem squinted at it.

It's a tower.

It was close enough to glimpse the stonework even through the creeping vines and moss.

Alem shimmied back down the tree as fast as he could without falling and breaking his neck.

◆ ◆ ◆

"Some more of this wonderful wine, please." Brasley gestured to his empty glass.

One of the copper-haired women with the milk-white skin smiled and bowed and refilled Brasley's wine. She spoke not a word of Brasley's language, but a gesture to an empty glass was clear enough. They seemed delighted to serve.

Brasley was delighted to let them.

Dinner had consisted of perfectly prepared roast chicken, rice, and a long green vegetable Brasley had never seen but turned out to be tasty enough. Where they'd been hiding chickens these past centuries was anyone's guess. The servants simply disappeared behind their doors that led somewhere behind the walls, and then they'd return later with wine or food or warm bathwater or whatever the guests desired.

With Olgen acting as interpreter, they'd confirmed to the best of their ability that *guests* and *servants* were indeed the appropriate words to describe their relationship with the white-skinned women. They each had been shown to their rooms. The women had poured hot water for baths. Brasley had even had his clothes laundered and his boots shined. All requests to the servants went through Olgen, who often had to try half a dozen times to get the translation right, but eventually the servants understood.

By the time the servants brought dessert—some strawberry pastry lighter than a cloud—Brasley's glass needed filling again.

"We're not on vacation, you know," Talbun said to him from the other end of the table.

They'd been served dinner in a formal dining room, long table, chandelier with miniature versions of the light globes hanging low and casting soft lighting over the meal. Thick and exotic rugs beneath them. A half dozen of the servants stood along the wall, waiting to cater to their every whim. The platters were silver, as was the cutlery. The wine-glasses crystal.

"I notice you didn't say no to the wine," Brasley said.

Talbun hunched over her end of the table, scribbling on a piece of parchment with a quill. She answered without looking up. "This wine is so I can tolerate *you*."

"Yes, very amusing," Brasley said. "You can at least come down to this end of the table and insult me to my face like a civilized person."

"This is where the servants put the place setting."

"Will you just come down here?" Brasley insisted.

The wizard sighed and stood, snatching up her wineglass. She made to gather her quill, inkwell, and papers, but a servant rushed forward, placed the items on a tray, and followed Talbun to the seat at Brasley's right.

Olgen looked at Brasley expectantly, like a puppy hoping to be tossed a piece of rawhide. His place setting was in the exact middle, equidistant from Brasley and Talbun.

"Yes, you too," Brasley said. "Come on, then."

Olgen shuffled down to sit on Brasley's left.

"See?" Brasley said. "Now we can talk without shouting across the room at each other."

"Uh-huh." Talbun was back at her scribbles.

Brasley squinted at the parchments. "What are you doing anyway?"

"I've been working with Olgen on ancient Fyrian," Talbun said. "It's close enough to modern Fyrian, I think I can get the hang of it. My inflections were all wrong, though."

"And you're still conjugating incorrectly, milady," Olgen said.

Talbun looked up at him, eyes narrow, mouth tight.

"Uh, but you're *improving* rapidly, milady," Olgen added hastily.

Talbun frowned, drank wine, and returned to her parchments.

"Not that the language lessons aren't fascinating, but shouldn't we be talking about how to get out of here?" Brasley asked. "I'll admit

I'm quite content for the moment, but this place will seem like a posh prison soon enough."

When they'd asked about a way out, the servants had indicated they should go back to the lifting platform that had brought them up in the first place. When Brasley explained—through Olgen—that the lift had been wrecked (leaving out he'd been the one to wreck it) the servants had only returned a blank stare. Apparently they hadn't been instructed in how to deal with such contingencies.

Brasley had the bright idea to follow them into one of the side doors that opened into the wall, the ones they used to fetch wine or food or perform other servant duties. Attempting to do this caused the politest uproar Brasley had ever seen. One of the white-skinned women had placed herself directly in front of him, shaking her head even as she bowed obsequiously. The message was clear: *I am so so so terribly sorry, but you can't go in there.* Trying to walk around her had summoned another of the servants to stand in front of him, and when Brasley had switched directions to circle around her the other way, a third appeared. Ten minutes of trying to dodge around them had produced a dozen of the women, all shaking heads and bowing and muttering prefabricated apologies. Unless he wanted to hack a path through them with his sword, he wasn't getting through the door. Brasley wasn't yet ready to get that extreme.

Brasley had ordered Olgen to plead their case in a number of different ways, but the answer was always the same. The little doorways were for servants, and Brasley wasn't a servant. Olgen eventually became flustered, straining the limits of his ancient Fyrian, and Brasley had given up.

Not to be so easily thwarted, Brasley then waited until none of the servants were around and attempted to open one of the doors himself. It was impossible. When the doors were closed, they blended in perfectly with the rest of the wall, no crease or seam to be found. The door might as well not have been there at all.

"The point being that eventually with enough time and wine these odd, pale creatures will start looking good to me, and I'd like to be gone from here before that happens." He drained his glass and noticed the servants no longer waited for his signal to refill it again.

So they can learn. Noted.

Talbun frowned at him. Sometimes she appreciated his sense of humor. Other times . . . not so much.

"Getting out of here isn't the priority," she said.

"It's *my* priority," Brasley insisted.

"No. It's not." She fixed him with one of those iron glares. "Rina sent you to help me. We haven't done what we came here to do yet."

Brasley rolled his eyes. *This* again. "And that would be . . . ?"

"That's what we're here to find out, isn't it?"

Brasley quickly gulped wine before he said something to piss off the wizard. He knew he'd had too much. Usually he was a jolly drunk, but felt himself going in a disgruntled direction this time. Somewhere in the Great Library—*maybe*—there was a tattoo that did . . . something. How had he been roped into this fool's errand?

"We still have the same problem either way," he said. "We've got to get out of here."

"Well, the servants consider us guests, not masters. They'll only obey commands in that context," Talbun said. "They were created to serve the wizards."

"*You* are a wizard," Brasley pointed out.

Talbun paused in her scribbling, sat back, and crossed her arms. She frowned again, but this time in thought, not displeasure. She nibbled her bottom lip, thought some more. "You talk so much, I suppose it shouldn't be a surprise that you'd eventually stumble across a good idea."

After the women had captured him and taken the final component, Knarr had been taken to a small room. Chair. Waste bucket. A narrow cot. A window, too high up and too small to crawl out of. It was a damn sight better than the dungeon cell he'd expected, but he was still definitely a prisoner.

One last delivery and he would have had the gold and that would have been it. He could have picked up the rest of his money where it lay hidden and headed south to warmer climes. He'd always wanted to see Sherrik, although he'd heard the rumors along with everyone else that it had been sealed and would soon be under siege. But maybe he could still catch a ship to the Red City. His gold would go far there. Perhaps he could even sail all the way back to his homeland in the Southern Scattered Isles.

Not that he remembered anything about it. He'd been an infant when his parents had taken him north. His father had been accepted as a novice scholar at Tul-Agnon—an honor nearly unheard of among the Southern Scattered Islanders. And when Knarr was old enough, he'd been accepted too, had even lasted quite a while before they expelled him.

He probably should have spent more time studying and less time learning the best way to fence stolen artifacts from the Great Library.

Still, it was good money.

Except now he'd been caught, and just because he hadn't been tossed in the dungeon yet, didn't mean it couldn't happen any time. He had a pretty good guess why he wasn't there already. They might have questions about the item they'd confiscated from him and wouldn't feel like tramping all the way down to the dungeon to ask.

He sprawled on the bunk. He got up again and paced. He looked out the window.

The view was of a tall stone tower broken apart at the top. The "prayer tower," the locals called it. Tavern gossip had it that the top had been torn to pieces by some winged beast but the duchess had single-handedly driven the creature away.

Drunk talk. Obviously.

He waited. And waited some more.

At last the door swung open. It was one of those Birds of Prey and two more behind her, swords dangling from belts. Some dumb part of him said *They're only women* and thought maybe he could push past them and make a run for it. A smarter voice in his head reminded him he'd met too many dangerous women in his time.

"Come with us," she said.

Knarr followed the women through the castle. He recognized they'd taken him to some nicer wing, probably where the nobles lived and worked. Maybe he was being taken to the duchess for pronouncement of sentence, although the same gossipers reported she wasn't in Klaar at the moment.

They entered some kind of library. Bookshelves and well-appointed furnishings. The fireplace stood open. Well, that didn't look right. They led him down a passage behind it.

Knarr entered a large chamber. Smooth walls curved up to the ceiling. A group of people waited for him, more armed women, a greasy-looking man who looked like he might try to pick your pocket as soon as you turned around, and a shorter, haughty woman in a fine dress and a demeanor that tilted between regal and an irritated nursemaid.

The crowd split apart, revealing something on the far wall.

An intricately carved archway. Ten feet tall and half again as wide. It was the exact sort of thing to mark a pass-through from one castle hall to another. But instead of an opening, there was only solid stone. An archway to nowhere. Detailed markings had been carved at various points around the archway, and a glittering gemstone nestled in the center of each group of markings. The only place absent a gemstone was the cluster of markings at the very top of the—

Knarr blinked. Comprehension hit him like a sling stone to the forehead.

A portal. I never thought I'd see one. I'm looking at an actual portal.

Knarr realized everyone was looking at him as he stood with his mouth hanging open.

The haughty woman took three steps forward, hands clasped in front of her.

"Master Knarr?"

He nodded. "Yes."

"I'm Stasha Benadicta, steward of Klaar. I understand you might know something about this portal. It is in your best interest to tell us everything you know."

Knarr cleared his throat. "Where would you like me to start?"

CHAPTER
EIGHTEEN

They'd given Bishop Hark and Rina each their own rooms. Rina was glad for a chance to bathe and get out of the black armor. It fit her well but was still armor. A silk lounging dress and light slippers were a welcome change.

The duke had insisted his personal physicians inspect every inch of her after her tumble on the veranda, but she wasn't injured. Just fatigued from her long trek out to sea in Zin's mind.

She sat in her room and heaved a great sigh. *They don't believe me. They think it's impossible there could be so many ships in one fleet.*

Maybe she wouldn't have believed it either.

There was a tattoo that let her possess a falcon and fly across the sea, but there was none to make anyone believe what she'd seen there. No matter what the duke of Sherrik had planned with his little toy soldiers, there was no way he could stand against what was coming.

I have to talk to someone, convince them. Somebody has to believe me.

Rina left her room, walked to the end of the hall, where a guard stood at a crossroads of corridors. He snapped to attention at her approach. She told him who she was looking for, and he obliged her with directions. Unfortunately, it was near the top of the pyramid. The guard told her the nearest and most direct passage to the top was a steep spiral staircase, not a pleasant climb, he conceded.

She tapped into the spirit and sprinted up the stairs. It was a frivolous use of the magic, but Rina was in no mood for some endless trudge. She followed the guard's direction, found the correct door, and knocked.

A moment later, the door swung open and Maxus Fench stood there.

"Your grace." He didn't seem surprised to see her.

"Apologies for calling unannounced," Rina said.

"Please think nothing of it," Maxus said. "Would you like to come in?" He stepped aside and gestured a welcome.

Rina entered, eyes raking the room, taking in everything. In a way, the place reminded her of Weylan's cave. Old books, numerous oddly shaped bottles, various dried herbs hanging from a length of twine over a table where a spotty adolescent—an apprentice, probably—ground something with mortar and pestle. The place smelled old and musty but simultaneously sweet and fresh.

Maxus's room had a better view than Weylan's cave. A big window allowed a pleasant breeze and afforded a view of the ocean. The vantage was high enough now to see down into the harbor. Maxus Fench would have a fine view of the war.

"I was hoping to speak with you about something." Rina's eyes shifted momentarily to the apprentice.

"Rikken, why don't you go get yourself a meal," Maxus suggested. "You can finish that later."

Rikken bowed curtly and left the room.

"I can assure you we have privacy here," Maxus told her.

"You serve the duke? You're loyal to him?"

"Yes."

"Then help him," Rina said. "Help him understand what's coming."

"Ah." Maxus paced a moment, then said, "The duke is young."

"I'm young," Rina said. "Young doesn't mean stupid."

"But it does sometimes mean inexperienced. His grace relies on his military advisors. For the most part, they are good men. He has no reason to doubt them."

"I've given him a reason."

"You've given him *too much* reason, Duchess Veraiin. You've presented him with a situation so dire that no matter how he deploys his figurine army, it simply won't matter. As you might imagine, it's not a scenario the duke would be eager to believe. Hopeless scenarios aren't popular."

"At least you seem to believe me," Rina said.

"I don't believe you'd lie," Maxus said. "But whether or not you saw ten thousand ships, I couldn't say."

"It was your idea to send the falcon," Rina reminded him. "What's the point if you're not going to accept the results?"

"I didn't say I didn't accept them. I simply have no way to *verify* them. If there's even an outside chance your estimation is accurate, then it's worth taking seriously."

"That's something at least."

"I'll ponder how best to swing the duke's opinion," Maxus promised. "In the meantime, we can discuss the other matter that's brought you to see me."

"What other matter?" And the question sounded like such a lie coming out of her mouth that she realized with a start it was.

"Come, Duchess, let us speak plainly, shall we? When I asked you to demonstrate your ability with the familiar tattoo, it was for my own curiosity. Yes, getting a good look at the enemy fleet was a good opportunity, but my motivation was more personal. I wanted to see you tap into the spirit. To see one of the tattoos being used."

"It wasn't much of a show," Rina said. "Me sitting there with my eyes closed."

"It was more interesting than you might think."

"You're right," Rina admitted. "I did want to talk to you about something else. As soon as you mentioned your interest in ink magic, I knew I had to ask you."

"Then please. Ask."

"Do you have one?"

Rina held her breath as she waited for the answer. Anticipation was like something that had a tight hold on her, something that squeezed harder each second that passed. It shamed her slightly how eager she was. She didn't think of herself as the kind of person who sought power, but she knew the answer she wanted. Her eyes never left the wizard's as she waited.

An eternal few seconds passed as he considered. Then he turned away from her and opened a small chest on a table behind him. His back blocked her view. She grew impatient and chastised herself. She was acting like some sort of addict, and that thought disturbed her.

Later. Think about that later.

Maxus turned back to her, an object in each hand.

Rina took a step forward to look, her heart picking up its pace with excitement.

A small inkwell rested in his left palm. Through the clear glass she saw the ink inside, a dark green—no, more of a blue really. It . . . Wait, actually a kind of deep burgundy with—

It's changing! Going from one color to another.

The ink swirled within, never settling on one color for too long.

In his other hand, Maxus held a square of shiny brass, some pattern cut out in the middle of it.

"A stencil," he explained.

Rina squinted at it, realized it was the figure of a small bird, its wings spread, about the size of a coin.

"How did you come by it?" Rina's voice was barely above a whisper.

"That would be a long story and would betray too many confidences," Maxus said. "It goes in the little hollow of your throat. And I can put it there, if you'll let me."

"I suppose it will hurt."

"Oh, yes. Just like the others."

"And I suppose you want something for it?"

"Must we be so cynical?"

"Do you want something or not?"

"Yes."

"Out with it."

"It wouldn't be terrible if you helped us. Sherrik is about to come under attack, and if there really are ten thousand ships, then our situation is even worse than we thought," Maxus said. "You are powerful, Duchess Veraiin. If this tattoo adds to your power, then maybe you'll remember who your friends are when the time comes."

Rina's eyes narrowed with suspicion. "I was always going to help. I think you know that. There's something else."

"Yes."

"Then tell me."

"Knowledge."

"You're going to have to use more words," Rina said.

"Ink magic has been a passion of mine for many years," Maxus said. "When I said before that I'd crossed paths with Weylan many years ago, it was because I'd sought him out. I was hungry to learn. I burned with curiosity. He told me some things. Other things he kept secret. Obviously, he wasn't about to share the secret of inking the Prime. The tidbits of information he doled out only whet my appetite for more. This stencil and the tattoo I can ink with it"—he nodded at the little brass square—"means nothing unless someone has the Prime first. I know there are ink mages in the world, but they are few and far between. You are the first I've met in person."

Rina shook her head, confused. "Wait. I don't understand. Do you think I have some information to trade you? How does giving me this tattoo add to your knowledge?"

"The stencil and ink came to me under unusual circumstances. I have the ink and the stencil, and I know how to apply it. What I don't know is what it does. I want you to help me find out. I can ink it on your throat. I'll be careful, I assure you. I hope that once it's on you, it will be something beneficial."

Maxus shrugged. "Although at that point, of course, it will be too late."

CHAPTER
NINETEEN

Floating in complete darkness.

The cold seeped into her bones. She was too afraid to expend the spirit it would take to fend off the chill. Instead, Maurizan focused on keeping the fear at bay.

You're dead already. What does it matter?

No. Panic wouldn't help. Nor would despair.

She began to shiver but ignored it. Maurizan opened all of her senses. The great beast's thrashing had subsided, which was some consolation. She'd been afraid it would burst through the wall and continue its pursuit of her. But the complete silence that accompanied the total darkness was unsettling in quite a different way.

Stay calm. You just need to decide a direction. Then you start swimming.

Going back the way she'd come was obviously not a choice. *Okay, stop fretting. Forget about monsters. Pay attention to what you're trying to do.*

She cleared her mind. What did she hear, smell, feel, see ... Well, she couldn't *see* anything.

She floated, waited. Then on one side of her face, she felt it. A current pushing against her, a fraction warmer. The water had to come in from someplace. Maybe it was a way out.

Maurizan swam in the direction of the current. Slowly. She wasn't eager to smash her face against a stone wall. When she did finally come to a wall, she felt the current on her feet. She groped her way down to an opening with rough edges, just big enough to squeeze through, scraping her hips only a little.

She kept swimming, the current getting slightly stronger and warmer as she went. She chose to take it as a hopeful sign. Warmer water had to mean it came from somewhere up and out, didn't it?

It seemed she'd been swimming for ages, and she reminded herself she was going slowly and carefully. If she rushed, she could make a mistake and hurt herself.

On the other hand, she couldn't hold on to the spirit forever. It had already been too long.

A sudden feeling of space.

Maurizan stretched her arms out to both sides, turned a complete circle. She explored, feeling her way around. She'd swum into some kind of large chamber. She circled it again, confirming the way she'd come in was the only way back out.

Damn it. Please no. I don't want to swim back and start over.

She opened her senses again, really more as an excuse to pause and think. She'd wanted the Prime from the time she could understand what it meant, just like her mother and grandmother. She'd been bitterly angry when she'd learned the wizard Weylan's dying act had been to give the Prime to Rina Veraiin. It was the selfish feeling of a child, but she couldn't help it. The Prime was meant to be *hers*, and the duchess had slipped in ahead of her and taken it.

Just like Rina had taken Alem.

And just when Maurizan was winning him back, she had to go drown herself in some long-lost fortress. Foolish girl. How many centuries until some explorer found her bones? If ever. *Yeah, morbid thoughts like this really aren't going to help—*

She heard something.

She looked up, but of course saw nothing but darkness. The sound was distant and muffled in that way sounds are underwater. She swam toward it. A few seconds later her hands touched hard stone above her. She felt along until the stone gave way to an opening, and she swam up through it.

The sound grew louder the farther up she went, a constant churning, chugging sound. It sounded familiar.

Water. It was fast-flowing water splashing above her.

She swam faster, kicking hard. No more moving slowly. No more caution. Enough.

It was time to get out of here. She could feel her hold on the spirit slipping.

She streaked upward through the water, the sound growing louder and louder and closer until—

Maurizan broke the surface.

She gasped and sucked in a lungful of air. It was pure reflex. The gill tattoo had let her breathe underwater without trouble. But there was something about a lungful of air. Something simple and basic.

She was alive. And would stay that way a little longer. She let herself feel relief.

She treaded water in the small pool, deciding what to do next. It was still pitch-black, but she heard a huge downpour of water falling into the pool a few feet from her, a constant mist spraying over her face and shoulders.

She felt around the wall until her hand fell into an opening. Some kind of ledge. She crawled onto it. She felt around some more and thought the opening kept going, maybe a room or a hallway.

Maurizan released her hold on the spirit.

And passed out.

CHAPTER
TWENTY

Alem staggered naked, knee deep in the surf, the sun beating down on him.

He hadn't wanted the bother of drying his clothes again, so he'd lashed a few pieces of driftwood together with vines, and pushed the makeshift raft ahead of him, floating his sword and clothes as he'd paddled the short distance to the island with the tower.

Once out of the water, it didn't take him long to dry under the relentless sun. He dressed and belted on his sword. He looked up the hill, wondering the best way to go about it. From the other island, the slope had looked steeper. Still, it would be a long, hot climb. He wished he could have figured some way to bring fresh water with him from the other island. Maybe he'd get lucky and stumble across a stream. The fruit he'd eaten had been sweet but hadn't really filled him up. *I'm missing all the food I ate in Klaar.* He wished he had something more substantial. A mutton shank or a pork chop. Potatoes.

What was that saying his old stable master, Nard, had been so fond of? *Wish in one hand and shit in the other. See which one fills up first.*

He was a long way from the castle stables in Klaar. A long way from home.

I thought I'd live and die within sight of that castle. Never thought I'd see the world. Not like this.

He left the beach, trudging into the tree line, and three minutes later he was already tromping up the hill. It really wasn't much of an island, a little hiccup in the ocean. It rapidly grew steeper as he climbed, thick tufts of coarse grass springing up sporadically between the rocks. Crooked trees grew at odd angles from the hillside.

He leaned forward as he climbed, trying to compensate for the slope. He tripped over a fallen tree trunk and hit the hill face-first. He lay there for a few minutes, thinking that this was not what he'd planned for his life.

Alem heaved himself up. He looked back. The beach lay below him. He was surprised how far he'd come. If he slipped, really seriously lost his footing, he'd tumble a long way. Probably break something.

Why was he here again? Oh yeah. The tower. If that's what he saw. It seemed stupid now to swim to another island and climb a hill just because he thought he saw stonework through a bunch of weeds and vines.

Like you've got anything else to do.

The slope abruptly went from steep to straight up. The hill had stopped being a hill and had become a wall. Alem pulled apart the creeper vines clinging to the surface. Slick green moss underneath. He rubbed it away.

And there it was. Large gray interlocking stones. The top of the hill wasn't some quirk of nature. It was definitely man-made. It took him almost an hour to circle the tower, precarious footing promising to send him ass over elbows back down the hill. He'd hoped vaguely for a door or window or some useful marking that might identify the structure. He got none of that.

He looked up, estimated the top was maybe thirty more feet. Alem closed his eyes and pictured what he'd seen from the other island. The tower had a flat top. Maybe a landing. No way to tell from where he was.

Alem tugged on some of the thicker vines. They held. He began climbing.

It was slow work, and often he had to switch to another vine or climb sideways for a while until he found the best way up. Sweat ran into his eyes and down his back. The need for water would soon outweigh everything else, but he tried to put that thought out of his mind.

At the top, he discovered the vines and weeds had obscured the crenellation design. He pulled the weeds out, removed the vines, and heaved himself between two battlements. He sprawled on his back and gulped air, arms and legs sore.

A few minutes later—or maybe it was an hour—he heaved himself to his feet and began to explore the top of the tower. It was carpeted with a mix of dead vines and live ones. He walked carefully. He wasn't sure, but it felt like solid stone under all the vines. When he reached the far side of the tower, the floor beneath his feet sagged and creaked. He stepped back abruptly.

With one foot he prodded the area. Three feet by three feet. He went to his hands and knees and clawed at the accumulation of vines. He wondered how often a really big storm blew through and cleared out the foliage. It was sweaty work, and his shirt was soaked through by the time he was finished.

He stood, hands on hips, looking down at what he'd found.

A wooden hatch. The same sort you might find at the top of any other tower. Much of the wood was rotten, and the hinges were completely rusted.

But it was a door. He could get inside.

And why in Dumo's name would you want to do that, thicko?

Because if he were just running away from something, he could have stopped in Kern, found a job, and had his safe little life. But he'd taken to the sea with Tosh and Maurizan and the others. Had gone all the way to Sherrik, all the way to the Red City. He'd come a long way to find something—admittedly he wasn't sure what exactly—but he wasn't about to back down now. They'd been close to the spot on Maurizan's map when he and the gypsy had gone overboard in the storm. Maybe this was the place they'd been looking for.

Really there was no choice at all.

He bent, grabbed the iron ring, and pulled. The rusty hinges moaned and creaked. Halfway open, the ring came loose from the rotted wood and the hinges crumbled to dust. The hatch and the remnants of the hinges fell and clanged and clinked down into the opening. It seemed to go on forever, bouncing and falling down the stone steps, the clamor echoing back up to him.

Alem stood, held his breath, waited.

If the racket had disturbed any ghosts below, they didn't swarm up to confront him. He looked over the edge and down into the dark opening. Stone stairs spiraling down and down and down.

Things he didn't have: A torch. A lantern.

Even if he could fashion a torch from some of the dried vines, how would he light it? He didn't have flint. He wouldn't get far if he couldn't see. He didn't like the idea of climbing back down the outside of the tower, but if he couldn't figure out how to—

Thicko. You have a light.

Alem drew the sword.

It glowed, not as bright as a lantern, but in complete darkness it would be more than enough.

He took a deep breath and began his descent, blade out in front of him to fend off the darkness.

CHAPTER TWENTY-ONE

In through the nose. Out through the mouth.

Empress Mee Hra'Lito sat cross-legged and focused on her breathing, eyes closed. She was afraid all the time. Afraid for the fleet she'd sent to Helva under Thorn's command. Afraid it wouldn't come back. Afraid what would happen while they were gone. The fate of the entire Perranese Empire hinged on her decisions, yet she'd never felt so helpless. The fear might paralyze her if she let it.

Meditation helped only a little.

In through the nose. Out through the mouth.

A knock at the door.

These were her personal apartments. Any knock on the door—disturbing her—meant trouble. She was not prepared to receive. She wore only a loose gown and slippers. No ceremonial makeup. Her hair was loose. It was all highly inappropriate.

Mee had the sick feeling the proprieties no longer mattered.

The knock again.

"Come in," said the empress.

The door swung open, and a man entered. It took her a moment to recall his name. Bel'Fre Logan. Third steward. At least two ranks below anyone who should be in the imperial apartments.

This was bad.

Bel'Fre Logan fell to his knees and bent forward, his forehead touching the floor. "Abject apologies for disturbing you, your imperial majesty."

Mee forced her voice to be calm, even icy. "Why are you here, Bel'Fre Logan? Where are the first and second stewards?"

"It is with great regret that I report their demise," said the third steward.

"Explain."

"The first and second stewards led a mutiny within the palace," Bel'Fre Logan said. "When it was put down, they were slain. Order has been restored."

Fear rose within her. She smashed it down. The empress offered the outward appearance of calm. "Please tell me what instigated the mutiny."

"The city is lost, your majesty," reported the third steward. "The city watch is gone, and the citizens have stormed the outer wall. Your personal guard has retreated to the palace and sealed themselves within. Some felt the situation desperate and . . . elected to effect a change in leadership."

Mee thought about that.

In through the nose. Out through the mouth.

"My compliments to those who remained loyal."

"Thank you," the third steward said.

"How long can we hold out?" she asked.

"The palace is sealed, and we have provisions for many weeks."

Provisions. It was a lack of provisions that had caused the riots in the city in the first place. A hungry population would be coming for those provisions. How long her personal guard could keep them out remained to be seen.

The city was lost. Perhaps the Empire too.

A slim thread of hope remained. That the fleet would conquer Helva and return victorious.

"Good work, Bel'Fre Logan," she said. "Please see to the palace's defenses and keep me informed."

◆　◆　◆

Bremmer had dreamed often since slaying Glex during the Great Reconstitution and bringing Mordis back from the realm of the gods. Nightmares vague but heavy with dread.

But this dream was so vivid and realistic that when Bremmer awoke, he thought he was still on the island. He saw through the eyes of some unknown pilgrim. A temple being torn asunder by some great conflict. One in spiked armor, circled in flame. The other looked like a woman, a bright glow about her. Powerful but losing the struggle.

Debris fell all around him, the temple shaking apart. Bremmer screamed, threw up his arms to protect his head from the falling rubble. He blinked, drew in a sharp breath.

He was in his own room, on the floor next to his bed, his nightshirt soaked with sweat, hair matted.

The door flew open, and a figure stood there holding a lantern, flooding the room with light. "Abbot Bremmer? We heard a scream."

"It's . . . it's okay." Bremmer staggered to his feet. "Get my robes, acolyte. Help me get dressed."

"At this hour?"

"Now," Bremmer snapped. "I must consult with Mordis."

The acolyte blanched and swallowed hard. "M-Mordis?"

"Stop wasting time, fool. Get me dressed."

Moments later, he had his robes and furs on. Even the short walk from the abbot's lodge to the great temple was too bitterly cold to go without the furs. The Mother Temple of Mordis was located high in the frozen wastes.

Probably some sort of test, building the temple here, Bremmer thought. Pilgrimages up to the mother temple wouldn't mean so much if the road were lined with cozy taverns and warm inns.

The acolytes with him paused at the temple door.

"Go back to the lodge," Bremmer said. "I'm going in alone."

Their relief was palpable. They bowed quickly, then scampered back along the path to the lodge, stepping and looking back to see if the abbot would actually enter.

Bremmer paused, took a deep breath, then went inside.

Even prepared for it, the presence of a god almost knocked him to his knees. The entire temple vibrated with raw power.

Mordis sat on the altar as if it were a throne. He hadn't moved from that spot since arriving via the Great Reconstitution. He sat with the blur of heat around him, skin glowing red, fire pulsing below the surface like lava. The heat coming off him made it hard to breathe. Bremmer felt like his lungs were being seared.

None of the other priests could endure Mordis's presence for more than a few seconds. Since Bremmer had been the one to initiate the Great Reconstitution, he thought it possible the ritual had created some bond with Mordis that let them communicate.

Not that Mordis had been very talkative. All Bremmer knew was that something big was coming, and Mordis was waiting.

But the dream was different. Some instinct told Bremmer to come to Mordis.

Bremmer bowed low. "Exalted One."

"I did not summon you." Mordis's voice was a rumble that filled the temple. It felt like a thousand horses stampeded past him, the vibration coming up through the soles of his feet and into his bones.

"Your pardon, Exalted One," Bremmer said. "But I've had a dream."

He realized how feeble it sounded as soon as it was out of his mouth. *A dream. So what?*

But Mordis didn't smash him flat like the insect he was. He simply said, "Tell me," and again the deep rumble.

So Bremmer told him. A temple on an island in a lake. Two gods locked in battle. The beautiful woman and the monstrosity in the spiked armor.

"Zereen—goddess of clouds, mists, and fogs—is dead," Mordis intoned.

Bremmer felt his heart twist with the news. He had no special feelings for Zereen, had never even met any of her worshippers.

But a goddess slain? That's unheard of. If the world is ending, is this how it starts?

"What do we do now?"

Bremmer hadn't really meant it as a question. He'd simply spoken his fear out loud. What do they do now? What *can* be done? If gods are killing each other, how can simple men like Bremmer possibly live through such times?

But Mordis chose to answer. "A great change is coming."

Mordis's voice was like a great weight placed on Bremmer's shoulders. He went to one knee, gritting his teeth, bones vibrating with each syllable. Surely the temple was about to shake apart.

"The battle for dominion has begun," Mordis boomed. "And it will come to our very doorstep."

Before Bremmer could even form a question, his mind filled with understanding. Mordis poured the knowledge of what was to come directly into Bremmer, as if he were an empty vessel waiting to be filled. Bremmer went blind, vision flaring white as he fell to the steps before the altar, writhed there as Mordis opened his consciousness to the cosmos.

Bremmer filled to bursting with knowledge no mortal should ever glimpse. This was the price to be the chosen of Mordis.

When he finally blinked his eyes clear, Bremmer was staggering down the steps in front of the temple. He had no recollection of how he'd gotten there. Had Mordis dismissed him, or had Bremmer fled?

His knees went watery, and he pitched forward down the stairs, landing face-first in the deep snow.

A moment later, he felt himself being lifted. The acolytes had decided to wait for him after all. They had him under each arm, dragging him back toward the lodge. Bless their stupid, dogged loyalty.

"Abbot Bremmer, are you okay?"

Bremmer tried to talk. His mouth felt swollen and numb. His whole face pulsed with his heartbeat. He still wasn't sure what had just happened to him. He was alive, and a part of him found that miraculous. What had Mordis done? Bremmer knew things he couldn't put into words.

"It's happening." Bremmer panted, felt dizzy. "It's all changing. He's coming. I tell you, he's coming!"

The acolytes exchanged puzzled looks. One asked, "Who's coming?"

"Akram!" Bremmer shouted. "The god of war!"

◆ ◆ ◆

"The god of *what*?" Brasley asked impatiently.

"The god of grass and clover, Baron Hammish."

Brasley frowned and massaged his temples. "Look, I have a blistering hangover, and if that's your idea of a joke, I'm not in the mood."

"A joke?" Olgen's face was blank with noncomprehension.

"Why in blazes would grass need a god? I thought you were going to tell me about this blasted mural." Brasley gestured at the artwork in front of him.

The mural took up the entire wall between Olgen's bedroom door and Brasley's. It was exquisite and detailed work, and after passing it a number of times, Brasley finally decided to pause and have a look. It was a scene in a garden, a lot of gods and goddesses—a *lot* of them—all standing in admiration of a single goddess elevated on a glowing throne. When Olgen saw Brasley admiring the illustration, he volunteered to hold forth, at length, on the historical significance of the depiction.

Brasley admitted he didn't realize there were so many gods and goddesses. The mural was practically overflowing with them. Olgen pointed out that not all gods and goddesses were popular enough to have temples and worshippers but did agree there did seem to be an absurd number of them. It was then that Olgen had begun to list a number of the lesser deities, including Elizir, the god of grass and clover.

"I mean, yes, he's literally the god of grass," Olgen explained. "But it's more than that. It's what grass represents. That's how it is with all the gods."

"And what, pray tell, is grass supposed to represent?" Brasley asked.

Olgen shrugged. "Well, I don't quite know really. Not my field."

"Grass is not your field?" Brasley scolded. "Is that another bad joke?"

"I just mean, I only know the basics from a historical context," Olgen said. "I'm no theologian. Grass might mean a carefree stroll on the lawn on a spring morning. I don't know. But I'm told all of the gods and goddesses represent something literal but also something more abstract."

Brasley scoffed. "How do you know these are even gods and goddesses at all? Could just be a random bunch of poncy overdressed bastards flitting about a garden."

"Well, Dumo's throne is clearly rising on a wave of heavenly light."

"Okay, that's a fair point."

"Also, this is one of the most famous scenes in religious history," Olgen said.

Brasley shuffled his feet and cleared his throat. "Of course it is. It's obviously the . . . the scene of . . . It's on the tip of my tongue."

"The crowning of Dumo," Olgen said.

"The crowning of Dumo," Brasley repeated quickly. "I was just about to say that."

"It's fanciful, of course," Olgen said. "We have no way to know if the gods actually *crowned* Dumo per se. How they work out their hierarchy among themselves is a mystery and has been debated by scholars for years."

"And also, why would they crown a goddess who's already in charge, eh?"

Olgen looked confused. "Baron Hammish?"

"Dumo has always been supreme," Brasley said. "Sort of redundant to crown her."

Olgen looked slightly embarrassed. "That's not *quite* true, milord."

Brasley blinked. "It's not?"

"Each epoch marks the ascendance of a new god or goddess as supreme," Olgen explained. "But Dumo has been dominant for so many centuries, it certainly can seem to the layperson as if she's always been that way."

"That's what I meant," Brasley said. "That such a painting might be confusing to the layperson. Who do you suppose was supreme before Dumo?"

Olgen looked genuinely perplexed. "You know . . . I don't know actually."

"Perhaps the god of grass."

"Probably not," Olgen said.

No, probably not.

Brasley leaned forward, squinted at the mural. There certainly were a lot of them. He supposed if they had a god for grass, then they could have a god or goddess for any old thing, and that would explain why there was such a mob of them. The turtle god? The goddess of dusty cupboards? The god of missing socks? There might be no end to them.

"At least they all look like they're having a good time," Brasley said.

"Of course, milord," Olgen said. "It is a celebration of Dumo's ascension."

"All except for that guy?"

One of Olgen's eyebrows shot up. "Milord?"

"That one all the way on the far end," Brasley said. "There's always one. Every party has that one fellow whose job it is to sour everything. Probably because he can't get a girl."

Now Olgen leaned forward, scanning the mural. "Milord, I don't . . . I'm not sure I see . . ."

"Right there." Brasley pointed to the extreme right of the mural. "Skulking in the shadows. Probably the god of being an asshole or something."

Brasley stepped closer. Pointed directly at a figure standing under the low-hanging branches of a gnarled tree. The artist, Brasley suddenly realized, had been far more skilled than Brasley had originally thought. A quick glance at that section of the mural, and one saw only a shadowed area. A closer examination revealed the vague shape of some looming figure. The more Brasley stared at it, the more it came into focus, a hulking man in spiked armor, red eyes glowing from the depths of a great helm.

Brasley saw Olgen's eyes widen and knew the young man had at last seen the god he was talking about. "Oh my."

"Indeed. A party pooper if I've ever seen one."

Talbun approached from behind, looking over their shoulders at the mural. "Is this where you two have been? Gawking at the artwork?"

Olgen pointed at the intimidating figure in spiked armor. "I believe I know who that is. The god of war. Akram. He's often depicted in such armor."

Talbun gasped so sharply that the other two spun to look at her.

"I know him," she said.

Confusion crossed Brasley's face. "You *know* him?"

"At the Temple of Kashar," Talbun said. "He massacred all of my men. And slaughtered the monks there." She swallowed hard. "And killed the great serpent god, Kashar."

Brasley shuffled nervously. "Well, see there. I told you. The quintessential party pooper."

CHAPTER
TWENTY-TWO

Like all young, brash, overconfident military officers, Kasmis Urlik would not have believed it if someone would have told him he was about to die.

He would have been doubly incredulous to hear that his death was the direct result of the poor decision he was about to make. He was a lieutenant in Sherrik's First Lancers Cavalry and by definition invincible.

Such was his limited experience.

When Urlik saw the squad of Perranese soldiers, he raised his cavalry saber and prepared to sound the charge.

A world-weary sergeant spoke up immediately. "Sir, we were told to observe, not engage. Do you think it wise to—"

"It's five men, Sergeant," Urlik said, voice dripping with contempt. "I think thirty mounted lancers can handle it. I also think it would be rather nice to have a prisoner to question, but we'll miss our chance if we let them vanish into the trees. Now come on!"

The sergeant's next objection was cut off as Urlik lifted his saber and shouted, "Charge!"

The thirty lancers thundered toward the fleeing Perannese, horses' hooves digging up turf as they left the road and headed for the tree line. The Perranese made the trees just ahead of the lancers, but they'd completely lost their head start.

We have you now, Urlik thought. *My very first action, and I'll be bringing back prisoners.* He imagined with pleasure what the decoration would look like on his dress uniform.

Once the lancers were within the tree line, the arrows rained down, at least a hundred of them. Men screamed and fell from their saddles. Horses reared. Urlik looked up, saw the higher limbs of the trees swarming with Perranese, all loosing arrow after arrow.

An ambush. The bastards!

He turned his horse and spurred it back toward the road. "Withdraw!"

White-hot pain exploded in his shoulder. The world blurred past his face, and something slammed him hard, knocking the wind out of him. The ground. He'd fallen from his horse and hit the ground. He rolled onto his side. An arrow must have hit in the small gap where his breastplate and back plate buckled together. One of these Perranese sons of bitches was either a very good shot or awfully lucky. He tried to reach the arrow sticking out of his shoulder but couldn't.

Well, this was bloody embarrassing. Urlik had gone from capturing a prisoner and earning a medal to getting shot out of the saddle and sprawling helplessly on the ground.

He saw a bunch of boots, craned his neck, and looked up at four dour-looking Perranese warriors. One had an eye patch and jabbered in his heathen language to the others.

Urlik managed to summon some bravado. "Looks like you win this one, chaps. Well done. I suppose you'll want to take me prisoner now."

One of the warriors leaned over casually and stabbed Urlik through the eye.

CHAPTER TWENTY-THREE

Having a tattoo inked on a shoulder or an arm or an ankle was one thing. Having one inked on her throat offered an entirely new form of discomfort. The pinprick sting of the needle was familiar enough, but keeping her head back so long so Maxus could apply the tattoo had put a stiff crick in her neck.

And having the needle work the ink into her flesh directly over her larynx was no picnic either.

If Rina moved or spoke, it might disrupt and ruin the process.

But *inside* she complained loudly.

Hurry up, you stupid old wizard!

An eternity later, Maxus stepped back from her, eyes wide with wonder. "It's finished . . . I think."

"You think?" Rina's hand shot to her throat, but all she felt was smooth skin. "What is it? What's wrong?"

"I don't think anything is wrong," Maxus said. "It's just not what I expected."

Rina stood, feeling her throat with both hands now. "Damn it, tell me what you're talking about."

"Wait. Hold on." Maxus turned away, rummaged through a chest of random items, then turned back, handing her a mirror the size of a saucer. "Look for yourself."

Rina examined the bird in the reflection. Small, but intricately detailed. It looked like a colorful songbird, wings spread, head up, tiny beak open as if singing. Its wings were a deep blue with pink underneath. Its belly yellow. Somehow the colors all worked together and— no. She'd been mistaken. The wings were a bright green, and the pink underneath was more orange. No red. No . . .

The colors! They keep changing.

Before her eyes one color melted into another, constantly swirling and changing.

Dumo help me. If the eye tattoos draw stares, then what will this *do?*

She looked up from the mirror and realized Maxus was looking at her expectantly.

"It's beautiful work," Rina said. "But I think I'll be wearing high collars from now on."

The wizard cleared his throat. "But what does it *do?*"

Rina had momentarily forgotten that the tattoo was supposed to do something besides just look garish. She tapped into the spirit. The songbird hummed like a new warmth at her throat. The Prime recognized it, fed power to it. It was ready and waiting to do whatever it had been made to do.

She felt it pulsing on her throat but had no idea how to command it. It taunted her, and she couldn't do a thing with it.

"Well?" Maxus prompted.

"I don't know how to work it."

"What do you mean?"

"I mean I don't know what it does, and I can't make it do what it's supposed to do if I don't know what it does."

Maxus made a short noise in his throat halfway between fatigue and frustration. "Don't you have some instinct or something?"

"Look, I'll keep trying. I don't know, okay?"

The wizard's eyes narrowed. "With respect, your grace. You wouldn't be keeping certain information to yourself, would you?"

Rina had forgotten how mistrustful wizards could be. They were especially stingy about sharing magical secrets.

"I'm not holding anything back, master wizard," she said. "I'm not keen on this mystery any more than you are."

Maxus had at least enough manners to look chagrined. "I beg pardon, your grace. I'd been so anxious to at last determine the function of the tattoo. Forgive my impatience."

"Look, it does . . . something." Like a lost word just on the tip of her tongue, she felt she could almost tell what the tattoo was for. It *wanted* to be used. The magic was right there for her, waiting to be triggered. "I'll figure it out, and I'll tell you as soon as I do."

"Thank you, your grace. I've waited this long. I can wait a little longer."

Rina hoped they had time to wait. It would be nice to find out if the tattoo did anything helpful before the Perranese began climbing over the city walls.

CHAPTER TWENTY-FOUR

She'd been awake for a while but simply hadn't wanted to move. Grit under one cheek as she lay flat against the ground. Wet mist from the falling water on the other cheek. She was cold but not enough to shiver.

Of course, it was still pitch-dark.

Maurizan sat up, took hold of the little orb still hanging between her breasts, and gave it a hard shake. The little fish flashed dim light for a second, then faded dark again. They were all used up or needed rest or something. She had no idea.

She turned away from the water falling into the pool and felt her way deeper into the opening. It must have been a tunnel or hallway or something. She kept going, slowly, hands up in front of her to keep from walking face-first into a wall.

The farther Maurizan moved from the pool and the waterfall, the cleaner the floor felt beneath her bare feet. She suspected the level of the pool might rise or fall depending on the tides or rainfall or maybe the season. When the level rose, it carried grit and sediment farther down the hallway, but not this far.

Her hands bumped against something cold and smooth. She ran her hands all over the surface. Hinges, a ring. It was an iron door. She pulled on the ring, and the door swung open toward her, surprisingly smooth, the hinges not even creaking.

The air on the other side seemed stuffier, but drier. She hesitated only a moment, then stepped inside.

Lights flickered around her so brightly and abruptly that she thought she might be having some kind of fit. She stumbled back over her own feet, drawing both daggers, and ended up on the floor. She scrambled back up into a fighting crouch, daggers out in front of her, panicked and panting, heart flailing against her chest.

She started to tap into the spirit and stopped herself. There didn't seem to be any immediate danger, and she desperately needed to let her well of spirit replenish itself.

The room was not like anything she'd ever seen before. The floor was so black and so glossy, she didn't know if it was glass or highly polished stone or what. It didn't even look like a material she'd ever laid eyes on. The walls were like highly polished silver, and the room's furnishings seemed to grow right out of the floors and the walls.

But none of that was as startling as the lights. They were perfectly shaped glass spheres hanging down from the ceiling on thin metal poles. There was no flicker of flame. They were nothing like candles or torches. They simply glowed all on their own.

It has to be some spell. They come to life when somebody walks in the room and needs light.

She lowered the daggers and proceeded slowly into the room. Her bare feet felt cold on the perfectly smooth floor. Nothing in here was dusty or dirty. Along the far wall was a line of glass boxes, a half dozen of them, five feet from the ground and almost as wide.

Maurizan approach slowly, and as she drew closer she saw that some of the glass had been broken. She stood at the foot of the first box and looked inside.

A skeleton lay in the box as if it were a glass coffin, arms folded in a pose of final rest. Whoever it had been had once worn fine velvet robes of deep blue, but the color had faded and the fabric fallen to tatters. Additionally the robes looked disheveled, as if the corpse had been searched and not gently. Broken glass littered the floor between that glass box and the next, where she found a similar scene. This time the corpse wore robes of a rich burgundy, tattered as before and also showing signs of ransack.

The corpse in the third glass box had been vandalized to the point that bones were scattered every which way, arms and legs pulled apart and stacked to the side. The dead man's robes had been completely shredded.

Between the next two boxes, she found something new.

A skeleton. Not a corpse from one of the glass boxes, but somebody else. Still some dried meat on the bones. Not much. She wondered if there were rats down here to take care of such things, but looking around, she supposed not. The place seemed far too clean, almost as if it were immune to the dirt and grime of the outside world.

Maurizan noticed the skeleton on the floor wore no clothing, not even tatters, but there was a cracked leather belt around its waist with a rusty short sword. She looked down at herself. Completely nude except for the belt and the daggers.

Uh-oh.

She bent, looked closer, and saw the corpse's skeletal hands clutched a leather satchel. She leaned in, took hold of the satchel's leather strap between thumb and forefinger, taking special care not to touch any part of the corpse. Maurizan had stabbed grown men with her daggers while looking them in the eyes as the life left their faces, but suddenly the idea of touching any part of the skeleton appalled her. In fact, the eerie cleanliness of this chamber creeped her out much more than did the rest of the ruined fortress.

At least she wasn't being chased by a giant sea creature anymore.

She had to tug hard to pull the satchel free from the skeleton's grip. There was a short series of dull snaps as the skeleton's fingers broke off and clattered across the floor. She pulled the satchel clear of the corpse, fussed with its rusty buckle, then slowly opened it, hoping the contents wouldn't be something terrible and deadly.

The satchel contained two items.

The first was a scroll case. She'd seen simple wooden ones many times, carrying messages for her mother, but this was something different. It was about eight inches long and carved from something that might have been ivory. All she knew with certainty was that it looked fancy and expensive.

The carving displayed a stormy sea, large waves coming down hard on a small fishing boat. The design of the boat didn't look like anything she'd ever seen in Helva. Everything about the scroll case was foreign and exotic, even the aquatic wave designs on the silver end caps. She grabbed one of the end caps, made ready to twist it off.

She froze.

What are the odds I can read whatever I find in there? If it's something magical, I might set it off.

It was a job for a wizard. Not her. She put the scroll case back in the satchel.

The other item was a small square of brass with pieces cut out of it. She had to look hard to figure out the picture it made, a stylized cloud with an angry face on it, lips pursed and lines coming from the lips, as if the cloud were blowing out a candle.

Realization hit her like a bolt from the sky.

It's a stencil! These things are for ink magic!

Fear, fatigue, every worry vanished with the excitement of what she'd found. She broke out in goose bumps, her body tingling. She'd come for the Prime and had also been given the gill and swimming tattoos. The ruined fortress of the ancient wizards just kept on giving.

She giggled wildly as she placed the stencil back in the satchel and then swung the strap over her shoulder.

The next box was the same, glass broken, corpse ransacked.

Maurizan shifted to the final glass box and gasped.

It wasn't broken, and the man inside was intact.

Not *alive*, but not vandalized either.

He hadn't been that old, perhaps in his middle fifties. Or maybe wizards had ways to stay younger, longer, Maurizan mused. His hair was white, but his beard was black with only thin streaks of white. Maurizan thought he looked rather wise, fine features and clear complexion, although his skin had gone a waxy gray and had shrunken against his cheeks and hands. Whereas the other skeletons had clearly been collecting dust for centuries, this dead body merely looked a few months old. What peculiar brand of magic had slowed its decay, Maurizan couldn't guess, nor did she care because it was the objects the dead man held that drew her full attention.

In his clawlike grip, he clutched another scroll case. Unlike the other, this scroll case was jet black, some smooth glossy substance that seemed to drink the light. The end caps were gold without engraving or marking of any kind. In his other hand he held the stencil.

Another tattoo. Right there. Dumo. I can't believe it.

She went over every inch of the glass box looking for a way to open it but already knew she wouldn't find anything. There was a reason the glass had been smashed out of the other boxes—the scavengers or tomb raiders or whatever they were called hadn't been gentle about their looting.

Maurizan turned one of the daggers around in her hand, holding it by the blade. She lifted it over her head, prepared to bring the hilt down hard on the glass.

Wait. What if I actually took a second here and used my brain?

She lowered the dagger. Something bothered her about the skeleton she'd found on the floor, the dead scavenger from whom she'd taken the satchel. She presumed he would have gone on to loot the final box if not for . . .

What? He couldn't have just spontaneously dropped dead.

Could he?

She went back to examine the skeleton, still loath to touch any of the grimy bones. She squatted next to it, letting her eyes roam up and down, trying to get a clue of what might have happened.

Three of its ribs on the left side were broken and caved in.

Maurizan's hand went to her own ribs. She'd thought the beast's tentacle had cracked one when the thing had given her a hard squeeze, but suspected now it was only a bruise. Still, it ached something fierce, and if the monster had squeezed her a little longer and a little harder, it could have crushed her ribs, no problem.

So once upon a time an explorer came looking for ink magic. A hideous sea creature mortally wounded him, but he escaped and made it this far before giving up the ghost.

She shivered thinking about ghosts.

Okay, let's just say he died. I've got enough problems without adding restless spirits to the mix.

Satisfied she'd deduced the cause of the scavenger's demise, she went to the final box and smashed the glass with her dagger hilt.

She spun the blade the right way round in her palm again, going into a fighter's crouch, daggers up for action.

No ghosts sprang forth to carry her away to the netherworld.

And if they had, then what? You can't stab a ghost.

She reached into the box, careful to avoid the jagged glass, and plucked the scroll from the dead wizard's grip.

The second she did, there was a soft hiss of air, and the wizard's skin dried to dust, falling away from his bones. His eyes caved in to his sockets, hair falling out.

Maurizan jerked her hand back in surprise and disgust.

The magical lights above shifted to a deep red, and she felt a rumbling in the floor through her feet.

Oh . . . shit.

The room washed suddenly in red light was even more disturbing, and Maurizan glanced back over her shoulder at the door she'd come through, thinking it was time for a hasty departure.

The stencil!

Without it the scroll might be useless. She reached in again and snatched it quickly, putting both it and the scroll case into the satchel.

The rumbling increased, and at the far end of the room, the wall split in half, opening outward. From the darkness beyond she heard them before she saw them—a clunking, plodding, metallic sound accompanied by odd sporadic hissing bursts.

And then a fraction of a second later, she saw them.

Three enormous men in full plate armor came stomping through the new door in the wall, armor gleaming strangely in the red light, face guards down on their great helms, so tall their heads almost scraped the top of the doorway as they marched through.

Except . . . they weren't men.

Maurizan tapped into the spirit.

And everything slowed down.

With the calm of the spirit came the cool logical workings of the mind; she took in every detail of the situation in an instant.

The lumbering suits of armor were shaped like men, but they were something else. Where the arms and legs joined the torso, she saw gears and pulleys through the gaps in the plate. Nozzles in the knees and elbows randomly spurted long gouts of steam like hissing teakettles. In one gauntleted hand, each gripped a long sword with a straight blade. The other arm grew into a spiked mace.

The things were quite obviously constructed for a single purpose. To kill people.

To slay intruders like Maurizan.

A portcullis slammed down, blocking the door she'd come through. The walls behind the armored men were slowly swinging closed again.

Maurizan calculated she had about thirty seconds before she was trapped in the room with the killing machines.

She sheathed one of the daggers and bolted toward the clattering armored warriors. That she was tapped into the spirit was the only thing that gave her a chance. She had perfect vision of the melee as it unfolded in slow motion before her. She saw the way they stood, postures, how they lifted their weapons. Every little move telegraphed what the armored men would do next.

In two seconds, Maurizan had charted her path past the knights.

She ran straight for the first knight and dropped a split second before a horizontal slash would have taken her head off. By the time the knight recovered and hacked at her with the back swing, she'd already tucked and tumbled away.

A glance was all she needed to know what she was going to do next. She saw some kind of tube that ran down the interior of the armored leg in the back, looping out at the ankle before plugging back into the heel. At the same time, she leapt to the side as the second knight brought his mace arm down hard, cracking the floor where she'd been a moment before.

The third knight was going to be the tough one. He'd already seen Maurizan's moves and positioned himself to compensate.

In another few seconds, the wall behind her would close enough to cut off her escape.

The knight must have sensed what she was trying to do. Instead of attacking, he stopped, went into a crouch, legs wide, weapons spread to either side.

Maurizan threw one of the daggers. It tumbled end over end toward the knight. With its weapons spread, the knight was vulnerable. It brought its arms up to block the dagger but too late.

The dagger's tip flew straight into one of the helm's eyeholes. There was the harsh grinding sound of jammed machinery, and the knight took a halting half step to the left as if trying to right itself. Even as steam shot from the knight's helm, it resumed its defensive stance, legs spread.

Which was what Maurizan had been counting on.

She was already diving through the knight's legs as it brought the mace down hard, nearly shattering her ankle but slamming a crater into the floor instead, dust and shards of stone flying up. As she passed, she drew the other dagger and cut the tube at the metal man's ankle. More steam hissed, the tube flailing loose behind the knight's foot.

Maurizan rolled through the doors just as they were closing. Soon it would be a wall again, but she'd be on the other side.

At the last second, an armored arm shot through the door and grabbed her by the ankle.

She tried to yank free, but its grip was too tight. If it squeezed any more, it threatened to crush bone. Slashing at the metal fingers with her dagger accomplished nothing.

The walls closed on the knight's arm, and for a moment, Maurizan thought that was it, but then there was a deep grinding down from deep within the floor, and the walls started to move again, slowly crushing the arm, the metal bending with a groan. A sudden pop, and steam shot from the creases at the wrist and elbow.

As the steam subsided, the metal fingers around Maurizan's ankle slowly released her. She crawled away, pulling her legs up underneath her, trying to get as far away from the arm as possible.

The steam was spent, and the arm went limp. The walls closed, pinching the metal arm in half and clunking shut, plunging Maurizan again into complete darkness.

CHAPTER
TWENTY-FIVE

Maurizan released her hold on the spirit. Pain and exhaustion flooded her, but not enough to make her pass out this time. She sat back, leaning against the cold stone, panting and trying to force her racing heart to calm.

She gave herself a few minutes to rest, then forced herself to her feet and felt around the interior of this new space. It was a small room, just big enough to contain the three armored non-men. She felt nothing that might be an exit.

Maurizan burst into tears.

She hated herself for it, but just fuck it. She indulged herself, letting the tears flow, great wracking sobs shaking her body.

Okay, you're frustrated and tired and just fuck this place already, but stop it. You're done now.

She swallowed her next sob, mastered herself, and wiped her eyes with the heels of her hands. A few deep breaths.

Okay, what haven't you thought of yet? She went to her hands and knees and methodically felt every square inch of the floor. Nothing but smooth stone.

When she stood again, she felt something bump against her chest. It was the glass orb swinging from its leather strap. She took hold of it and gave it a hard shake.

Light flared, the little fish circling frantically, and her hope soared, but a second later the light dimmed again. Apparently they hadn't had enough rest.

But in the brief burst of light, she glimpsed something on the wall to her left.

She went to the wall, feeling around frantically. There! An iron bar stuck into the wall, about a foot wide. Two feet above it, another one. She'd missed the ladder rungs when she'd felt around the walls the first time, her hands groping right past them.

I knew it! There had to be some way in and out to service those metal monstrosities.

She climbed carefully, giddy and giggling. She fully realized how tired and light-headed she was, and that made her laugh even harder.

Then she bumped her head, making a deep, hollow *klung* sound.

Ouch.

She felt above her. An iron wheel attached to a hatch. She turned the wheel and pushed the hatch open, climbed through to the next level. When she was through, she let the hatch fall closed again with a harsh clang.

More groping. She found stairs going both up and down and started upward without hesitation. She climbed.

And climbed.

At last she reached some sort of landing. She bent over, her hands on knees, panting, rib sore and ankle flaring pain. She was matted with sweat. The air here was so hot and stuffy, it made her miss the cool, watery depths below.

Well, no. Not really.

She eased her way across the floor. Hands up in front of her. Stepping softly.

And hit another set of stairs going up.

Fuck you!

She slumped to the floor at the foot of the stairs and groaned, leaned back against the wall. At the moment, it was difficult to think of anything more appalling than climbing more stairs. Every muscle in her body screamed.

Just rest. Just a minute. Close your eyes and just count to thirty before getting up again.

She dozed. It was difficult to tell dream from reality, slumber from wakefulness, opening her eyes to darkness or closing them again to see some scene from her imagination. She was with Alem again, walking hand in hand through the Red City's waterfront bazaar, immersed in the sights and sounds. Such a brief time together.

I'll never see him again.

She opened her eyes, saw a light floating down from above. No. Obviously she was still dreaming. It was the moon low against the horizon. She lay on the deck of Miko's little scow as it bobbed in the swell, Alem beside her, both of them bathed in moonlight, letting the ocean breezes cool them.

The glowing moon twisted into the wrong shape and floated slowly down, swaying back and forth like a leaf falling. She blinked, and Alem was holding the light. In the dim glow he looked like one of the ghosts she'd been so worried about. If only he were real. If only he were here now.

She blinked again and he was kneeling in front of her.

"Maurizan!"

What?

"Maurizan, are you okay?"

How much has happened since I've been away?

"Maurizan, it's me. Alem. Are you okay? Talk to me."

No. This was impossible. She was dreaming him.

He held a glowing sword.

Okay, I am definitely *dreaming him.*

But when she reached for his face with trembling hands, he was solid. Flesh. She started crying again but this time didn't try to stop herself. She pulled his face in close and mashed her lips hard against his, arms going around him, crying and kissing, tasting him and tasting the salt of her own tears.

And then he was lifting her, taking her back up the stairs, and she buried her face into his chest, tears flowing, and it felt like she was being whisked away on a cloud.

◆ ◆ ◆

She emerged from the hatch at the top of the tower, and the sunlight hit her face. That's when Maurizan truly believed it. She wasn't going to die. She breathed in the air, balmy with ocean currents.

She wore Alem's shirt, heavy with his sweat. It didn't matter. Nothing could make a dent in her joy and relief. The shirt hung just low enough on her for decency.

More or less.

When Alem had seen the tattoos on her, his eyes had shot wide. Of course, he'd seen the Prime before. On Rina. He'd started to overflow with questions, but Maurizan had stopped him. She'd promised to tell the whole story later, but at that moment all she'd wanted was *out*.

Alem had an arm around her waist to help her stand. In no way did she need help standing. In no way was she going to suggest he remove his arm. She clung to him, leaning in, her head on his shoulder. She had resigned herself to death. Now she wanted to live more than anything in the world.

Mother always said never give up, because fate can turn things around on you in the blink of an eye.

Alem pointed across the narrow channel of water to the next island. "The cave where I found the body and the sword is halfway down the hill. There's a stream with fresh water. Fruit trees too."

"Good." As soon as Maurizan heard the word *water*, she felt a fierce thirst. All she could think was how much she wanted to get to Alem's little island, to eat and drink.

A flash of white caught her attention on the blue water. She pointed out to sea. "What's that?"

"The ocean."

She laughed, pointed more earnestly. "No. *That.*"

Alem shaded his eyes against the sun, squinted in the direction she was pointing. At first it wasn't easy to spot the little scow among the whitecaps, but once he saw it he couldn't believe he'd ever missed it. The little sailboat was incredibly close, sails full and heading more or less straight for them. "It's them! I can see Miko at the tiller. That's Tosh up at the bow. It's them! It's them!"

Alem jumped up and down, screaming and waving his arms. "Hey! Over here!"

Maurizan was already throwing one leg over the battlements to climb down. "Come on!"

Alem rushed to her. "Wait, are you okay to—"

"Try to stop me."

By the time they were at the bottom, they saw the boat plowing through the surf toward them. They were close enough now to see Tosh's big grin. He waved frantically at them.

Alem and Maurizan ran through the trees toward the beach, whooping joy and giggling.

Her arms and legs ached. The bruised rib flared pain every time her feet hit the ground, as did her ankle, but she didn't care. She ran ahead of Alem, laughing and carefree.

Maurizan burst from the tree line, bare feet sinking into the hot sand of the beach. The water looked cool and inviting. She felt so happy to see the shabby little scow, she thought she might dive in and swim all the way out to—

Sudden movement in her peripheral vision caught her attention. She started to turn her head—

Pain exploded across her face.

The world spun. She tried to keep her feet but stumbled. Trying to make her legs work was like stepping in deep holes, and a second later she was on her hands and knees, spitting blood into the sand. She ran her tongue along her teeth. Two on the left side were loose. Through the ringing in her ears she heard Alem yelling her name and running fast toward her.

She looked up. Kristos stood there, naked, glistening, and wet. He'd obviously just come out of the water. He held a spear with a long, thin head. Maurizan had obviously taken the blunt end of it in the face.

Alem stood next to her now, sword up. "Get away from her!"

If Kristos tapped into the Prime—and certainly he would—Alem wouldn't have a chance. She tried to warn him back, but she'd bitten her tongue. She spit more blood. Her whole face throbbed.

Kristos stood casually, leaning on the spear, taking almost no notice of Alem. He smiled down at Maurizan. "You got past the guardian, I see. I had a good feeling about you."

She worked her jaw, the pain in her mouth subsiding just enough to talk. "How many have you sent down there?" The words came out thick. Her tongue was swollen, and she had a fat lip.

"A half dozen or so over the years," Kristos said. "I knew there was more ink magic in the fortress, and after the creature nearly killed me, I wasn't about to chance it again. But I knew from talking with the Moogari where the treasures were likely hidden. You found the hall of the inventors, yes? According to the Moogari, each was preserved with his or her greatest tattoo. The great wizards invented hundreds of them during the Mage Wars. I send others to do my searching for me. They come from everywhere, explorers and adventurers lured by the legends of the ancient wizards. Most don't make it as far as these islands. They go the wrong direction or get caught in a storm; ships sink. But I find a castaway now and then. You're the first one to succeed. And now that you've cleverly found another way in and out, I can explore at my leisure without risking the guardian."

"By all means." Maurizan gestured up the hill. "Explore to your heart's content."

A wide grin. "I will." Then the grin fell, and he reached out a hand. "But first, I'll take that satchel. Simply hand it over, and you and this lad can join your friends in the boat. You're lucky, you know. Few people who fall overboard in these waters are fortunate enough to find themselves afloat again."

"She's not giving you a damn thing," Alem said, wagging the sword at him for emphasis. "Swim away."

"You're a second from death, boy." Kristos squinted at the sword. "That's an interesting toy. Do you know how to use it?"

"I hold the handle," Alem said. "Pointy end toward you."

Kristos laughed and turned back to Maurizan. "Truly, your bodyguard is an opponent to be reckoned with. If you don't want him to die, hand over the satchel."

There wasn't a doubt in Maurizan's mind that Kristos meant it. She had to give him the satchel. Dumo bless Alem for good intentions, but he didn't have a chance against an ink mage. She had to hand over the satchel right now.

But she didn't.

The items in this satchel are mine. I earned them. My tattoos. I risked my life for them. They're mine.

Then Maurizan heard her mother's voice, warning her. She'd had the Prime less than forty-eight hours and already she wanted *more*.

Hadn't she been cautioned against this very occurrence? The power just made one want more power. It was never enough.

I don't care!

She tapped into the spirit.

For a long moment, the three of them waited, frozen, taut as a bowstring.

Alem gripped his sword hilt tighter, and the slight movement was enough to set them off.

Kristos brought the spear down for a strike, lightning quick and yet still too slow. Maurizan rolled out of the way, drawing her daggers, the spearhead striking the sand.

Kristos might have been able to follow up with a deathblow to her back, but Alem moved in with a clumsy sword swing. The Fish Man parried it with a backhand swing of the spear, then spun it in his hands, bringing the butt end down atop Alem's head. Alem's eyes rolled up, knees buckling, and he went down.

The Fish Man turned to see Maurizan's daggers coming at him. He sidestepped the lunge of the first dagger and deflected the next with the spear.

Maurizan pressed the attack. She hadn't rested enough since the last time she'd tapped into the spirit. She didn't know how long she could keep this up. The only hope for victory lay in ending this *fast.*

She swiped, jabbed, and lunged with the daggers, all the while remembering what her mother had told her. *The Prime doesn't give you anything extra, but it does give you complete access to everything you already have.*

Since she was a toddler and old enough to hold the daggers, Maurizan had been taught her people's way of fighting. Quick and lithe, a blade in each hand. A style as much dancing as fighting—duck, dodge, strike, withdraw. Tapped into the spirit, she remembered every lesson. Every move. Perfect technique. Maurizan was the master of a fighting style her people had passed down from generation to generation.

And she struck with all her strength.

Her dagger drew a red line down Kristos's left leg, a shallow gash, but blood sprayed.

He came back at her with a flurry of strikes with the spear, blade end and butt end falling alternately. Maurizan crossed her daggers and fended off each blow. The Fish Man had more experience with the Prime, but she'd had more training fighting.

They traded blows and blocks until he slipped in with the blunt end of the spear and took the air out of her with a blow to the gut. She bent, backed up out of reach of the spearhead, sucking for breath.

Seeing his chance, he moved in for the kill.

Something streaked down through the air and landed on top of Kristos's foot with a meaty *thuk*.

A crossbow bolt. Blood pooled around the entrance wound, dripped down both sides of his foot. Kristos registered no pain on his face. He didn't scream with the shock of it, but his attack pulled up short. He leaned to one side, hopping on the good foot.

A split-second glance told Maurizan what was happening.

Kalli, Lureen, and Viriam rushed forward, knee deep in the surf, heading for Maurizan's spot on the beach. They each held one of the long Perranese swords in a two-handed grip. There'd been no time for armor, and they charged in bare feet, breeches rolled up above the knees, loose shirts knotted under breasts, hair pulled back and tied with leather laces. Their faces were stone, eyes intense.

Close behind them, Tosh tried to fumble another bolt into his crossbow.

Maurizan wanted to shout a warning but was still trying to catch her breath.

Kristos's next move was a blur. He pivoted on his good leg, swinging the spear, arms fully extended to achieve the greatest reach. The spear tip sliced a line straight across Lureen's throat. She dropped her sword, tipping backward in the water, eyes big as she grabbed her throat, blood flowing through her fingers. She went down with a splash, bobbed in the surf.

Kristos brought the spear back fast and stabbed Viriam in the leg. She screamed and hobbled back out of range. The spear spun in the Fish Man's hands, and he blocked a thrust from Kalli.

Maurizan was already up and leaping at Kristos. She tossed a dagger as she flew at him.

He blocked it easily, but that left him open, and Maurizan barreled into him, knocking him on his back in the sand with her on top. He shoved the spear shaft under her throat to push her away, but Maurizan's dagger had already slipped under his guard.

She shoved the blade slowly into his throat. He didn't scream or thrash. His eyes slowly widened, then just as slowly closed again. He went limp and dropped the spear.

Maurizan rolled off him and sprawled in the sand. She released the spirit, panting, heart hammering against her chest. A minute later, she sat up, looked around. Alem was just sitting up too, groaning and rubbing his head.

Maurizan lurched to her feet, headed for the water. Lureen bobbed facedown, dead.

Tosh had pulled Viriam's head into his lap, foamy water sloshing around them. Kalli had gone to one leg, slapped both hands over the wound in Viriam's leg. The blood just kept pumping out of her. It made a red cloud in the water all around them. Maurizan couldn't believe one body could hold so much blood.

Tosh gently rocked her, brushing wet hair out of her eyes with one hand. "Shh. Just rest. It's okay. I've got you. Keep still."

"I . . . I'm cold," Viriam said.

And then she was gone.

CHAPTER
TWENTY-SIX

"I've sent for Giffen," Stasha Benadicta said.

Knarr sighed. "That's probably for the best."

They'd spent hours fussing with the magical doorway. The Birds of Prey who had been tasked with guarding him sat cross-legged on the floor across the room, passing the time with some dice game.

Stasha Benadicta had paced and glowered. Knarr felt her eyes on his back when working. The woman had a sort of fierce bureaucratic efficiency about her that intimidated him more than the girls with the swords.

He felt sure he'd inserted the gems into the mountings correctly at the various stations around the doorway. The settings were what caused the problem. Actually the fact that he didn't *know* any of the settings. In an effort to remain useful, Knarr had been pretending he did. The mountings turned like dials, clicking into place at various runes that meant nothing to him. He'd been dialing in random combinations, hoping something would work. One combination caused all the gems to glow, a low-level hum vibrating the doorway. But it didn't open.

Giffen had been taken away early in the process—nobody really liked having him around—but Knarr now conceded he was stymied and any information Giffen might have couldn't hurt.

Two Birds of Prey escorted Giffen in a few moments later. He looked well fed and well rested. Knarr had heard that Giffen had struck some kind of deal that kept him out of a dungeon cell, and he seemed to be taking full advantage of it.

"I understand you're having some trouble with the doorway," Giffen said.

The mock concern in Giffen's voice made Knarr want to punch him in the mouth. No wonder the man was so reviled around here. Knarr didn't know the extent of the man's crimes in Klaar, but he'd heard whispers. Nobody would miss the man if he suddenly tripped and accidentally fell on several daggers.

That the steward tolerated the man was proof enough how badly she wanted the doorway to work.

"It has been assembled properly. I'm sure of that at least," Knarr said. "But the settings. I don't know them."

Giffen's face remained carefully blank. "Oh?"

"I thought you might have some notion," Knarr said.

"Notion?" Still blank.

"Since you'd spent a lot of money on the missing gems and other parts to repair the doorway, I thought it likely you had some plans to use it," Knarr said.

"Oh. I see," Giffen said. "Yes, I suppose the door would be useless unless someone knew the proper settings." He smiled at the steward. "*Utterly* useless."

"Giffen, enough," Stasha Benadicta said, voice sharp with barely concealed impatience. "Do you know the settings or not?"

"And if I did, how might that benefit me?"

Stasha's eyes narrowed. "Do hot meals and a soft bed bore you already? Have you forgotten what it was like in the dungeon? Perhaps we should go back to the old way and bring in Bune and Lubin for these conversations."

"I'll never talk that way," Giffen said. "Not anymore. And if you kill me in a fit of anger, it might take you years to stumble upon the right combination of runes."

Stasha Benadicta took a long, deep breath, then let it out slowly. "What do you want?"

"Better wine and food. Better clothing. A bigger room with a window."

"Very well."

"Not so fast," Giffen said. "Those are just the little things. I want something else, or just forget about getting any information from me."

"Go on."

"When that doorway opens, I want to go through it."

"Don't be ridiculous."

Giffen sneered. "I'm not suggesting you let me off your leash, Lady Steward. I simply mean that I want to see what is on the other side. I spent a lot of time and energy and *money* to get this doorway working again. I want to at last see the result."

Stasha thought a moment. "Okay."

Giffen grinned and rubbed his hands together. He approached the doorway and started turning the gem housing, each to a specific rune setting. When he'd clicked the last setting into place, the gems glowed and again the entire doorway hummed as if magic flowed through it.

The Birds of Prey stopped playing dice, stood, and came closer, eyes wide.

Darshia arrived just in time to see. The group formed a semicircle, all facing the door in wonder. Giffen stepped back.

The stone wall within the arch turned black as night, then started to swirl, other colors bleeding in one at a time. At first it was all just a mess of colors and shapes, but slowly it started to form into something recognizable.

At long last, the doorway had opened.

CHAPTER TWENTY-SEVEN

At the end of a long hall in the living quarters there was an ornate set of double doors made of some glossy dark wood, inlaid with gems. No ring or knob to open them. Like the doors hidden in the walls and used by the servants to come and go, this door had also been forbidden to the guest. *Politely* forbidden, but forbidden nonetheless.

Brasley, Talbun, and Olgen stood in front of the door again, pondering how to get inside.

"We could take one of the beds apart," Brasley said. "And use the headboard as a battering ram."

"The doors look pretty sturdy," Talbun said. "You might scratch it, I suppose."

"I don't think the servants would like it if we tried to bash down one of their doors," Olgen said.

"Probably not." Brasley shuffled his feet, yawned.

Talbun stepped forward and knocked on the door. Loudly.

Predictably, three of the white-skinned servants appeared behind them, bowing and jabbering apologies.

But not opening the door.

Talbun lifted her chin, summoned her most regal manner, and addressed them in the ancient Fyrian she'd been practicing with Olgen. The servants exchanged puzzled glances. Talbun tried again, speaking more slowly.

She got blank stares in return.

"Damn it!" She turned to Olgen. "Ask them what's on the other side of the door."

Olgen and one of the servants exchanged words.

"That is the hall of the great masters," Olgen said.

"By masters does she mean the wizards?"

Olgen shrugged. "I believe so, milady. Although I can't be sure."

"Tell them I *am* one of the masters," Talbun said.

Olgen stared at her.

"*Tell* them."

Olgen relayed the message. There was a fat pause as the servants exchanged disbelieving looks. Then they started shaking their heads and jabbering again. Olgen listened intently, frowning as he tried to follow what they were saying.

"Do they think I'm lying?"

"Not quite, milady," Olgen said. "The chamber on the other side of the door is indeed reserved for wizards only, but you are not known to them. It's rather that—hmmm, what's the word—you're not on their *roster*, so to speak."

"Turn one of them into a fruit bat," Brasley suggested. "That should establish your credentials well enough."

"That's not a bad idea," Talbun said.

"I was *joking*."

"I don't mean I'm going to do anything harmful to them, idiot. But it might help to show them who I am."

Talbun stepped forward, spitting out the syllables to the spell, making her hand gestures a little more dramatic than they needed to be. *I'll show these pale bitches who's one of the masters.*

A globe of white light the size of an apple sprang into existence, hovering in the air a few inches above Talbun's open palm. The servants shrank from the sudden brilliance. They jabbered quickly to one another, then scurried into one of the servants' doorways. It quickly closed behind them, becoming a smooth wall again.

"You have a spell that makes light?" Brasley asked. "Would have been nice if you'd used that back when I was fumbling in the dark for a lantern."

"Once I use the spell, it's *gone* until I study it again from a spell book," Talbun explained. "So I was saving it. Anyway, you found the lantern, so stop complaining."

Brasley frowned. "I'm just glad I didn't trip and fall down the—"

A loud clunk drew their attention back to the doors. Slowly they opened inward, lights flickering to life in the chamber beyond.

"It worked," Brasley said breathlessly.

"I'm a little surprised too," Talbun said.

The three of them slowly entered, pausing just inside the doorway. Talbun muttered a few words, and the sphere of light dissolved into the air. They stood a moment, gawking at the large chamber.

The ceiling was too far above them to be seen. The chamber simply rose and rose into the dizzying distance. Chains hung down, holding up a cluster of the magical light globes thirty feet over their heads. The floor and walls were the same glossy black they'd seen before, gold trim around the edges. Numerous shelves with many leather-bound books. Tables to the left and right with arcane devices, beakers and potions and magical miscellany. A huge stone structure like a tomb dominated the chamber, humping up from the floor as if carved from the same material. Before the tomb stood three pedestals, a different object atop each. Not a speck of dust anywhere.

"Don't touch anything," Talbun whispered. "Just follow me."

Slowly they approached the tomb.

Calling it a tomb turned out to be a good guess. A figure on top lay carved in stone, hands crossed over chest as if in his final rest. The carving was expertly detailed, an old man in wizard's robes, bald and wrinkled, a moustache but no beard.

"Do you think . . . Is it possible this is the last resting place of the master magician?" Talbun's voice was heavy with reverence.

"The Great Library was his stronghold," Olgen said. "I mean . . . well . . . it's possible, I suppose. Look. Runes."

Neither Talbun nor Olgen could decipher the runes at the foot of the tomb. Brasley didn't even try.

Instead he turned his attention to the objects on the pedestals.

The first object was a book. Everything in this place was in a language long dead, so why bother? He skipped to the next pedestal. A thick bracelet of silver, more unreadable runes all the way around it. He leaned in to take a closer look. There didn't seem to be anything special about it. Talbun had told them not to touch anything, but really where was the harm?

He picked it up slowly between thumb and forefinger, braced himself for the world to end.

Nothing happened.

He held it in the palm of his hand. Heavy. Solid silver. Certainly valuable.

But a place of honor at the foot of the tomb of history's greatest wizard? Obviously, Brasley was missing something. Maybe if—

"I can't believe it," Talbun said suddenly.

Brasley hastily shoved the bracelet into the pocket of his breeches. He didn't want to be caught touching things without permission, and the wizard's scoldings were far from pleasant. He hastily moved down to the third pedestal to pretend he was examining the object there.

"I just can't believe it," Talbun repeated. "This is the master magician's workshop. Every wizard alive would give her left arm to be here."

Brasley breathed a sigh of relief. Talbun hadn't noticed what he'd done. Still, just to be on the safe side, he pretended to examine the—

He lost his train of thought as he stared at the object on the pedestal.

Three objects actually. One was a flat square of brass. Pieces had been cut out in roughly the shape of a hand but with numerous designs Brasley didn't recognize. All of this magical nonsense confounded him. The second object was a scroll case, gleaming silver with no decoration at all. The final object looked like an inkwell, but he could see through the clear glass that it was empty. Why an empty inkwell should rate a pedestal—

Brasley looked closer. The inkwell seemed empty, but there was some sort of distortion inside. He realized it wasn't empty at all, but filled with some kind of clear liquid. At a glance it seemed nothing was there at all, but when he squinted, the scene through the clear glass seemed to bend.

Clear ink? Maybe it's magical, or . . .

He stood up straight, eyes wide. "This is it."

Brasley turned to the others. "This is it! A tattoo. The stencil and the ink. This is what Rina sent us to get!"

Talbun stood at the first pedestal, running a hand over the book, eyes filled with wonder. "This is the master magician's spell book. Keep your tattoos. I don't care about anything else." A slow smile spread across her face. "This book is mine."

CHAPTER
TWENTY-EIGHT

Rina went out with all the others to watch the approach of the enemy ships. Dozens from the ducal palace stood watching from the top floor. From there, they could see miles out to sea but also down into the harbor. They all crowded the rail—maids, valets, soldiers, petty functionaries, and one ink mage. All shoulder to shoulder, wide eyes, as one ship rolled in after another and after another and after another and . . .

There's too many. I tried to tell them.

She tapped into the spirit so she could focus her eyes the best she could. From here she could just make out the delegation on the harbor wall. The duke and his advisors and Maxus. A delegation from the Perranese ships came across the wharf and stood shouting up at the duke. No matter how much she strained, Rina couldn't hear what they were saying. Even tapped into the spirit, it was too far. But she could guess.

The Perranese are demanding a surrender, I bet. Telling the duke he can save a lot of lives if he capitulates now. Emilio is probably telling him to sod off.

It was a good enough guess. Nobody had lost anything yet. After it got bloody, the delegations would meet again.

It might be too late by then.

She jammed a chuma stick into the corner of her mouth and smoked it while she watched a while longer. More ships came over the horizon as the two delegations said whatever they said, probably predictable things, threats, appeals to reason, bravado. She didn't know that much about Emilio, but what Rina did know didn't make her optimistic. She couldn't imagine anything they might be saying that would avert a battle, blood, and death.

She smoked and watched.

Eventually the Perranese returned to their ships, and the duke and his delegation left the wall.

The ships kept coming.

Instinctively, Rina knew nothing had been accomplished. Formalities had been observed.

Those around her kept watching, wide-eyed. Their fear was so thick, Rina almost couldn't stand it. She had no words of comfort, no reassurances. These weren't her people. She moved away from the balcony, looking for a private corner to be alone and smoke and try to figure out what she was supposed to do here.

The death priest's words plagued her. *The southern path pays a debt.*

She'd fought a battle, been captured, escaped, and made her way south when every other sane person was fleeing north, yet she still had no idea what Krell's words meant. The city was under siege. Maybe she could help. That's all she could guess. Looking at the ships crowding the harbor, it seemed less and less likely she could do a damn thing. Coming here had probably been a mistake.

She smoked. She paced. She avoided eye contact with everyone around her.

These people are going to die, and there's not a damn thing I can do about it.

Fifteen minutes later, a runner in the duke's livery found her, red faced and out of breath. Rina wondered how many flights of stairs he'd run up looking for her.

"Your grace." The runner paused to suck in deep lungsful of air. "The duke requests you attend him."

Rina took a last pull on the chuma stick, blew out a long gray stream that swirled away on the breeze. "Tell him I'm coming."

The duke leaned on the table, glaring at the model of his city, toy soldiers lined along the miniature walls. He looked haggard and unhappy. He was surrounded by various generals and military advisors in armor only slightly less garish than his.

Rina approached, offered a slight nod. "Your grace."

The duke sighed. "You've been watching?"

She didn't need to be told he meant the ships. "Yes."

"My advisors say it will take hours for all of them to arrive, and then another day to position themselves. It would seem . . ." He cleared his throat. "It looks like you were right about the number of enemy ships. It still seems impossible."

For a long moment, nobody said a word.

Then the duke drew his sword and smashed the model city, sending figurines flying. Rina flinched at the sudden violence. All of his men took a step back as he smashed the model again and then once more. He tossed his sword on top of the wreckage with a curse.

The duke took a few moments to master himself, then in a calm voice said, "All those hours of planning. Doesn't seem fair really."

He looked up, saw everyone watching him.

"Gentlemen, may I have a few moments with Duchess Veraiin?"

His advisors bowed and hurried away. Rina thought most of them looked relieved to be going.

"I apologize for the display."

"Think nothing of it." She pulled out a chuma stick. "May I?"

The duke snapped his fingers, and a servant hurried forward to light it for her.

"Thank you, your grace."

"Please. I've asked you to call me Emilio."

She puffed, then said, "Have you sent a rider to Baron Kern? Maybe he can send reinforcements."

"I've already sent a rider telling the baron not to bother," Emilio said. "He could send all the ships he has, loaded to overflowing with every man, woman, and child big enough to hold a spear, and it wouldn't matter. Not against what the Perranese are sending. In fact, I've warned him to look to his own in case the Perranese break off a portion of their fleet to sail north and harass him."

Rina puffed and thought about that. That the duke would consider the welfare of others and not just his own people gave her some comfort about the man.

Not a lot. A little.

"As you see, none of my plans amount to a hill of beans now," Emilio said. "I was wondering . . . that is, I was hoping you might have some suggestion."

She rolled the chuma stick from one corner of her mouth to the other. A silly habit she'd started. The way she was going through chuma sticks, she'd be out before the Perranese even attacked. "I'm not sure what you mean. I'm no tactician."

"I understand, but, well, I wasn't looking for military advice so much as I was hoping for something . . . uh . . . magical?" He rubbed the back of his neck, embarrassed. "Forgive me. We've all heard the stories of what you can do. It's hard to separate truth from exaggeration."

"I see." She thought about it. It's *all* she had been thinking about since arriving in Sherrik. What could she do, fight the entire Perranese army single-handed?

She sighed out a long stream of smoke. "I can fight with you. And die with you. But I have no idea how to stop what's coming."

CHAPTER TWENTY-NINE

Tosh paid Miko to take them back to Sherrik. Rina had given Tosh more than enough money to carry out the expedition as he saw fit. He'd tried to be frugal, and thought—hoped—there was enough left to get them home again after this was all over. Miko's little scow-schooner was really more suited to island-hopping than it was for the open sea, but the weather was calm. They'd had some luck.

Luck. Don't make me laugh.

He'd brought five volunteers with him on this trek, five women who'd trusted him, and he was coming back with one. And they weren't home yet. Dumo help him if something happened to Kalli too. How could he look the others in the eye when he got home? Why should Tosh be alive and the others dead?

Luck. He leaned over the gunwale and spit. *That's for luck.*

"You okay?"

Tosh turned, looked up at Alem. "I just want to get home."

"Me too."

"I thought you were running *away* from home."

"I was." Alem sat next to him. "I did."

Tosh wasn't really in the mood for company but didn't object.

"It wasn't a *place* I was running away from," Alem said. "I was running away from how I felt, and that's pretty stupid because there's no place far enough to run away from that."

They sat a while in silence. The sun set.

"You gave those women something, you know?" Alem said.

A noncommittal grunt from Tosh.

"They followed you because they didn't want to be whores anymore."

"They were alive when they whores," Tosh said.

"They made a choice. You showed them they *had* a choice, that they could take a different path. I'm sure Kalli wants her sister back. I'm just as sure she wouldn't go back to the Wounded Bird."

Tosh sighed. *No. None of the girls would go back. You can see the pride in the way they walk now, in their eyes, and how they hold their heads up. They'd never give that up. They'd die first.*

None of that made Tosh feel one bit better.

Miko shouted something from his place at the tiller, the words lost in the wind and the sound of the boat plowing through the waves. Maurizan came forward. She'd put on some clothes: breeches of the lightest material she could find, which she'd cut off at the knees, and a cotton shirt, the top two and bottom two buttons left undone. The heat seemed to hit her harder than everyone else.

Maybe Tosh would cut off his own breeches at the knees too. It was pretty damn hot, although it helped a little when the sun went down.

Maurizan pointed ahead of them. "Look."

Tosh and Alem squinted ahead into the darkness.

But it wasn't completely dark. A tiny dot of orange light in the distance. No. Many tiny dots.

"Sherrik?" Tosh asked.

"Almost," Maurizan said. "Those are ships. The Perranese have arrived. Miko says he can take us a little closer, but he won't risk trying to run the blockade to take us to Sherrik."

"I don't blame him," Tosh said.

"What do we do, then?" Alem asked. "Go back? Or around?"

"Miko isn't going to sail us all the way back to Klaar," Tosh said. "He's nuts, but he's not crazy. If not Sherrik, then I don't know what."

"Sherrik," Maurizan said.

Tosh cast a questioning glance at her. "Oh?"

"Miko will take you up the coast away from the Perranese," Maurizan said. "You can walk to Sherrik from there."

"They've closed the city," Tosh said. "You remember what it was like when we left."

"I'll open it for you," Maurizan said. "I can swim in, find a drain or culvert or something. I'll tell them you're coming. Make your way around to the north side of the city. I'll get you into one of the gates. I promise."

Alem frowned. "Now wait a minute. I don't think you should risk—"

"I don't think I asked you," Maurizan said. "You don't pick and choose my risks."

Alem opened his mouth. Closed it again.

"Okay, then," she said. "As soon as Miko gets us a little closer, I'm going."

When they were close enough to barely discern the outline of a Perranese ship, Miko declared they were as close as he was willing to risk. Beyond the ship they saw the lights of Sherrik, a city on the edge of war.

Miko had ordered no lamps be lit. No loud talking. Noise carried in the night. They bobbed in the darkness.

Maurizan started to unlace her breeches, and Tosh abruptly excused himself.

Alem didn't.

Maurizan handed Alem her breeches and then her shirt. She stood naked, and a sudden gust of cool wind broke her out in gooseflesh.

"I don't want you to go," he said.

"Miko gave me this lambskin," Maurizan said. "It's wax sealed. I can put my things in here, and it should keep the water out." She wrapped her daggers, clothes, sandals, and a few other belongings into the lambskin and tied them tight with strips of leather.

"Did you hear me?" Alem asked. "I don't want you to go."

Maurizan tied a leather strap to her wrist, tied the other end to the lambskin bundle. "I'll be fine unless I catch a current or something. Dumo, I hope there aren't sharks."

"Aren't you listening to me?" Alem asked. "I said I don't want you to—"

Maurizan slapped him across the face. Hard.

His hand went to his stinging cheek, eyes going wide.

"Do you think I want to do this, you stupid asshole?" she said. "Don't you think I'd love to sail back to the Red City with you and stroll the bazaar and forget about all of this? We can't, okay? All of Helva is in peril, my mother and my people, everyone in Klaar. What I found in the ruined fortress might not mean a thing. Or maybe it does. I don't know. I don't know anything except that we have to try. We have to do . . . something. I don't know what. Okay? I don't have answers, but we have to try. We have to keep going."

She blew out a long sigh, as if all those words flying out of her mouth so fast had sapped her. The two of them looked at each other, no words good enough.

Abruptly, Alem gathered her on his arms and kissed her. Her arms went around him, and she kissed back.

They finally broke apart, breathless.

"I can't believe I finally got you naked, and now you're leaving," he said.

She started crying first and then laughed, wiping her eyes. "You're such an . . . ass. You had your chances, you know."

"I want *another* chance," he said.

She kissed him once more, then turned and dove into the sea.

CHAPTER
THIRTY

Stasha, Giffen, Knarr, Darshia, and the rest looked through the magical doorway in wonder, eyes wide, only partially understanding what they were looking at.

It was as if they were looking at a scene blurred by water, a painting at the bottom of a clear pool, figures frozen in motion. And yet not *completely* frozen. As they watched, it seemed that the two men and one woman were moving extremely slowly. They were in some unfamiliar room, walls of black gleaming stone.

"That's Baron Hammish, isn't it?" Darshia said.

"Yes," said Stasha Benadicta. "And the woman is the wizard Talbun. I don't know the boy."

"I don't understand why they're frozen like that," Giffen said.

"They're not," Knarr said. "Not quite. They're moving but very, very slowly."

Giffen frowned. "That still doesn't explain why. I expected a doorway, not a shimmering, blurry window looking at some glacially moving fools."

"Who knows how far away they are? Maybe that has something to do with it," Knarr said. "It's a magical portal after all. You didn't really think it was going to swing open like a barn door, did you? You're the one who chose the setting."

"I don't know where they go," Giffen admitted. "The old duke had them written down. I knew they were for the doorway. There was no other information."

"Enough," said Stasha Benadicta. "The obvious way to test any door is to walk through it. I believe you have the honor, Lord Giffen."

Giffen's head jerked around to glare at her. "Me?"

"I believe you made going through the doorway a condition for your aid."

"But . . ." Giffen gestured at the shimmering tableau. "What if I get stuck in slow motion like those idiots?"

"It's a risk, I suppose." Stasha's smile was cold, didn't touch her eyes. "One I'm more than willing to take."

♦　♦　♦

Talbun sat at one of the tables, hunched over the master magician's spell book. She'd been there for hours. Brasley and Tosh had left to eat a meal and returned to find her sitting in the same place. Brasley tried to open a conversation with her, but the woman waved him away. She didn't want to be disturbed.

He poked around the master magician's workshop. None of the books meant anything to him, and he considered off limits all the beakers and bottles and strange vials of liquid, because they might explode or something if he messed with them.

Leave all the wizard nonsense to the wizards.

Hit with a sudden and uncharacteristic pang of responsibility, Brasley thought somebody should attempt to find out what the stencil, scroll case, and inkwell were for. After all, digging up some useful ink magic had been the whole point of the expedition in the first place. Talbun might suddenly be obsessed with the spell book, but duty demanded that proper care and attention be paid to the task at hand. Rina was counting on them. Time to get to work.

Brasley delegated Olgen to look into it and then sent one of the servants for a pitcher of wine.

Olgen opened the scroll case and began to read. Brasley drank wine. *A good thing I'm here to stay on top of the situation.* An hour later the pitcher was empty, but a servant—possibly the same one; they all looked so similar—brought a new one just in time.

Talbun hadn't budged.

Brasley took the silver bracelet out of his pocket. Scanning the runes again, he confirmed he couldn't make heads or tails of them. A glance over his shoulder told him nobody was paying attention to him. He slipped the bracelet onto his left wrist, held it up to catch the light. Not bad. Yes, after all, why shouldn't he have a little something for his trouble? Taken away from his new bride and dragged halfway across Helva, he deserved a little something, didn't he?

Yes, I'd say I've earned it. A little bauble. What could it hurt?

He remembered that expeditions to the Great Library were obligated to turn over whatever artifacts they discovered upon exiting, but obviously they were going to take the ink magic back to Rina. Might as well smuggle the bracelet too.

Brasley wandered past the tomb to examine something on the far wall. An archway carved into the black stone, like an enormous picture frame with no picture. Large, different-colored jewels set at various places around the arch, and a collection of unfamiliar runes circled each jewel.

He shrugged. *Whatever.*

Brasley went to Olgen, looked over his shoulder at the scroll. "And how's it going over here?"

"Slowly, I'm afraid. Ancient Fyrian again," Olgen said. "But I'm having a good bit of trouble with the vocabulary. It's all very technical. Much of it is simply instructions for applying the tattoo."

"But what does it *do*?" Brasley asked.

"I couldn't even make a guess, milord."

"Ah." Brasley sipped wine. "Well, keep at it."

Brasley missed Fregga. Was she okay? She made him feel . . . what?

Like I'm not just a drunken womanizer. Like I'm somebody worth marrying.

He vowed things would be different if he could just make it back to her. And she was a good wife, not some bit of eye candy he'd be stuck with if he picked out his own wife. Fate had done him a favor. A big one. He just hoped she wasn't too lonely back in—

Talbun stood abruptly, knocking her chair over. It clattered on the floor.

She took one halting step, then almost collapsed, grabbing the table to keep herself upright.

Brasley rushed to her, took her by one arm. "Talbun! Are you okay?"

She turned to look at him, no recognition in her bloodshot eyes, skin pale and clammy, hair matted with sweat. "Where . . . where am I?"

"The Great Library," Brasley told her.

She blinked at that, turning her head slowly to take in the entire chamber. She suddenly looked back at him. "Who are . . . Brasley?"

"Yes." *What in blazes is wrong with her?*

"I . . ." Her eyes fell to his goblet of wine. She grabbed it out of his hand, tilted it back, and drained it. She gulped breath and shoved the goblet back at him. "More. And food."

Brasley screamed for the servants. Five minutes later, Talbun was seated at the table again, spooning a thick stew into her mouth. Brasley thought he smelled lamb. There was a fresh pitcher of wine too, and a dark brown loaf of bread. She ate manically, eyes darting around between bites like someone might sneak up and steal her food.

"Remember how I told you that when I cast a spell, it goes out of my mind?" Talbun slurped wine. "Until I cast it, the spell is cooped up in there with all the other spells, just buzzing around, wanting to get out."

"I feel like maybe you need some sleep," Brasley said. "Maybe we should get you back to your room."

"Maybe you should shut your face."

Ah.

"S-sorry." Her eye twitched. She took another long drink of wine, a tremble in her hands. "Just listen."

He nodded. "Okay."

Olgen came up behind him. "I've almost got the name of this tattoo. The translation's tricky, though."

Brasley ignored him.

"How many spells a wizard can hold in her head at one time depends on the strength of the wizard's mind and her willpower," Talbun explained. "A wizard just finishing his apprenticeship might hold three or four. A journeyman wizard's mind is more disciplined. Might hold five or six or seven. My old master never told me how many he held, but I think it was close to a dozen."

She twitched again, so violently it startled Brasley.

"Heart beating . . . so fast." She gulped more wine.

"It's something like Feeding a God," Olgen said, squinting at the scroll. "Or a Meal for God. No, that's not quite right."

"Not now, Olgen," Brasley said.

"I've b-been reading the master magician's spell b-book," Talbun said. "The spells are . . . amazing. So . . . p-powerful." She wiped sweat from her forehead. "B-been m-memorizing them."

Brasley swallowed hard. "How many, Talbun?"

Talbun rubbed at her eyes with her fingers, her breath coming in short gasps. "It's a b-bit loud in there. A b-bit crowded."

"Talbun." Brasley made sure to make eye contact, kept his voice calm. "How many spells?"

She blinked. "Twenty-nine."

Ohhhhhhhh, fuck.

Olgen snapped his fingers. "Got it. The tattoo is called the God Eater."

CHAPTER
THIRTY-ONE

A knock at the door. The little office was tucked out of the way on the first floor of the ducal palace, across the hall from the guardsmen's barracks.

Captain Sarkham looked up from the parchments strewn across the little wooden table—supplies, troop numbers, guard rotations, all the clerical minutia that made a war happen. He was captain of the city guard, but the Perranese invasion obligated him to put his troops under the command of the army generals. The transition hadn't been smooth. There'd been some dispute about exactly who commanded which companies.

He rubbed his eyes and said, "Come in."

Three people entered, two city watchmen in leather armor, a short girl between them. He looked at her but couldn't see much in the dim office. He took the single candle and circled the table, holding up the light to get a better look at her.

She wore men's breeches cut off at the knees and a shirt of some incredibly thin material. He knew it was incredibly thin, because the fabric clung wetly to her in a way that left little to the imagination. Sarkham could tell the girl had striking red hair and very fair skin even though at the moment the hair was matted and wet and she had a hue of deep pink across her nose and cheeks from recent time in the sun.

One of the guards held up a belt from which dangled two sheathed daggers. "She had these on her when she snuck into the city."

Sarkham raised an eyebrow at the blades. "She give you trouble?"

"No," the guardsman said. "Said she wanted to talk to somebody in charge."

She said, "I need to—"

"We'll get to you in a minute." He'd said it firmly but not too harshly. He asked the guardsman, "She came over the wall?"

"No," the guardsman said. "Under it."

"What?"

"She told us she came in through one of the deep drains."

"And you *believed* her?"

"Well . . ." The guard shrugged. "She's wet."

"Do I need to dignify that with a reply, trooper?"

The guardsman had the good sense to look chastised but said, "We found her at one of the high-tide gates this side of the inner wall. On the *other side* of the *locked* high-tide gate."

"Huh." Sarkham scratched his chin. "Then someone put her there."

He could see she was aching to speak but forcing herself to be patient.

"How about it, girl?" Sarkham asked. "Someone put you in there?"

"I guess that would be more believable," she said.

Sarkham chuckled. "You wanted to talk to somebody in charge, eh?"

"Would that be you?"

"I'm about as far up the ladder as you're going to get."

"I have friends," she said. "A boat dropped them up the coast. I need to arrange for them to come into the city."

"The duke's sealed the city," Sarkham said. "That's his order. Not a thing I can do about it, and you're not likely to see him. Probably asleep by now anyway." He glanced at the guardsmen. "Unless he's still up asking Duchess Veraiin how to save the city." He smirked as if it were a private joke.

The girl's eyes shot wide at the mention of the name. "Rina's here?"

"Rina?" Sarkham looked her over again as if possibly he'd missed something the first time. "You know the duchess?"

Her face hardened a little, subtle but enough to be noticeable. "Yes. I know her."

◆ ◆ ◆

Maurizan hadn't been nervous down in the captain's simple office with its rough wooden table and bare stone walls. Sarkham seemed like a man who took his business seriously, but there was nothing especially cruel about him. Even with her hair dripping and the guards holding her weapons, she'd never felt small or intimidated.

She supposed the duke's reception hall had been specifically *designed* to intimidate. High ceilings and hard floors, the sounds of boots echoing, men along the walls with spears, thrones raised on a platform—all designed to make her feel small amid the relentless *bigness* of the place. Castle Klaar's reception hall looked like the inside of some tavern with delusions of grandeur.

I swam in the sunken halls of the ancient wizards. What's this compared to that?

Maurizan lifted her chin, hardened her eyes. She was determined to at least *look* unafraid. Mother's words rang in her ears. *Show them the person you want them to see.*

A side door swung open, and a man in a red silk robe entered with a brace of men in plate armor. She thought he'd climb the stairs to the platform and look down at her from one of the thrones. Instead, he walked straight toward her. He seemed too young and handsome to be a duke. Wasn't Helva ruled by sour old men?

"Is this the girl?" he asked.

"Yes, your grace," replied Sarkham.

Another man followed the duke into the hall through the same side door, older but tall, powerfully built with a barrel chest, dressed like a priest or—*is that the bishop of Klaar?*

And then the duchess walked in.

Rina saw the gypsy girl and gasped. "Maurizan?"

"So you *do* know her?" the duke said.

"Yes . . . I . . ." Rina abruptly turned back to Maurizan. "Is he . . . I mean is everyone else okay? Are they with you?"

"Tosh is up the coast . . . with the ones who made it," Maurizan said. "I'm here hoping to get them into the city."

Maurizan could see the question on Rina's face. *I'm not telling you if Alem is among the living. You can just wonder.*

Petty? So what? Let Rina hurt like she'd been hurt. Hadn't Maurizan felt loss and resentment and pain? *He's mine now.*

"Rina, are you aware this woman claims to have swum *under* the wall to get inside the city?" the duke asked.

Rina looked from Maurizan to the duke and back again. "I didn't even know she was here until a moment ago."

Maurizan pinned Rina with a hard gaze. "Rina. This is important."

"Emilio, I sent her and some of my people on a mission south," Rina said. "I need to talk to her. To find out what happened to them."

"I understand," said the duke. "And I'm sure we can work something out. But we're on a war footing. She's lying about coming under the wall, and that means she came in some other way. I need to know how and plug the hole before we're all neck deep in Perranese infiltrators."

Rina looked at Maurizan, the question plain on her face.

Everyone else looked at Maurizan too, waiting for her to explain herself.

Maurizan unbuttoned her shirt, turned, and lowered the garment to her waist. She looked over her shoulder to see the expression on Rina's face.

Rina stared a long time. Maybe she didn't believe what she was seeing. Or didn't want to.

The duke, Bishop Hark, Sarkham, everyone in the room looked to Duchess Veraiin, awaited her reaction.

"Those tattoos," the bishop whispered behind her.

"The Prime," Rina said. "She's telling the truth."

CHAPTER
THIRTY-TWO

Brasley frowned up at Olgen. "Boy, can't you see the lady is having a problem? Go away and— wait, did you say the God Eater?"

"Yes, milord."

"That's rather ominous."

"Yes, milord."

"Well, what does the tattoo actually do?" Brasley asked.

Olgen shrugged. "Eat gods?"

Brasley shook Talbun by the shoulders. "Listen, woman, we need some wizarding. We've got a tattoo to figure out, and the boy here is useless."

"Honestly, milord, I'm trying my best to—"

"Oh, shut up."

"*Shhhh*, shut up, both of you!" Talbun tapped the side of her head with trembling fingers. "So much jabbering in here. I can't take your jabbering too. There's too many. Too many spells. Got to let something out."

"Careful!" Brasley said. "We don't want to be fried or zapped with lightning or melted in a puddle of goo. Let's be calm about this."

Talbun rocked back and forth in her chair, a strained bleating coming from deep in her throat. "I can't I can't I can't I can't."

Shit, she's going to pop. And when wizards pop . . . what? Well, not anything good, probably.

"Look, Talbun old girl, you've got to pull it together before—"

There was a dull thud from somewhere in the depths of the library, almost like an explosion or somebody dropping an enormous barrel of water onto a cow. That's the problem with distant thudding sounds. Very hard to identify.

When it happened again, it was closer, and the floor shook.

Definitely something smashing something else.

Talbun shot to her feet, eyes suddenly focused, hands rock steady. "What was that?"

"Something utterly and terribly bad," Brasley guessed.

When it happened again, it was a sharp crack that sounded more like an explosion with all the fire and destruction that entailed. Mostly it shook the room so hard that Olgen and Brasley went hard to the floor. The spherical lights overhead swayed and trembled. One broke free and smashed to the floor next to them with a startling pop.

Brasley raised himself to his hands and knees, looked up at Talbun.

She still stood upright, face stoic, no sign any longer she was losing her mind.

Typical. Now that I'm about to shit my pants, she looks right as rain.

The doors to the magician's chamber slammed open.

A tide of milk-faced servants flooded into the magician's chamber. In spite of the fear radiating from them, they were calm and orderly. Hundreds of them crowded the room in seconds, turning as one and slamming the doors shut again. They pressed forward, the front line of them putting their hands against the door to hold it shut. The next line pushed the backs of those in the first line, and the third pushed the second and so on. Whatever was on the other side of the door, the servants wanted it to stay there.

Brasley gawked at the display and felt cold sweat drip down his back. "Oh, that can't be good." He turned to Talbun. "We've got to get out of here."

But she didn't hear him. Arcane syllables flew from her lips impossibly fast, her mouth a blur. A flash of red light engulfed her. It was brief but so bright that Brasley had to turn away. When he shut his eyes, he could see the glowing shape of full plate armor and a helm outlined in red.

Before he could figure that out, something slammed against the doors. It made him jump, and he drew his sword. He'd forgotten he'd even had it. His palm felt sweaty on the hilt. Another slam on the door rattled the hinges, and Brasley had to exert all of his self-control to keep his bladder in check.

He spared a glance at Olgen. All the blood had drained from the boy's face.

Talbun babbled another spell, and Brasley felt something in the air that made his hair stand up on his arms and the back of his neck. He didn't know what she was doing but guessed it was something powerful. A bright yellow light formed around her fists. The more spells she cast, the calmer she seemed to be as her mind became less crowded.

"Hey."

She looked at him. "What?"

He swallowed. "You okay?"

Talbun locked eyes with him a moment, and then an insane smile spread slowly across her face. "No."

The next thunderous smash, and the doors flew open inward, crushing a number of servants against the walls and sending others flying backward into the crowd. They shrank back, leaving an open semicircle for the intruder. Every part of Brasley went watery with fear. He would have thrown down his weapon and fled if there'd been anywhere to run.

The intruder was a huge brute of a man, bald, muscles from head to foot. Tattoos covered every inch of him save for his gleaming metal leg.

An ink mage! What else could he be?

Except for the slightest hitch in his step, the metal leg might have been a natural part of his body. He stomped into the room, backhanding servants out of the way. Some flew far enough to hit the wall with a sickening crack, eyes rolling back as they slid into a limp heap. The other servants rushed past him, making for the wrecked doors. They squealed in a single, uniform, high-pitched sound, none of them looking back with any concern for Brasley, Olgen, or the wizard.

The chamber cleared of servants, and the hulking ink mage doggedly moved toward Brasley and the rest. When his flesh-and-blood foot came down, the room shook with the sound of a bass drum. When the metal foot came down, it cracked the stone with an earsplitting clang.

"Give me the ink magic," he bellowed. His voice had been magically augmented somehow and filled the chamber, cowing Olgen and Brasley. "I want it now!"

Olgen looked down at the inkwell, stencil, and scroll case in his hands and went white as a sheet. He rushed to Brasley, dumping the items into his arms. "I think these are yours, milord."

Brasley had to drop his sword to catch the items. "What are you doing?"

"My fists are thunder! My voice is a storm! To stand against me is to stand in the path of an avalanche!" shouted the ink mage.

Each word made Brasley flinch. His knees almost gave out. Panic stricken, his eyes darted around the chamber for a hiding place. Olgen was already scooting under the table.

Talbun lifted her hands, both still glowing with yellow light. "If you're looking for easy fodder, you've come to the wrong place, you big son of a bitch!"

Her hands flared blindingly bright, and two yellow streaks of light crossed the room in a flash, striking the ink mage in the chest. He stumbled back, wincing pain, metal foot scraping a deep gouge across the floor. He righted himself immediately and came roaring back.

"That attack would have killed a mountain bear," Talbun said.

"What do we do?" The words came out of Brasley's mouth embarrassingly high-pitched.

"Run."

I'm going to die I'm going to die I'm going to die.

Talbun spat more words, and a two-handed sword glowed red in her hands. She charged at the ink mage, screaming a war cry so savage, Brasley almost didn't recognize the woman.

He bent down and shouted at Olgen under the table. "Come on!"

"I'm not going out there!" Terror in his eyes.

Talbun swung the sword, but the ink mage's skin had turned a dark metal. The glowing blade scorched a dark mark across his chest, but it didn't penetrate. He punched Talbun square in the face with a huge iron fist. Brasley gasped, waiting for Talbun's head to fly off, but the glowing outline of armor appeared around her upon impact.

She flew back and smashed into the table, the magical red armor saving her again. She shattered the table into kindling, her and the debris tumbling away and leaving an exposed Olgen, squatting with his arms over his head.

The ink mage strutted forward and opened his mouth so wide it almost seemed like his jaw had come unhinged. An orange light stirred in the black abyss of his throat.

Brasley froze. *Oh no.*

The ink mage belched a long gout of fire that completely engulfed Olgen and Brasley. The sudden searing heat shocked a prolonged scream ragged and hoarse from Brasley's throat. He stopped screaming abruptly when he realized he wasn't being burned to death. But he still heard a scream.

Olgen writhed on the ground, every inch of him aflame. He screamed and screamed, and Brasley thought it impossible the boy could still live, but he continued to scream as the skin melted from his bones and he slowly turned black. The smell of charred hair and flesh—

Brasley fell to his knees, dropping the magical items, and vomited. It splashed hot and acrid in front of him. He spit, feeling dizzy, gagged once, again, then turned his head toward Olgen, who finally lay still, contorted body turning to charcoal.

Dumo help the poor bastard.

An enormous shadow fell over him, and he looked up into the smirking face of the ink mage.

"You intrigue me, little man," the ink mage said. "Why aren't you a cinder like your friend?"

Brasley's eyes shifted to the inkwell, scroll case, and stencil, half-covered with his sick.

The ink mage followed his gaze to the items and grinned. "Alas, no time for curiosities. I see what I came for." He bent to reach for them.

The ink mage suddenly flew straight up, slamming into the ceiling. The ink mage grunted in pain.

Brasley gathered up the ink-magic items and staggered to his feet. He turned his head and saw Talbun holding out a hand toward the ink mage pinned to the ceiling.

"I can't hold him long!" she yelled. "Get out of here."

"Where?"

"Anywhere!"

He hesitated, wondering if he should stay and help her. *She's a wizard with spells overflowing her head. If that's not good enough, then there's nothing I can do.* Still, just to run off and leave her . . .

Brasley ran for the doors, understanding it would take him right beneath the spot where Talbun had trapped the ink mage.

Just run!

But the hesitation cost him.

A strangled cry escaped Talbun's throat, and the ink mage dropped from the ceiling, landing ten feet in front of him, smashing a crater in the stone floor, cracks radiating from him in every direction.

Brasley turned on his heels and ran back the other way.

"Little man!" roared the ink mage. "You have something that doesn't belong to you."

Just drop it all. Let him have the tattoo.

But he found some hidden storehouse of courage or perhaps just foolishness and clutched the items to his chest. He ran for the tomb. It was the biggest, most solid thing in the chamber, and he meant to hide behind it. As he ran, he spared a glance for the wizard.

Talbun had drawn her dagger and cut a deep slice in her thumb. She sucked a mouthful of blood and then spit it as far as she could. Before the blood drops could hit the ground, they grew and formed into shapes at an incredible rate. In two seconds, a dozen drops grew into exact duplicates of Talbun. They were naked, but that didn't stop them screaming and running straight at the ink mage.

Brasley dove behind the tomb, popping up again just enough to watch the scene unfold.

One of the ink mage's forearms and fists had grown into a giant stone hammer. He swung it back and forth, swatting away the fake Talbuns, a crack and crunch of bones each time the hammer connected. The Talbun bodies piled up around the ink mage's feet.

With an overhand swing he brought his hammer fist down on the last duplicate's head. It exploded in a mist of blood, chunks of brain and skull flying.

Brasley felt a strange vibration and turned to look at the archway he'd examined earlier. Where once there had been stone, there now swirled a shimmering darkness, color and light slowly bleeding into the mass as it turned in a clockwise motion. He gasped as it resolved into the scene of a room with people in it, but it was blurry, like he was looking into the room through a glass window smeared with a thick layer of chicken grease.

He looked back at Talbun.

The ink mage crossed the room so fast, Brasley almost didn't see it. The brute grabbed Talbun in an unbreakable bear hug, lifting her from her feet. She babbled another spell and grabbed the ink mage's shoulders. Blue lightning erupted from her hands and played all over the ink mage's body. The ink mage went stiff, gritting teeth.

Brasley looked back at the archway. It bubbled out toward him, and then the surface broke and a man stumbled out, knocking into him. Both were equally surprised.

Brasley blinked at the man. "Lord Giffen?" He'd met the man on a few occasions when he'd still been Duke Veraiin's steward. Before he turned traitor. "What are . . . how . . . ?"

But Giffen was looking past him at the battle between the ink mage and the wizard, his mouth falling open at the sight.

The hulk had nearly let her go after Talbun's shock attack, but he recovered quickly and took her head in his meaty hands.

Don't.

With appalling ease, the ink mage twisted. The snap was so loud, it made Brasley flinch even from across the chamber. His mouth fell open to scream.

"No!"

The brute's mouth twisted into a contemptuous grin as he let the limp body fall from his hands. Brasley watched it happen in slow motion, almost like she was floating, eyes closed, face peaceful, hair floating up around her. It was as if life had been some tremendous weight, and now that it was gone, her shell drifted down to the floor like a dry leaf.

Talbun's body hit with a dull thud that brought Brasley back to reality.

He turned without another thought, knocked Giffen out of the way, and ran full speed for the shimmering doorway. He dove for it, and even as he did, he saw that the surface was bubbling up again. Somebody else was coming through.

He saw the pretty face of a tall red-haired woman a split second before her eyes shot wide, and he slammed into her, his momentum carrying both of them back the other way.

Then there was a moment he felt like he was frozen in the center of a block of ice, not cold but immobile, like the entire world had stopped around him. In the next instant, Brasley felt like he was being pulled down a long hallway, stretched thin, and just when he was about to come apart, he popped out the other side, falling onto the red-haired women. He fell to the stone floor, looking up into the other gawking faces in the room, and immediately recognized Stasha Benadicta.

"Close it! Close it!" Brasley screamed. The redhead was trying to shove him off her, but he ignored her. "Close it now!"

Stasha's eyes shot wide. "Baron Hammish, what are you—"

"There's no time!" Brasley shouted. "He's coming! Close it now!"

Stasha made a violent gesture at a dark-skinned man Brasley had never seen before. "Do it!"

The man rushed forward and pulled a red gem from its housing at the top of the arch. Immediately, all of the other gems went dark. The shimmering portal vanished, leaving only the smooth stone wall.

Brasley fell back against the stone floor, a groaning sigh leaking out of him. "Thank Dumo."

And abruptly he started to cry.

♦ ♦ ♦

Ankar released his hold on the spirit. Steam rose from his sweat-slick skin. He'd drunk deeply from his spirit well but hadn't reached his limit. Many times he'd pushed himself further. He would again. He felt something coming. Something that would test him.

Ankar would need rest. The wizard bitch had sprung some surprises on him.

He kicked her limp form with the metal foot. Her head lolled to one side, eyes open and vacant. A shame. A good-looking bit of ass. But he was glad she was dead. One less dangerous thing to worry about.

Some slight noise drew his attention. His eyes narrowed, head cocked to listen.

It was coming from behind the great slab of a tomb.

Ankar circled the tomb and found him cowering up against it, a greasy nebbish of a man. He tapped into the spirit. Just a little more. Enough to finish off the straggler they'd left behind when the magical gateway had closed.

The man threw up a hand to fend him off, a gesture more of fear than defiance. "Please, no."

Ankar grabbed a fistful of the coward's robe and hauled him to his feet. "Calm yourself. I'll make it quick. It will only hurt for a second."

"Ankar, wait!"

The ink mage paused at the sound of his own name. He looked at the man, again reached back into his memory. Tapping into the spirit gave him perfect recall, and it only took him a fraction of a second to realize where he'd seen the man before. "Klaar. You were General Chen's puppet. He put a local in charge to help keep the native rabble in line. Giffen."

"Yes, exactly," Giffen said. "We're on the same side."

"I'm on my own side. Now make peace with whatever deity you prefer."

"No, please!" Giffen pleaded. "I can help. I can open the portal again. Let me serve you, and I can tell you many things. I am privy to many secrets. They can be yours."

Ankar considered. There was not a single thing pleasant about the man. It would probably be in service to the greater good to snap his neck and leave him here. On the other hand, Ankar sensed he was getting close to the end of a long journey, and the ending was still in doubt. Information could be helpful. And if the man really could make the portal work . . .

"Very well," Ankar said. "Talk."

CHAPTER THIRTY-THREE

Lugg was the master sergeant on duty at General Braxom's side door as the day slowly slid into evening. He stood atop the wall looking out at nothing at all, just empty countryside and forest. Empty was good. A lot better than a harborful of enemy ships. The regular army had to deal with that. As a city watchman, he had the easy duty on the northern wall.

Okay, that was sort of bullshit. There was no easy duty, not these days, but Sergeant Lugg had pulled some strings to get himself assigned to General Braxom's side door. He wasn't keen to face the brunt of the Perranese attack. He wasn't, frankly, keen to fight at all. Word had been spreading rapidly through the troops that the situation was hopeless.

Ten thousand ships? Fuck that.

The good thing about being assigned to the side door was that Lugg could make a quick escape if the Perranese topped the wall and overran the city. He had saddlebags packed and a horse picked out and set aside. Frankly, he was seriously contemplating cutting out before the attack began, but after fifteen years in the city watch, he didn't like the idea of everyone remembering him as a coward.

But ten thousand ships? Fuck. That.

"Corporal!"

A kid ten years his junior hurried to stand in front of him, snapping off a salute. "Sergeant?"

"Sundown in a few minutes," Lugg said. "Make sure the shift change goes smoothly. See to it, then report back."

"Yes, Sergeant." He saluted again and scurried away.

Lugg shook his head and laughed. Easy job.

Still, tomorrow or the next day. Soon. He'd need to quit the city. He'd been saving his pay for years. He'd head north, maybe west over the mountains.

A gleam coming out of the forest caught his eye, a flash of light from the setting sun on something metal. Lugg leaned out over the rampart, squinted. A line of mounted men in armor emerged from the tree line, twenty-five or thirty of them.

Shit.

The Perranese had circled around to attack the north wall. He knew he should have headed north when he had the chance. Now the whole fucking city was surrounded, and Lugg would have to work even harder to sneak away.

He drew breath to shout the alarm.

Then stopped himself.

They wore the armor of the Sherrik army and the ducal livery. It was one of the patrols returning. That puffed-up popinjay Urlik, Lugg guessed. The way they slumped in the saddle with their heads down, they obviously hadn't accomplished anything.

Relief flooded Lugg. Still, that fool Urlik today could be a legion of Perranese warriors tomorrow. Yeah, that decided it. Lugg would take off tomorrow. He'd make some excuse and ride out tomorrow and wouldn't look back.

He yelled down for the gate guard to lower the bridge and raise the portcullises. Urlik's patrol crossed single file, and when the last horse had entered the narrow tunnel into the city, Lugg ordered the bridge raised again.

He took the side stairs down from the wall to the courtyard to take Urlik's report, dispatch grooms for the horses.

In the courtyard, the patrol dismounted, none of them speaking. They were even more somber than they looked from a distance. Poor bastards having to follow that empty set of armor, Urlik. The man was all big talk. Just because he was from a prominent family, he thought he was a leader and a hero. Lugg found that to be a common error among the nobility.

Whatever. Not his problem.

The man wearing the officer's sash had his back to him, but it had to be Urlik. He approached, trying to summon an air of respect.

"Milord, how went the patrol?" Lugg asked.

Urlik turned, took two quick steps to close the distance, and jabbed a dagger into Lugg's throat.

Lugg opened his mouth to scream but . . . well . . . a dagger in the throat. Blood came out instead, dripping hot down his chin.

The man stabbing him wasn't Urlik. A foreign face. A sneer and an eye patch.

Lugg tried to fall down. That's what you did when you were being killed, right? You fell down. But two other soldiers had moved in to hold him up. Lugg just kept bleeding and bleeding but never fell down.

But he did die.

◆ ◆ ◆

"Don't let him fall," Yano said. "The ones on the wall will see."

The other soldiers held him up and walked him out of sight. Yano gave orders for men to sneak up the stairs and take out the guards on the wall. The rest made as if they were taking saddles off horses and securing gear. A few minutes later, one of his men signaled down into the courtyard. The other guards were dead.

"We have the side door and the inner courtyard," Yano told his men. "The sun will set completely in minutes, and then we'll lower the bridge and bring in the rest of the men."

"And then?" asked his second in command.

Yano grinned. "And then we take the city."

CHAPTER THIRTY-FOUR

The view from the throne platform was off-putting.

Looking up at the seven thrones had been one thing. Looking down the length of Sherrik's great hall from the same perch was another.

Rina decided she didn't like it. Her parents had been murdered before she'd been ready to be duchess. She'd been a child. She could see that now. Spoiled and safe, with no concept her world could ever be disturbed. But it had been—completely turned upside down. She'd been forced to grow up, to take responsibility. Had it really only been a few months? She looked back on the girl she'd been and almost couldn't recognize her.

But she didn't recognize the woman sitting to Duke Sherrik's right either. The little girl she used to be would have adored the silk dress of deep green, high collar, matching gloves. Emerald earrings. The duke had been generous with his hospitality. It surprised her how much she itched to get back into the black armor. Part of her hated it, hated the *need* for it. But what was she accomplishing sitting there on display in a pretty dress? Every moment she spent sitting idle seemed another moment closer to doom. The Perranese ships were nearly in position. Already troops disembarked and crowded the wharfs.

She didn't like sitting there on the platform, looking down at people. Didn't like sitting in one of the high seats with the duke, Maxus, and his advisors, and Bishop Hark too. It was an honor she didn't deserve. A responsibility she didn't want.

Get over it, she thought. *It's just a chair. So I don't like the view. So what? It will be over soon.*

The doors at the far end of the hall opened, and she nearly came out of her chair. She was that anxious. Eager.

A squad of the duke's personal guard in gleaming plate ushered in the small group. Too small. Maurizan had warned Rina that not all of the people she'd sent south had made it. Tosh walked beside a fierce-looking woman with a scar, one of his Birds of Prey, obviously. Behind them, Maurizan walked next to—

Alem.

Rina's heart slammed against the inside of her so hard that she actually reached up to touch the middle of her chest. She gulped a lungful of air to calm herself. Tears almost came to her eyes, but she willed them away. This wasn't the time, wasn't the place. No way would she allow herself to make a scene like some little girl.

But it's Alem. Alem!

She realized she was grinning like an idiot but didn't even try to stop herself.

He'd been in the sun, cheeks red, hair bleached a little lighter than she remembered. It seemed like decades since she'd seen him, held him. Why had he run away like that? Oh, yes. The nonsense with Gant. She'd explain. She'd fix it.

Alem!

The guards brought the small group before the platform, and Tosh bowed low, the other following his example.

"Your grace," Tosh said. "I know it's a time of war. No time to be letting strangers into your city, but you have. We thank you for this."

Simple words from a simple soldier, but Rina approved. Brasley would have stretched the speech out to five minutes with flowery talk.

The duke stood, and so did the others on the platform.

"You are most welcome," the duke said. "Duchess Veraiin is a friend to Sherrik, and as you are her people, then naturally our hospitality extends to . . ."

His voice faded to benign background chatter. All Rina could do was stare at Alem. He was real. He was alive. Why wouldn't he look at her?

When Rina finally did catch his eye, he didn't return the smile. He seemed nervous.

Something's wrong.

A knot of worry formed in her stomach.

Maurizan saw the exchange of glances, and defiance lit her eyes. She scooted closer to Alem, and her hand found his down at their sides. The gypsy girl held the hand tightly, possessively. Her mouth flattened into a tight line. The defiance in her eyes hardened to a challenge, as if to say, *Mine now. Just try to take him back.*

The worry in Rina's gut turned to a heavy, sick dread. This wasn't happening.

But it was.

Alem looked away. Embarrassed. But he didn't let go of Maurizan's hand.

"Duchess Veraiin?"

She started, realized the duke had been speaking to her. "Wha—" Words stuck in her throat. She swallowed hard, then said, "Your pardon, Emilio. I'm so happy to see my people, I was just lost in the moment."

"Of course," the duke said. "I thought you might like to address them."

Rina turned to Tosh and the others. She tried to force a smile to her face. She might as well have tried to lift a draft horse over her head. "Tosh, I want to thank you. I understand you've been through difficulties. That you've lost people because I asked you to do something for me. There's no time to thank you properly. No time to hear your story. But you have my promise if we live through this war, I'll think of a way to reward you."

Tosh opened his mouth as if to say something but then simply nodded.

"You've had a long journey. You're weary in probably too many ways to count," Rina said. "You need food and rest, and the duke has kindly offered you his hospitality. I think we all know there's hard work ahead, but for now, be at ease."

She titled her head toward the duke, pitched her voice low so only he could hear. "I need the gypsy girl, the red-haired one."

"Of course," the duke whispered back. "I have a place set aside. You can eat and drink with your friends and catch up on—"

"No," Rina said. "I mean, thank you, but there's no time. I need the girl. And Maxus. Let the others rest. But the gypsy found something, something that could help. Do you trust me, Emilio?"

He didn't hesitate. "I trust you."

"Then bring her to the wizard's workshop," Rina said. "And we'll see what Maxus can make of what she's brought us."

◆ ◆ ◆

The two ink mages sat glaring across the table at each other as Maxus read the scroll, his eyes slowly growing wider and wider. Rina didn't know the wizard well enough to get anything out of his reaction. Maybe he was pleased. Maybe frightened.

Maybe anything.

"This . . . this is amazing." Wonder and awe in Maxus's voice.

"What does it do?" Maurizan asked.

"Can you put it on us?" Rina asked at almost the same instant.

The two women shot each other hard looks.

The wizard's eyes came up from the scroll, landed briefly on the stencil and inkwell before looking at the women. "Before we proceed I feel I should say two things."

"Go on," Rina said evenly.

"The inkwell is small," Maxus said. "If I try this and botch it, there might not be enough ink for a second attempt."

Rina wanted to tell him just to try his best. That's all anyone can do. Instead she said, "So don't botch it."

Maxus cleared his throat, rubbed the back of his neck. "Uh . . . right. Good advice."

"What's the other thing?" Maurizan asked.

Rina shot her another look. *Why don't you keep your damn mouth shut and let me ask the questions here?* She hated her, hated the sight of her, hated the sound of her voice. She indulged in a brief fantasy where she leapt across the table and took Maurizan by the throat, choking the life out of her.

Except Maurizan had the Prime now too. She was an ink mage. Was she as strong as Rina, as fast? That Maurizan also had the Prime infuriated Rina as much as seeing her with Alem.

And that should be a warning sign, shouldn't it? Come on, act like a duchess. Act like an adult.

"The other thing," Maxus said, "is that such a small amount of ink makes it quite obvious I'll only be able to apply the tattoo once. To one of you." His eyes flitted back and forth between the two women, as if knowing this news would not elicit the happiest of responses.

Rina and Maurizan stared at each other for a long time. The gypsy girl wouldn't give in and returned Rina's hard look without flinching. Maybe Rina didn't blame her. How many hundreds of miles had Maurizan traveled, what had she gone through to recover these items that would give her a brand new tattoo? The woman across from her was an ink mage. There was nothing Rina could do that would intimidate her.

Rina relented, turned back to Maxus. "What does it do?"

"Ah." Maxus brightened as if comforted to be turning to another topic. "The tattoo is called the Breeze and the Gale. An inelegant translation but close enough. The tattoo goes on the back of your hand. It lets you control the winds."

"The winds?" Rina didn't immediately see how that was useful.

Maurizan's reaction was blunter. "What use is that?"

"Well, if you were becalmed at sea, you could fill the sails of your ship," Maxus said. "How far you could sail depends on the ink mage, I suppose."

"What do you mean?" Maurizan asked.

"Remember, these tattoos are fueled by the store of spirit within you," Maxus said. "One ink mage might be able to power it all day. Another perhaps only a few hours. I've studied ink magic for years, and one thing is clear: many of these tattoos are only as strong as what you put into them."

Maurizan nodded as if she understood.

But as Rina let the wizard's words sink in, she realized the gypsy didn't understand, not fully.

A long moment stretched, and then Rina said, "You have to give the tattoo to me."

"What?" Anger flared in Maurizan so brightly, it was almost as if there were heat coming off her. "Just like that? Because you say so?"

"You can't do what needs to be done."

Maurizan pinned Maxus with her eyes, half demanding, half pleading. "You can look at the ink and figure out what's in it, right? And then you can make enough for both of us."

Maxus scratched his chin, considering. "It's possible."

Maurizan turned back to Rina. "You see?"

"No."

"What's *wrong* with you?" Maurizan said. "You don't know what I went through to get that tattoo. And now you're just going to take it away?"

"Yes. Because I can use it better than you can. Because it's the only way."

"Fuck you!" Maurizan barely kept her fury in check. "It isn't fair. I'm the one who found it."

"You found it because I sent you to find it," Rina said. "You got the Prime. It's what your mother wanted for you. Whatever else you found was to come to me."

"That's because you stole the Prime from me. If Weylan—"

"If Maxus tries to duplicate the ink, it might work or it might not," Rina said. "Either way, I doubt he can do it fast. And if he fails, he might ruin the ink and then nobody gets the tattoo."

"It's true, I'm afraid." Maxus looked embarrassed to admit it.

"This is because of Alem, isn't it?" Maurizan squeezed her fists so tight, some of the knuckles cracked. "You just want to hurt me back."

Yes.

"No," Rina said. "The fact is you can't use this tattoo, not in a way that will make a difference. I can."

"How do you know?" An edge of desperation crept into Maurizan's voice. "How can you even say that?"

"Because"—Rina tugged the glove off her left hand, showed the palm to Maurizan, the skeletal tattoo, the mark of death—"I have one of these."

CHAPTER
THIRTY-FIVE

Maurizan watched from the shadowed alcove at the other end of the hall. How long had it been? Going on two hours maybe. It didn't matter. She'd wait forever if she had to.

A few minutes later, Rina Veraiin emerged from Maxus's workshop, pulling on her gloves. Maurizan pressed herself back against the stone wall of the alcove, but the duchess didn't even turn her way, heading instead for the stairway down.

A sigh eased out of Maurizan. She waited another minute, then went to the door and knocked.

Maxus opened the door almost immediately, maybe thinking it was Rina returning. The surprise was plain on his face when he saw it was Maurizan.

"I want you to put a tattoo on me," she told him.

"I'm sorry, child," Maxus said. "As I told you, there was only enough ink for one."

"I want to offer you a trade," she said.

"I'm listening."

"Not in the hall."

Maxus stepped aside, gestured she should enter.

She pulled a scroll case and stencil from the satchel around her shoulder. The scroll case was a glossy, jet black. She handed it to the wizard.

Maxus turned it over in his hands, handling it with reverence. "You kept this from her."

"I couldn't help but notice that the inkwell for this one is just as small as the other inkwell," Maurizan said.

"Yes, I suppose you're right," Maxus said. "Not enough for two."

She watched him open the scroll case with care and take out the rolled-up parchment. He read slowly, nodding, seeming intrigued.

He looked up at her. "You said something about a trade."

"Once you've put it on me, I won't need the scroll anymore. Nor the stencil either."

Maxus chewed his bottom lip, thinking. "But without ink . . ."

"You'll have time to figure out the ink," Maurizan said. "Are you a wizard or not?"

Maxus glanced back at the scroll in his hands, up again at Maurizan. He started nodding, decision made. "We'll need to wash your feet."

◆ ◆ ◆

Alem looked out the window, paced, returned to the window again. It would normally have been a spectacular view of Sherrik's harbor, the sea stretching beyond, so many lights twinkling in the darkness.

Too bad each of those pretty lights represents an enemy ship full of people who want to kill us, Alem thought.

And yet with ten thousand ships on the city's doorstep, there were other worries uppermost in his mind. Every time he remembered the look on Rina's face, it made him queasy. He couldn't help but think it had been unfair for her to see him with Maurizan suddenly like that.

His feelings for the gypsy girl were strong and real, but she had an undeniable vindictive streak, which had reared its ugly head at the exact wrong time. For days, Alem had felt like the injured party, knowing that Rina was arranging a marriage behind his back, but now he felt like he needed to find Rina and apologize.

He had been told she was busy.

So Alem had waited. He'd been given a chance to bathe. The duke's servants had brought him a new set of clothes, a black velvet doublet and matching breeches, high hard boots polished to a blinding shine. He'd probably never looked so good in his life, and with his new sword buckled around his waist, he thought he cut a rather dashing figure in the mirror.

He wished Maurizan could see him. But then he wished Rina could see him too.

Neither of the women was to be found.

So he'd gone to dinner with Tosh and Kalli. He'd almost mistaken Tosh for a lord. A shave and a new set of clothes had done wonders for the man, although he slouched around in the new garments as if he were embarrassed. Likewise, Kalli looked elegant in a green dress with lots of lace and a neckline that left little to the imagination. But her scar and gruff attitude kept wandering eyes from lingering on her cleavage for too long.

A number of the lesser local nobility had joined them for dinner. Mostly young men who fancied themselves heroic and had stayed to weather the siege. They displayed a uniform inability to recognize that he, Tosh, and Kalli simply wanted to dine in peace before retiring for a long sleep. They'd pressed the trio for stories of their adventures.

Tosh had scowled until they'd left him alone.

They'd decided to leave Kalli alone after the third son of a minor baron had tried to slide his hand up under her dress. A fork in the man's thigh had set him straight.

After much badgering, Alem had agreed to "regale them with a tale of his journeys," as they'd put it. He told them about being washed overboard and finding himself on a humped-up bit of rock in the ocean and then swimming to another island—only *slightly* bigger—and having to find food, water, and shelter and eventually discovering a magical sword.

They'd gone nuts at the words *magical sword* and had demanded to see the blade in question. Alem drew it from its scabbard and held it aloft to the appreciative cheers of the onlookers, who ordered an alarming number of wine pitchers so they could toast him appropriately. This was followed by many slaps on the back and compliments for the intrepid "Lord" Alem.

There was nothing Alem could do to disabuse them of calling him that. It was the first time Alem had heard Tosh laugh in days.

It had actually been a pleasant distraction. For a while.

Now Alem paced the room, pausing to look out the window.

He needed to talk to Rina.

He wanted to see Maurizan.

Where in blazes were they?

When he heard the knock at his door five minutes later, he almost broke his neck tripping over himself to open it.

Maurizan entered.

"Where have you been?" Alem demanded. "I've been waiting hours."

"You know what I found in the fortress was important. That wizard and Rina—" Then she broke off, looking Alem up and down. "Wow."

"They're just new clothes."

"You look like a lord."

Alem frowned. "Don't say that. What were you doing?"

"The tattoos were important," Maurizan said. "Never mind. I'm here now."

"I think I need to talk to Rina."

Maurizan's eyes narrowed. "What?"

"You saw how upset she was," Alem said. "I need to explain to her."

Maurizan put her arms around Alem's neck and pulled him close. "And who explained to *you* when she was finding a husband?"

"I just—"

"I just think you should remember what's right in front of you right now," she said. "I think I've been very patient."

One hand trailed down his chest, started to unbutton his doublet. She leaned in, kissing him softly on the lips. She finished with the buttons, slipped a hand inside his doublet and ran it over his chest. Her next kiss was firmer, and with the next she slipped her tongue into his mouth.

Alem's arms went around her, pulling her body against his. She felt him grow stiff through his pants.

Her hands fell to the laces of his breeches, frantically tugging them loose. "*Very* patient."

They pulled at each other's clothing desperately. Alem lifted Maurizan's shirt over her head and tossed it aside. He bent his head down and took a nipple into his mouth, sucking sharply. She gasped, ran fingers through his hair. She grabbed a fistful of it and moved his head over to her other breast so he could suck that one.

She hooked her thumbs into her breeches and pushed them down, grabbed Alem's hand and pulled him to the bed. He kicked off the rest of his clothing and crawled in between her legs, kissed her stomach. He kissed lower and she gasped, a shiver rolling through her body.

"Come up here," she said. "Come on."

She rested one of her ankles on his shoulder, reached down and guided him inside.

He pushed inside, so slowly at first. Then he rocked back and forth, picked up speed, found a rhythm.

"Alem." Her voice was hoarse. She closed her eyes. "Alem."

He leaned down, kissed her hard on the mouth, thrusting faster, his body trembling.

Her body began to shake. "Alem." She arched her back, thrusting her hips to meet him. "Alem!"

He shuddered, grunting.

She wrapped her legs around him, finishing next, tears running from the corners of her eyes. "Alem, I love you."

◆ ◆ ◆

They lay next to each other, tangled in the sheets. Maurizan on her belly, hugging a pillow, Alem next to her, trailing a finger down her spine. The tattoos were exactly the same as Rina's and yet looked completely different on Maurizan. Maurizan's skin was different. Her back and hips were different.

Alem kissed her on the hip. Her legs were different too. He kissed them.

She giggled. "What are you doing?"

He kept kissing down the length of her, kissed her ankle. He took her by the heel, lifted her foot, and kissed her toes. She sighed.

He looked at the top of her foot. There was a tattoo there. The same tattoo on top of her other foot also.

"How long have these been here?"

"Something I found deep in the old fortress," Maurizan said. "Before you saved me."

He ran his hands lightly over each tattoo. The skin was smooth and soft, as if the tattoos had always been there.

"Do you like them?" she asked.

He looked closer, realized there was some trick to them. At first, the tattoo looked like an image of swirling smoke. But when Alem turned her foot one way or the other, the smoke gelled into a figure of a person in a robe, hood up to hide the face, his pose a stealthy crouch. When he turned the foot again, the image dissolved back into smoke.

"That's incredible," Alem said. "Rina doesn't have these. I would have seen."

"Do you really think I want to hear about which of Duchess Veraiin's body parts you've seen?"

"Sorry. What do they do?"

"Maxus says the tattoos are called the Phantom Walker. They're supposed to let me—"

Somebody shouted something just outside the door. It was followed by the jangle of metal, like men running in armor.

Alem sprang from the bed and pulled on his breeches. "Something's happening."

"Go look."

Alem threw open the door. Men rushed down the hall, hastily buckling on armor and sword belts with a palpable sense of urgency.

"What's happening?"

One of the men turned to shout back at him without pausing. "It's started! The Perranese are assaulting the harbor wall!"

Alem turned back to Maurizan. "It's started."

She'd already pulled on her clothes. "Get dressed." She belted on her daggers and grabbed her boots.

Alem reached for his doublet. "Okay, after we're dressed, then what?"

"Damned if I know," Maurizan said. "But if there's a war, I'm sure they'll find something for us to do."

CHAPTER
THIRTY-SIX

General Thorn watched the assault from his flagship, moored just beyond bow range.

Preparations had taken far too long. The ships with the assault gear had fallen behind on the crossing and had arrived last. By normal standards, the wharves and docking facilities were huge, no surprise for a port city like Sherrik, but for landing fifty thousand fighting men, support units, gear, and supplies, the place got very crowded very fast. The docks roiled with chaotic activity, officers screaming into the turmoil, trying to bring some kind of order to the mess.

At last, the companies had been organized and order established. The blare of multiple horns rolling over the wharves sounded the charge, and the troops with the scaling ladders ran screaming for the walls, covered by several companies of bowmen. A flight of arrows returned from the men on the wall, taking a tithe of death from the Perranese troops.

In some ways, Thorn had been fortunate. Sherrik had enjoyed such rich trade with so many other lands for so long that the notion of siege had only been addressed as an afterthought. The walls were high and strong, but they had no catapults or ballistae that could harass the ship from the walls.

A junior officer ran across the deck to intercept him, red faced and puffing. He looked barely old enough to shave. Probably his first action. He snapped off a smart salute.

"Report," Thorn told him.

"A signal from the battering-ram squad," the boy said. "They are in position."

"Is it really a better choice than assaulting one of the landside gates?" Thorn mused out loud, but already knew the answer.

The junior officer took it as a real question. "The engineers assure us the landside gates are thicker and much stronger and better defended." He pointed across the waterfront at the knot of men making their way to the last gate all the way to the right of the harbor wall. "The gate on the far end is the best choice. The bulwark overhangs there, making it difficult for the archers to target the area below."

Thorn almost told him he knew all of this already but let it go. The boy was nervous.

"Tell them to proceed," Thorn said.

The officer saluted again and ran off, shouting at the men with the signal flags.

A few minutes later, Thorn heard the iron-capped battering ram strike, a low booming sound that echoed across the harbor.

Thorn smiled, wondering what it must sound like within the city.

It sounded like a long, lazy clap of thunder rolling slowly down the empty city street, Yano thought.

He grinned. Good. That meant the assault had started. Yano had hoped to bump into a Perranese patrol before infiltrating the city so he could coordinate with whoever was in charge. Never mind. He'd improvise. And when the leadership found out what he'd done in aid of the battle, maybe they'd make him an officer. Shit, maybe they'd even grant him a lordship.

He chuckled to himself.

Yano was surprised how far they'd penetrated the city without being spotted. Usually a couple hundred armored men stood out. Most of Sherrik's troops were on the walls, and an alarming number of citizens had fled. The ones who hadn't had shut themselves in their homes . . . probably now wishing they *had* fled.

It also helped that a platoon of his men still wore the Sherrik armor and livery. He sent them ahead to scout, making sure they had a clear path.

He glimpsed the ducal pyramid between buildings. They were almost there. He'd send the men in the stolen livery ahead to scout, but Yano could guess the situation. They'd probably sent nearly every available man to the walls, leaving only a token house guard.

In which case Yano would very soon take over management of the place.

◆ ◆ ◆

Sarkham watched the company of men double-time it out of the palace gates and turn toward the harbor. That left maybe a score of men from the palace guard to mind the ducal pyramid. Not that it mattered. If the walls held, then they were secure enough. If not, then it wouldn't make any difference how many men they had.

In fact, Sarkham had earlier approached the duke in a private moment and as tactfully as possible suggested that plans for escaping the city should be made so the duke could get safely away if the city fell. The duke had brashly declared he would not take any action that projected cowardice. Sarkham pointed out that if everyone were dead, then nobody would be around to judge him—although he phrased it more diplomatically.

Duke Sherrik had relented, telling Sarkham he could make whatever plans eased the guard captain's mind. And Sarkham had made plans. Quietly. Discreetly. The duke was confident the city would stand.

The rhythmic boom of the distant battering ram told a different story.

CHAPTER THIRTY-SEVEN

Bedlam had erupted in the halls of the ducal palace.

Servants waffled between fulfilling their normal duties and finding places to hide. The young nobles who'd been staying at the palace as the duke's guests vacillated between strapping on swords and pretending they couldn't find them. And so the chaos was split into two camps: make ready for war or find a way to escape.

Rina stood amid the tumult, second-guessing her choice. Black armor. Rapier at her side. Two-handed sword strapped to her back. She was ready for battle but would have preferred hopping on a horse and riding away from Sherrik as fast as possible.

But I can't do that. People here are counting on me. People I care about.

She felt a sharp pang thinking of Alem. But there was also Tosh and Hark and an entire city full of people. There was more than that too.

She looked down at her hands, black gloves hiding tattoos. The new one Maxus had just applied and the skeletal hand of the death cult. She thought of Krell, the priest of Mordis. His words haunted her: *The southern path pays a debt.*

She tried to thread her way between the frenzied people in the hall. It was like trying to get through the market at high hour with an armload of produce.

Fuck it.

Rina tapped into the spirit.

She zigged and zagged between people as if they were statues and then flew down the stairs hardly touching them. On the third landing down, she stopped abruptly when she saw a guardsman with an officer's plume in his helmet, startling a gasp out of him.

"Where's the duke?" she asked.

"Apologies, your grace, but I don't know."

"Sarkham, then."

"Five minutes ago, he was in the courtyard, dispatching troops."

Rina flew down the stairs, dodging wide-eyed people, until she slammed to a sudden stop in a cloud of dust in the courtyard. He spotted the guard captain. "Sarkham!"

He jogged toward her. "Your grace."

"I need Emilio. Now."

"I'm sorry, your grace," Sarkham said. "He's gone with a squad of his personal guard to the harbor wall. He felt he needed to be there with his men."

"Send a runner for him," Rina said. "I have something to tell him, which might change the entire battle."

Sarkham hesitated, the conflict clear on his face. He didn't want to disobey a duchess, but he clearly didn't believe his master wanted to be pulled off the wall in front of all his men just as a battle was starting.

Being tapped into the spirit didn't bless Rina with additional intelligence or special knowledge, but it did let her think clearly, allowed her to clear the clutter from her mind and focus on the problem at hand with cold logic. Out of respect for her position, Sarkham would heed her requests . . . up to a certain point. He wasn't blind to the duke's shortcomings, but he was the sort of man who'd be loyal to a fault. He'd obey the duke even if ordered to charge a score of Perranese warriors with nothing but a gentleman's blade.

Rina needed some way to sway him, and the battle had already started.

"We can't win this battle with the men we have. I'm sure the men of Sherrik are brave. I'm sure they're ready to fight with everything they have. But it's not going to be enough. I think you know that." And now came the lie. "The duke explicitly told me to send for him if I found some other way to win. He *told* me to send for him."

The songbird tattoo at her throat flared hot and tingled. Rina had to fight hard to keep the surprise off her face.

What just happened?

Sarkham said, "At once, your grace." He turned and shouted, "Runner!"

A young man in light leather armor shot over and stood at attention in front of Sarkham. "Go to the harbor wall and fetch the duke back immediately. It's of the highest priority, and the fate of the entire city is at stake."

The runner saluted and sprinted away at top speed.

The tattoo. It made this happen somehow.

She realized Sarkham was looking at her, waiting for her to speak again.

"Are there dungeons below the palace?"

"Yes, your grace."

"Filled with criminals?" Rina asked. "Murderers? Rapists?"

"Some, yes."

"You need to go get them," Rina said. "And bring them to the top of the palace."

Sarkham frowned.

"The duke ordered this," Rina said. "And I need you to obey."

The songbird tattoo tingled again.

Lies. The tattoo works when I lie.

"At once, your grace!"

Sarkham barked the orders to bring the criminals up from the dungeons.

And even tapped into the spirit, Rina couldn't fend off a chill, knowing that her plan would come with a price, understanding with sick certainty she'd taken an irreversible step into the darkness.

CHAPTER THIRTY-EIGHT

"This way!"

Alem led Maurizan through the frantic hallways of the palace, pulling her along by one hand. He didn't want to let her go, didn't want to risk losing her in the crowd.

"Where are you going?" Maurizan shouted.

"I don't know."

"Who are you looking for?"

"I don't know."

Maurizan squeezed his hand and tugged him to a stop. The crowd flowed around them.

"Maybe some kind of plan," Maurizan suggested.

"I thought getting out of here as fast as possible was a pretty good plan," Alem said.

"Out of where?" Maurizan asked. "The palace? Then what?"

If the situation hadn't been so dire, the blank look on Alem's face would have been comical. "Well . . . uh . . . out of the city?"

"You mean out of the sealed city I busted my ass getting us *into*?"

"Uh . . ."

"We can't catch a ship, for obvious reasons, and even if we could get out of the city, we don't have horses," Maurizan said. "Want to take another stab at that plan, champ?"

"Tosh," Alem said. "He'll know what to do."

"Sold."

They weaved their way back through the throng to Tosh's door. Alem had raised his hand to knock when the door suddenly swung inward. Tosh stood there, strapping on a studded bracer. He wore a gleaming steel breastplate with chain mail underneath. A long sword belted to one side, a long dagger on the other. Shin and thigh plates. A simple helm that came down below his ears but without a face guard.

"Good," Tosh said. "You're here."

"Where'd you get the gear?" Alem asked.

"Asked for it. Ah, here's Kalli."

The girl came down the hall toward them, outfitted the same way as Tosh, her hair spilling from under her helm. The only difference was that she carried the curved Perranese-style sword. She'd trained with it.

"I thought we'd got out of here but—" Alem began.

Maurizan talked over him. "—I reminded him the city was *sealed*—"

"—but if we could get some horses—"

"—as if the army is just going to let you take some of their horses—"

"Hey," Tosh said calmly. "Shut up."

They shut up.

"Follow me," Tosh said. "And keep it tight. Kalli, bring up the rear."

Kalli's hand fell to her sword hilt, chin up, eyes bright. "You got it, boss."

"It's pretty crazy out there," Alem told him.

"See how shiny this armor is?" Tosh said. "Watch and learn."

Tosh waded into the crowd and bellowed, "One side! Make a hole."

Everyone moved.

Tosh didn't run. He acted exactly as if he knew where he was going, marching steadily with purpose but not in a panicked hurry. It was almost a relief to the onlooking rabble. At least *somebody* seemed to know what he was doing. Alem, Maurizan, and Kalli fell in behind him, matching his stride.

They made their way down and out of the palace in this fashion, Tosh clearing a path with shouts and grand gestures.

The courtyard just inside the gates was as chaotic as the inside of the palace had been. Grooms pulled horses out of the way as a column of men marched through the gates. Duke Sherrik scowled at the front of them.

Tosh spotted Captain Sarkham jogging across the courtyard to meet the duke.

Tosh looked over his shoulder at the others. "We need Sarkham. He's the only one around here with his head screwed on right."

He led the others to Sarkham but pulled up short when he realized the duke was raking the man over the coals.

"How dare you call me back from the harbor wall!" Duke Sherrik shouted. "Don't you know the battle's begun? Can't you hear it, you fool?"

The dull boom of the battering ram echoed across the city.

To Sarkham's credit he stood straight, met the duke's eyes, although his face looked pained and confused. "I was simply obeying your orders, your grace."

"Orders?" Sherrik's face grew red.

"Duchess Veraiin," Sarkham said. "She said you left orders to—"

"Damn the woman! What's she done?"

"I don't know, your grace. She claimed some scheme to aid in the battle, but I don't—"

The duke looked past Tosh. "Lord Alem, do you know anything about this?"

"I'm not really—" *Forget it. No time.* "I don't know, your grace. But if she has something in mind, I think you need to trust her."

The duke rubbed his chin, clearly not liking the situation. "Where is she now?"

"The top of the palace, your grace," Sarkham said.

"The top of the . . . ? Damn the woman. Damn her eyes. Sergeant Larz!"

A burly man in the duke's livery rushed forward, coming to attention in front of the duke. "Your grace."

"Send your fastest runner to the top of the palace," Sherrik said. "If Duchess Veraiin is there, ask her to join me immediately. Be respectful but insist."

Larz saluted. "As you command, your—"

An arrow sprouted from his neck with a *thip*, and Larz's eyes went wide. He opened his mouth to scream, and blood foamed out.

"Alarm!" somebody yelled.

Larz twitched and fell in a clamor of armor, pawing at the arrow in his neck, blood squirting from the wound.

"Protect the duke!" Sarkham shouted.

But already men were drawing swords and moving to surround Sherrik.

Alem drew his sword, felt himself jostled by the sudden rush of soldiers.

Maurizan grabbed his arm. "Stay close to me."

Alem looked to the gate. Perranese warriors poured through by the score. The single line of armored troops in Sherrik livery wouldn't hold them for more than a few seconds.

"Withdraw to the palace!" Sarkham's voice. "The palace!"

The crush of bodies shifted, men in armor trying to push past. Alem was knocked to the ground.

Maurizan dragged him back to his feet. "Come on!"

Alem risked a glance behind him.

The tide of Perranese slammed into the line of the duke's men, weapons falling, rising red again and trailing blood on the next swing.

Men screamed and fell. The battle crowded the courtyard as more enemies poured through the gate. Men slipped in blood as they tried to find footing. They stabbed, slashed, hacked. The duke's men fought hard, but the Perranese pushed past with sheer numbers.

Alem felt somebody grab a fistful of his doublet, and he was shoved in with the rest of the people trying to crowd up the steps and through the front doors of the palace. He bounced off one armored body and into another, and when Maurizan pulled him from the press of bodies, he looked up to see he was back inside the palace.

Duke Sherrik leaned against a wall, panting, sword in his hand and a brace of guards on either side of him. "Get those bloody doors closed!"

Men rushed to push them shut. Two others waited with a thick, heavy length of wood to bar it.

Between the closing doors, Alem saw the Perranese charging up the steps to the palace, screaming war cries, weapons held high.

Oh no. This is going to be close.

The enemy troops slammed into the other side of the door before the duke's men could close it, reaching into the gap to hack and jab with swords. The duke's men jabbed back through the crack, drawing screams and blood. The guards at the duke's side rushed forward to help shove the doors closed, leaning their shoulders into it and grinding teeth with the effort.

"Shut them, damn you!" screamed the duke. "Put your backs into it!"

Arrows flew through the crack, clattering against the wall over Alem's head. He flinched, cursing, and looked around until he saw what he wanted.

"Follow me," Alem told Maurizan. "Hurry!"

"Where are we going?"

"I think there are stairs this way," he said. "Rina's at the top of the palace."

Maurizan hesitated. "So?"

Tosh rushed past them. "He's right. I don't know what she's doing, but she might need help."

Maurizan's eyes flashed annoyance, but she followed without complaint.

They found the stairs, and the three of them stormed upward, blades in hands, ready for anything. By the time they reached the third floor, they were puffing and red faced, but kept going. The halls were deserted now, debris littering the floors, evidence of hasty, panicked departures. The palace's inhabitants had found either places to hide or a back way out.

They were winded by the time they made it to the top, where a wide veranda circled the entire floor. Alem went to one knee, leaning on his sword and panting heavily. Back outside, the thump of the battering ram reached them clearly.

Tosh and Maurizan went to the balustrade, looked down at the harbor.

"Look at that," Maurizan said breathlessly. "You're a soldier. Have you ever seen anything like that?"

Tosh shook his head. "Little skirmishes. Border bandits. Nothing like that."

Perranese warriors swarmed the harbor wall like insects, climbing hundreds of assault ladders. The duke's men raced along the battlements, shoving the ladders back, but here and there Perranese topped the walls. Pockets of fighting broke out. Perranese packed the wharves below, standing shoulder to shoulder, tens of thousands of them waiting to storm up the ladders or charge through the gates once the battering ram had done its work.

"The harbor wall will fall and then the inner wall and then the city," Tosh said. "This is hopeless."

Alem stood, looked up at the platform that topped the palace, ducal banners hung from poles, and there was a large brazier for lighting signal fires. To the right of the brazier, a huge horn rested in a large stone cradle. Alem realized it was made from some enormous animal horn, banded in brass. He didn't know what animal, but he would not have wanted to meet one. The sailors on the *Witch of Kern* had told him stories of great horned whales. The bell of the horn was as high as Alem was tall and faced the harbor. The horn ran down along the cradle and curved back up, a brass mouthpiece the perfect height to blow.

Rina stood next to it.

"Rina!" Alem ran up the narrow stairway to the top of the platform.

He stopped ten feet from her. She faced the harbor, watching the battle unfold.

"Rina?"

Rina turned, expression calm. "I was hoping you were Captain Sarkham."

"Oh?" Alem wasn't sure what to say to that. "He was in the courtyard when the Perranese attacked. I haven't seen him. I don't know if he made it." Many of the duke's men had fallen. Alem had no idea whether the captain was still alive.

Silence stretched between them. The din of battle and the slow drumbeat of the battering ram rose from the harbor.

"Do you love her?" Rina asked.

Alem felt his throat tighten.

He'd been so angry when he'd seen her with Ferris Gant, heard their talk of marriage. He'd been hurt beyond his ability to express. She'd done that to him. Rina. The woman he'd trusted most in the world.

And yet looking at her now, he felt an overwhelming urge to apologize. To beg forgiveness, to insist he'd have done anything to not have hurt her.

"I . . ." He groped for words. Failed.

"Never mind." A wan smile. "I mean, I suppose we have bigger worries." She made an offhanded gesture to the thousands of enemy ships below.

Alem swallowed hard.

Tosh and Maurizan stood together; they'd turned from the battle to look up at Rina. He shouted up at them. "Duchess Veraiin!"

"I need Sarkham!" Rina shouted back. "I sent him on an errand. It's urgent."

Tosh shrugged. "I don't know. It's chaos down there. He could be anywhere."

"Well, that's it, then." She said it quietly enough that only Alem could hear. "There goes the city."

"There must be another way out of the palace," Alem said.

"And then what?" Rina asked. "If Sherrik falls, the Perranese will roll north with nothing to stop them between here and the capital."

"But . . . the king. His armies."

"Damn the king." There was little heat in her words, only defeat. "Damn all of them."

"That's it, then?" Maurizan had come up the stairs behind Alem, Tosh in tow. "You're just going to quit? The mighty ink mage. Don't make me laugh."

"What do you want me to do?" She'd said it calmly, but the muscles in her jaw tightened.

"*Try!*"

"Fucking try yourself!" Rina flared. "You're an ink mage now. It's what you've always wanted, isn't it? You think it makes you a god, that you have the answers for *everything*? Can do *anything*? You're in for a rude awakening, girl. If I had unlimited power, do you think I'd have let you—"

She cut herself off, looking away, cursing under her breath.

Alem opened his mouth to say something.

Maurizan shot him a look. "Don't."

He shut his mouth.

Maurizan pointed at Alem but addressed Rina. "*He* told us to come up here, said you had a plan. Maybe I don't have faith in you, but he does. So do a lot of other people. The least you can do is to tell them what you thought you were doing up here."

"Yes, Duchess. By all means."

They all turned to look at Duke Sherrik staggering up the stairs.

"Please. Tell us what you had in mind." The duke bled from his side, down his left leg. His once gaudy and gleaming armor was black with soot, streaked red with blood. He held his sword, the blade slick with gore. The left half of his face was charred black with burns, hair singed on the same side. He winced in pain with each step but kept coming, the fire of fury burning in his eyes.

"After all," he said. "You called me away from the wall, my men. Are you really going to tell me it was for *nothing*? That I fought my way up here for *nothing*?" He winced again as pain lanced through his side.

Tosh stepped forward to help him. "Your grace."

The duke waved him away. "Don't touch me."

"What happened?" Rina asked.

Sherrik gestured to the burned side of his face with a bloodred hand. "What? This? The third floor of the palace is on fire. Can't you smell it?"

Alem had smelled it earlier but had thought it something from the battle. "How?"

"Because I *ordered* it," the duke said. "We couldn't get the door closed. The Perranese bastards overran us. We know the layout of the palace. They don't. The fire won't block every passage, but it will slow their progress."

"Then we're trapped up here," Tosh said.

"An astute observation," Sherrik said dryly. "My men and I could have made our way to another stairway and a back exit, but I was told *this bitch*"—he pointed at her with his bloody sword for emphasis—"was implementing some grand scheme on top of the palace to win the battle. Well, Duchess? What miracle have you conjured for us?"

Rina sighed. She stuck a chuma stick in her mouth but had no way to light it. She rolled it from one side of her mouth to the other. "I didn't like you at first, Emilio. A spoiled little duke playing with his toy soldiers. But I think you're okay really. I think you would have been a good duke if you'd lived long enough to grow up."

The duke's face twisted with rage. "You stupid little—"

All heads turned at the rusty squeal of hinges. A hatch opened across the rooftop, black smoke coming up from the opening.

Alem gripped his sword tighter, palms sweaty on the hilt. *This is it. The Perranese have found a way up.*

A battered, blood-spattered person emerged from the hatchway. Sarkham. He was smudged black, and one side of his head was bloody where he was missing an ear. He coughed as he cleared the hatch, gulping for fresh air, and then turned to beckon the next man out.

The next man wore rags, leg irons and chains, wrist manacles. So did the next three.

"Hurry!" Sarkham shouted down the hatchway. "Move your asses, you lazy sons of bitches, or burn alive for all I care."

The duke turned and hobbled back down the stairs, cursing and wincing with each step as he made for Sarkham. The others followed.

"Captain!" Sherrik barked. "What is this?"

"Prisoners up from the dungeon, your grace."

"Care to explain why?"

A dozen prisoners had come through the hatch, and there appeared to be more on the way.

"Duchess Veraiin's orders," Sarkham said.

The duke wheeled on Rina, trembling with barely controlled rage. "Compliments on your kindheartedness, Rina, but would you like to tell me why saving cutthroats and rapists is a priority at this particular moment?"

"I'm not saving them," she said.

The prisoners lay around the open hatch, coughing and gasping for air, at least twenty of them now. The next man through the hatch was a soldier in the livery of the palace guard.

"Who's behind you?" Sarkham asked.

"Just one more," the soldier said.

"Can the Perranese get through?"

"No chance," said the soldier. "It's an inferno back there."

The soldier climbed out. The last man up was a large, barrel-chested man, wearing a once-bright suit of full plate armor, now streaked and smudged with blood and grime. He held a mace dripping red. He slammed the hatch shut again.

Rina's face brightened, and she ran to him. "Bishop Hark!"

She threw herself on him, hugging, her face against the dirty breast-plate of his armor. He hugged back best he could with one hand.

"Glad you're not dead," she said.

"Never without permission from your grace."

She smiled up at him. "How did you happen to fall in with Sarkham?"

"Frankly, I was a bit lost," Hark said. "I donned my armor when everything started happening. The palace was in an uproar, and nobody seemed to be able to find anyone else. I ran into Captain Sarkham and one of his men supervising these prisoners and thought he could use some company."

Sarkham laughed. "Some company, the man says. A pack of screaming Perranese descended upon us, and if it hadn't been for the bishop wading in with that mace of his, we'd all be dead."

Hark smiled down at Rina. "I heard you had some scheme to save us all. Poor gratitude if I didn't fight my way up here to help."

Rina's smile fell.

Alem was close enough to hear what Rina said next even though she whispered.

"I think I have a way," Rina said. "Pray to Dumo for my soul."

Confusion clouded the bishop's face. "Your grace?"

Rina stepped away from him, turned to Sarkham, her expression iron. "Captain, please line the prisoners up at the foot of the stairs to the platform."

Sarkham hesitated, his eyes flicking to the duke.

Emilio Sherrik staggered back into the conversation. He looked pale, had lost a lot of blood, hair matted with sweat. He was near to collapse, but his anger was still ready to boil over.

"Wait just a bloody minute," the duke said. "I give the orders here."

He's only partly angry with Rina, Alem thought. *He hates that he's helpless.*

"I demand you explain what's happening right fucking now!" the duke bellowed.

Rina took three quick strides and grabbed the shoulder strap of the duke's breastplate, yanking him close. If her chuma stick had been lit, it might have burned him.

"I can beat them. I can do it," she said. "But every second I'm trying to explain to you is a second away from doing it. You understand? And even if I did explain what I'm about to do, you might never sleep another night all the way through again. Listen. I need your help. So shut up your fucking whining and help me. Can you do that? Can you be a man instead of a boy and help me?"

Alem almost felt sorry for the man.

Miraculously, the duke pulled himself together. "Promise me," he said. "Promise me you can do it."

"I promise," she said, releasing him. "But I meant what I said. I need you."

"Tell me what to do."

"Keep them off me," she said. "I don't know how long it will take me, but you have to keep the Perranese at bay."

The duke smiled slowly, his upper lip trembling, sweat beading on his forehead. He was obviously in pain and just as obviously trying to hide it. Dumo damn it, Alem admired him. Didn't *like* him, but admired him.

"I'll hold them," the duke said. "My men are guarding the south door on the level below. They won't get through us. I swear to you."

"One more thing," Rina said. "Is there a way to call your men back from the harbor wall?"

"Call them back? The Perranese will overrun—"

"Is there a way or not, Emilio?"

"I don't have any flagmen with me to send a signal, but . . ." His eyes drifted to the great horn on the platform. "The signal for general retreat is a long blast followed by two short blasts, then another long blast. They're good men, trained. They'll retreat properly, not some panicked rout."

"And I'll need Captain Sarkham," Rina said. "To manage the prisoners."

The duke shifted his gaze to the ragged men lying around the roof in chains. His expression made it clear he didn't want to know. "Sarkham is yours."

The duke turned to go, and Bishop Hark fell in behind him.

"I'll stand with you, your grace," Hark said. "There's no work for my mace up here."

Tosh nudged Kalli. "You ready to get to work?"

Kalli drew her sword, her grin making her look predatory. "Right behind you, boss."

They jogged after the bishop.

"Me too." Maurizan's hands fell to the hilts of her daggers. "Let's see what an ink mage can do."

Alem looked down at the faintly glowing sword in his hand.

"No," Rina said. "I need you here, Alem."

Maurizan's eyes narrowed. "What?"

"You know he's no good with a sword," Rina said. "And I'm going to need help."

The gypsy thought about it.

Maurizan went to Alem, grabbed him by the doublet, and pulled him close, planted a hard kiss on his lips. "I'll see you later."

She shot Rina a last defiant look, then ran off after Hark and the others.

"Sarkham."

"Your grace?"

"Keep the prisoners in line at the base of the platform," Rina told him. "When the time comes, I'm going to want you to bring them up one at a time. If they all see what I'm doing, they'll riot."

Sarkham almost asked but stopped himself. He didn't want to know either. He moved away to organize the prisoners.

"What do you want me to do?" Alem asked her.

"When I signal you, I'll need you to sound the retreat," Rina said. "You heard the duke. A long blast, two short ones, and another long."

"That's what you need me for? To blow a horn?" Alem gripped his sword tight enough to turn his knuckles white. Everyone else was fighting. *Maurizan* was fighting. Alem didn't want to be in a battle, but if he just stood around waiting to blow a horn he'd feel like a coward.

But she's right. I'm not trained with this sword. I can swing this sword around like a club, but I don't really know what I'm doing.

"Alem." She put a hand on his shoulder, tentative, as if wondering whether she still had permission to touch him. "I need somebody I can trust at my back. Just so I know I'm not alone. I know things are different now, but . . ." She cleared her throat, looked away for a moment, nervously. "Something's going to happen, Alem. And afterward, you're not going to be able to look at me in the same way. I wanted to say I still . . . I wanted to say I'm sorry."

She let her hand drop from his shoulder.

Alem wanted to ask her about it. Maybe if she explained. Maybe he could help somehow. Maybe . . .

"I'm here for you," Alem said.

She nodded, a brief smile lighting her face for a moment. Then she turned and headed up the stairs to the platform. Alem took a deep breath and followed.

Rina stood atop the platform between the brazier and the great horn, looking down at the battle, her face impassive. Alem stood behind her. Thousands of men still fought for possession of the harbor wall. The boom of the battering ram continued. It seemed impossible the gates could hold much longer.

"Well. I wonder if this has ever been tried before."

Rina tugged off one of her gloves, and Alem saw the tattoo on the back of her hand. A cloud with a stylized face, cheeks puffing as it blew a long stream of wind.

She slowly held the hand aloft, fingers spread, as if she were defying the sky itself.

At first, nothing happened. Then slowly Alem felt it, the wind kicking up behind him, blowing past and out to sea. It made Rina's short hair flutter. A few seconds later, a gust almost knocked him off his feet. Gray clouds gathered overhead.

A minute later the gray clouds turned black, blotting out the sun. The bright day had dimmed almost to night. The wind rose again, buffeting them constantly at the top of the platform. The banners rippled and snapped.

Alem looked down and saw whitecaps forming on the water. Some of the smaller ships were beginning to feel the effect.

"Better blow the horn," Rina said. "They'll need time."

Her voice startled him. She sounded so strange, distant.

Alem went to the horn, stood at the mouthpiece. His mouth felt suddenly dry. He licked his lips, turned his head, and spit.

Then he took a deep breath and sounded the retreat.

CHAPTER
THIRTY-NINE

The falcon dove low, flying along the harbor wall.

Rina saw through Zin's eyes, close enough to see both battle rage and abject terror on the faces of the men. Screams of rage and pain. She smelled the blood and sweat, bowels loosened in the throes of death.

The duke's men looked up at the sound of the great horn from the top of the palace.

Get out of there, Rina thought. *Hurry!*

The duke had spoken true when he'd said the men were well trained. Squads formed to hold off the Perranese atop the wall as others made a quick and orderly retreat down the inward stairways. Many were already running at a full sprint across the market grounds and through the gates of the inner wall.

I hope that's enough. I hope the inner wall saves them.

When it was time for the rear guard to turn and flee, archers covered their retreat. The men of Sherrik were disciplined and skilled, but hundreds of them were cut down as they fled.

She told Zin to fly out across the harbor.

The ships had been caught by surprise, the typhoon winds seeming to come out of nowhere. Crews scurried across the decks, pulling on lines, and sailors crawled through the rigging.

A wave lifted one of the smaller ships and dashed it down again against the stone wharf, a span of the hull cracking and splintering like kindling. It listed away, taking on water and then bobbing on waves. The crew scrambled to save it, but it was obviously hopeless.

She'd seen enough. She told Zin to get to safety, then released her hold on him.

Rina blinked and was back on the platform atop the ducal palace.

She stood with her legs spread, braced rock steady against the howling wind. One arm still raised as she continued to summon the storm, building it stronger with each passing second.

Just as she'd predicted, her store of spirit had already nearly exhausted itself. The tattoo that controlled the winds behaved just like the others. The more she asked of it, the faster it drained spirit.

The moment Rina had been dreading had come at last.

She turned back to Alem, who was waiting patiently, wind pulling at his hair and clothes. "Tell Sarkham I need the first one!" She had to shout to be heard over the gale.

He nodded and ran for the captain.

Rina thanked Dumo she was tapped into the spirit. She was able to shove her fear and guilt and self-loathing into some dark corner of her soul, lock it away, ignore it. Cold logic told her what needed to be done.

She turned and saw Alem escorting a prisoner toward her, an emaciated man in gray rags, filthy and barefoot, hair greasy and matted, skin fish-belly white. How long had he been in the duke's dungeon? Months? Years?

"Come here," Rina told him.

The prisoner took a look at her, one hand held high in command of the storm, black armor, a fierce expression on her face. He took a half step back.

"It's okay," Rina said. "No harm will come to you."

The songbird tattoo flared at her throat.

The prisoner shuffled to her, chains hampering his movement. He knelt, looking up at her, eyes wide and trusting.

She told herself the man was a criminal. He'd probably raped some young girl or murdered a child. She told herself what she needed to believe, tried to summon anger or disgust at this man, whatever made her next actions okay. Any excuse to justify it.

Rina tugged off her other glove with her teeth. Seeing the skeletal tattoo on her palm was still a shock. She would never get used to it.

"I'm sorry," Rina said to the prisoner.

She reached out to take him.

CHAPTER
FORTY

General Thorn clung to the gunwale to keep from being thrown to the deck.

The waters churned. One of the escort ships was thrown into them, rattling both vessels. This time Thorn *was* thrown to the deck. He picked himself up again with as much dignity as he could muster. The sky had darkened suddenly, the storm catching them all completely by surprise, but Thorn had ordered the attack on Sherrik to continue. He'd vowed to take the city, and he'd be damned if he'd stop for anything. Not even a hurricane. Then he heard it.

Or rather *didn't* hear it.

The slow, pounding thud of the battering ram had stopped.

"Lieutenant!" he shouted over the howl of the wind.

The junior officer ran across the tilting deck as quickly as he could while still keeping his footing. A sloppy salute. "General."

"Has the battering-ram squad broken through the gate?"

"No, General."

"Then why have they stopped?"

"The enemy has abandoned the harbor wall. A company has been sent to secure the gate from the inside."

Something is very wrong, Thorn thought. *It shouldn't be this easy.*

The harbor wall was a much better defense than the inner wall. Yes, it would have been taken eventually, but to abandon it so soon?

"Tell the flagmen to signal they should not advance beyond the inner wall until the scouts have assessed the situation."

The lieutenant saluted and sped away to give the order.

Thorn cast a glance upward. The sky roiled with black clouds. The storm was getting worse.

Still, calling off the attack wasn't an option. His men would press on and take the city.

Let the bloody winds howl.

Smoke filled the hall, and they could feel the heat of the fire coming around the corner.

A mob of Perranese charged around the other corner.

The duke lunged in weakly. The enemy batted his blade aside and came en masse, a press of bodies that pinned the duke against the wall. He struggled to free himself. A Perranese warrior lifted his blade to hack at him.

And was immediately smashed in the face by the bishop's mace, the crunch and splat of bone and blood, shattered teeth flying.

"I'm here, your grace!"

Bishop Hark grabbed the duke by the collar and yanked him back, practically throwing the man behind him. A backhand with the mace snapped another man's collarbone, and he went down, bleating like an animal.

There's too many, Hark thought. *Only the narrowness of the hallway keeps them from overwhelming us, but they'll still wear us down in time.*

Time. That's all they were doing really, buying time so Duchess Veraiin could do whatever it was she thought would help. The bishop simply had to trust her. And she'd said she needed time. They'd followed the duke down the stairs to the level below and had met a dozen of the duke's men retreating back toward them. They hadn't looked happy when the duke ordered them to turn and stand their ground, but they obeyed.

Fighting had been fierce and desperate. Half the duke's men fell as they gave ground a foot at a time.

We won't last long like this.

"Pick him up!" Hark shouted. "Retreat to the landing at the foot of the stairs."

Kalli and Tosh pulled the duke to his feet, but he struggled out of their grasp.

"No, stand—" Coughs wracked his body. He spit blood. "Stand your ground." Pain shot through him, and he went down on one knee.

"Forgive me, your grace, but there's a heavy wooden door at the landing, banded with iron," Hark said. "We can hold there longer."

The duke didn't agree, but neither did he object when Tosh and Kalli each grabbed him under an arm and dragged him back toward the landing. Two more of the duke's men died covering their withdrawal.

Maurizan rushed forward, a dagger flashing in each hand. Her graceful movements, so quick and fluid, made everyone else look slow and clumsy. She slashed and stabbed and dodged, cutting the back of a knee, stabbing the armpit through a gap in the armor, then stepping aside as enemy blades tried to find her.

The enemy fell back momentarily, stunned by the little red-haired girl dealing death among them.

Hark and the rest had retreated to the other side of the door. "Come on, girl! We're closing it! Hurry!"

Hark watched her in awe.

She spun, slashing a dagger across an enemy throat as she turned to run back down the hall. She seemed to have eyes in the back of her head, knew exactly when to zig or zag as arrows flew past her. She dove through the doorway a split second before Hark slammed it shut.

"Quickly," she said. "Bar it."

Hark put his shoulder against the door, as did three more of the duke's men. "Would love to, young lady. Alas, it bars on the other side."

The enemy slammed the door, jarring Hark and the others holding it.

"Push, lads!" Hark shouted. "I think we'd all prefer they stay on the other side, eh?"

Tosh rushed forward to put his shoulder against the door with the others.

"A dagger," Sherrik croaked. The duke sat against a wall a few feet away, sword held limply across his lap. The burn and the other wounds had taken their toll. His complexion on the unburned half of his face had gone a clammy gray. "Wedge it."

Maurizan went to her hands and knees, reaching in between the legs of the men holding the door, and jammed the dagger into the crack below.

"Bishop, your mace."

He handed it down to her.

She used it like a mallet, hitting the hilt of her dagger once, twice, wedging it in tight.

"That's got it."

The Perranese kept hammering from the other side.

"Better keep your shoulders to it, gentlemen," Hark said. "We've wedged it shut, but they'll knock it loose if they can. Still, we can hold here a good long time."

The dull thuds against the door stopped, replaced a few moments later by the sharp hacking sound of axes.

Hark cleared his throat. "Well, then. Maybe not quite as long as we'd hoped."

◆ ◆ ◆

The prisoners huddled along the wall of the platform, the wind lashing them. Their wide eyes watched the sky growing darker and darker.

Sarkham almost pitied them. Then he remembered that the denizens of the ducal dungeons were made up almost exclusively of murderers and rapists and the worst dregs of the city.

Still, the duchess wanted them. For what, he couldn't imagine. In fact, why had he obeyed her when she'd asked they be brought to the top of the palace? Somehow Sarkham had gotten the idea that it was in accordance with the duke's wishes. This notion had gradually seemed less likely, but the duke had been here, talked to Duchess Veraiin, had told her he'd hold off the Perranese while she . . .

Did what?

Looking again at the line of prisoners, Sarkham couldn't begin to guess why he'd been sent for them, why they were here, what use they could possibly be. The Perranese were attacking the city, and he was playing jailer. This didn't make sense. There were more important things that should have been occupying the captain's attention.

And yet the duke had given his orders.

Still . . .

Sarkham gingerly touched the side of his head, wincing at the contact where his ear had been. He dreaded what his wife would say. She'd always thought him so handsome. She'd be horrified at his mutilation. In the heat of battle, it had been a quick, sharp sting. Now it was an excruciating throb.

He didn't think the sky could grow any darker in the middle of the day, but it did.

And then the horn sounded. Sarkham didn't think it possible any sound could drown out the howling wind, but the unmistakable signal for retreat did just that. This couldn't be right.

"Stay here," Sarkham said to the first prisoner in line.

He looked up at the captain, eyes vacant, the possibility he might go anywhere else utterly ridiculous.

"Captain Sarkham!"

Sarkham looked up the stairs. It was the boy in the black doublet with the glowing sword. "Milord?"

"Duchess Veraiin says to send up the first prisoner."

Sarkham pulled the prisoner to his feet, pointed up the steps. The prisoner went with the boy.

Sarkham thought about it. No, this couldn't be right. He needed to check on this, to see for himself.

He climbed the stairs.

The prisoner knelt next to the duchess. She pulled off a glove with her teeth.

And reached for the prisoner.

CHAPTER
FORTY-ONE

"I'm sorry," Rina said again.

She didn't even know whether the prisoner heard her above the wind.

Rina grabbed him, the skeletal tattoo on her palm flat against his forehead. Immediately she began drawing the man's spirit. His eyes went wide. His mouth fell open to scream, but he was frozen, a strangled croak trying to escape the depths of his throat. Her grip didn't waver as he trembled, his face going waxen and pale.

The man's spirit flowed into her, refilling the well she'd drained creating the storm. Rina felt the power surge through her, but there was an unwholesome feel to it, like a slick oily layer on the surface of an otherwise pure pool of water. She drained the prisoner and he slumped over, eyes rolled back. He looked shriveled. Lessened.

Dead. Whatever he was, good or bad, is finished now. I did that. Maybe he deserved it, but how do I know? Who am I to make these decisions?

She'd never wanted power. Never wanted to decide between life and death. Her father had told her many times that such decisions were the burden of leadership. As duke he might have to order men into a situation that meant their deaths. He couldn't hesitate when the greater good was at stake.

Rina looked at the dead man at her feet. *But this . . . this can't be the same. It feels wrong.*

She turned back to Alem. The appalled look on his face would have broken her heart if she hadn't been tapped into the spirit. This was no time for emotion. No time to second-guess. Resolve steeled her.

She saw Sarkham watching from the top of the stairs. He also seemed disturbed by what he saw. It didn't matter.

"Bring me another one," Rina said.

Sarkham looked at Alem, but Alem turned away.

"Bring me another one," she repeated more firmly.

A hesitation, then Sarkham nodded and went back down the stairs, came back a moment later with another prisoner, a man with coarse black hair and a deep scar down his face. He'd been a man of muscles before wasting away in the dungeon. Like the previous prisoner, he balked when he saw the woman in black armor, one hand held aloft, commanding the storm.

"It's okay," she said. "You'll be all right." Again the songbird flared at her throat.

He nodded and went forward. Rina signaled him to kneel.

Her palm against his forehead. She drained him.

Like before, the oily feeling repulsed her. But now there was the other feeling too. She'd been expecting and dreading it. The sweet thrill of the power. It lurked there under the oily corruption. A part of her loved it. Another part of her despised the part that loved it. Weylan's words came to her yet again. He'd warned her when he'd inked the Prime down her spine. The power was seductive. She could get drunk on the spirit. Use too much, and she'd burn herself out.

In a way, the fear of burning out was the only thing keeping an ink mage in check. The only thing reminding her to pull back was the idea she could kill herself draining her own spirit.

The Hand of Death changed that, the tattoo of the skeletal hand.

She could take as much spirit as she needed—*wanted*—as long as there were live bodies to take it from.

And what could stop an ink mage then?

She looked down at the ships tossing in the harbor, knocking into one another. She looked at the dead prisoners at her feet, one fallen across the other.

Rina commanded the winds to blow stronger. Already she was draining herself again.

She looked back at Alem. "Tell Sarkham to bring me another one."

Alem stared back at her, not moving. He looked lost.

"Alem."

He snapped out of his daze, went to tell Sarkham.

Alem belonged to the gypsy girl irrevocably now, she realized. If there'd ever been a chance to change things, it was gone.

He'll never look at me the same way again.

There was no going back.

◆ ◆ ◆

They stepped away from the door, weapons up and ready. The Perranese were coming through, axes hacking through the door, rattling the hinges. Woodchips flew. It didn't matter that they'd wedged the door shut with a dagger, because in another minute the door wouldn't exist.

I wish I'd used somebody else's dagger, Maurizan thought. *Only having one blade feels strange.*

The gypsy fighting style was two-handed. She pulled a skinning knife from her boot to fill the empty hand. It wasn't as good as the long fighting daggers, but the blade was sharp and it was better than nothing.

They stood in the small landing at the foot of the stairs leading up to the top of the palace behind them. In addition to Maurizan, Tosh, Kalli, and the bishop, four of the duke's men had survived. They had tight grips on their sword hilts and looked scared. The duke himself still clung to life but was in no shape to fight. His armor was stained with the blood of his enemies as well as his own.

The axes hacked away from the other side. Through the cracks, they could see the Perranese bunching on the other side preparing to storm through. One of the hinges popped off and clanged on the stone floor. It would be a matter of seconds now.

"This was a mistake," Maurizan said suddenly. "There's no room to fight here. We should go up top."

"Rina told us to hold them off as long as possible," Hark said.

"I can fight better with room," Maurizan said. "You and the others can fall back to guard the platform. You have to trust me."

"She's right," Kalli said. "We start swinging swords in this tight space, we're as likely to hit each other as we are them."

Hark looked at the duke for guidance, but the man's head lolled in a daze.

"Okay," Hark said. "Everyone topside!"

Two of the soldiers grabbed the duke under the arms and dragged him up the stairs, the others following close. They heard the racket of the door smashing in behind them just as they emerged onto the roof.

They were all nearly knocked over by the hurricane-force winds.

Maurizan had tapped into the spirit, so she could take in the situation in an instant. She was still getting used to how everything seemed to slow, as if the world were giving her a chance to scrutinize every detail. Captain Sarkham marched a prisoner in chains up the stairs to the platform. There'd been a score of prisoners earlier. Now there were only three. From this angle, she couldn't see what was happening up on the platform, but considering the angry black clouds and the way the wind tore through the sky, Rina must have gotten the hang of her new tattoos.

She glanced back at the harbor. A number of the ships were half-submerged, swamped by enormous waves. She felt a pang of awe. *Rina must be using an incredible amount of spirit.*

But there was no time to be impressed. The Perranese were already spilling up the staircase and spreading toward them.

"All of you get up to the platform!" Maurizan shouted at the others. "Hold there if they get past me."

"Alone?" Hark said.

"You'll just be in my way," she said. "Now go!"

Hark and the others rushed up the stairs, dragging the unconscious duke with them.

Maurizan turned back to the charging Perranese, dagger in one hand, knife in her off hand. *Okay, Rina's putting her new tattoo through the paces. Now it's my turn.*

She sprinted toward the Perranese warrior in the lead, and when she got within three feet, the man swung the sword two-handed, the blade slicing straight down the middle of her skull.

Instead of a fantastic splatter of brains and blood, the image of Maurizan swirled away like smoke. Maurizan appeared ten feet away, knife slipping into the throat of a completely different warrior, blade entering flesh just above the collar of his armor. Blood sprayed, and the man lurched back a step before dropping. Another warrior stabbed Maurizan through the back.

Again, Maurizan's image dissolved into smoke, flying away on the wind. She reappeared a dozen feet away, stabbing up and under the rim of a helmet into the base of a warrior's skull. Others slashed at her to no avail, the blades passing through her as if she were a ghost.

The tattoos on her feet were called the Phantom Walker, and now she fully understood why. She spun and danced among the enemy, slashing and stabbing, and by the time they saw her, she was already gone, leaving just a ghostly image like a memory.

Enemies dropped by the second. The illusion they were fighting a ghost sowed fear among them. Many of them backed toward the stairs, considering escape. Maurizan showed no mercy or pity. Her hands dripped red with the blood of the enemy.

A seductive song of power sang in her ears. She neared her limit, spirit draining so fast. And yet another little voice enticed her on. *Just a little bit more.*

In her peripheral vision, she saw a handful of the Perranese had gotten by her and were heading for the platform. In a split second, she calculated she couldn't get there in time to do anything. She killed three more warriors in the time it took to think this.

◆ ◆ ◆

Bishop Hark reached the top of the platform and saw the bodies piled in a semicircle around Duchess Veraiin, emaciated men in chains. The bishop gasped, realizing they were the prisoners he'd just seen alive not so long ago.

The duchess stood with one hand lifted to the roiling sky. The other hand grasped a kneeling prisoner by the forehead. A moment later, the prisoner fell limp on top of his brethren.

Dumo, protect us. What has she done?

Hark was a big man in full plate armor, but the winds redoubled again, almost knocking him over. *Was Rina doing this? Of course she was. The ink magic.*

A commotion behind him drew his attention. Perranese warriors topped the stairs. The last of the duke's men died bloody on enemy blades.

Kalli slashed one across the face, and he dropped his sword, clutching at himself and screaming as he fell back into his comrades.

Another warrior surged past the fallen man and thrust his blade deeply into her arm.

She trapped her own scream against gritted teeth, and it came out like an animal growl. She batted his blade aside with her own but gave ground.

He lifted his blade again for another strike, but Tosh was there and stabbed him in the leg. The man went down, and Kalli kicked him in the head.

More warriors rushed them. Tosh and Kalli swung their swords wildly, trying to keep them at bay. Some of their strikes landed, but three warriors slipped past them.

"Hark!" Tosh yelled the warning.

But the bishop was already charging. He swung the mace in a wide, backhanded arc and caved in the chest of the first warrior with a crunch of armor and bone, sending him flying off the platform. He blocked a sword thrust from the second warrior.

The third made it past him.

◆ ◆ ◆

Rina's entire body pulsed in time with her heartbeat. She felt as if she were the entire world, that she inhaled and exhaled eternity. The power that flowed through her was beyond measure. She was an ink mage, and she was invincible.

Some distant part of her recognized the madness, knew these claims to be lunacy, a fiction brought on by insanity.

But it's such a sweet story. I like it. Is this how madness works, when we start believing the story we tell ourselves?

Still, there was no denying the feeling, the sheer bliss of the power. The feeling of oily corruption was a distant memory, burned away by the blinding bright power that was hers to control.

Rina had drained all the prisoners. That they had given themselves so she could feel this way was only right. Anything that gave her this kind of power, that lifted her up past the rest of mewling humanity, was right and proper. The world existed to feed Rina's hunger.

The vague awareness of something going on behind her caused her to turn her head.

Hark knocked one of the enemy warriors off the platform. The man tumbled through the air. Rina looked at his face and saw the instant he realized that everything he'd been or ever could be was over. She watched the light go out of him a split second before he landed. She nearly imagined she could see the soul leak out of him, floating away to whatever distant and indifferent deity he worshipped.

One of the enemy warriors broke past the bishop, running straight for Rina, screaming, sword raised. He moved so slowly. Rina had other things to occupy her, no time for trivia, and yet she spared a moment to examine this man. He was that brutal type, weathered face. One eye covered with a black patch. The girl who'd once been Rina Veraiin would have once upon a time found the man terrifying. Now he was a mild curiosity. An amusement.

A slight smile on Rina's face.

The man in the eye patch saw the smile as he raised his sword. It was enough to make him hesitate, just for a moment.

A glowing sword blade erupted from his chest.

Rina's smile grew into a grin. *Good-bye, little man.*

Alem stood behind him. The blade had gone through armor and man as if they were soft cheese. Alem stepped back, and the man slid off the blade, landing with a dull thump on top of the dead prisoners.

Seeing Alem helped Rina find the part of her humanity that had been hidden away, buried under the delusions of ecstasy. Her grin wilted, and she turned back to the business at hand, summoning all of the power within her.

Okay. Let's do this.

CHAPTER FORTY-TWO

They'd lost at least a hundred ships, and that was just General Thorn's estimate based on what he could observe from the flagship's foredeck. The real toll wouldn't be known for some time. He cursed the storm. They couldn't even dock and disembark. The ship's captain assured him the risk of being dashed against the wharf if they tried to tie up was far too great. All they could do was trust their seamanship and ride out the storm.

In the meantime, there was still a battle to be won.

The signalmen reported that the enemy had withdrawn behind the inner wall and had shut the gates. The company in charge of escorting the battering-ram squad had requested to move forward and begin work on one of the inner gates, which were far weaker than the outer gates. They felt confident they could knock down the gate in a matter of minutes.

A hesitation here could be costly. So could blundering forward into an unknown situation, but the scouts had reported nothing untoward.

"Tell them to proceed," Thorn told his junior officer. "Smash the gate into splinters."

The officer saluted and ran to tell the signalman.

Good. I don't like to wait. Let them spring whatever surprise they think they can manage.

The men poured slowly through the outer gates. They'd completed the first stage, and once they were past the inner wall, the city would, for all intents and purposes, be theirs. Pockets of resistance would be mopped up sooner rather than later, and then the port city of Sherrik could be put to use in service of the Empire. First by landing the rest of the occupying force and serving as a base of operations for conquering the rest of Helva, then eventually as a convenient port from which they could export foodstuffs back to the home island of the Empire.

And when the Empire was strong again, when it had recaptured its former glory, they would return to the colonies who'd thrown them out and make them pay. And in a thousand years, none of them would be able to imagine any other life than that under Perran rule. Thorn would be long dead, of course, but his descendants would forever honor his contribution to the eternal Empire.

But first things first. There was a city to take.

A moment later, the dull, rhythmic thump of the battering ram resumed, barely audible above the gale-force winds. Good. It wouldn't be long now, and then—

The city began to rise. Thorn blinked, looked again.

No, of course it wasn't. Was the ship sinking?

Thorn went to the railing to look but was thrown to the deck before reaching it, the planks below him tilting violently. Men screamed and fell from the rigging, landing on the deck with a crunch of bones. If it had been a rogue wave, the ship would have righted itself, but it was stuck at an awkward angle.

What's happening?

Thorn scrambled to his feet, went to the railing. The ship was stuck in the mud. All over the harbor, ships found themselves in a similar predicament, lodged in the mud at various awkward angles.

"The water." Thorn gaped, unable to make sense of it. "Where's the water?"

Men behind him screamed, pleading to their gods.

General Thorn turned and looked. His eyes went wide, a cold and terrible fear gripping him by the spine.

"Oh no."

◆ ◆ ◆

Rina Veraiin's body trembled, her hand held high, and demanded the wind obey her. The wall of water towered a hundred feet over the harbor, helpless ships dotting the muddy floor below. She couldn't hold it much longer. She'd drained twenty men of their spirit and had used every drop.

And yet she couldn't let go, couldn't release the spirit and the pure pleasure it offered, the sweet, unending ecstasy, even as another part of her screamed for her to stop before it was too late.

A voice called her name from some distant place, maybe a thousand miles away.

Alem was still behind her. She saw his mouth form her name as he shouted, but he couldn't be heard above the wind, or maybe she was someplace so deep within herself she couldn't be reached.

Tears streamed from the corners of her eyes. Was she so far gone?

Alem shouted her name again, sounded like he was at the bottom of a deep well. Darkness closed in on her vision, and the world grew cottony and soft around the edges. This was it.

Just let go.

This was the end.

Let go now.

Soon there would be nothing left of her.

Let go let go let go let go let go let—

She let go.

The wind ceased to roar.

Untold tons of water crashed back down, instantly smashing the ships below to bits. A huge rolling wave swept over the harbor and smashed the wharves to rubble, the same wharves that had seen thousands of ships and centuries of trade from every corner of the world. Now debris tumbling along the bottom of the harbor.

The massive wave washed over the men there, drowning most of them instantly, slamming bodies up against the harbor wall, which itself didn't last long. It was plowed under almost immediately, such was the force of the rushing water. It swept across the waterfront market, smashing buildings large and small and scooping up warriors uselessly attempting to flee.

The water crashed hard into the inner wall. Miraculously, the wall held.

The gates didn't.

They were blasted off their hinges, and water poured into the inner city with incredible force. The men of Sherrik were knocked off their feet as the water splashed through every street and alley, filtering throughout the entire city. Men on top of roofs helped pull their comrades to high grounds.

Others weren't so lucky. Those who didn't drown immediately were smashed into stone walls, breaking bones and cracking skulls. The byways of the city were choked with the dead.

At last the roar of the water subsided, replaced by the moans of the dying.

CHAPTER FORTY-THREE

The dark clouds had already begun to part, the sun breaking through in places.

Why was Rina looking up at the sky?

She turned her head, saw Alem's face. He carried her and looked worried. Was that because of her? Was Alem afraid for her? He spoke, but she couldn't hear. There was a fierce ringing in her ears. Her head felt so light.

She closed her eyes, just for a second. So tired.

When she opened them again, she was in a smoky hall, the ring of steel on steel nearby. Alem still had her. She wanted to tell him something important but couldn't remember what it was.

Then she went away for a little while.

When she came back, she was underwater. Many hands grabbed her, lifted her back into the air. She sputtered, coughing and gulping for breath.

"I'm sorry. I tripped." Alem's voice from somewhere.

She tasted salt.

Rina blinked her eyes clear. Each of her arms was around the shoulder of someone. They dragged her through waist-deep water. She looked to her left. Alem. She looked to her right.

Maurizan.

"Don't think this suddenly means we're best friends, Duchess," the gypsy girl said.

Rina wanted to say something, didn't know what that might be, and was pretty sure she didn't have the strength anyway.

The world spun and she saw water, then sky. They were lifting her. A second later they set her down again. She lay in the back of a wagon. The duke was next to her, unconscious. Rina turned her head, saw another woman, her chin down on her chest, also unconscious. It was the one who'd come with Tosh. Rina had forgotten her name. She looked pale. Blood had already seeped through the makeshift bandage they'd tied around her arm.

"Rest, your grace. We're taking you out of here soon."

She looked up, saw the face of Maxus looking down at her. He sat in the driver's seat of the wagon.

"The men are scattered," Maxus said, "but what troops remain are rallying behind the north gate. We're passing the word to anyone still alive. I'll take us there."

Rina worked her mouth to say thank you, but only a croaking half whisper came out.

"I looked for you when the battle started," he said. "No idea you'd gone to the top of the palace. I suppose it offered the best view for what you had to do." He gestured at the flood all around them. "This is your handy work, I take it."

Instead of answering, she tapped into the spirit. It was dangerous and foolish. She was already so weak, but she had to see something for herself.

She called for Zin.

The falcon flew low over the flooded city toward the harbor. Water shimmered between every building. Stranded citizens called to each other from rooftops, and small bands of surviving soldiers moved in a general northerly direction, presumably headed for the rallying point.

Zin landed on a rampart of the inner wall. Rina looked through his eyes down into the flooded disaster that had once been the market quarter between the inner and harbor walls. Bodies spun slowly in the currents among the debris, the water already receding. The harbor wall might as well have not ever been there for all the evidence that was left of it.

Someday it might be rebuilt, but Rina doubted Sherrik's waterfront would ever be quite the same again.

Rina scanned the horizon. Not a single ship was visible.

She told Zin to get closer, and the falcon dove toward the water, pulling up at the last second to perch on a barrel that bobbed along with the dead.

The defeat of the Perranese was as complete as it was terrible. At least it was finished.

One of the bodies stirred, splashed, and the falcon turned to look.

Against all odds, one of the Perranese warriors had survived the cataclysm. He stood, the water coming up to the middle of his chest. And then another stood.

When a third one broke the surface near Zin's barrel, it sent the falcon flapping and squawking into the air. Dozens of them rose from the water. No. Hundreds.

Thousands.

Get closer. I've got to see. I've got to know.

Zin balked at the command. He didn't want to go near them.

The Perranese slowly formed into lines and began to advance across the market quarter, heading toward the inner wall, marching slowly through the water.

Please, Zin.

The falcon dipped low, making a quick pass along the forward-most line of men. Their eyes were vacant, mouths slack. One's head tilted awkwardly to the side, neck obviously broken, but he marched on all the same, not bothered by it.

Rina couldn't hang on much longer, not enough spirit to—

She was back in the wagon. She tried to talk, so weak, mouth so dry. "The . . . dead . . ." Barely above a whisper.

"Yes, the dead are many," Maxus said. "A dark day for Sherrik."

"No . . . the . . . the dead." Rina took a deep breath, summoned all of her strength to get the words out. "The dead are coming."

CHAPTER
FORTY-FOUR

Stasha Benadicta refilled Brasley's wineglass.

"Thank you." He sipped, more slowly this time. It had taken two glasses to stop his hands from shaking. He'd had a rough time of it, she guessed.

They all had. One way or another.

They sat in the duke's old library upstairs from the portal room. It seemed the most convenient place for Baron Hammish to pull himself together, with its comfortable chairs and a good stiff drink or two. Or three.

Darshia and two more Birds of Prey frantically searched the rest of the library all around them.

Brasley cast them a glance. "What are they doing?"

"Searching for something that might help us operate the portal."

"Ah." Brasley sipped wine, clearly no longer interested in what the women were doing.

"Is she really dead?" Stasha asked, pitching her voice low enough so only he could hear.

He cleared his throat, looked uncomfortable. "Yes, afraid so. Her neck was . . . uh . . . well, snapped." He took another big gulp of the wine. "Oh, and Olgen was burned alive right before my eyes. I . . . I don't think I'll ever forget that smell as long as I live." He held out the empty goblet. "Sorry, hate to be a pig, but . . ."

"Of course." She refilled it. "I'm terribly sorry, Baron Hammish, but I don't know who Olgen is."

"Oh, yes. How stupid. He was the young student hired as our guide in the library. A good . . . a good lad."

He was slurring his words now, swaying in his chair. He would come crashing down soon. Stasha had seen it before at the Wounded Bird. Men who'd been on the edge too long. Something eventually had to give.

"Maybe you'd better lie down," Stasha suggested.

"Perhaps you're right," he said. "I was wondering if I might be able to arrange a horse after that. I need to get back to the lodge. Fregga is there."

Stasha looked past Brasley. "Darshia, can you escort Baron Hammish? I think you can probably guess which room will be best for him."

Darshia smiled. "Yes, Lady Steward."

Brasley rose slowly from the chair, like the weight of the world hung around his neck. He gestured to the items on a nearby table: the inkwell, stencil, and scroll case. "Guard those, please. They're important, I think. The reason for the whole trip. The reason for everything."

"You have my word, Baron Hammish."

He nodded as if satisfied and followed Darshia out of the room.

Stasha Benadicta went to the table and looked down at the items Brasley had brought back from the library, the items the wizard Talbun had died for.

If Brasley Hammish said they were important to Duchess Veraiin, then it was Stasha's duty to figure out a way to get them to her as soon as possible.

And Stasha Benadicta took her duties very seriously.

◆ ◆ ◆

Brasley thanked Darshia and entered his room. He was so tired, but it was more than that. He felt like he'd been turned inside out.

"Brasley?"

He turned, started at the voice. "Fregga!"

"They told me you were here."

"I thought you were at the lake lodge."

"I was, but the steward invited me to stay while you were gone," Fregga said. "She's ever so nice. She knew I was all alone and—"

Brasley swept her into his arms and kissed her hard on the mouth. Her arms went around him. They broke the kiss, and he nuzzled her neck, rocking back and forth, holding her tight, never wanting to let go.

"I'm never leaving you again," Brasley said.

"Good."

He looked at her, touched her face. "You okay?"

"Yes. I just missed you is all."

He put a hand on her belly. It had grown since he'd seen her last. "I mean, not just you, but everything."

"We're both just fine."

"Good." He smiled, nodding, suddenly at a loss for words. "Good."

She squeezed his arm. "They said you had a bad time of it."

He shrugged. "Well, you know. Nick-of-time stuff. It was a close call. To be honest, I didn't think I was going to make it."

"But you did."

"Yes, I was lucky. A couple of the people I was with, well, they . . . they weren't quite as lucky, I guess. I mean, I guess . . ."

He burst into tears, and she grabbed him and pulled him close. He sucked for breath, his shoulders heaving with sobs.

"It's okay." She rocked him gently, patting his back. "It's okay."

Ankar drank fine wine and ate a good meal.

Whatever the ancient wizards had been, they lived well, he thought.

When it seemed the coast was clear, the white-skinned servants had emerged from their hiding places in the walls and began to clean up. They carried away the bodies and removed the debris from the battle. They set up a table and brought refreshment. Tattoos around his mouth and inside his ear canals let him speak and understand any tongue. They seemed all too pleased to serve him even though he'd recently killed dozens of them.

Whatever race of people they are, they certainly don't hold a grudge.

So he sat there, eating and drinking, watching Giffen fiddle with the settings on the portal. The battle with the she-wizard had depleted him, so he'd been satisfied to eat and drink and rest, but now he grew impatient.

"I thought you said you knew the settings for the damn thing."

"Your pardon, master," Giffen said. "I'm doing this from memory. A little trial and error and I'm sure I'll have it soon."

"Don't call me 'master,' you obsequious turd."

"My pardon, your . . . uh . . . lordship?"

"My name is Ankar."

"Ankar, then. I remember the setting back to Klaar well enough, but they must have removed one of the guidance gems from its housing on the other side, because I can't get it to open."

"I don't want to go to Klaar."

"Well, I don't blame you for that. A squalid little backwater."

"The other settings open the portal to other places?"

"Yes."

"Where?"

"Well, that's where a bit of guesswork comes into play," Giffen admitted. "But I have reason to believe my guesses are good. Klaar might be a shit hole, but it's the seat of one of the *old* houses of Helva. It stands to reason that other portals might be similarly located. Ah, here. For example, if I were to readjust this final guidance stone to the next rune over, I believe it might open the portal located deep within the hidden dungeons of Sherrik. The portals were generally kept hidden. Wouldn't want just anyone messing with them, now, would we?"

Ankar pushed back from the table, stood, and approached the portal. "Do it, then. Show me."

Giffen reached up and slowly clicked the guidance stone into place. The wall shimmered into a portal again just as it had before, and Giffen grinned triumphantly.

An enormous gout of water the size of the portal itself shot into the room and sent Giffen tumbling back against the far wall.

Ankar tapped into the spirit and turned himself to stone and stomped slowly, one step at a time, against the raging torrent of salt water spewing against him. At one point, he almost lost his footing, but he leaned into the spray and finally reached the portal. He snatched the gem from its housing at the top of the arch, and the portal became a stone wall again.

Ankar sloshed across the room to where Giffen had washed up against the far wall. He grabbed a fistful of his cloak and hauled him up. Giffen sputtered and coughed, looking like a drowned rat.

"Are you sure that was Sherrik?" Ankar asked. "Or was it perhaps the *bottom of the fucking ocean?*"

"Apologies," Giffen said. "Perhaps we should try some other setting."

"Yes. Let's."

"There is another setting, one I didn't tell anyone else about," Giffen said. "I think I can remember it. I just need a bit of time to remember."

"Get on with it, then," Ankar said.

Giffen went back toward the portal archway, wringing out his robe.

Ankar looked around the chamber and sighed. *Looks like those pale-faced bitches have another mess to clean up.*

CHAPTER
FORTY-FIVE

The makeshift camp twenty miles north of Sherrik was a ragtag collection of carts and wagons and hastily erected tents. It served as the rallying point for the slow trickle of soldiers slugging out of the city. Any civilians who happened by were urged to continue on, although many wanted to stay near the soldiers, feeling they offered some semblance of safety.

The battle surgeons had set up the largest tent available to treat the wounded. The cots within had filled almost immediately, and many of the lesser wounded had simply found a place to lie down outside the tent and shut their eyes, exhausted. Many of the eyes never opened again.

Alem spotted Tosh kneeling next to one of the cots and went to speak to him. Kalli was lying in the cot, sleeping peacefully, and when Alem saw the bloody bandage around the stump of her arm, he gasped.

"Took it off at the elbow," Tosh said. "Nothing they could do to save it. It's not her sword arm. That's something at least."

"Damn." Alem shook his head.

"She's tough," Tosh said.

Her eye flickered open, a wan smile. "You talking about me, boss?"

"You're the toughest lady I know, aren't you?"

"Don't say that in front of Darshia," Kalli said weakly. "I don't want to have to prove it." She turned her head just enough to see her stump, and her smile drifted away. "Well. Look at that."

"Forget it," Tosh said. "You just rest."

"Damn. I was really working on those two-handed lunges, you know?"

"We'll fix you up with a rapier," Tosh said. "Or a short sword."

"Yeah . . . sure." She closed her eyes again.

"They gave her something for the pain," Tosh told Alem. "Makes her sleep too."

"Do you know where they've put Rina?"

"Down at the other end." Tosh pointed.

"I'll come check on you both later," Alem said.

"Sure."

He found Rina lying in her cot, skin ashen, breathing shallowly. There was no wound on her. Something that simple wouldn't bother an ink mage who could heal herself. This was something deeper. She'd tried to explain once that there was always a danger, that she could push herself too far.

"I think I know how she feels," said a voice behind him.

He turned. "Maurizan."

"I felt it after the battle," Maurizan said. "It wasn't just like being tired. It's like using up part of yourself."

"Is she going to be okay?"

"I don't know," Maurizan said. "This is still new for me. Alem?"

"Yes?"

"I can't do it again. I can't love you and then you leave me for her. Just tell me now."

"Just because I'm concerned about her doesn't—"

"Please. I know. I'm not accusing you of anything. Honest. I just can't . . . I won't. It hurts too much."

He reached for her hand. She let him take it.

"Don't worry," he said. "It's not an issue."

She smiled at him. He smiled back.

Then his eyes shifted to the man entering the tent. It was Maxus the wizard, and a soldier in leather armor. They went to a nearby cot. Captain Sarkham stood there, a bloodstained bandage around his head.

Alem realized the man in the cot was the duke of Sherrik. He was shirtless, had a bandage around his torso. He'd been cleaned up, but the burn covering half his face looked just as terrible as before. It must have been excruciatingly painful.

"Something's happening," Alem said. "I'm going to eavesdrop."

"Tell me what you find out," Maurizan said. "I want to check on Kalli."

Alem gave her hand a quick squeeze as she left, and then he edged into the semicircle of men surrounding the duke's cot. *Just keep quiet and act like you belong here.*

"This man's patrol has just come from the city," Maxus said. "I've brought him to you just as you ordered, your grace. So you can hear for yourself."

The duke propped himself up on one elbow, wincing at the effort. His eyes looked alert and concerned. "Okay, then. Let's hear it."

"It's true, your grace," the man said. "My patrol found them just inside the merchant's quarter, marching in a line like any army would except . . ."

"They were dead?" asked the duke.

"I don't know about such things," the man said. "But we filled a half dozen of 'em with crossbow bolts, and they didn't so much as blink. Just kept marching right for us. I'm glad we had horses. We got out of there and came back right fast."

"How long until they get here?"

"The water's slowing 'em up a little, not much. A couple hours, three maybe."

The duke sighed, nodding as if he'd been expecting bad news all along. "Thank you, trooper. Rejoin your men. Get a hot meal if you can."

"Your grace." The soldier bowed and left.

"Well, gentlemen, don't get too comfortable," the duke said. "I want us packed up and moving within the hour."

"That might be difficult, your grace," Maxus said. "You've seen the men and the wounded, and there are civilians too. They're all dead on their feet."

"Dead on their feet, you say? An interesting choice of words," the duke said. "Because apparently the dead are on their way. If anyone is too tired to move on, if they feel they had a hard day, then just remind them what's coming, and we'll see if that motivates them."

Maxus cleared his throat. "As you say, your grace."

"Your grace, if I could make a suggestion," Sarkham said.

"Go on."

"I've done a quick head count," Sarkham said. "We've lost a lot of men and have plenty of wounded, but I can scrape up five hundred men still hale enough to hold swords. We could fight a rear guard, give the wounded and the civilians a head start, buy you some time."

"An excellent suggestion, but not here," the duke said. "The village of Millford north of us is a better spot. A stone bridge crosses the river. A stand there might be more fruitful. Does that meet your approval?"

"Most certainly, your grace."

"Go make your preparation, then."

Sarkham saluted and left quickly.

"I want all the wagons and carts for the wounded. Conscript abled-bodied civilians to carry whatever meager supplies we have," the duke ordered. "Ah, Lord Alem, glad you could join us."

Alem reddened, shuffled his feet. "I apologize, your grace. I didn't mean to intrude."

"Nonsense. Maxus, can I have a moment with Alem? I'm sure there's something wizardish you should be doing."

Maxus nodded respectfully and left.

"Rina told me you're quite the horseman."

Alem was surprised. "She talked about me?"

"We had a few opportunities to pass the time with idle chatter, and the subject of horses came up. She told me you were the best rider she knew."

"I'm flattered."

"I didn't bring it up to flatter you," the duke said. "I have an enormous black stallion picked out, and I want you on it and riding north in the next twenty minutes."

Alem blinked. "Your grace?"

"As you just heard, an army of the dead is coming for us," the duke said. "We're heading north. I need my cousin Pemrod to take us in. Behind the walls of Merridan is where I'll feel safest, but it's a long road and we'll never make it. I need you to carry a message. The king needs to send his army out to meet us. The sooner he gets the message the better, so if you're half the rider I've heard you are, Lord Alem, then you're the man for the job."

"Your grace, I have to tell you. I'm not a lord. I'm not anything or anyone."

"I see. To be frank that's not very important right now. You get to the king on time, and I'll make you a lord. I'll make you earl of this fucking tent or anywhere else you want."

"Don't you want an officer for this?" Alem asked. "Somebody important?"

"I'm sorry for this, but you're forcing me to be blunt," the duke said. "I need my officers. And remember I was on top of the palace too. I heard Rina say you're no good with a sword. That makes you useless to me here. But you can ride, and that's what I need right now. I find myself with precious few resources at the moment, and I need to be as smart as possible about how I allocate them."

Alem's heart beat faster. He felt flush and ill. He didn't want this responsibility.

"The horse I've picked for you is a good one," the duke said, "but you have my permission to run his legs off. I'll give you a bag of silver. Buy as many fresh horses along the way as you need."

Alem nodded, trying to find his voice. "Yes, of course. Whatever I can do to help."

"Good man. I knew I could count on you." He took off his ring and handed it to Alem. "As stationery is a bit hard to come by at the moment, I can't write you a letter of introduction. My signet ring will prove I've sent you."

"And I can warn others as I go," Alem said. "Tell the people in each town and village what's coming."

"No."

"No?"

"I'm sorry, but no," the duke said. "If you warn them, they'll take everything that isn't nailed down and flee. I have hundreds of refugees, and we'll need food and supplies along the way. We'll pay fair prices and warn them as we pass through, but I can't have you scaring them off. Likely word has spread ahead of you already anyway, but that can't be helped. Your good intentions do you credit, but I hope you understand my position."

Alem was sure he might throw up. He looked around for a place to do it.

"Think of it this way if it makes you feel better," the duke said. "You'll be riding *away* from the dead army that wants to kill us all."

"Why does it have to be *you*?"

"I told you," Alem said. "I'm the best rider available, and I'm shit with a sword. I'm elected."

"Then I'll get a horse too," Maurizan told him. "I'll go with you."

"That's not how this works." Alem stuffed the bag of silver into the saddlebag with the meager ration of food he'd been given. At his request, they'd also dug up a crossbow for him and a quiver of bolts. "First, they can't spare another horse. Second, if they could, it wouldn't be as fast as mine, and I can't wait. The whole point is for me to ride as fast as I can."

"There's got to be a way we can both go together."

"Well, if we both had lightning bolts on our ankles we could," Alem said. "But we don't."

"What does *that* mean?"

"Look, nothing, okay? I'm going crazy," Alem said. "You think I want to leave you? I don't."

He grabbed her and pulled her close. "If I get killed, what's the last thing you want me to remember? That you were screaming at me, or that you gave me the best kiss of my life?"

One of her hands went to the back of his head and pulled him down. Her lips met his. She kissed him softly at first, then gradually harder. Her mouth opened, her tongue finding its way into his, and after an eternity she pulled away slowly, the taste of her lips lingering on his.

A shiver ran through him. "That actually might have been the best kiss of my life."

Maurizan fixed him with a hard glare. "That does *not* mean you have permission to die."

CHAPTER FORTY-SIX

Brasley rolled over in bed, his eyes opening slowly. There was a horrifying disoriented moment before he remembered where he was.

You're in Klaar. You're safe.

Gray light leaked in through the shutters, still very early in the morning.

His wife curled next to him. He scooted in closer, his erection growing against her softness. She made a purring sound and wiggled back against him. He reached around her and grabbed a full breast. His wife was so incredibly soft. He could just sink into her in a way he was never able to with other women.

I'm going to treat you right, he thought. *I'm going to be the husband you deserve.*

She reached down and guided him in, a little gasp escaping her. He stopped suddenly.

"What is it?" she asked.

"Are you sure it's okay? I won't hurt the baby?"

She threw her head back and laughed so loudly it startled him.

"Yes, my magnificent husband," Fregga said. "You're so massive you could hurt our unborn child."

"Hey!"

She laughed again but gently. "You know you please me. You've more than enough for the job. But you're not going to hurt anything. Go ahead and enjoy yourself. It's not like you can make me any *more* pregnant."

Well . . . he didn't have to be told twice.

He thrust into her from behind, picking up speed, holding on to a breast the whole time. He groaned into her neck as he shuddered and finished.

"I love you, Fregga."

"I love you."

"Give me twenty minutes, and we can do something for you this time," Brasley said.

She turned her head and kissed him. "I can do some things to bring you back faster than that."

"You are the best wife ever."

A knock at the door.

"Are you fucking kidding me?"

Another knock. "Forgive the hour, Baron Hammish. The steward asks you to join her."

A woman's voice. Probably one of those warrior women. What had they started calling them again? The Birds of Prey? He supposed it had a certain ring to it.

"If we're quiet, maybe she'll go away," Brasley whispered.

Fregga patted him on the cheek. "Get dressed and see what Stasha needs, darling. I promise you can attend to my needs when you get back."

◆ ◆ ◆

The Bird of Prey that had come knocking was a petite and pretty brunette, arms and legs tightly muscled, high cheekbones, hair woven into a long single braid that hung down her back. She'd introduced herself as Nivin. Just a few short months ago, Brasley would have made a complete idiot of himself trying to get inside her armor. How had he ever found such a woman attractive?

She has the body of a child. Not like Fregga's round curves and ample—

Brasley cut off that line of thought immediately when he realized he was making himself hard again. Not now. Later. He'd dispose of whatever favor Stasha wanted and get back to his wife as quickly as possible.

Nivin took him through the library where Stasha had offered him wine the day before and down the secret stairs behind the fireplace to the portal chamber. Stasha waited for him there. There were also three other Birds of Prey stacking backpacks against a wall and checking weapons: swords, crossbows and bolts, and various daggers.

That black-skinned fellow was there too. Knarr.

"Thank you for coming so early, Baron Hammish," Stasha said. "I have some exciting news."

"You know the best place for exciting news?" Brasley said. "Upstairs where they're serving breakfast. Who wants eggs?"

"But if we were upstairs, I wouldn't be able to show you this."

Stasha signaled Knarr.

He twisted one of the gems on the archway, and the stone wall swirled and shimmered into a portal.

Brasley gawked.

"I've assembled a team of volunteers to go in with you," Stasha said.

Brasley blinked. Then blinked again. "You've assembled a what to do what now?"

"Darshia has volunteered to lead a squad of the Birds of Prey, and Knarr's going too, in case there's a problem with the portal on the other side. We worked all night to figure it out. We couldn't have done it without Knarr."

"Uh . . . ," Brasley said. He pulled himself together and then said, "Um . . ."

"You made it clear how important it was to get those items to Duchess Veraiin as quickly as possible," she said. "I'm so glad we could do this for you."

Ohhhhh . . . shit.

CHAPTER
FORTY-SEVEN

As promised, the stallion was fast.

Alem leaned low in the saddle, the wind whipping his hair, his black clothing and the black horse making him look like a dark streak along the King's Highway. He headed north, passing through tiny villages in an eyeblink, already gone by the time farmers pulling weeds in the garden looked up to see what was happening.

A day and a half north of Sherrik he crossed a river over a narrow stone bridge into a village that could almost be called a town, or at least it was more than a collection of shabby huts clustered around a muddy crossroads.

He watered the horse in the main square. It was a good animal. Alem had been given money to buy new mounts as needed, but this horse had plenty of go left in him.

As the horse drank, Alem glanced about. People seemed to be going about their business. Across the square, a blacksmith at his anvil hammered at a plow blade. A gangly man standing in front of his butcher's shop wiped his hands on a bloodstained apron. A man with a nose like a big red turnip stumbled into a shabby tavern.

If they've heard what's happened in Sherrik, they sure aren't letting on.

A young woman waddled toward him, two children in her wake. One of the little girls looked maybe ten or eleven years old. The other one was a toddler. The woman was *very* pregnant. They weren't coming toward him, Alem realized, but toward the well. The mother and the older girl carried a wooden bucket in each hand.

She stopped abruptly and looked at him with open curiosity. She wasn't any older than Maurizan. Alem thought about how he must look in the black breeches and doublet. The clothing had been provided to him by the duke, and even dust covered, they were probably the finest garments in this little town. The stallion was probably also the best animal in a hundred-mile radius.

"Are you from Sherrik?" she asked, a heavy county accent in her voice. "Has the siege started?"

A nervous jolt made Alem shuffle his feet, the duke's warning not to alarm the locals foremost in his mind. "No," he said a little too quickly. "Just passing through."

"Oh, that's a shame." She set the buckets down and rubbed her back, stretched. "My man's in the duke's army. I was hoping for news."

Alem felt queasy. Her man was either drowned or killed by the enemy. The odds he was alive among the refugees were too long to offer hope. "Sorry. I don't know anything about it."

"Oh. Well, sorry to bother you." She signaled the older girl to start drawing water from the well.

The toddler picked random weeds from between the paving stones to hold in a little bouquet in her tiny fist.

Alem glanced back at the bridge he'd crossed coming into town. "What town is this?"

"Millford, milord."

The bridge. That's where Sarkham's going to fight his rearguard action. The war's coming right here.

Alem cleared his throat. "Do you have family somewhere?" He tried to sound casual, just making conversation. "I mean since your man is away." He gestured at her belly. "Someone who could help you?"

"My sister and her man live in Sawmouth on the coast." She waved vaguely east. "Fishing village."

"You should go there."

She shook her head. "She's got four kids to feed. Can't feed hers and mine both."

The toddler presented her with the bouquet of weeds, and she smiled down at the child. There was a tooth missing at the edge of her smile, but it still brightened her face.

Tell her. For Dumo's sake, the dead are coming. Tell her so she can get out of here.

He climbed back on the stallion. "I'm sure your man will be back with you soon." He hated himself the second the words were out of his mouth.

"Good travels, milord."

Alem clicked his tongue and trotted away.

He yanked on the reins, turned the horse around, and reached into the purse, fishing out one of the coins the duke had given him. He leaned in the saddle. "Take this."

She reached out her hand, and he placed the silver in her palm.

She looked from side to side, maybe expecting some trick.

"That will feed you," Alem said. "Go to your sister's."

He turned and rode away without waiting for a reply.

At the edge of town, he urged the horse to full speed, the wind in his ears drowning out his thoughts.

◆　◆　◆

Tosh squinted at the sky. It would be night soon. He sat on the back of the wagon, legs dangling over the side, muddy wagon ruts passing slowly between his feet. He sat in the middle of a long line of wagons, creeping along at the pace of a casual stroll.

Escaping should feel faster. I should just steal a horse and get out of here.

But he couldn't. He looked back into the bed of the narrow, rickety wagon. Kalli slept next to Duchess Veraiin. He'd managed to snag one of the few blankets available—a ragged, threadbare thing—and had thrown it over the women. Kalli had proven to be incredibly strong willed. She'd accepted the loss of her arm with surprising aplomb. She breathed easily and slept untroubled. Rina, on the other hand, slept fitfully without waking. Occasionally she would twitch violently, startling the shit out of him.

She's gone someplace where no one can help her. Dumo only knows what will happen.

The sound of a galloping horse drew Tosh's attention, and he leaned out of the wagon, looking forward along the wagon train. A man on a horse came toward him. There weren't so many horses available, and most of them were pulling wagons, so the rider must have been of some importance to rate a mount.

As the rider galloped closer, Tosh saw it was Sarkham.

He waved a hand. "Captain Sarkham! What news?"

Sarkham reined in his horse next to Tosh's wagon. "Scouts have gone ahead to the bridge. I'm forming companies to make a stand there."

Tosh wasn't eager about what he was about to say but felt he had to make the offer. "If you need another sword, I can help." Somehow he'd come through the fall of Sherrik unscathed. He felt too guilty just sitting back and letting others handle the fighting.

Sarkham's eyes shifted briefly to the women in the back of the wagon. "Stay with your people. We'll need at least a few good men to guard the wounded."

Tosh nodded, feeling relieved.

"What I'm most anxious about are the scouts I sent back down the road to—wait." Sarkham stood in the saddle, looking south along the road. "They're coming now."

A half dozen riders trotted toward them from the south, one holding a pike streaming the duke's colors. They halted in front of Sarkham and saluted.

"Well?" demanded Sarkham anxiously.

"Following us up the King's Highway six abreast," the soldier reported. "Perfect lines, disciplined as you please. You'd think they was any old army, except they're dead. Vacant stares and faces all clammy and white."

"How fast are they coming?" Sarkham asked.

"Not fast. Marching a normal pace," the soldier said. "But they'll catch up to us just the same. They don't rest. They don't stop to sleep or eat or drink or piss. They just keep coming. If we camp for the night, they'll be on us in the morning."

Sarkham contemplated that for a few seconds, then said, "Very well. Head forward with the rest of the muster. I'll have orders for you soon."

The men saluted, then galloped north.

Sarkham sat in his saddle, head down, chewing his bottom lip.

"What do we do?" Tosh asked.

Sarkham sighed. "We march through the night. No rest for any of us. Not with the dead on our heels."

Brasley had balked at the offer to go through the portal. If there was one thing he excelled at, it was making excuses. He was far too fatigued from his ordeal at the Great Library and needed to recuperate. He was a newlywed, and his wife needed him.

And how did they know this new portal place was anywhere they wanted to go anyway?

Complaints along these lines had stalled the expedition two full days.

He stuffed a spare set of clothes into a travel pack. He slipped the silver bracelet he'd taken from the Great Library onto his wrist. He had reason to believe it was something of a good-luck charm. Dagger. Sword. A purse of silver. So many problems could be solved with a purse full of silver.

Brasley sighed, tossed the pack on the bed. "This is ridiculous. I have a pregnant wife. Obviously my duties are here."

"Of course," Fregga said. "You're a good husband."

"I mean, I just got back, for crying out loud."

"No one would blame you."

"I'm just going to tell them I've already done my part and that I'm staying right here with my wife."

"I'll support any decision you think best," Fregga said.

"I suppose you're going to say that Rina is my friend and I owe it to her to do this, or some such nonsense."

"You're a good man, my husband. I'm sure you know what's right without anyone telling you."

They stood quietly a moment.

"Damn it!" Brasley snatched up the pack and slung it over his shoulder.

Fregga took his arm. "I'll walk you down."

"How did you do that?" Brasley asked as they walked.

"I didn't do anything," Fregga told him. "You just needed time to arrive at the right decision on your own. Which you did. Because you *are* a good person even though you try to hide it."

"It's a lot of work being a good person."

"You're a baron. That comes with a lot of responsibility."

"You act like you *want* me to go."

She stopped them in the middle of the hallway, turned to him, touched his cheek. "Sometimes I think you say intentionally stupid things just to test me. Of course I don't want you to go. I'll be worried sick every moment you're away. But if you stay you'll feel guilty about it and you'll start acting like a brat."

"I wouldn't."

"You would, and we both know it." She kissed him, prolonged and soft. "Now, come on. They're waiting."

They entered the library and took the stairs behind the fireplace down to the portal chamber.

Stasha, Knarr, and three of the Birds of Prey waited for them. Knarr and the Birds of Prey had their packs and weapons ready to go. They'd obviously been waiting for Brasley to show up.

"Darshia will lead the Birds of Prey," said Stasha Benadicta. "They're good fighters. Trust them."

Brasley hoped there wouldn't be any fighting, but if there were, he would happily leave it to the ladies with the armor and dour expressions. They all looked like they had something to prove, Nivin especially. She was so petite that at first glance it was difficult to think of her wielding a sword with any credibility, but one look at her face would give anyone pause.

"And what if this portal doesn't take us where we think it will?" Brasley asked.

"That's why Knarr is going with you," Stasha said. "We'll close the portal after you go through, but leave the settings as they are. Knarr feels confident he can open it again from the other side."

Well, that's nice, Brasley thought. *I'm glad* somebody *is confident.*

"Let's get on with it, then," Brasley said. He hoped he sounded braver than he felt.

Knarr twisted the gem at the top of the arch to its rune setting. The wall shimmered as the portal opened.

All faces turned to look at Brasley.

He kissed Fregga, then lifted his chin and eyed the portal with an expression he hoped communicated the appropriate amount of bravado. "Well, then. Follow me."

Brasley stepped through.

CHAPTER
FORTY-EIGHT

Bremmer curled in bed, the heavy blankets over his head. The icy winds rattled the windows.

He heard voices on the wind. Were they from the dream?

"He's gone mental, he has," said one voice.

"Don't talk blasphemy," said another voice. "You know Abbot Bremmer is special. What you see as insanity is simply Bremmer communing with the gods. It is beyond our meager abilities to understand."

"He crapped himself in the bed," the first voice said. "And we had to clean it up. There wasn't nothing holy about it."

Two acolytes, Bremmer realized. Not ghost voices on the wind. They'd been set to watch over him, obviously. Bremmer struggled to open his eyes and sit up so he could berate them. Especially the mouthy doubter.

But the dream pulled him back down. Was it a dream, or was it some sort of vision?

Bremmer fell through fire and into the sky. He looked down as he was falling, the world spread out wide and green and peaceful.

It was a lie.

Anything could look peaceful from a distance, but up close one saw all the gruesome details. As if obeying some subconscious command, the landscape zoomed in closer to a city on the sea.

This must be Sherrik, he thought.

He'd never been there, but he'd seen it on maps, knew it was the most significant port city in that part of the world. But something had happened. A wall along the southern part of the city had been smashed. The once great wharves were a jumble of stone. Water slowly receded from the flooded city, and lumber and debris from smashed ships spun in the eddies.

Bremmer no longer felt he was falling, but flying. Not that he was in control, far from it. Something guided him. He was being shown all of this, but why and by whom he could only guess.

He headed north along the King's Highway and was shown a long line of marching soldiers. They were dead, all of them, skin white, eyes glassy and haunted. In some cases bodies had been twisted and mangled in grotesque ways, but they felt no pain. They marched doggedly north without the need for rest.

Bremmer suddenly felt an icy stab of dread, some presence casting a pall over the scene. He looked back and felt his heart clench with fear.

A giant figure stood ten stories high, looming over the marching army, a menacing warrior in spiked armor with a huge mace gripped in one hand, the other hand open palmed, as if commanding his legions onward. The behemoth looked ghostly and transparent, as if Bremmer was being allowed to see something hidden from the rest of the mortal world.

It's Akram, Bremmer thought. *The god of war commands his army of the dead.*

An instinct told Bremmer that the flooded city had some connection with Akram and his army being on the move. *He was waiting for this. Something has started.*

Bremmer realized it had nothing to do with instinct. Mordis had opened Bremmer's mind, allowed him a glimpse into the vast machinations of the cosmos. It had nearly driven Bremmer mad. Maybe it was driving him mad still, and this was all a vision of the insanity.

He told me a change was coming. And Akram is bringing it.

A new epoch approached, and Akram was vying to make himself supreme. Bremmer didn't completely understand the details of this. Nobody could. Mortals might nip at the edges of understanding the gods and their intentions, but to truly understand the gods was beyond the greatest wizards and wisest scholars in the world. Bremmer had been allowed to see as much as he dared without his mind melting under the heat of total cosmic understanding.

But Bremmer had seen just enough.

He's owed this somehow. Akram has been granted this army of the dead as part of some bargain.

Bremmer could almost figure it out, in his mind's eye could almost see—

An icy chill hit him so hard he could feel it in his teeth.

He turned to see the great ghostly form of Akram reaching for him, hand the size of a country cottage about to close around him. He screamed and felt something warm and wet running down his left leg. His scream went on and on as the giant hand closed into a fist and—

He sat up in bed, stiff and straight as a board, throwing off the heaving covers and still screaming.

The acolytes flinched and yelped, startled by Bremmer's display.

Bremmer panted, his entire body cold with sweat, yet the sheets between his legs were warm with his own piss.

The dead are on the march. Mordis said the trouble would come to our doorstep. Here. The dead are coming here!

"Call the brethren together," Bremmer commanded. "We must make ready for battle. We must send for arms!"

The acolytes looked at each other, then back at Bremmer.

"Right fucking now!" screeched Bremmer, voice edged with madness.

They tripped over each other running out the door.

"And bring clean sheets for this bed!" Bremmer shouted after them.

CHAPTER FORTY-NINE

The stars floated overhead, glittering and cold and distant. The rattle and creak of a wagon. A horse whinnied.

Rina blinked. *Where am I?*

You're flat on your back in the bed of a wagon. The night sky was clear and cool.

She turned her head. The woman who'd arrived with Tosh slept next to her. Kalli.

Rina sat up, looked around. Wagons in front of her. More wagons behind. A long train of them heading . . . She looked at the stars again, got her bearings. North. They were going north.

A man sat slumped on the rear edge of the wagon, snoring lightly. "Tosh."

Tosh started awake with a snort, rubbed his eyes, and looked back at her. He looked groggy and bewildered by cool starlight. "Rina?"

"Where are we?"

"Are you okay?" Tosh asked.

She thought about that. She didn't feel bad at all, exactly as she would have felt after a long night's deep sleep. She'd drained her store of spirit to rock bottom but had healed while she slept. Was that it? Destroy a city and sleep it off?

Rina relived the enormous wave crashing down and destroying the harbor wall. She could see it in her mind. It washed over enemy soldiers and friendlies alike. She only had to think about it for a second to feel queasy, her stomach turning over.

How many dead because of me? How many thousands?

But I had to. There was no other way. The Perranese would have over-run the city.

Right?

"I'm okay," she said. "I need to find the duke."

"Up near the head of the wagon train," Tosh said. "We're heading north on the King's Highway."

Rina hopped over the edge of the wagon and onto the road. "I've got to see him."

"Rina," Tosh said. "What you did . . . back in Sherrik . . ." Tosh couldn't find the words, didn't even know how to form the question.

"I don't know." She wasn't even sure what she meant. *I don't know how one person could cause that much destruction. I don't know how to feel about it. I don't know if it was worth it. I don't know what will happen next. I don't know anything.*

"Is this going to be okay?" Tosh's voice was barely above a whisper.

She thought about it a moment. "I hope so."

Rina offered him an encouraging nod, then turned and jogged toward the front of the long line of wagons. Men and women, soldiers and civilians—wounded, defeated, just flat out exhausted, their heads and shoulders slumped.

The forward group of wagons was surrounded by a dozen mounted soldiers trotting along as an escort. They challenged Rina as she approached but let her through when she said who she was.

She found the duke nestled in pillows and blankets in the back of his own wagon. That he was alive at all was a miracle. He'd been wounded and burned last time she'd seen him. He looked better now. The burned half of his face looked like melted pink candle wax, but it was an improvement over the crispy black char. He seemed weak but not in pain.

"Maxus fussed over me with various potions and spells," the duke told her without lifting his head from a silk pillow. "I'm afraid most of the ladies at Pemrod's court will be disappointed to find I'm not as pretty as they've heard. If we make it that far."

"Emilio, I have to go," Rina said. "There's something important I need to do."

He frowned. "You're leaving?"

"I'm sorry. I have to leave immediately. I'll need to travel fast, so I'm going alone."

The duke propped himself up on one elbow, and now a stab of pain did mar his expression. "You *destroy* my city, and now when we need you you're leaving?"

"The waters will recede," Rina said. "Your people will rebuild."

"If we live long enough," the duke said. "The army of the dead follows after us. An army *you* created."

"I didn't know that would happen," Rina said. "I'm sorry. It's why I've got to go. I've got to find out."

"Go, then, and be damned." He fell back on his pillow.

She wanted to tell him something, maybe that she could make it right, but she didn't want to add lies to what she'd already done.

She jogged ahead until she was clear of the wagon train, then tapped into the spirit. Rina felt the lightning tattoos flare hot on her ankles, and she ran full speed north on the King's Highway.

Sleeping villages blurred past. A quiet, peaceful countryside, so deceptive at night. She ran for hours. A stone bridge over a river, a town.

Dawn humped up a dirty orange on the horizon. Soon she'd turn off the road, taking a more direct route through the countryside.

Her well of spirit seemed deeper than usual. Rina thought she would have needed to rest by now, but she still ran at full strength. Was the spirit like a muscle in some way? She thought it must be. The more she worked it, the stronger it became, the longer she could last. There would be a time to rest, but not yet.

She ran through a dim forest, early morning light filtering through the leaves. She ran in a line as straight as possible for the Temple of Mordis she'd visited twice before. Instinctively she knew the priest would be there waiting for her, the old man who'd plagued her with riddles.

Rina planned to ask him some very pointed questions. Dumo help the man if he didn't answer.

CHAPTER
FIFTY

The stallion had lasted much longer than Alem had thought it would. He couldn't bring himself to run such a fine animal into the ground, so at a shabby crossroads village, he'd traded it for a flea-bitten gray nag, a half dozen apples, a loaf of black bread, and some dried venison.

The nag got him as far as a reasonably decent-size town, where he purchased a brown mare. Strong and young, a good runner. He rode the mare through the night and traded her at a village for a speckled gelding. He'd made a dent in the duke's silver, but there'd been no time to haggle.

He did this twice more and finally arrived at the outskirts of Merridan on a tall, reddish-brown mare he'd named Blaze in the hopes the horse would take some pride in the name and run faster.

He fell in with the flow of people headed for the main gates and realized a lot of people had packed up and were heading for the safety of the walls, peasants with lumpy packs on their backs and children in tow and middle-class merchants with wagons or carts piled high with worldly possessions. The traffic was decidedly flowing in one direction only. In, not out.

They know, Alem thought. *Somehow word's gotten here ahead of me, and they know something bad is coming.* Merridan had the same vibe that Sherrik had when they'd left it for the Red City, and people had crowded the docks looking for a ship to take them away.

Fear. The city hummed with it.

The crowd grew the closer everyone got to the bottleneck of the huge gates. Guards stood aside, gawking as people filed inside. Alem was one of the few riding high on horseback and was spared the press of the mob, but there was a tension just below the surface of the crowd. They moved along in an orderly way, but it was a fragile thing. This time tomorrow the story might be completely different.

The crowd squeezed through the gate, then spread out again on the other side as people filtered away in multiple directions. Alem reined in the horse and allowed himself a moment to gawk. Merridan was enormous. He'd grown up in Klaar, which he'd thought a large place compared to the lakeside village where his grandmother lived. A laughable notion now. Alem had seen Sherrik and been to the Red City. Merridan dwarfed them all, the buildings higher, the streets wider and more crowded.

"Milord, if you please."

Alem looked down to see a guard waving him on. "Traffic's heavy today. Don't want to block the road."

Alem had reined in his horse just inside the gate, and the pedestrian flow had to split to walk around him. "Your pardon." He clicked his tongue, and the horse moved on.

Even by horse, the royal palace was an hour away. He didn't have to ask where it was. It sat on a slight rise, dominating the cityscape. He wound his way through the city streets, steering the horse generally uphill. A narrow alley opened abruptly into a broad cobblestone square. The palace loomed on the other side, and as Alem approached, he realized he had nothing resembling any kind of plan.

Arriving at the front gate and announcing "I'm here to see the king" seemed very similar to declaring "Hello, I am an insane person."

He needed to ask for someone of lower rank and work his way up. *Okay, how would Brasley do this? All bluff and bluster, I bet.*

He approached the gate, chin up, a slight sneer of superiority on his face. His heart was beating up into his throat, but he didn't let it show. Two fairly bored-looking guards leaning on halberds stepped out of their guardhouses on either side of the gate to meet him.

Alem dismounted in front of them and handed his reins to one of the guards without so much as glancing at him. To the other guard, in his best spoiled-Brasley voice, he said, "Fetch me your captain immediately." He tugged off his riding gloves and used them to beat dust from the sleeve of his doublet. "I've just ridden all the way from Sherrik without rest to convey a message from the duke. It is an utmost urgent matter of life and death."

The slightest hesitation, and then, "Yes, milord. If you'd please wait here, I'll fetch him back immediately." He left at a fast jog, armor rattling.

The captain turned out to be a brusque but efficient man who asked Alem to follow him into the palace after examining the duke's signet ring. The captain handed him off to a clerk, who in turn passed him off to one of the palace's lesser chamberlains. Alem's nerves subsided slightly. He was working his way up the ladder of authority, and as soon as he'd passed along the duke's plea to someone of sufficient importance, he could breathe easy.

There was a long wait during which his nerves crept back again, but he was at last taken to a man introduced as Kent, the lord chamberlain of Helva, an old man, gaunt and swimming in a black robe. He wore a close-fitting velvet skullcap and lines in his face from a lifetime of frowning.

Kent turned the signet ring over in his hand, squinting at it with curiosity. "You're from Klaar, you say?"

"Yes, Lord Chamberlain."

"How did you find yourself as far south as Sherrik?"

Alem stifled a sigh. Fatigue weighed heavily on him, but he didn't want to give offense to King Pemrod's right-hand man. "I traveled with a party on an errand for Duchess Veraiin. It's kind of a long story."

Kent's eyes came up from the ring and pinned him, as if he were deciding whether Alem was being impertinent. Kent didn't pursue it.

"An army of the dead, you say?" Kent raised an eyebrow. "And Sherrik destroyed?"

"Flooded," Alem said. "Not completely destroyed. I'm sure it can be restored once the waters recede." *And once thousands of dead bodies are cleared away.* "I know it sounds crazy but—"

Kent held up a hand. "Word has already reached the palace. Your eyewitness account merely confirms this tragic news. We thank you for your efforts. Rest assured, the king is aware."

The king is aware? Is that all?

"Lord Chamberlain, Duke Sherrik pleads for help. His refugees are on the road now, and soon the dead army will overtake them. There's no time to—"

"The king is aware," Kent repeated. "You need trouble yourself no more about it. You must be tired from your journey. I'll have you shown to a place where you can rest and take refreshment."

Alem opened his mouth to protest, but upon seeing the lord chamberlain's dour expression simply said, "Thank you. That's very kind."

◆ ◆ ◆

Alem slumped at a long table in an empty dining hall. He was bone tired and wanted a bed, but the lure of a hot meal won out by a hair. He waited, chin in his hand, having been told someone would be along to attend to him. He wondered whether they'd forgotten about him. He dozed.

The sound of a door opening and closing behind him started him awake.

It's about time. I'm starving for meat and potatoes.

An arm went around his neck from behind, getting Alem in a tight headlock.

Alem's eyes went wide. "What the—"

Whoever had him in the headlock tussled Alem's hair with his other hand.

"Look at you, dressed all fancy. They must be paying stable boys much better these days."

"Brasley?"

Brasley let go of him. Alem stood, and the two men embraced, slapping each other loudly on the backs.

"What are you doing here?" Alem asked.

"Working various miracles, of course," Brasley said. "You wouldn't believe what I've been through since I've seen you last."

Alem blew out a dramatic sigh, shaking his head. "Trust me, I can match you story for story."

"I suspected as much," Brasley said. "But not on an empty stomach. When I heard you were in here, I rushed down to keep you company. Let's get some food in front of us. Then we can see which of us will provide the bards with their next legendary songs."

"I've lost track of the time," Alem admitted. "Are we late for breakfast or early to lunch?"

"Halfway to dinner," Brasley told him.

A sturdy-looking woman in an apron showed up eventually with plates of roast pork and little red potatoes and hot biscuits. Brown bread and baked apples and a dish of sliced cucumbers with vinegar. Alem dug in immediately, letting Brasley tell his story first. Alem hadn't been so famished since the day he'd knocked fruit out of a tree with his magic sword.

Brasley sent away a pot of tea and asked for flagons of beer. He related his tale to Alem between foamy sips.

"Well, after Rina was captured, Talbun and I headed north," Brasley said. "Bishop Hark went after her. I was hoping to find the both of them here in Merridan."

Alem almost spit out a mouthful of beer. "Rina was *captured*?"

"You didn't know?"

"She didn't mention it when I saw her," Alem said.

"You *saw* her?"

Both men began talking at once.

Brasley held up a hand. "Wait. Whoa. One story at a time."

He glossed over the barge ride up the river to Tul-Agnon but related with relish his cleverness in getting his expedition moved to the front of the line to enter the Great Library, how he'd almost been killed by a lift—feat of engineering or not, it had been bloody terrifying—meeting the milk-skinned servants who were apparently somehow immortal even though their masters, the ancient wizards, apparently were not.

"The most important thing is that we found another tattoo," Brasley said. "It's why Rina sent us there in the first place. Talbun thought it might be something to help with . . . well, with all this shit that's been going on."

Brasley's face clouded. He pushed food around his plate with a fork, suddenly looking uncomfortable. "It's not all good news, I'm afraid. We lost the wizard."

He told Alem about Talbun's death, the appearance of the ink mage with the metal leg. By the end of his account, the words were coming with difficulty, something thick in his throat. He signaled the serving woman for the strongest wine she could find.

The woman brought a pitcher and two goblets. Brasley gulped down a gobletful quickly, and that seemed to steady him.

A minute later, he astounded Alem with his explanation of the magical portal that allowed someone to cross hundreds of miles in an eyeblink.

"Of course there's a moment where you feel you might vomit up all your innards," Brasley said. "But it soon passes. That's how we made it to Merridan so quickly."

Alem raised an eyebrow, a forkful of pork halfway to his mouth. "We?"

Brasley resumed his story, concluding with Brasley, the Birds of Prey, and somebody Alem didn't know named Knarr crossing through the portal and finding themselves in the dank depths of Merridan's dungeons. They'd stumbled around in the dark for a while before the palace guards had rounded them up and taken them to the lord chamberlain.

"It took some quick talk to assure him we meant no harm," Brasley said.

"I've met the man," Alem said. "I got the feeling he's sick of the words *Klaar* and *Rina Veraiin*."

"A sober fellow," Brasley agreed, "but hospitable enough. We were given comfortable rooms as opposed to cells in the dungeon. Anyway, I get the feeling they have their hands full right now. The palace is practically buzzing."

"That's because they know there's bad news on the way," Alem said. "There's a whole army of—"

"No, no, start at the beginning." Brasley slurped wine, wiped his mouth on his sleeve. "It's your turn to entertain me now."

Looking back, Alem found his decision to run away from Klaar a bit childish now, and he moved through that part of the story quickly. He fought Perranese on the high seas, escaped Sherrik just before they sealed it, and ate food in the Red City that almost melted his tongue. Then he got into a boat that was *way* too small and would surely sink in a storm. And then was in a storm. And was washed overboard. And stranded on a deserted island, where he found a magic sword (which Brasley immediately demanded to see). Then he swam to the next island, entered an ancient fortress, rescued Maurizan, and fought an ink mage. Alem admitted Brasley might have the better of him here, as the ink mage they fought didn't have a metal leg. Also, Alem admitted he did very little of the fighting.

Did I really live through all that? Was that me?

Alem had impressed himself. When it had all been happening to him, Alem hadn't had time to think anything. Mostly he was terrified. But telling it to Brasley, it really *did* seem like a bard's tale.

By this point in the story, they'd completely obliterated two pitchers of wine, and Brasley called for a third. Alem suspected standing up might be a problem and decided to put off trying until later. When sleep finally came, it would hit hard. Deep fatigue plus the wine had him dizzy.

The dining hall had filled up around them, various other guests in the palace wandering in for a meal, but nobody disturbed the two old friends catching up on their adventures.

"Rina's . . . different," Alem said.

Brasley poured wine. "Oh?"

"The Perranese were already there when we returned to Sherrik." Alem explained how they'd gained entrance back into the city. How they'd brought Rina the new tattoo Maurizan had found in the ruined fortress.

"We stood at the very top of the duke's palace, and she commanded the wind," Alem said, voice strained with the memory. "I don't know how to describe it, Brasley. It frightened me. She commanded the ocean to rise up into a giant wave." Alem told it like something from a legend, how the wave crashed down, smashing the enemy fleet and flooding the city.

"That's . . . incredible," Brasley said with awe. "I can't even imagine what that must have looked like."

"That's not all," Alem said. "That's not the most frightening thing." Brasley watched him intently, expectant.

"She had prisoners brought up from the dungeon," Alem said. "Criminals, I guess. Bad men. But she . . ." He cleared his throat. "She *used* them."

"What do you mean?" Brasley's voice was barely above a whisper.

"She took their . . . I don't know." Alem rubbed his eyes. He was so tired. "She took something from them—their lives, their souls, *I don't know*—but she used them to fuel her spell. I watched. I saw the dead bodies pile up around her as she destroyed ten thousand ships."

Brasley didn't say anything, his expression a mix of horror and disbelief.

Alem ran his fingers through his hair, blew out a long sigh. He drank wine.

Brasley drank wine.

"I just want to *talk* to her," Alem said. "I just want to help her. I don't see how I can, but she must feel alone. She needs to know she isn't."

Brasley leaned forward, lowering his voice. "You should know there are things happening in this palace. Things not generally known." He lowered his voice again to a barely audible whisper. "They say the king is dying. He sees only a handful of people, and one of them is Gant."

"Ferris Gant?"

"The same," Brasley confirmed. "I know how you feel about Rina, but Gant has a fair reputation as a swordsman. And no offense, my good friend, but magic blade or not, you're no fencing champion. Brave? Yes. Lucky beyond imagination? Yes. A swordsman? No."

"It's not like that," Alem insisted. "I care about Rina, yes, and I want her to be okay, but we're not . . . There's somebody else."

Brasley looked interested. "Tell."

"I'm really not sure I should—"

"You listen to me," Brasley said seriously. "I'm an old married man now. I need to live vicariously through you young gadabouts."

"Maurizan."

"The gypsy girl?"

Alem nodded.

"You sly bastard!" Brasley leaned across the table to slap him on the shoulder. "You saved the best part of the story for last."

Heads in the dining hall turned to look, and Alem sank in his seat, going red.

"I always said she was a better match for you. Nothing against Rina obviously, but the little spitfire is right for you," Brasley told him. "I've *always* said so."

"You have?"

"Well, I thought it."

Alem rubbed his eyes. "I have to go. I have to sleep."

"But we're drinking."

Alem stood. "No. I need sleep."

His legs felt like noodles. The room wobbled. *Get a hold of yourself.* He took deep breaths. He'd be fine. He just needed a bed.

Alem took a step.

And fell down.

CHAPTER
FIFTY-ONE

Sarkham's men bivouacked along the riverbank on the Millford side of the bridge. Sarkham himself stood at the end of the bridge, impatiently waving the wagon train across.

Maurizan watched from the shade of a tree atop a nearby hillock. She sat in the grass. She missed Alem, worried about him, hoped he was thinking about her.

Why do two people pick a time like this to find each other, when the whole world is coming apart?

A wagon ground to a stop in the middle of the bridge, the mule pulling it refusing to budge. Maurizan could hear Sarkham's enraged bellowing even from her spot under the tree. He was on edge, at his wit's end like they all were.

"Commanding men is troublesome enough," said a voice behind her, "without also having to contend with stubborn animals."

Maurizan turned her head to look at the man who'd come up behind her. "Bishop."

Hark stood with his hands clasped behind his back, watching the spectacle on the bridge. He had dried blood splatter across his armor, his face lined with fatigue, yet he still managed a cheerful tone. "I've been in the town having a look around."

"Millford, isn't it?"

"Yes. I asked why it was called Millford. Had to ask nearly a dozen people before someone knew. A funny thing. You grow up in a place, and it's just called what it's called because it's always been that way. Some of them looked at me a bit crossways for even asking the question."

"So why *is* it called Millford?" Maurizan asked.

"There used to be a mill with a rather large waterwheel. Burned down nearly a century ago." Hark gestured at the bridge. "And there used to be a ford there before the bridge. Nobody could tell me when the bridge was built."

Sarkham and a squad of soldiers managed to dislodge the mule, and the line of wagons began moving again.

"Most of the people in the town are leaving," Hark said. "The duke told them himself from the back of his wagon in the town square. Two soldiers helped him stand. He told them the army of the dead was coming. Maybe his half-melted face helped convince them. Scouts report the dead have burnt the villages and fields as they pass through. No reason to expect they'll have any mercy here."

"Are you going with the wagons?"

Hark looked down, absently kicked at a root with the toe of his boot. "I thought I'd stick around here. Maybe I can be of some use."

Maurizan didn't doubt it. Whatever his duties as bishop, the man was also a formidable warrior. If she closed her eyes, she could picture him during the battle with the Perranese atop the ducal pyramid. Everywhere the bishop swung his mace, screams, broken bones, and the crunch of helms and armor followed. What would a man like that do with the Prime inked down his back?

"And you?" Hark asked.

She wanted to keep going. Alem was somewhere up ahead. And anyway these weren't her people. The gypsies—her mother, grandmother, Gino—were building a new life around Lake Hammish. They had a place now, wanderers no more.

Thanks to Rina.

So do I owe her?

She took Alem from me.

But I took him back.

And when the army of the dead kept killing and burning its way north, what would happen when it reached Klaar? This was Maurizan's fight as much as it was anyone's in Helva.

"I guess there's no point being an ink mage if I can't show it off," she said. "I'll stay too. The wounded and the civilians need time to escape. We'll buy time for them."

"Proud to fight alongside you again," Hark said. "May I offer a suggestion?"

"Please."

"I'm impressed with your two-dagger fighting style," he said. "Very graceful. It's something to watch."

"But?"

"I've heard the duke's scouts have filled the dead with arrows without effect," Hark said. "Your daggers might not be enough. Rumor says a good beheading does the trick. I suggest a sword or maybe even a sturdy axe if you can dig one up."

Maurizan considered it. Her fighting style and the bishop's were as far apart as it was possible to be. She slashed and dashed and stabbed. She was a deadly hummingbird floating on a breeze. Hark's mace was a clap of thunder wherever it struck.

"I'll catch Sarkham when he's not cursing at mules," Maurizan said. "See if he has arms to spare."

Hark nodded but didn't say anything.

They watched the wagons cross the bridge.

Two hours later, they'd all crossed and were through the town, heading north.

The last man across was a mounted soldier on a horse foamy with sweat.

Maurizan and Hark went down from the hillock to get the news.

The rider set off north after the wagons just as Hark and Maurizan arrived.

"What's the word?" Hark asked.

Sarkham sighed. "Three hours if we're lucky." He turned his head and spit. "Dumo knows why we'd suddenly get lucky."

"Forgive me, old friend, but I have to ask," Hark said. "Do you have a plan?"

"Hold out as long as possible," Sarkham said. "Give the wagons as much time as we can to get away. I expect I should get some kind of barricade across our end of the bridge. I'll get some men on it next. If we jam them up on the bridge, we can hold them a good long time, I think. It's two hundred yards from one bank to the other, and the current is swift."

"Do you have any ideas for harassing them once they're stuck on the bridge?" Hark asked.

"Normally a crossfire from the archers, but word is arrows don't do much since they're already dead." A mirthless smile crossed Sarkham's face. "Don't be shy, Bishop. If you have ideas, I'm all ears."

"I'm not a military man," Hark said. "But I was in town earlier and did some poking around. There's a storehouse with a half dozen barrels of lamp oil inside."

Sarkham thought about that for a moment, then smiled again, more genuine this time. "I see." He looked at Maurizan. "And you, milady? Any suggestions for how we might arrange our defenses?"

"You don't have to 'milady' me. I'm a gypsy. We don't do that," Maurizan said. "But if I can trouble you for a battle-axe, I'll do my best."

◆ ◆ ◆

Sarkham, Hark, and Maurizan crouched behind a barricade on the Millford side of the bridge. They'd overturned a cart and stacked empty barrels around it, completely blocking the passage across the bridge. A hundred soldiers waited behind them, each on one knee, ready to spring forward and replace the fallen.

Plug the gap and keep it plugged, Maurizan thought. *Simple enough strategy. So how did I end up in the front row for this?* She held her weapon in a white-knuckled grip. Sarkham had found her an axe with a double-edged head. She'd need two hands for it, not a weapon she was used to.

She'd realized what should have been obvious all along. This wasn't a battle meant to be won. Sarkham's orders were to delay the dead as long as possible, and if that meant getting killed in the process then so be it.

Not me. I'll do my part and then go. I've been through too much to die for some fucking bridge.

But she didn't know what she would do, not really. She was afraid to run. Afraid to stay.

When the time comes, I'll tap into the spirit. Then I'll know what to do.
She hoped.

The rest of Sarkham's men were spread along the bank to either side of the bridge, hunkering low behind wheelbarrows, overturned hand-carts, assorted furniture, or anything else that could be looted from the town to be used as cover. They all waited in silence, throats dry, hearts beating too fast. This wasn't like the battle at the top of the ducal palace back in Sherrik. That had happened suddenly, so fast. This was different. The waiting, knowing what was coming, was insufferable. Maurizan was suddenly so thirsty.

They waited.

The unmistakable sound of marching boots reached them before they saw anything. As the sound grew closer, Maurizan looked around at the men. They exchanged nervous glances, fidgeting, and she was sure some would run, but none did.

But I wouldn't blame them. Not one bit.

The army of the dead came out from behind a stand of trees where the road curved toward the bridge. They marched six abreast, stepping in perfect time. Other than the crunching footfalls on the sandy gravel road, there was an eerie silence about them. No shouts or commands.

"They march like any other army," Hark said.

"Better," Sarkham said. "It's like one mind controls all of them."

They kept coming, more and more rounding the bend, thousands upon thousands. They marched right up to the far end of the bridge and stopped abruptly without any discernable command or signal.

Behind the first company of dead soldiers, another company split in half, marching deliberately and without rush to take up positions along the opposite riverbank on either side of the bridge. They formed two lines. The first line kneeled, and both lines raised bows.

"Incoming!" Sarkham yelled.

The dead released their arrows, and they flew in a perfect arc, falling among the men on the other side of the river. Men who had shields covered their heads. The arrows *thukked* into the wood of the barrels and carts and tinged off armor. Here and there a scream rose where an arrow found flesh.

Maurizan ducked low, hugging a barrel. "So what's the plan here? Just duck and take it?"

Sarkham crouched next to her. "I hate to say it, but if letting them shoot at us means they're not advancing, then I think we're doing our job."

"They'll pick us apart a little at a time," Maurizan said.

"Yes," Sarkham agreed. "But slowly."

A second volley of arrows fell, and with the third volley, the lead company of dead warriors started across the bridge, dogged but unhurried.

Sarkham looked at Hark. "It's your idea, Bishop."

"Wait until they're almost across," Hark said. "Bunch as many of them on the bridge as we can."

When the front line of warriors came within twenty feet of the barricade, Hark nodded. Sarkham waved at a man behind him, who stood and nocked an arrow, pulling the bowstring back to his ear. Another soldier lit the arrow with a flaming brand he'd kept handy, and the soldier with the bow let fly.

The arrow trailed smoke as it arced over the front few lines of advancing warriors and dropped down in the middle of the bridge. Maurizan rose up enough to see over the top of the barrel. She didn't want to miss this.

The lamp oil ignited immediately, and the flames spread back along the bridge to engulf the dead soldiers massed there waiting to cross. The flames came forward also, stopping within ten feet of the barricade.

Maurizan watched, wide-eyed. Every warrior on the bridge burned, flames engulfing dead flesh and hair. If they'd been living men, there would have been screams and panic, men leaping off the bridge into the water. But the dead simply marched on, unflinching, as if they didn't feel the flames crawling over them at all.

The flaming warriors in front drew their weapons and advanced on the barricade.

Hark rose, gripping his mace. "I'd had rather high hopes that would work."

Sarkham drew his sword. "We'll have to do it the hard way."

"Less talking. More hacking." Maurizan tapped into the spirit and lifted her axe just as the dead warriors struck.

She watched them come in slow motion, the spirit allowing her to take in every aspect of the melee at once, absorbing even the tiniest detail. The dead man swung, and she let the blade pass before stepping in to strike. Maurizan didn't have Rina's bull strength, so she had to angle it perfectly. She swung hard with both hands.

The axe swept clean through the dead man's neck. His head popped off, tumbling back flaming and smoking, and landed among his comrades two rows back.

In her peripheral vision, Maurizan saw Bishop Hark bat aside a sword thrust, then bring down his mace hard, crushing the dead man's helmet and skull nearly flat. He fell in a clatter of armor, but already more of his dead brethren pressed forward against the barricade.

With so many flaming bodies pressed against it, the barricade caught fire.

Sarkham stood back from the heat. "We may have miscalculated."

More of the enemy crowded close, threatening to topple the barricade.

"Spearmen!" Sarkham yelled.

The crowd of soldiers behind them parted, and a dozen spearmen rushed to the barricade, jamming the spears into the bodies of the dead men attempting to climb over the barricade, which was burning out of control now. The length of the spears was just enough to keep them back from the blazing heat. The spearmen stabbed faces, pierced armor, and slashed flesh.

None of it mattered. The dead were already dead. Sarkham's men were simply trying to keep the burning warriors behind the barricade. Sarkham's orders had been clear. This was the bottleneck. This is where they had to keep them at bay.

"Hold them!" Sarkham shouted. "Hold the unholy bastards!"

More men ran up to push the backs of the spearmen, who in turn pushed all of the flaming dead men off the barricade. Others stepped over the bodies to take their place, but the men of Sherrik wouldn't budge.

One of the dead warriors managed to climb to the top of the barricade. He raised his sword high, looked like he might leap down among the spearmen. The sword slipped from his hand. There was the briefest pause, and then he fell, body sprawled unmoving across the barricade.

Maurizan slapped Hark on his armored shoulder and pointed back along the bridge. "Look!"

The dead warriors had come to a halt amid the flames. Slowly they dropped, falling across each other, the fire charring them black. They stacked on top of each other like cordwood, stiff and soundless save for the crack and pop of their dead flesh burning.

"It doesn't hurt them, but it consumes them," Hark said. "It just took some time."

Sarkham thrust his sword into the air. "Burn, you bastards!"

A cheer went up from the men behind him. The bridge was impassable, choked with the smoldering dead. Their orders had been to hold them at the bottleneck, and they'd put a cork in the bottle.

The cheer trailed off, and again the only sound was the crackle of the fire. An eerie pall hung over the scene, the army of the living staring across the river at the army of the dead. The rattle of armor could be heard among the living as they shuffled nervously. The dead might as well have been statues, staring back across the river with glassy, vacant eyes.

"Now what?" Maurizan pitched her voice low, afraid to disturb the silence.

"Now nothing," Sarkham said. "They can stand there like that for a week as far as I'm concerned." He turned his head back toward the men. "Hold your positions!"

They all stood that way for a minute. Two.

Then the dead along the opposite bank stirred. These were the warriors who harassed the men of Sherrik earlier with the volleys of arrows. They dropped their bows and drew swords. The kneeling front row stood.

And both rows marched for the river.

Maurizan's eyes narrowed as she watched them. "What are they doing?"

"Drowning themselves, I hope," Sarkham said.

"They're already dead," Hark reminded them.

The first row marched down the bank and entered the water. They were waist deep by the time the second row entered. The dead archers on the other side of the bridge were doing the same thing, marching into the water, swords drawn. A few seconds later the river swallowed both rows of warriors. No sight of them. Like they'd never existed. Beyond, the rest of the dead army stood impassively.

"Are they going to swim it?" Maurizan asked.

Sarkham shook his head. "Not in armor. Not in that current."

A minute went by. Then two. Then five.

Maurizan grabbed Hark in the crook of his elbow and dragged him along. "Come on!"

Hark's eyes went wide. "Oh, okay."

She dragged him down the bank to the side of the bridge where the piling went down into the water. Maurizan let go of Hark and pulled off her boots, tossing them aside.

"I'm not sure what you intend," Hark said.

She pulled her top off and tossed it to him.

He caught it. "Oh . . . uh." He turned away.

"We need to know." Maurizan shimmied out of her breeches and threw them at Hark. "Please, this is no time to worry about being proper. Guard my back."

Hark held her clothes. "But what are you going to do?"

Maurizan splashed forward into the water and tapped into the spirit. "Scouting ahead."

She dove into the river and swam deep.

It was dark and murky below the surface of the water. Maurizan swam toward the opposite bank. The current was indeed strong. If her tattoos hadn't allowed her to swim better than a fish, she would have been swept away in a second. She swam farther. The river here was deeper than she'd anticipated. And the light from above barely penetrated.

She pulled up and hovered in place, arms treading water against the current.

Nothing. Just the gray-green depths of the river. The current had taken them, Maurizan realized. They'd done it. They'd halted the advance of the dead army. They'd blocked the bridge, and the dead couldn't cross the river. Relief flooded her. All they had to do was hold the bridge and—

A pale hand shot out of the murk to grab for her.

She darted away like a guppy, hovered there in the water and watched them come.

With armor and weapons, the dead were too heavy to swim, but they didn't need to. They plodded forward, bracing themselves against the current. One step, boots sinking into the mud, next step, and so on. A slow but inevitable advance.

Maurizan swam back as fast as she could, a white streak in the water.

She stood when the water was waist deep, releasing the spirit and staggering ashore toward the bishop. "They're coming!"

She took her clothes back, frantically pulling them on. "Tell Sarkham. The current won't take them. They're not swimming. They're just walking across the bottom. It's slow going, but it's not like they need to breathe. Tell Sarkham to line up the men as close to the water as possible. They'll gain some small advantage getting them as they come out. No point letting them reach good footing on dry land."

Hark ran to tell Sarkham as Maurizan sat on the bank and pulled her boots on, clothes clinging to her wet skin.

To think I was worried about Alem. That's a laugh. He's long gone, and I'm here beheading dead men with this fucking axe.

◆ ◆ ◆

Hark relayed Maurizan's suggestion to Sarkham, and the captain shouted the order. His men lined up three rows deep along the river, the first row standing ankle deep in water, waiting with iron grips on swords and axes.

The bishop watched from behind. He'd taken his turn at the bridge and would again but didn't pass up the opportunity for a rest. He was getting too old for this. He'd honestly thought his combat days were over when he'd been assigned as bishop in Klaar. Never in a million years had he dreamed he'd be donning his plate armor again and following Rina Veraiin into the wilderness.

And where is she now? I swore to help her, and nobody can even tell me where she's gone.

They all watched the water.

Time crept by, and a low murmur worked its way through the soldiers. Maybe the current had swept them away after all. If the dead army couldn't cross the river or use the bridge, then Sarkham's men had done it, hadn't they? It would take at least two days to find a ford or another bridge across the river, and by then the civilians and the wagons of wounded would be far enough ahead to be safe.

But soldiers know better than to hope, and when the dome of the first helmet rose up through the water like a surfacing turtle, they knew. The dead had crossed.

The dead had arrived.

"Don't let them out of the water!" Sarkham shouted. "Take their heads off!"

The men of Sherrik went into the water to their knees just as the dead lurched forward, raising their weapons, and a split second later the riverbank erupted in an uproar of battle cries and the clang and crash of metal on metal.

Heads flew. Men screamed agony as some of the dead pushed through and drove steel through living flesh. When a soldier fell, a man from the line behind would fill the gap, swinging and hacking knee deep in water at the enemy.

Bishop Hark's eyes shifted from the battle to the rest of the dead across the river. They were on the move now, thousands of them, marching slowly but with perfect discipline down toward the water.

We could kill a thousand, and it wouldn't matter, Hark thought. *They'll just keep coming.*

Hark turned and ran for the hillock he'd been on with Maurizan earlier. The slight elevation gave him a better view. He looked at the small town, looked to the east and west. The King's Highway ran through the middle of the town. To the west was a forest with thick undergrowth. No easy passage there. The river wrapped around the town to the east and emptied into a large lake.

In short, marching straight through the town was the only timely way to keep traveling north.

He ran back to Sarkham, arriving out of breath.

"Are you okay, Bishop?" Sarkham didn't take his eyes off the battle.

"The rest of the dead army," Hark said. "They're crossing."

"I know."

The first ranks were already entering the water.

"They'll overrun us."

"Our task is to slow them as long as we can," Sarkham said.

"Taking an army through the forest would be very slow going, and there's a lake to the east," Hark said. "The only fast route is through Millford."

"So?"

"So burn the town," Hark said. "Burn it all."

CHAPTER FIFTY-TWO

If the Temple of Mordis looked deserted before, it looked twice as deserted now. Grass grew high between the paving stones. No fires burned. Not a soul living or dead in sight. Rina walked slowly across the grounds, grit and gravel crunching beneath her boots.

She entered the temple. Some of the candles had burned out. The rest had burned down to nearly nothing.

Rina climbed the steps to the domed room. Krell waited there with his back to her. The cosmic show plated above him. It was more frantic this time, ringed planets hurtling by at alarming speeds, comets colliding in fantastic explosions.

Krell held his hands up to display. "Behold, Rina Veraiin. A reality in chaos. But we're very near the end. Soon there will be order again. But whose order? That's the question."

"I did as you told me, Priest," Rina said, voice tight. "And now a city is destroyed. The dead come for the living."

"I commanded you to do nothing," Krell said. "I simply informed you of a looming choice."

"But not how to choose," Rina said. "Or what it might mean."

"That is life for nearly every human being in the world," Krell said. "We are but tiny things swimming through reality, often against the current, making the best decisions we can with imperfect information."

"I'm tired of games," Rina said. "No more riddles. No more guessing. You said the way south paid a debt."

"Yes."

"Then I'm done with you," she told him. "With you and your god."

The priest laughed, a sick, dry sound, and turned to face her. He was skin and bone. There seemed to be less of him each time Rina saw the man. "But is he done with you, Duchess?"

"Talk straight, damn you."

"You're living in a time of transition," Krell said. "One epoch dies as another is born. The transition is a time of turmoil and upheaval. The gods contend for supremacy. Little mortals such as ourselves are merely the instruments of their will."

"No," Rina said. "I won't be used. Gods or not."

"You have been used already," Krell told her. "It is inevitable."

"No."

"Yes, Duchess," Krell said. "Do you know what kind of god Mordis is? What is his relationship to the others?"

"I don't care about your god," Rina said.

"You want answers," Krell said. "These are my answers. Listen or go."

Rina said nothing.

"Some say Mordis is a servant to the other gods," Krell explained. "This isn't completely accurate, but we'll set that aside for the moment. When a god's worshippers pass from this realm, it is Mordis who escorts him to the afterlife. Death is but a bridge from one reality to another, and Mordis reigns over this bridge. The debt you paid was to another god. Akram."

"Who's Akram?"

"The god of war," Krell said. "Eons ago another god was supreme." The priest waved his hand absently. "Never mind which one. It doesn't matter. But the lore says the next god ascendant was Akram, who would have plunged the world into eternal war, an epoch of ongoing conquest and conflict. I don't pretend to understand how the gods choose their successors. I am sure it is beyond our understanding, but somehow Akram was cheated. Or at least he *felt* cheated. I don't know. He was passed over, and Dumo was raised instead."

"If you're going to explain, then explain," Rina said. "I don't want a lesson on the entire pantheon."

"Akram could not have been thwarted if he hadn't been weakened," Krell said, ignoring her outburst. "It was Mordis who arranged for Akram to be weakened. It was Mordis who prevented the world from being thrust into eternal war."

Rina paused, curious now. "Go on."

"Gods get their strength in part from their worshippers," Krell said. "As I've already mentioned, Mordis ferries the dead of each god to their own particular afterlife. When men die in battle—*regardless* of their religious preferences—they belong to the god of war. But Mordis stopped taking dead for Akram, relegating them to some other reality. It weakened Akram just enough to allow Dumo to ascend instead. Akram felt cheated, and accused Mordis of wrongdoing. So Mordis made Akram an offer. When it came time for a new epoch to begin, Mordis would return the dead souls he'd stolen from Akram."

Rina chewed her bottom lip, thinking. She looked down at the glove covering the skeletal tattoo on her palm. "The dead army."

"The southern path pays a debt," Krell said.

"I killed thousands of men," she said.

"In battle," Krell said. "They belong to Akram now. If he can cover the globe in war, he can grow powerful enough again to reign supreme."

"Then I really am finished," Rina said. "I've paid your debt."

The priest's dry laugh again. "No, you are not finished. Only the gods say when they are through with us."

Her hand fell to her sword hilt. "No."

"You've been set on a path, Duchess Veraiin."

"I won't follow it."

"You have no choice," Krell told her. "Nor do I. Nor any of us. The path will unfold before your feet wherever you tread."

"No." She tapped into the spirit.

"Do not be tiresome, child." Impatience in Krell's voice. "We've all come this far together. The finish line is in sight. The final end to a long journey. I speak not for myself. Do you think the gods will allow you to upset their machinations, plans thousands of years in the making? Don't be a fool."

"I said no!" The rapier flashed from its scabbard, the blade a gleaming blur.

Off came Krell's head. It bounced on the ground, mouth and eyes frozen open. The priest's body fell next to it, landing so lightly it might have been a robe stuffed with straw. No blood oozed from his neck. It was as if there were no humanity left in him, one foot already in the realm of death.

Above her, the swirling cosmos went dark, planets and stars winking out, until there was only a dull stone dome lit dimly by a flaming brazier across the chamber.

Rina released her hold on the spirit and left the temple. Her hands shook, heart beating so fast. Halfway down the front stairs she felt her legs give and sat down hard on one of the steps.

She put her face in her hands and cried.

He dreamed of Tenni, of fingers through her blond hair. The scene morphed like scenes do in a dream, and Tenni was so cold, eyes open and skin waxen, flecks of blood on her lower lip. He called to her but was far away, voice echoing like he was at the bottom of a dark mine shaft.

Something nudged him firmly in the ribs, and Tosh started awake. He'd been rocked to sleep by the sway of the wagon.

It was Kalli. She nudged him in the ribs, now pointed back south. "Look."

Tosh looked. A column of black smoke rose into the air. "Millford?"

"I don't know," Kalli said.

Tosh looked at Kalli. She was sitting up, eyes clear. The color had come back into her skin. "You look better," he said.

"I feel better," she said. "Plenty of sleep. Where's the duchess?"

"I don't know. I don't know anything. You got any money?"

"Not much. A little."

"I've got a bit left from what Rina gave us. Can you ride?"

"I think so."

"At the next village maybe we'll buy a horse," Tosh said. "Or we'll borrow one of these. I don't think they'll come after us. They've got bigger worries." He tried to picture the map he'd seen. "I think sooner or later another road will fork off from this one. The one that goes on to Kern and ends up being the Small Road up to Klaar's Back Gate."

Kalli frowned. "It sort of feels like running away."

"We've done our part." Tosh thought about Tenni's little girl, Emmon. Tosh's little girl now. She had nobody in the whole world. Just Tosh. "It's not running away. It's going home."

◆ ◆ ◆

Rina lit a small fire with the flint and steel she'd found among the debris of the deserted village on the temple grounds. She wasn't cold. There was just something comforting about a fire.

And anyway, she wanted to light her chuma stick.

She sat and smoked and stared unblinking into the fire.

Where are you, Alem?

Rina felt utterly alone, aimless, and defeated. An entire city destroyed because of her. For what? Because one god owed another a favor. How was she supposed to make sense of the world after that?

Oh, Alem. I'm sorry. Sorry things got so messed up. It's all such a big mistake.

She wiped her eyes. *No, don't start that again. It's too late now anyway. Too late to fix it.*

She smoked. She watched the fire.

When she'd smoked the chuma stick down to almost nothing, she flicked the butt away and stood. She considered the possibilities. Which direction? Rina tapped into the spirit, the lightning bolts flaring on her ankles as if they knew what to expect. Rina made her decision.

And ran.

CHAPTER
FIFTY-THREE

Sarkham had only been given ten horses for his scouts and had been reluctant to give up two of them, but he supposed Maurizan and the bishop had earned them. They bid farewell to each other, and Hark and Maurizan rode north as fast as they could, Millford burning in their wake.

They passed through two villages, both deserted, but took the opportunity to rest and water the horses before moving on. A half day's fast ride caught them up with the wagon train.

Maurizan kept her eyes open for Tosh and Kalli as they galloped past the wagons but didn't see them.

They arrived at the duke's wagon and the head of the train, and Hark nodded respectfully. "Your grace."

The duke sat up in the back of his wagon. "What news?"

"We weren't able to hold the bridge quite as long as we'd hoped," Hark said. "So we . . . uh . . . made other arrangements."

"Such as?"

"We set Millford on fire. The King's Highway through the town is utterly impassable."

"I . . . see." The duke thought about it. "The lake is to the east."

"Yes, your grace," the bishop said. "And a thick forest to the west. Sarkham says they'll be delayed at least a day. With any luck, two. He remains behind with his men to harass and delay the dead army further."

"That helps," the duke said. "A drastic step, but I commend the decision under the circumstances. But we'll still need my cousin Pemrod's army to cover us while we get all the civilians and wounded into the city."

"You grace, I'd like to make a suggestion that might serve both our purposes," Hark said. "I know you sent a rider ahead to alert the king to our needs, but anything can happen on the road. I'd hate to think some harm came to the man. I have business in Merridan. Let me carry your message to the king, and it will double our chances. If your rider has made it safely, then no harm done."

"I have no hold on you, Bishop Hark," the duke said. "Your help is appreciated. Go where you will, and Dumo go with you."

They said good-bye, and when Hark and Maurizan had trotted a quarter mile or so ahead of the wagons, Hark said, "Will you come with me to Merridan?"

"Yes."

"Thank you," Hark said. "My guess is Rina's gone one of two places. If she's gone home to Klaar, then so be it. If she's gone to Merridan, then she might need our help. The capital is full of snakes and backstabbers."

"As far as I'm concerned, Rina Veraiin can take care of herself," Maurizan said. "I can't say the same for Alem. That's why I'm coming along. I've invested far too much time in that boy to let anything happen to him."

"Good enough," Hark said. "I plan to ride fast and rest little."

"If you're waiting on me, you're already behind."

Maurizan spurred her horse into a run, and Hark was only a split second behind her.

◆　◆　◆

Brasley sat on his bed, pulling on his boots.

Darshia ran past his door and down the hall. Fast.

Brasley blinked. "What the bloody . . ."

He had taken to leaving the door to his room open. His room was in a guest wing of the palace, and he'd learned that if he watched the flow of people moving down the halls at certain times of the day, and if he followed the crowd, it would often lead to some reception or a meal or some other entertainment.

I wish Fregga were here. I could escort her to these things, and she could look at me lovingly, and all the daughters of the barons and counts will wonder why they couldn't get to me first.

But mostly he just missed his wife and wanted her around.

Nivin ran past his door, followed by the other Birds of Prey, boots making a tiny stampede.

Something is going on.

"Hey!"

A second later, Nivin stuck her head in the door. "Rina's here!"

She was gone again just as quickly.

Rina!

Brasley jumped up and tore out of the room after her.

He caught up with them at the end of the hall, where they all got down on one knee in front of Rina. She wore that dreadful black armor that Brasley hated and was covered in dust and road grime.

But you're a sight for sore eyes, lady.

"Darshia." Rina took her by the hands and lifted her to a standing position and gave her a big hug. Darshia hugged back. "What are you doing here?"

"We came looking for you," Darshia said.

"We all did!" Nivin piped up, then suddenly looked embarrassed.

"I'm sorry that I don't know all of you," Rina said. "But it's so good to see people from home."

They took that as an invitation to stand and all talk at once, bombarding Rina with questions.

Rina look past them and saw Brasley, her face brightening with a wide grin.

"Brasley!"

She rushed past the others and threw herself on Brasley, gathering him into a huge hug.

"You might be wearing armor, but I'm not, you know." But he returned the hug, and they laughed.

"You can take it, big strong man."

"Where's Bishop Hark?" Brasley asked. "Last time I saw him he was riding off into the wilderness to rescue you. I would still think the Perranese had you, if Alem hadn't told us—"

"Alem's here?"

"Around here someplace," Brasley assured her. "He came in with the news that you drowned Sherrik, and then he *insisted* on getting drunk."

"That's not funny," Rina said sharply.

"I'm sorry," Brasley said. "I thought I'd try a little gallows humor. Bad choice. I guess I miss Klaar. And my wife."

She hugged him again, sighing, this time holding on to him for support as if suddenly tired. "Somebody told me we're getting near to the end of this thing. Do you think it's true? I hope so."

"I hope so too," he said. "Hark?"

"Alive when I saw him last. I had to travel fast, so I left him in good company. What about Talbun?"

Brasley's face clouded. He shook his head.

Rina ran her fingers through her hair, grabbed a fistful, and closed her eyes tight. "Oh no."

"Forget it," Brasley said. "There's something more important. We found it."

Rina blinked. "Found it?"

Brasley lowered his voice. "The reason you sent us to the Great Library. The *tattoo*."

Understanding dawned in her face. Talbun's death hadn't been for nothing.

"Rina." A voice behind her.

She turned, sucked in a quick breath. "Alem."

He looks so good, Rina thought. The black doublet and breeches suited him. He'd recently bathed, hair combed. She'd loved him just as much with hay in his hair and stinking of horse straight from the stables. *I'm not going to cry. I'm never going to cry again.*

She went to embrace him, hesitated.

Alem grabbed her into a hug, whispered in her ear, "It's okay. We're friends."

Friends.

Don't cry. Don't cry. Don't cry.

The hug only lasted two seconds, but Rina considered tapping into the spirit, making time slow, stretching the moment forever.

But she didn't.

Alem released her. "Glad you're okay."

"You too."

The sound of someone clearing his throat.

Rina turned. The Birds of Prey had parted as Kent strode toward her, looking grim and inhospitable beneath his black skullcap. A brace of armored guards stood behind him.

"Forgive the intrusion," Kent said. "I know you're reuniting with your people, but King Pemrod summons you, and time is of the essence. Several things have to happen very quickly if we're to dispatch the army to Duke Sherrik's aid."

"Of course." Rina looked back at Alem. "We'll visit more later. All of us," she said, including the rest.

Brasley leaned in and whispered, "Invited to see the king, eh? Better you than me."

"Brasley, my boy!"

Brasley looked up and saw Count Becham behind the guards, gesturing for him to follow. "You too. Come along now. It will be good for you to see how things get done in the capital."

"Just . . . shit," Brasley muttered under his breath.

CHAPTER FIFTY-FOUR

Kent ushered Rina, Brasley, and Count Becham into an anteroom adjacent to King Pemrod's private bedchamber. The guards closed the door and took their positions on either side of it. There were three other men there waiting. One was a broad-chested man in a gleaming breastplate, high black boots, with a saber hanging from his belt, a short dagger on the other side. He held a plumed helmet under one arm, and Kent introduced him as Lord General Denrick. Next to him was a fat man with a pointed white beard known as Count Harlan, evidently one of Pemrod's advisors. The third man was . . .

"Ferris Gant," Rina said, attempting to sound pleasant. "I wondered if you'd be here. Good to see you again."

"And you, Rina." Gant's voice was tight. He seemed nervous. "It seems we're all going to be forced to make hard decisions a little sooner than we thought."

Rina didn't like the sound of that but wasn't given the chance to pursue it.

"Give me just a moment to make sure his majesty is ready to receive." Kent went into the next room and returned in less than ten seconds, gesturing them to enter.

The king's bedchamber was enormous and ornate, with thick, exotic rugs on the floor and a glittering chandelier hanging from the ceiling. Three guards stood at attention in three different corners. King Pemrod sat up in a huge canopied bed in a nest of silken pillows. He wore a simple nightshirt. The covers were pulled up to his waist.

"I'll ask you to excuse the intimate setting." Pemrod said it in a way that made it clear he didn't really give a damn what they thought of the setting at all. "Since I've taken ill, it's become convenient to conduct the realm's business from here." He looked at Rina, eyes narrowing. "Ah, Duchess Veraiin. Glad you could join us. I understand you've just arrived. Forgive me for summoning you before you've had time to freshen up, but time grows short in more ways than one."

"It's okay," Rina said. "I just hope your majesty will feel better soon."

"Well, I won't," Pemrod said. "I'm dying, and I'm told it will happen sooner than later. Some damn disease eating me up from the inside. All the wizards and physicians at my disposal, and nobody can do a thing about it. I'm told it's excruciatingly painful. Fortunately Kent has whipped together one of his tonics that keeps the pain at bay. But that's neither here nor there. To business. My grandnephew tells me he broached the subject of matrimony and that you're thinking about it."

"Oh. Yes, your majesty," Rina said. "When your delegation visited Klaar."

"Well, the time for thinking is over," Pemrod said. "And the time for acting is at hand. When you were here in Merridan before, I laid out what I thought were some convincing arguments for such a union, but you were unmoved. Was Ferris able to sway you by other means?"

Rina had no idea what to say. Her eyes shifted to Gant.

"Rina, I told you how it could be agreeable for both of us," Gant said. "You remember? I . . . well, let's just say that everything will go more smoothly if you agree. You'd make a wonderful and courageous queen."

A long pause.

"Thank you for that, Ferris," Rina said. "But I'm sorry. The answer is no."

Gant's shoulders slumped. Everyone else in the room stood perfectly still, waiting to see what happened next.

Pemrod took a white handkerchief from beneath his bedcovers and coughed into it. Rina saw bright red flecks of blood on the fabric.

The king dabbed at the corners of his mouth, then said, "I see."

"I mean no offense to you or your family, your majesty. Ferris is a fine man, but I hardly know him," Rina said. "And I'm not ready."

"I understand," Pemrod said.

Another long moment crawled by.

"Lord General," Pemrod said.

The general snapped to attention. "Your majesty."

"Once the order is given, how long will it take you to mobilize a sufficient force to cover my cousin's retreat from the dead army pursing them?" Pemrod asked.

"The Light Cavalry Third Brigade can be saddled and on its way in two hours," said the lord general. "A division of royal pikemen can follow three hours later, but of course infantry will move more slowly."

"The sooner the better, then," Pemrod said. "It seems I have much to think about for such an important decision. Yes, much to consider."

Rina blinked. "Your majesty, you will send help, won't you?"

"Will I?" Mock innocence on his face. "Why is that?"

"But . . . to save their lives!"

"Their lives are in *your* hands, Duchess," Pemrod said. "Do you have some convincing argument for moving faster?"

Rina took a deep breath. "Are you saying you won't help those people?"

"What if I am?"

"But they're *your* people," Rina said.

"So are the people inside this city," Pemrod said. "If the dead surround the city, and we're under siege for weeks or months, who will feed them? Letting in Sherrik's folk will increase the number of mouths to feed. These are the life-and-death decisions a king must face. Often ugly decisions, but these problems don't go away just because we wish they would. You are young, Duchess, and if you're lucky enough to grow older, you'll learn hard decisions make a person hard too. What happens to Helva if I die with no successor? I try to assure a smooth succession for my heir because I'm a responsible ruler. If I pass with no heir named, the long knives come out of every shadow, and Merridan plunges into chaos."

Gant looked at Rina with pleading eyes. "Marry me, Rina. It's the best way. You'll be saving lives."

"Never mind her, boy," Pemrod said. "You'd think she'd want to save the survivors of the city she destroyed? I suppose some people just have no sense of responsibility."

Rina gasped. *He knows. Somehow he knows what I did in Sherrik.*

And was he wrong? Would Rina's pride and stubbornness cost lives? She looked at Brasley, who returned a bewildered gaze.

And then she remembered what Krell had told her. That she was on a path from which she couldn't escape. Fate had decided for her. She trembled with rage that she would have so little control over her own life.

"You're the king," Rina said. "The responsibility is yours."

"Rina, please." Gant tried to communicate something with his eyes, but Rina was too angry to care.

"You're a monster," she said. "That's on you. That blood is on your hands."

"A monster, am I?" Pemrod tsked. "I've been called worse, I suppose."

"Rina." Gant's voice begging.

She ignored him. "And history will call you worse, if you let this happen."

Gant turned to Pemrod. "Tell me to marry anyone else, and I will. Anyone you think best. Let's settle it once and for all."

"No, I don't think so," Pemrod said. "This whole episode has made me reconsider if you're cut out to be a monarch. And I won't be sending troops to rescue my dear cousin Emilio, I'm afraid. We'll order the gates closed and make the city safe."

"You bastard!" It was all Rina could do not to reach for her sword.

"Uncle, don't," Gant said. "Send troops to help Sherrik. I'll do whatever you say."

"Every word you utter screams weakness," Pemrod said. "Only confirming I'm right to pick another to be my heir."

"I'm sorry, Uncle."

"I'm sorry too," Pemrod said. "I'm sorry for Helva."

"No, Uncle," Gant said. "I mean, I'm sorry."

He whisked his sword from its sheath, and in the same quick motion thrust it through the king's chest. Pemrod slumped over onto the bed, the breath leaking out of him like a long, wistful sigh.

Rina screamed.

Behind her, she heard Brasley utter, "Oh, fuck!"

The lord general drew his saber in one hand and his dagger in the other.

Then he plunged the dagger into the back of the fat count with the pointy beard. The count screamed and fell.

"The king! Assassins!" Count Becham clumsily drew the small dagger on his own belt.

"Count Becham, don't!" Brasley tackled him to the floor.

Gant jerked his sword loose from the king's chest, spraying blood across the white sheets, and slammed the hilt into the face of the guard coming up swiftly behind him. The crack of a broken nose, more blood spraying.

The lord general spun and faced the other two guards in the room. When one lunged, he parried it easily and moved in to kill the other. On his backswing, he caught the first on the arm, a deep gash that made him drop his weapon. The lord general finished him off with a quick thrust.

The door slammed open, and the two guards from the anteroom rushed in, blades naked and ready.

Kent, almost forgotten, stepped out of the shadows, muttering blurred arcane syllables, and tossed a pinch of blue powder in the air. The guards' eyes rolled up, and they fell in a heap.

"You're a wizard?" Rina said.

"It would appear so," Kent said dryly.

Brasley helped Count Becham to his feet.

"Why did you do that?" demanded the count.

"Because it was doubtful you could affect the outcome of this unfortunate incident, and I'll be damned if I'm going home to tell Fregga her father is dead if I could have prevented it," Brasley said.

"Oh, yes." It was clear by the expression on Becham's face that he was only just now considering his own mortality. "Thank you, my boy. Thank you."

Gant crossed the room and kissed the lord general on the lips. "How many of the other men and officers are with us?"

"Not many," the lord general said. "But the right ones."

"Secure the palace first," Gant said. "Then the rest as we discussed."

The lord general gave Gant's arm a squeeze, then left at a run to carry out his tasks.

"I didn't know you were going to do that," Rina said.

"I wasn't quite sure myself if I'd go through with it or not," Gant said. "No turning back now. I still wish you'd have married me. The nobility would have accepted me without question. I'm not quite sure how many will support me now."

"The lord general. He's your . . . ?"

"Yes. Nine years now."

"I'm sorry," Rina said. "I'm sorry it's going to be so difficult for you now."

"No, I'm sorry," Gant said. "It was wrong of me to make you feel obligated, to make you feel like it was your responsibility to solve my problems."

"Speaking of problems, I have a feeling it's about to get loud around here," Rina said. "I'd consider it a great favor if I could get horses for me and my people. And maybe show us the back door."

Gant laughed. "Kent has something better in mind. I'll leave you in his hands. Good luck to you, Rina Veraiin."

"And to you, Gant."

He turned to leave, but she grabbed his wrist. "Duke Sherrik."

"I'll send troops," Gant said. "I promise." And then he was gone.

It took about thirty seconds for Brasley to convince his father-in-law to go back to his estate and lock all the doors.

"Go and get your people," Kent said. "Then meet me, and I'll see you on your way. And hurry. The king's demise won't be a secret for long."

"Meet you where?" Rina asked.

"Our young Baron Hammish knows," Kent said.

"Oh, yes," Brasley said, realizing what Kent meant. "I believe I do."

◆ ◆ ◆

They should have been suspicious when there were no guards at the front gate of the palace. They entered and paused in the gigantic reception foyer, where a single man in palace livery sprawled on the tile floor, a pool of blood spreading from beneath him.

"Something's happening," Bishop Hark said.

Maurizan eyed him sideways. "You think?"

The racket of metal on metal followed by screams and shouts came from a hallway to the right. Hark grabbed Maurizan and yanked her into an alcove down behind the statue of some long-dead ruler holding a trident aloft. The racket entered the foyer, and Hark motioned for Maurizan to stay put while he peeked around the base of the statue. A small group of soldiers in the same livery as the dead man fought another group of soldiers in a different livery. Men on both sides fell before the battle moved on to another part of the palace.

"What was *that* about?" Maurizan asked.

"I don't know," Hark said. "But let's go in the other direction."

They headed down a hallway, past other dead bodies here and there, and ran into a frumpy woman in a maid's uniform coming the other direction. She seemed scared and started to flee back the way she'd come, but Maurizan yelled for her to stop.

"We're not part of this," Maurizan said. "We just want to find our friends."

The maid paused, still poised to run away, and then she came back. "Okay."

"Do you know Rina Veraiin?" Hark asked. "*Duchess* Rina Veraiin."

"No." The maid shook her head. "Sorry, no."

"Alem," Maurizan said. "Very good looking, rode in with a message for the king."

"No."

"Baron Hammish," Hark said. "Brasley Hammish."

The maid raised an eyebrow. "The one who always wants the wine?"

"Yes!" Maurizan said. "The lazy, drunken, lecherous wastrel that always wants the wine."

"Follow me."

She took them up two flights of stairs, then pointed down a long hall and told them it was the guest wing. That was as much as she was willing to do, and she turned and fled.

The hallway was filled with women frantically pulling on armor and throwing packs over their shoulders. It looked like they were trying to move out in a hurry.

And then there he was among them. He was there. He was alive and right in front of her eyes.

"Alem!" Maurizan screamed.

Alem turned, eyes wide, and the gypsy girl slammed into him, wrapping her arms around him as they both went to the floor. She kissed him hard on the mouth and kept kissing, heedless of the Birds of Prey, who gathered around and laughed.

A moment later, Duchess Veraiin was in the hall, chuma stick stuck in the corner of her mouth, expression emotionless. "Maurizan. Bishop Hark. Just in time to leave. Follow me."

◆ ◆ ◆

Kent led them down a narrow, winding staircase down below the dungeons. Rina was right behind him, followed by Alem, Brasley, Maurizan, Hark, Knarr, and the Birds of Prey. Deeper into the bowels of the dungeon didn't seem like an escape route, but Rina remembered Kork taking her out through a secret tunnel down in the dungeons when she'd escaped Klaar so long ago.

It seems like years. I'm not even the same woman.

"You asked me if I were a wizard," Kent said. "I am. I'm many things. I was admitted to the Abbey of Mordis when I was ten. I studied there. I went on to Tul-Agnon, where I not only attended the university, but apprenticed to a wizard. The Order of Mordis had big plans for me. I was meant to be close to the king. I was loyal to Pemrod but even more loyal to Mordis. My family has been among the faithful for eight generations. I believe I spent years just to be in the position for what I'm doing now."

They reached the bottom of the stairs and found themselves in a large chamber, a stone arch carved into the far wall, large gems at various points around the arch.

"Baron Hammish says you're going to send us through that arch," Rina said. "That it somehow becomes some kind of portal." She waved for Brasley to come stand next to her.

"I've set the archway to deliver you to the Abbey of Mordis in the Great Wastes," Kent said. "It's at the base of a mountain, and on top of the mountain is the mother temple of our order. We in the Cult of Mordis have for centuries prepared ourselves for this very day. It's fate that's delivered you to us at this time."

"I don't give a shit about your *fate*." Rina reached into the bag Brasley was holding and came out with the scroll case he'd found in the Great Library. She waved it under Kent's nose. "All I want to know is, how good of a wizard are you?"

CHAPTER
FIFTY-FIVE

Empress Mee Hra'Lito heard the clamor and knew what was coming, but she sat cross-legged on the mat and poured tea, waiting. She sipped, offering an outward appearance of calm.

There was a knock at the door. She'd been expecting it. "Come."

The door opened, and Third Steward Bel'Fre Logan entered. He held his left arm stiffly against his side, blood flowing freely from the shoulder.

"Pardon, your highness, but it is my unfortunate duty to inform you that the imperial palace has been breached," the third steward reported. "The bottom level is lost, but we're holding them at the mezzanine."

"How long?"

"There's no way to say with complete certainty, highness," he said. "But long enough for you to make . . . final arrangements."

"My thanks, Bel'Fre Logan," Mee said. "On your way out, will you please send my personal maids to me?"

"As you wish, highness." He bowed as well as his wounds would allow and turned to leave.

"One moment."

The third steward paused. "Highness?"

"Did we really never hear from the fleet?"

"Alas, no, highness. We made attempts to contact them by every means we could think of. It's as if they simply vanished."

"I see. Thank you."

He bowed again and left.

Mee sipped tea. *Well. That's a shame.*

A minute later, her personal maids arrived, a dozen of them, their hair pulled tight in glossy black buns. They wore identical silk robes in the imperial colors. She ordered them to bar the main doors to her apartments and then asked them to line up so she could address them for the last time.

"You are merely servants," Mee told them. "The ones who are coming have no quarrel with you. Surrender yourselves, and you will likely be spared."

Mee wondered if the lie was as obvious to them as it was to her. They kneeled in a line facing the door, heads bowed, waiting for mercy that would never come. If they were lucky, the mob would be so enraged, they would kill the maids on sight. If unlucky, they would be raped first.

She turned and left them, going to her private bedchamber. Mee opened the top drawer to her vanity and removed a hinged box of polished black wood. She opened it and took the dagger from within, gleaming and razor sharp. Her duty now was to plunge it into her heart.

Not yet. Just a few more minutes.

She threw open the double doors to her balcony and looked out across the city. Smoke rose in numerous places. As a child, she'd been taught that of all things, the Empire was eternal.

What other lies had she been told?

The harbor lay empty.

She heard a crashing racket elsewhere in the apartments, followed by the screams of the maids. Mee put the point of the dagger against her breast, hesitated. She hated to admit it, but she feared the pain.

Fists pounded the door to her bedchamber.

She let the dagger drop and climbed up on the wide balustrade, balanced precariously a moment, the wind tugging at her robes. She heard the door smash open behind her.

And jumped.

She wanted to think she was flying but knew she was falling. They'd all been falling for years.

CHAPTER
FIFTY-SIX

They stepped through into a blizzard.

Kent had warned them and given them heavy cloaks, but the bitter wind still cut through them. Snow slanting at them sideways. Rina pulled the cloak tightly around her, teeth chattering. She was glad she'd sent Zin away before going through the portal. He shouldn't have to endure this.

Neither should I, damn it.

She looked around. They'd come out of the portal to a wide landing on top of a tall tower. Snowcapped mountains rose up around them. The edge of the Glacial Wastes, Rina realized.

The rest of her people shivered in a semicircle behind her. They faced three men. The one out front raised a hand in greeting. The all wore heavy furs, and the two in back had their hoods pulled forward.

The one who'd waved his greeting had his hood pulled back, an old man, but with strong features and alert eyes, a full head of pure white hair.

"I am High Priest Bradoch!" he shouted over the wind. "Welcome to the Abbey of Mordis. The others have already arrived ahead of you." He gestured to the two men behind him.

The taller and larger of the two pulled his hood back, and Rina heard Brasley gasp behind her. She looked closer at the big man.

"I know you," Rina said.

"You should." Ankar swept aside the fur cloak, revealing his metal leg. "Your handy work."

Rina tapped into the spirit, and her sword was instantly in her hand. She noticed Maurizan had drawn her daggers just as quickly. The Birds of Prey had their weapons out a split second later.

"I saw you fall," Rina said.

"You know what a person can do when tapped into the spirit," Ankar said. "The world slows. I found an outcropping of rock to grab on to, then climbed down. It wasn't quite as easy as I'm making it sound."

"So now what? We pick up where we left off?"

"You've beaten me to two tattoos and taken one of my legs," Ankar said. "It occurs to me I might be fighting on the wrong side. I want to join you, Duchess Veraiin, not fight you."

"Rina, no," Brasley said. "He killed Talbun."

"And how many did you kill in Sherrik?" Ankar asked. "We pay a tithe in blood for what we do."

Rina flinched at that. There was some truth in what he said. Her hands weren't clean.

"How did you get here?" she asked.

The shorter man next to Ankar threw back his hood. "I showed him the way, *Duchess*."

Rina narrowed her eyes. "Giffen."

High Priest Bradoch shuffled his feet, looked embarrassed. "Forgive me, but I thought you were all comrades. It seems I was mistaken."

"We're old friends, aren't we, your grace? You didn't think you were rid of me yet, did you?" Giffen sneered. "Always people underestimate me, and always they pay for it."

"If you think you're going to join me, you're going about it the wrong way bringing him along," Rina told Ankar. "He murdered my parents."

"I can understand why that might be off-putting," Ankar said.

One of Ankar's huge hands shot out and grabbed Giffen by the back of the neck. A quick twist and a snap, and Giffen fell into the snow, eyes open and vacant.

"Well, then." Rina sheathed her sword. For so long she'd dreamed of killing Giffen with her own hands, but she was so tired. Giffen was nothing more now than a problem solved. She turned to Bradoch. "Can we continue this discussion inside? I'm freezing my ass off out here."

◆　◆　◆

"Why?"

"Why what?" Ankar asked from across the table.

They'd all been escorted to a rustic dining hall within the abbey. Fireplaces had been stoked, and they'd all been brought food and pots of hot tea. Rina wasn't especially hungry but spooned a thick brown stew into her mouth simply because it was warm. As a woman of Klaar, she'd been raised to endure harsh winters, but the Glacial Wastes were something else altogether.

She sipped tea, then said, "Why do you want to go with me to the top of the mountain?"

"Why do *you* want to go?"

Rina thought about it. It hadn't occurred to her to put it into words. "Because then it will be finished. Because I want my life to be my own again. Something's happening that could change the whole world. I need to see it through."

"I have spent my entire life making myself a being of power," Ankar said. "I don't mean a man who commands a city or army or a kingdom. Just me alone. Powerful. There is power at the top of the mountain. I want to face it."

I don't, Rina thought. *But I must.*

Krell's words haunted her again. Fate was guiding her, pushing her in this direction.

No. I make my own choices.

"Let me see the new tattoo," Ankar said.

Rina glanced around the rest of the dining hall. The Birds of Prey took up two tables near the fireplace. Alem and Maurizan sat at their own table, holding hands. Knarr and Brasley sat across from Bishop Hark. They all talked and ate and sipped tea. Nobody was paying attention to the two ink mages in the corner.

Rina slipped off her glove and held her hand out to Ankar, palm up.

"I see nothing," he said.

Rina tapped into the spirit. A skeletal hand identical to the one on her other palm appeared, except it shimmered and pulsed with a silvery glow. A strange power flowed through it. It felt nothing like her other tattoos.

Ankar raised an eyebrow. "What is it called?"

"The God Eater."

Ankar chuckled. "Can there be any doubt? Let us go to the top of the mountain and face this god together."

"And what do you want?"

"I told you."

"And what else?"

"That God Eater tattoo," Ankar said. "Give it to me."

"It won't do you any good."

"Let me guess," Ankar said. "There was only enough ink for one application. I've encountered this problem many times. I will hunt the world over for the right wizard to figure it out. This is my life's pursuit."

Rina looked down into her bowl of stew. "Let me think about it."

"Bradoch tells me there's a mad abbot at the top of the mountain," Ankar said.

"Oh?"

"His name is Bremmer, and it is said that he communes with Mordis. I'm given to understand he's become something of a problem, his acolytes more loyal to him than the order. I think Bradoch wants to help us because he wishes this Bremmer would go away."

"I'm no assassin," Rina said.

"Then all the better I'm coming along," Ankar said.

Ankar seemed to think it had been decided, which in fact, it had. Rina wouldn't stop the other ink mage from tagging along, mostly because she simply didn't care. It was his life to risk, and he might prove useful. It was the others she was worried about. The Birds of Prey were brave, but what could they do against a god? She couldn't ask them to come along.

But she couldn't send them away either. They'd come so far. Brasley wanted nothing more than to be home with his new wife, but he was here out of friendship. Hark felt he owed her. And Alem.

More than anyone else she wanted to send Alem away but had the least willpower to do so. *If I send him away now, I might never see him again.*

Rina drained her teacup and stood abruptly. She banged the cup on the table for everyone's attention. The conversation died away, and all heads turned to her.

"Ankar and I are going up the mountain," Rina said.

That caused a low murmur, which dried up when Rina started talking again.

"Many of you don't even know fully what this is all about," Rina said. "I'm not sure I do either except that what I do could change the world. I know how that sounds. I value each and every one of you, and I won't ask you to risk your life on something you don't understand or believe in. Nobody is obligated to do anything they don't want to do. I won't think less of you."

Bishop Hark was the first to stand. "I'm with you. Come what may."

The Birds of Prey stood next. Then Alem stood. Maurizan looked at him and frowned, but she stood too. Brasley's eyes shifted to Ankar. He didn't like the idea of the other ink mage coming along, but slowly he stood.

Only Knarr didn't stand, which wasn't a surprise. She barely knew the man, and he was only along to help in case there was a problem with the portal.

Rina looked at each of those who'd stood, nodding her gratitude. "Thank you. Thank you all. Now check your gear, pack food and water. We're leaving."

The place erupted with talk, the sounds of chairs pushing away from tables. Darshia yelled for her Birds of Prey to check weapons and armor.

"I'll tell Bradoch we need heavy traveling furs," Ankar said.

Brasley approached Rina after Ankar left. "Can we trust him?"

"No," Rina said. "But I don't think it matters."

"What is it you think we need to do up there?" Brasley asked.

"I think we might have to kill a god," Rina told him.

Brasley sighed, walked away shaking his head. "I *knew* I shouldn't have asked."

CHAPTER
FIFTY-SEVEN

They huddled in the heavy furs and bent into the wind as they trudged up the Skyway of Eternity. The trail narrowed to a single-file path, widening slightly where they passed skull shrines or rest points. But they didn't rest. The sky darkened as angry clouds gathered.

It was a long hike, and they talked little, concentrating on putting one foot in front of the other. The ink mages had taken the lead, and the Birds of Prey brought up the rear. Brasley marched in the middle, cursing himself.

Idiot. I could have stayed back down in that warm abbey. Okay, it wasn't very warm, but it was better than this. What was it I thought I could do to help? I'm no ink mage. I'm not a warrior.

And trusting Ankar? That just seemed foolish. But something had changed in Rina. Brasley could sense it. There was a single-mindedness about her, as if nothing else mattered, almost as if Ankar was a worry beneath her notice.

Endless hours later, Brasley looked up to see they'd stopped. He trudged ahead to stand next to Rina. "We're almost there, aren't we? What is it?"

Rina pointed. "They've blocked the path."

Brasley looked. The rock walls had risen up on either side of the path, and now somebody had piled a stone barricade across it. Dark figures moved frantically behind it. Beyond, Brasley could see some kind of building. This must be the summit.

And they've arranged a welcoming committee. How nice.

Something hissed through the air and struck Brasley in the fleshy part of his upper thigh. He screamed and went down, looked and saw it was a crossbow bolt. Blood gushed from around the wound.

Wow. That really fucking hurts.

◆　◆　◆

Rina tapped into the spirit, drew her rapier, and charged all before Brasley hit the ground. Crossbow bolts flew at her in slow motion. She leaned left to dodge the first, sidestepped right to avoid the next. In her peripheral vision, she saw Maurizan doing the same, a dagger in each hand. Ankar lagged behind with his metal leg but charged after them with surprising speed.

Rina kicked in with the lightning tattoos and pulled ahead, leaping atop the barricade while the astonished defenders were reloading their crossbows. She dropped down among them, spinning and thrusting and slashing until a half dozen lay dead and bleeding. Maurizan hopped over the barricade to find the work had been done.

To the right stood the great Temple of Mordis. To the left was a newer structure, and more acolytes in black robes with spears poured out the front door toward them. Rina and Maurizan charged.

Behind them, Ankar smashed the barricade with his mace, scattering the stones like pebbles. Darshia led the Birds of Prey through the gap, swords in their hands, battle cry high-pitched and terrifying.

A dozen acolytes broke off and charged them with spears in an uneven line. The women parried the spear thrusts easily, stepping inside their reach to thrust deep into soft bellies.

An acolyte ran at Darshia, a sloppy spear thrust. She caught it under one arm and brought her sword down hard on the hand holding it. Fingers fell away in a splatter of blood, and the acolyte fell back screaming and looking with horror at his ruined hand. Darshia dropped the spear and leapt forward to finish him.

The violent orgy of screams and blood lasted only a minute, and then suddenly there was silence, save for the groans of those who hadn't yet finished dying.

Nivin turned a slow circle, sword up as if expecting another opponent to come out of hiding. "These weren't warriors."

"No," Darshia said. "They were fanatics."

Hark and Alem came through the gap in the barricade, carrying Brasley between them. They'd yanked the crossbow from his leg and wrapped the wound tightly with strips of ripped cloth.

They all stood a moment, wondering at the needless death.

"These men were fools," Rina said.

A deranged laugh rode the wind and echoed around them.

Rina looked around until she spotted him.

He sat against the front door of the temple like a beggar, shrunken in his furs, face pale and eyes wide. He laughed again, more madness than mirth.

Rina mounted the steps and stopped one short from the top, looked down at the man huddled there. "Abbot Bremmer, I presume."

"Yes," Bremmer said. "The leader of the fools. The *last* fool."

Ankar and Maurizan came up behind Rina. Alem and Hark set Brasley on the bottom step, and the Birds of Prey gathered in behind them. They all looked up expectantly. They were at the front door of the mother temple of the Cult of Mordis, and nobody knew what was supposed to happen next.

"What happens if I go in there?" Rina's eyes shifted from Bremmer to the temple door.

"Madness," Bremmer said. "And death. Only *I* can talk to Mordis."

"Tell us what's happening," Rina said.

"You wouldn't understand." Bremmer twitched, swatted at something nobody else could see. "Nobody understands. He gave me a glimpse. Not much. Just a tiny peek at the workings of the cosmos, but it was more than any mortal should ever see."

"Tell us."

"No," Bremmer said. "Go away!"

"Bremmer," Rina said. "We're here to help you."

The songbird tingled at her throat.

Relief flooded Bremmer's face. "Are you really? Oh, that's . . . that's so nice to hear. I've been all alone. The acolytes couldn't understand. Nobody could."

"Understand what, Bremmer?" Rina asked. "Try to explain."

"Mordis used to be a man," Bremmer said. "Did you know that?"

Rina moved a little closer to him, knelt on one knee. "I didn't know. Tell me."

"Akram is coming," Bremmer said. "He makes war."

"Yes."

"No, you don't understand," Bremmer said. "He *is* war. At some level, a god is what he or she is god of. How can the god of death not *know* death? He has to be a mortal. It's the only way it works. As soon as Mordis moves from his altar—even a broken altar—he steps one foot into our world, the mortal world; he's vulnerable. And Akram's coming to kill him."

"Why would he want to do that?"

"Because Mordis is a check on all the other gods," Bremmer said. "*Especially* on war. War would go on forever if death didn't make men tired of it."

Rina stood, dusted herself off. "Sounds pretty serious."

Bremmer laughed his insane laugh again. "Understatement of the fucking epoch."

"Then I suppose I'll just have to go in there and have a word with this Mordis."

"Don't be absurd," Bremmer said. "You can't hear the voice of a god. It will rip your sanity from you and leave you a husk. Only my special bond allows me to communicate with Mordis, and I'm b-barely keeping it together myself." He twitched violently again.

Rina looked at Ankar.

"You know tapping into the spirit gives us perfect control," Ankar said. "I think we can shield our minds."

"Are you sure?" Rina asked.

Ankar grinned. "Absolutely not, but I'm here to test myself, remember? I'll risk it even if you don't."

Rina looked at Maurizan. "You don't have to come. Nobody's pressuring you."

Maurizan's face hardened. "What's that supposed to mean? I'm not brave enough?"

Rina frowned. "I didn't say that."

"Of everyone here, there's exactly three of us that can go in there and do anything," Maurizan said. "If the big guy is right, I mean."

"Listen to the gypsy," Ankar said. "Three ink mages fighting together has not happened in centuries. Maybe not since the Mage Wars. This will be one for the bards."

"I don't give a shit about the bards," Rina said. "But she can come if she wants. I'm glad for the help."

Rina turned to the others. "Wait here as long as you can. But get clear if it looks like things are going wrong."

That started Darshia, Bishop Hark, and Alem all talking at once.

"Shut up!" Rina shouted. "You heard what the crazy man said. You can't go in there. I'm not even sure *we* can go in there. Now do what I tell you. I don't want your deaths on my head."

Rina stuck a chuma stick in the corner of her mouth, looked at Maurizan, then at Ankar. "Come on. Let's get this shit over with."

CHAPTER FIFTY-EIGHT

The three ink mages entered the temple, the door slamming shut behind them with a deep, ominous thud. The interior of the temple was red orange with the light of low-burning braziers and torches.

Rina leaned into the brazier just inside the doorway and lit her chuma stick.

Kork was right. I smoke too much.

These things will kill me.

She laughed. The other two looked at her.

"Never mind." Rina puffed the chuma stick. "Come on."

They passed through a short entrance hall and down a short flight of steps.

And there he was.

Mordis sat on the rubble of the broken altar that had once been his tomb, skin cracked and glowing red all over, as if lava boiled just below the surface of his skin. He was ten feet tall and yet somehow smaller than Rina had expected. He turned and looked at them, something almost sad in his demeanor.

Mordis stood.

"I'm tapping in," Maurizan told them.

"I think that's a good idea," Rina said.

"Agreed." Some of the bravado had gone from Ankar's voice.

The god raised a hand.

"I've been waiting for you," Mordis said.

The death god's voice rolled over them like a clap of thunder.

Rina's hands went to her ears, tears leaking from her eyes. The Prime helped her discipline her mind, but it was still almost too much.

Ankar went to one knee.

Maurizan turned and grabbed on to a pillar for support, her back humping up as she vomited.

Perhaps it was some small mercy that Mordis didn't speak again. The three ink mages recovered, stood shoulder to shoulder to face the god.

Mordis took a step down from the ruined altar.

All three ink mages were tapped into the spirit, theoretically masters of themselves, masters of their own fear. But all three took a step back.

Mordis took another step, and there was a shimmer of pink light, almost like a curtain, as if Mordis had passed from one place to another.

What was it Bremmer had told them? He's one foot in the mortal world now.

Mordis held up a hand, almost gentle. Almost as if he were so very tired.

The sound of something ripping, like fabric, but ten thousand times louder shook the temple. Rina flinched away from a blinding light behind the altar, and when she looked back again, she saw someone else stepping through a hole torn in reality.

A dozen feet high, spiked armor, eyes glowing like coals from the deep black within his helm, a huge mace gripped in one fist. He advanced on Mordis, his footfalls clanging like metallic avalanches.

Akram.

The god of war.

Akram swung his spiked mace at Mordis. The god of death flinched back but still took a glancing blow in the shoulder, lava splashing from the wound like blood. Mordis went down, hitting the floor and shaking the temple to its foundations.

Akram stood over Mordis, mace raised high in both hands, poised for the killing strike.

Bremmer's words rang in Rina's ears. *How can the god of death not know death?*

"No!" Rina charged, her rapier flashing from her scabbard.

She gathered all of the strength from the bull tattoo, prepared to strike. She leapt at Akram, sword held high.

Akram backhanded her out of midair.

Rina flew across the temple and hit one of the stone walls with a crunch, her armor doing little to protect her. She bounced off the wall and hit the floor hard. She searched herself, took stock. Two broken ribs on her left side. A sprained wrist. A tooth knocked loose.

Already the healing rune worked to mend her.

Ankar leapt atop the altar and opened his mouth impossibly wide. He belched flames, bathing Akram in fire.

A scream of pain or perhaps merely annoyance escaped the god of war. He made a backhanded swing with his mace, but Ankar was tapped into the spirit, and his reflexes were as good as any jungle cat's. He sprang back, and Akram's mace missed his skull by inches.

Maurizan tossed one of her daggers. It flipped end over end and embedded itself in Akram's neck, a nearly impossible throw that found the small gap in his armor between his helm and his spiked collar.

Akram plucked the dagger from his neck like a rose thorn and flicked it away.

Rina lurched to her feet, willing the pain of her broken ribs into the background. The healing rune still needed time to do its work.

This was a mistake, she thought. *We're going to die.*

A deep rumble, and the ground shook.

Alem looked up. "Did you hear that?"

"Hear it?" Brasley said. "I felt it in my ass. I'm surprised the temple didn't cave in."

"Damn it, we have to get in there," Alem said. "They need our help."

"Don't be an ass," Brasley said. "You heard what Rina said. This thing is beyond us."

"Are we just going to stand around?" Alem demanded.

"I'm not going to stand at all," Brasley said. "I've been crossbowed in the fucking leg."

Alem's hand went to the hilt of his sword. "What's the point of having a magical blade if I can't do anything with it?"

"That won't keep your brain from being melted," Brasley said.

"I don't care. I'm going in there."

"Alem, don't."

"I have to." Alem headed up the stairs to the temple door.

"Alem!"

Alem paused, looked back at Brasley.

"Take this." Brasley slipped something off his wrist.

He handed it to Alem. Alem looked at it, a silver bracelet.

"It protected me from that one-legged asshole," Brasley said. "It's better than nothing."

Alem slipped the bracelet on his wrist. "Thanks."

"Alem," Brasley said. "Save her."

"I will," Alem said.

As he entered the temple, Alem wondered which one Brasley meant. And then he wondered too.

Ankar struck Akram with his mace. The god stumbled but then turned on the ink mage.

Akram jammed his own mace into Ankar's chest and started running. Ankar found himself picked up off his feet and flying backward. The god rammed Ankar against a wall. Ankar heard and felt bones crack. He slid down the wall and landed in a painful heap, wheezing as he tried to draw breath.

Akram reached down and grabbed Ankar by the throat, lifting him. Ankar kicked and struggled, clawed at the hands that held him. The ink mage was a big man and used to looming over others. Being handled like a rag doll was new for him.

He didn't like it.

Akram slammed the ink mage against the stone floor, once, twice, three times. The god held the bloody body up and stared at the mashed and mangled man like a curiosity, a small child who'd found a frog while playing in the yard.

Ankar spit blood. "You . . . y-you son of a . . . bitch."

The god slammed Ankar to the floor one last time. Ankar lay dead and bloody.

Akram turned to Rina. She pulled herself along the floor, wincing in pain, trying to hide herself from the furious god in the spiked armor.

Akram stalked toward her, the temple quaking with each step.

This is it, Rina thought. *I'm dead.*

Akram reached for Rina with one hand, raised his mace in the other.

Rina's eyes shot wide. *Please.*

Just as Akram was about to bring the mace down, he suddenly threw back his head and roared pain. The temple shook with his rage, dust and rubble knocked loose from the ceiling.

Rina looked to see what had happened. Alem stood behind Akram and had stabbed his glowing sword in the back of the god's thigh.

Idiot! You wonderful, gorgeous idiot.

Alem jerked the sword free and raised it for another strike, but Akram was already twisting to swing at him with the mace.

Run, idiot!

The mace fell, but Maurizan was there in the same instant, shoving Alem out of the way. He flew back, rolling across the stone floor. The mace struck Maurizan—

And her image dissolved into smoke.

Maurizan appeared five feet to the other side, and Akram swiped at her again with a backhand. Again her image dissolved into smoke and swirled away.

Rina gawked. *How can she do that? I can't do that.*

Maurizan appeared again next to one of the temple's fluted pillars, her back to it, crouched like she could dart one way or the other. Akram swung through the gypsy's smoke image again and smashed the pillar with a thunderous crack, chunks of stone flying. The pillar fell and crashed against the stone floor. A portion of the ceiling gave way, tons of stonework falling directly onto Akram in a cacophonous racket of destruction.

◆ ◆ ◆

Bishop Hark took one of the heavy fur cloaks from a dead acolyte and draped it over Brasley's shivering body. The baron looked pale. He had lost a lot of blood from the crossbow wound and really should get in out of the cold.

Hark motioned to the building across the courtyard. "I can't persuade the ladies to take cover." The Birds of Prey had insisted on staying near the temple entrance. "But we should get you out of this wind, Baron Hammish. You've been hurt."

Brasley smiled weakly. "And miss the show? Honestly, Bishop, sometimes I think you don't want me to have any fun at—"

A rumble and a crash came from the temple.

"Dumo help them," Hark breathed.

"Maybe we should move back a little," Brasley said.

Hark gripped his mace tightly. "Blast it. I feel useless standing out here."

"You don't happen to have a wineskin on you by any chance?" Brasley asked.

"Sorry, no."

"A pity," Brasley said. "It's the perfect time for a strong drink."

"I used to pray at times like this," Hark said. "But Dumo stopped answering. I thought I'd done something wrong, that I was being punished. But it's just that Dumo was in hiding. I wish it was just me. I wish none of this were happening."

"I briefly knew a student who explained to me that gods represent something literal but also abstract," Brasley said. "What did Dumo represent?"

"Dumo was god of rivers and streams." Hark made a wavy gesture to indicate the flow of a river. "Transitions. Going from one thing to another with order and reason."

"Considering all that's happening," Brasley said, "maybe it's time to try prayer again."

Hark looked at Brasley, considered, then slowly nodded. He went to one knee, groaning with aches and pains. The climb up the Sky of Eternity had sapped him. The entire journey had nearly done him in. He leaned on his mace.

Always have I been your faithful servant. If you have any strength or power to grant me, all I can say is that I'm here.

And he waited.

Rina staggered to her feet, coughing, waving away the dust from the collapsed ceiling. She looked at the pile of rubble that had buried

Akram. Nothing stirred. She checked herself. The healing rune had done its work.

She saw a dull glow through the dust on the other side of the rubble. Alem's sword.

"Alem!"

"Over here."

"Are you hurt?"

"Just bruises."

He started toward her, climbing over the rubble.

"Stay put, you idiot!" Rina said. "Where's Maurizan?"

"Here," echoed the gypsy's voice from somewhere Rina couldn't see. "I'm okay. I think. Is it over?"

"I don't know," Rina said. "Nobody move."

Mordis still lay near the remains of his altar, chest heaving with slow breaths. The air around him distorted and shimmered with the power he projected, but compared to the raw savagery of Akram, Mordis seemed diminished, almost shriveled.

Some instinct galvanized her, and she started toward the fallen god.

Akram erupted from the rubble. Huge chucks of stone tumbled past her, and she barely had time to dodge. Alem was knocked from his footing and went down with a yelp.

Akram slammed the mace down hard, cracking the floor where Rina had been a split second before.

She leapt atop a section of fallen pillar and launched herself at the god of war, rapier aimed between the glowing red eyes within the darkness of his helm. The bull tattoo tingled on her arm as she summoned all of her strength for the strike.

The sword shattered into a thousand glittering shards, as if it were made of glass.

Rina landed hard and rolled out of the way, barely avoiding getting her head smashed flat by the mace. She crawled away and scampered to her feet, realizing she no longer had a weapon.

Yes, I do.

She pulled off her glove. The God Eater blazed silver on her palm.

Akram came for her.

"Rina!" Alem ran up behind Akram, sword poised for a thrust.

"Alem, don't!"

Akram swung the mace behind him, almost lazily.

No.

It connected with Alem's chest, lifted him in the air.

Please, no.

The sickening crunch of bone echoed across the interior of the temple.

Oh no. No no no no no.

He landed on the far side, rumpled in a heap up against the wall, and lay there unmoving.

"Alem!" Maurizan screamed, and ran toward him.

Akram turned his attention back to Rina.

Rina held up her hand, palm out. *Come and get some.*

As always when tapped into the spirit, time slowed. A thousand thoughts raced through her head in an eyeblink. This wasn't right. This wasn't what she was supposed to do.

She turned and looked at Mordis.

The wounded god lifted his hand, reached out to her.

Rina ran for him.

Akram bellowed rage and chased her, his footfalls leaving a trail of spiderweb cracks in the floor.

Rina reached Mordis.

And took his hand.

In that first moment, she knew she must have made a terrible mistake. Power flowed from Mordis so fast it threatened to fill her to bursting.

Rina looked back over her shoulder. She'd figured it out too late. Akram was upon her, mace raised for a killing blow.

A huge armored figure crashed into Akram from the side, and both tumbled away in a deafening clamor of armor.

Bishop Hark!

He seemed a foot taller, younger, and full of power, a golden glow around him. He faced off with Akram, and a moment later they laid into each other with their maces, sparks showering where weapons struck armor, each blow sounding like the end of the world.

Rina's attention went back to Mordis. She still held his hand. He'd gotten smaller, and the lava seething below the surface of his skin had cooled. He looked at her, and she thought she saw relief in the ancient eyes.

Rina felt . . . lighter. A fire spread throughout her entire body, but it didn't harm her. There was no pain.

Something . . . was happening.

Maurizan cradled Alem's head in her lap.

"You're going to be okay." She blinked away tears. "I've got you. I'll fix it. I'll save you."

Alem's eyes were glazed, unfocused. He coughed, blood bubbling from his mouth.

Please don't die. Oh, please.

The two figures in armor drew her attention. It was the bishop! Fighting Akram!

They traded blows, each one of which would have knocked a bull across the temple. Sparks flew. The bishop hit Akram once, twice, three times in a row, and the god of war reeled, stumbled back. Hark saw his advantage, raised his mace, and screamed rage as he rushed in for the kill.

Akram swung his mace in a wide arc, catching Hark on the side of the head. The sickening crack of skull could be heard across the room. Hark took two halting steps backward and then fell.

Maurizan gasped.

It was almost comical that after all of the noise and racket of battle, it took only that slight gasp to draw Akram's attention. He stalked toward the gypsy and raised the mace to end her.

From behind, another figure grabbed the mace and squeezed. A crack and a flash, and the shards of the weapon clattered to the floor. Akram turned to face the new glowing figure that stood in defiance of him.

I don't believe it, Maurizan thought. *It's Rina.*

She no longer wore the black armor but was now a being of pure light. It pulsed through her, inside of her, around her. But the outline of her face was recognizable enough. It was Rina Veraiin.

Or what had once been her.

She was as tall as Akram, but her brilliance made Akram seem shabby and ridiculous in his spiked armor.

He roared and charged her.

Rina lifted a hand, reached out almost as if she might caress him.

There was a sound like a thousand screaming voices and a flash of light so bright, Maurizan had to turn away. She blinked, still couldn't see.

I'm blind!

But she rubbed her eyes and blinked again, and slowly her sight came back.

When she looked up, Rina was standing right over her, ten feet tall and pulsing with power. Maurizan could feel it vibrate in her bones.

Maurizan picked up Alem's sword, held it in front of her, knowing she was being ridiculous but too afraid to care.

At first, Rina looked as if she were made of pure white light, but Maurizan soon realized she was covered all over with tattoos, hundreds of little painted scenes. Maurizan could only glimpse them, because the light coming off Rina was so blinding that Maurizan could look at her directly for only a second at a time.

Maurizan tried to lift Alem while still holding the sword but couldn't. She stuck it in her belt, put one of Alem's arms around her shoulders and lifted him. She dragged him past the altar, glanced down.

An old man lay dead on the floor. He was emaciated, skin gray and blotched, but he had a peaceful look on his face.

"Come on, Alem," she said. "Let's go home."

She looked up at Rina one last time.

◆ ◆ ◆

Rina looked down at the girl and the boy. She knew them. Wanted to tell them things but understood it was a mercy not to. And anyway, her voice would have shattered them.

She sensed something from the girl. Fear. Rina remembered fear. What a peculiar thing to feel.

She gestured to the door. *It's okay. You can go. We're finished here.*

The girl seemed to understand. She nodded and left, dragging the boy with her.

Rina felt an odd pang, thinking of the boy, but it faded quickly. Already the small doings of the mortals grew less important. It was difficult to focus on such small beings and all of their mistaken beliefs and foolish choices. The mad one had been closest to understanding.

Death is a check on war. A check on all the gods.

But there was so much more. She was only just glimpsing it. A new epoch was beginning, but she now understood how short a time that was.

And she had so much to do.

The light from her expanded and brightened and filled the inside of the ruined temple. She felt herself being lifted. She had to go now.

Already she knew she'd have to return far too soon.

♦ ♦ ♦

"It's them!" Brasley said. "Lift me up."

"Your leg," Darshia said.

"Lift me up, damn it."

She frowned but did as he asked.

Maurizan came down the steps, struggling to bring Alem along with her. She glanced down as she passed Bremmer. She slouched in the corner of the doorway, blood from his nose and the corner of his eyes, obviously dead.

"Help me," she said.

Niven ran forward and helped Maurizan gently lay Alem on the ground.

"He's hurt," she said.

His eyes flickered open, focused on her as she knelt next to him.

"You're going to be okay," she said.

"No." He coughed more blood. "Feel . . . all wrecked inside. Sorry. Sorry it took me so long."

"No," she said firmly. "No."

"What is that?" Brasley said.

A brilliant white light shot into the sky. The stars flared, and suddenly a hundred comets shot across the sky, trails in a multitude of colors. Every face looked up, eyes drinking in the display.

Except for one head bowed.

Maurizan leaned down and kissed Alem on the forehead, fat teardrops falling on his face.

EPILOGUE

TWENTY YEARS LATER

The same night that the world saw the sky light up like never before, the army of the dead fell in their tracks and never moved again. Whatever had been pulling their puppet strings was either gone or had lost interest. Nobody knew, and the few who suspected didn't talk about it. Scholars would debate it for years.

Everyone else would clean up and rebuild, just glad that it was over.

In Klaar, the nobility argued for a month while lines of succession were explored and discussed and dusty old scrolls examined. Through a zigzag route of distant cousins and marriages it was discovered that Brasley Hammish's claim to the duchy of Klaar was shaky at best but also better than anyone else's.

Brasley made it clear he didn't want the job.

His wife, Fregga, set him straight.

Klaar enjoyed peace and prosperity for the next twenty years.

Brasley had daughters. They were very pretty, and Brasley was close on several occasions to banishing all the young men from Klaar to . . . well . . . anywhere else.

Fregga kept him sane.

Stasha Benadicta remained as steward, much to Brasley's relief. She ran the castle and, in fact, most of the duchy on a regular basis. She'd recently taken to her bed with pneumonia. She was expected to recover, but Brasley found himself thrust into the uncomfortable position of actually having to run things.

He sat at his office desk, sifting through a jumbled stack of parchments, his head swimming with numbers. The sun had set, and the candle on his desk burned low.

A knock at the door.

"Come in."

A pretty blonde, maybe thirty years old, stuck her head in the door. She wore the Birds of Prey armor, but the red sash marked her as captain. "Is this a bad time, your grace?"

"It is an abysmal time, Emmon." Brasley shook a piece of parchment at her. "Do you know what we pay for eggs?"

"No, your grace."

"Well, it's appalling," he said. "Never mind. How's your father?"

Emmon shrugged. "Tosh is Tosh."

At age fourteen, Emmon had surpassed Tosh's workmanlike approach to swordplay, and so he hung up his scabbard and resumed his duties as cook at the Wounded Bird. He occasionally scouted recruits for the Birds of Prey. Emmon had joined at age sixteen and was appointed captain ten years later.

"What can I do for you, Emmon?"

"The guest you're expecting has arrived, your grace."

"Already? Time flies. Please show her in."

Brasley stood and circled the desk just as she entered.

"Maurizan!"

They hugged. Maurizan now had the feather tattoos around her eyes, and Brasley thought of Rina every time he saw the gypsy girl. Maurizan's people had found a great mountain eagle to serve as her familiar. The sword Alem had found on the deserted island hung from her belt.

"What's it been?" Brasley asked. "A year?"

"Two."

"Has it really? Where this time?"

"I'm back from Fyria," Maurizan told him.

"I'm sure you have stories. We'll lay on a feast with lots of wine."

"Don't go to any trouble for me."

"Don't worry, it's not for you. It's for me," Brasley said. "You're just the excuse. How's your mother?"

"Her knees pain her. Otherwise fine."

The gypsies had built up a small, thriving town around what used to be known as Lake Hammish. People called it Gypsy Lake now, and Brasley had stopped trying to correct them.

"I need to talk to you," Maurizan said.

"Yes, of course."

"I found a wizard in Fyria who can ink the Prime."

"Ah." Brasley thought all that tattoo business had been long concluded. He couldn't guess where she might be going with this.

"My grandmother had the Prime and so did my mother," Maurizan said. "And so do I. My family is the keeper of one of the tattoos." She gestured to her eyes. "It's something of a family tradition, but I never married. I don't have daughters."

"I've heard you don't have to be married to have daughters," Brasley said. "Strictly speaking."

Maurizan smiled. "But you *do* have daughters." She took something from the pouch on her belt. "The oldest is what? Nineteen?"

Brasley rolled his eyes. "And the other sixteen. You're welcome to them. If I told you how many nights I stayed up late worrying about—" He stopped, suddenly realizing what she was suggesting. "Oh."

Maurizan stuck the chuma stick into the corner of her mouth and lit it with the candle from Brasley's desk. She blew out a long stream of smoke.

And grinned.

ABOUT THE AUTHOR

Victor Gischler is a world traveler and earned his PhD in English from the University of Southern Mississippi. He received Italy's Black Corsair Award for adventure literature and was nominated for both an Anthony Award and an Edgar Award for his crime writing.

He currently lives in Baton Rouge, Louisiana, and would grill every meal if his wife would let him.

Please join Victor on Twitter for hijinks and nonsense: @VictorGischler.